ARNOLD BENNETT

WHOM GOD HATH JOINED

ALAN SUTTON PUBLISHING LIMITED

First published in 1906

First published in this edition in the United Kingdom in 1985
Alan Sutton Publishing Ltd
Phoenix Mill · Far Thrupp · Stroud · Gloucestershire

First published in this edition in the United States of America
in 1994
Alan Sutton Publishing Inc.
83 Washington Street · Dover · NH 03820

Reprinted 1994

British Library Cataloguing in Publication Data

Bennett, Arnold
  Whom God hath joined.
  I. Title
  833'.912[F]   PR6003.E6

ISBN 0-86299-207-9 (paper)

Library of Congress Cataloging-in-Publication Data applied for

Cover picture: Signing the Marriage Register *by James Charles. Bradford Art
Galleries & Museums/ Bridgeman Art Library, London.*

Typeset in 9/10 Bembo.
Typesetting and origination by
Alan Sutton Publishing Limited.
Printed in Great Britain by
The Guernsey Press Company Limited,
Guernsey, Channel Islands.

BIOGRAPHICAL NOTE

ARNOLD BENNETT (1867–1931) was a successful, prolific and versatile writer, now best known as a novelist whose major works introduced the mainstream of European realism to early twentieth-century English literature. He presented the seamy side of provincial life, dispassionately recording its ugly and sordid features, sometimes ironically and always without censure, in a series of over thirty novels and collections of short stories. Yet he was the author of more than seventy books in all, a cosmopolitan and industrious journalist who performed at many levels of seriousness, a perceptive critic of contemporary music, literature and art, as well as a playwright and essayist who became a popular figure in the early twentieth-century literary establishment.

(Enoch) Arnold Bennett was born on May 27, 1867 at Hanley, Staffordshire, one of the 'Five Towns' (properly six) of the Potteries now comprising Stoke-on-Trent. The eldest of six children of a self-made Methodist provincial solicitor (who had also been a schoolmaster), he was brought up in an atmosphere of sturdy middle-class respectability and self-improvement of an uncommonly cultured and bookish household. He was educated at the Burslem Endowed School and the Middle School at Newcastle-under-Lyme, later attending a local art school (he painted charming watercolours to the end of his life). At the age of 18 he worked as a clerk in his father's office, where he contributed precocious weekly articles to a local newspaper.

He left the Potteries in 1888 for London where, after a period articled to a firm of solicitors, he soon put aside his law studies and laboured to establish himself in journalism. He wrote popular and sensational serial fiction, becoming assistant editor (1893), and later editor (1896–1900), of a women's magazine, *Woman*, where he wrote on a variety of topics from society gossip, fashion and recipes to book and, above all, theatre reviews. His writing was increasingly in demand from other magazines, including the leading critical journal *Academy*, and the popular press. Encouraged by the publication of a short story in the fashionable *Yellow Book* in July 1895, he embarked on a first novel, which was published in 1898 as *A Man from the North*.

In 1900 he resigned his editorship of *Woman* to become a professional writer, continuing to contribute free-lance short stories and serial novels to magazines. *The Grand Babylon Hotel* (1902), a sensational and popular work in the manner of Ouida, was published in the same year as *Anna of the Five Towns* (1902), a work of serious literary pretensions under the influence of George Moore and Émile Zola. This is now considered one of his best novels, describing against the fictional background of the Five Towns of the Staffordshire Potteries a heroine of honesty and compassion who refuses to compromise with provincial Methodist society.

In 1903, after his father's death, he moved from a farmhouse in the Bedfordshire countryside to metropolitan Paris, in the footsteps of the artists and writers whom he most admired. In Paris he conceived his greatest and best known novel, *The Old Wives' Tale* (1908), which established, and has since largely maintained, his reputation. This is a novel of finely drawn characters set against a vividly realized background: the heroines are two sisters, allegedly inspired by two ungainly elderly women whom he had seen in a Paris restaurant in 1903. When the *Clayhanger* trilogy appeared (1910–1915; reprinted 1925 as *The Clayhanger Family*), his stature as one of the leading serious novelists of the day was confirmed. Showing him as a meticulous and often comic dramatist and historian of life in the Five Towns, it concerns the gloomy life of Edwin Clayhanger and his desperate love for Hilda Lessways and, in the final volume, their life together.

In Paris, Bennett wrested free of his provincial attitudes, becoming a cosmopolitan inhabitant of the Paris of the end of the *belle époque*, a melting-pot of artistic and literary influences and experiment. An early admirer of the French masters, who had been among the first English novelists to learn from studying the technique of Balzac, Flaubert, the de Goncourts, de Maupassant and Zola, his criticism is of a high order; it demonstrates his early appreciation of the contemporary arts, of the Post-impressionist painters, of the ballet of Diaghelev and Stravinsky, as well as of the young writers, including Joyce, D.H. Lawrence and Faulkner. In 1907 he married a French actress, Marguerite Soulie, from whom he was separated in 1921.

When, after ten years in Paris, Bennett returned to England, he was a figure of the literary establishment, rich beyond the dreams of most authors, and offered a knighthood (in 1918; which he declined). He divided his time between London, Paris, a yacht and a country house in Essex, never returning to the Potteries except for brief visits, although they were to continue to provide the imaginative background to his novels. He wrote with remarkable facility, publishing novels and short stories, working as a journalist (particularly a powerful propagandist during the War years, and before them in A.R. Orage's brilliant journal, *New Age*) and writing a number of plays. The latter include *Milestones* (1912; with E. Knoblock) and *The Great Adventure* (1913; adapted from an earlier novel), which were popular successes.

A precursor of modernism who owed much to the example of the European realists, his reputation suffered a decline after the great novels of the pre-war years: the modernists condemned his technique as providing mere 'photography', for its excessively scientific and unstructured accumulation of details. From this it was retrieved by the publication in 1923 of *Riceyman Steps*, the last of his major novels and a popular and critical success. It is a brilliant achievement in technique and design, set in the dark and squalid suburbs of London. . . The sinister tale concerns a miserly second-hand-book dealer who starves himself to death and whose contagious passion for thrift dominates his household, with terrible consequences for his wife. Here Bennett's handling of atmosphere, his psychological observation and kindly tolerance of feeling contribute to a final masterpiece.

In 1924 Arnold Bennett was moved to complete the novella *Elsie and the Child – A Tale of Riceyman Steps* reintroducing Elsie from the original novel, now working with her husband

Joe in the household of Dr Raste.

The Journals of Arnold Bennett 1896–1928, a fascinating account of his life and times, were edited by Newman Flower (3 vols., 1932–3) after his death of typhoid fever in Marylebone, London, on March 27, 1931.

NICHOLAS MANDER

CHAPTER I

ON THE HILL

When I was young the road leading out of the heart of the Five Towns up to Toft End was nothing to me save a steep path towards fresh air and far horizons; but now that I have lived a little it seems the very avenue to a loving comprehension of human nature, and I climb it with a strange overpowering, mystical sense of the wonder of existence.

Bleakridge, a suburb of Bursley, oldest of the Five Towns, lies conspicuously on a hill between Bursley and Hanbridge; but Toft End, which may be called a suburb of Bleakridge, overtops Bleakridge itself by hundreds of feet. Immediately you have crossed the railway, the street, with its narrow brick pavement and cottage-rows on one side, and smoke-discoloured meadows on the other, begins to rise abruptly, and you feel that you are leaving things behind, quitting the world below, and gaining a truer perspective. You feel, too, that you are entering a mountain village, where primitive manners have survived. There are small potbanks in Toft End into which machinery has never penetrated; the shafts of the coal mines look as simple as wells; and there even remain, in a condition of habitable decay, a few of those Georgian mansions which earthenware manufacturers built for themselves a century ago and which in other parts of the Five Towns have either disappeared or been transformed into offices and warehouses. The women at the doors of the serried narrow cottages, each one of which is a little higher than its neighbour, stare at you for a stranger and ask why you walk so slowly and why you gaze so long at the glimpses of Bursley on the north and Hanbridge on the south – those cities of the murky plain mapping themselves out beneath. And suddenly you come plump into a new board school, planned with

1

magnificent modern disregard of space, and all red with
terra-cotta and roof-tiles; plants bloom in its windows, for the
powers down at Bursley have decreed that the eyes of the
children shall rest on beauty; you reflect that once the children
were whipped from their beds at three in the morning to work
till eight at night, and you would become sentimental over
those flowers did you not remember that all states of progress
are equally worthy, and that a terra-cotta board school is not a
final expression of the eternal purpose, though at a distance it
may resemble one. Close by is a cramped and tiny building of
aged brown brick, with no asphalt yard and no system of
ventilation and no wide windows and no blossoms; a
deplorable erection, surely! Carved over its modern stone
portal, in old-fashioned lettering, is the legend, 'Sunday
School 1806.' Oh wistful, unhealthy little temple of a shaken
creed, fruit of heaven knows what tremendous effort up there
in that village, the terra-cotta board school is not greater than
thou, and it shall not be more honoured!

And so you pass onwards, higher and higher, by cottages
new and old, by an odd piece of a farmstead with authentic
ducks on its pond, by the ancient highway from Hanbridge to
Moorthorne, by a new terrace of small villas with a sticky
grocer's shop for the sale of soap and perhaps stamps, by
Nonconformist chapels but not by a church, until you arrive
at the Foaming Quart Inn, which is the highest licensed house
in the Five Towns. A couple of hundred yards more, and you
are at the summit, in the centre of a triangular country which
on geological maps is coloured black to indicate coal. Turn
then and look. To the East is the wild grey-green moorland
dotted with mining villages whose steeples are wreathed in
smoke and fire. West and north and south are the Five Towns
– Bursley and Turnhill to the north – Hanbridge, Knype and
distant Longshaw to the south – Hanbridge and Bursley
uniting their arms in the west. Here they have breathed for a
thousand years; and here today they pant in the fever of a
quickened evolution, with all their vast apparatus of mayors
and aldermen, and chains of office, their gas and their
electricity, their swift transport, their daily paper, their
religions, their fierce pleasures, their vices, their passionate
sports and their secret ideals! Bursley Town Hall is lighting its

clock – the gold angel over it is no longer visible – and the clock of Hanbridge Old Church answers; far off the blue arc lamps of Knype shunting-yard flicker into being; all round the horizon, and in the deepest valley at Cauldon, the yellow fires of furnaces grow brighter in the first oncoming of the dusk. The immense congeries of streets and squares, of little houses and great halls and manufactories, of church spires and proud smoking chimneys and chapel towers, mingle together into one wondrous organism that stretches and falls unevenly away for miles in the grimy mists of its own endless panting. Railway stations, institutes, temples, colleges, graveyards, parks, baths, workshops, theatres, concerts, cafés, pawnshops, emporiums, private bars, unmentioned haunts, courts of justice, banks, clubs, libraries, thrift societies, auction-rooms, telephone exchanges, post offices, marriage registries, municipal buildings, – what are they, as they undulate below you in their complex unity, but the natural, beautiful, inevitable manifestation of the indestructible Force that is within you? If this prospect is not beautiful under the high and darkened sky, then flowers are not beautiful, nor the ways of animals! If anything that happens in this arena of activity seems to you to need apologizing for, or slurring over, or concealment, then you have climbed to the top of Toft End in vain!

In such a spirit I commence the history of certain human beings, including a man named Lawrence Ridware, at the point where Lawrence Ridware was riding a bicycle, with infinite effort and very little speed, up the steep slopes from Bleakridge to the summit of the Five Towns. But in what spirit I shall make an end of the history I cannot say.

Lawrence Ridware had reached the age of thirty-eight; nowadays, however, we have formed the habit of looking younger than our years, and Lawrence might have passed for thirty-two or so, except under the scrutiny of an expert observer who had learnt to judge age by the sure signs of the eyes' gaze and the limbs' gestures. He was an 'admitted' clerk in a solicitor's office. That is to say, he had acquired the right to practise for himself as a solicitor, but he did not practise for himself. Having spent five years of his life and some hundreds of pounds in an unremunerative apprenticeship, and having gone successfully through the ordeal of three examinations, he now, at nearly forty, earned three pounds a week – a salary quite exceptionally high and due to quite exceptional circumstances. Some years before he had been earning only two pounds a week for the same work from the same employer, Mr Charles Fearns, commonly called Charlie Fearns, of Hanbridge. Fearns had taken a young partner, and, having no further use of Ridware, had characteristically found another and a better place for him, in the office of his half-brother, a writer to the *Signet* in Glasgow, who wanted a sound general knowledge of English law in his establishment. Lawrence had thereupon definitely fixed himself and his wife in Glasgow. Then the young partner of Fearns had died with dramatic suddenness, and Fearns, characteristically once more, had demanded his old clerk from his half-brother by telegraph, and had got him, at any rate for the time being, on condition of a further increase in salary. Hence the three pounds per week. As Ridware had a private income of a hundred a year, he might consider himself, in the ranks of provincial admitted clerks, a rich man. But he felt no ardent interest in money, and he had allowed the half-brothers to dispatch him to and from like a parcel.

He was a thin man, fairly tall, with very thin arms and legs, black hair and moustache, and rather large black eyes. His pallid face was thin, but the nostrils were remarkably broad, and so was the forehead, a forehead bossy above the eyes. From the forehead downwards the face narrowed quickly till it came to a geometrical point at the extremity of the chin, which was sharp to an extraordinary degree and which protruded. If any reliance could be placed on chins and foreheads, Lawrence Ridware was such a person as makes his way in the world against incredible difficulties, and is induced afterwards to write articles in magazines for young men entitled 'How I cleared my first hundred pounds' or 'How I hit on my first discovery.' Chins and foreheads, however, are sadly unreliable.

He had beautiful, melancholy, contemplative eyes, whose lids seemed always a little anxious to close. His lips were thin and not very red, while his hands, strange to say, were of a full habit and reddish. He was neatly dressed: a very dark grey suit, black bowler hat, turned-down collar, and small olive-coloured tie. Women as a sex liked him, with a touch of disdain.

Such was Lawrence Ridware, a being wholly unsuited, by temperament and habits, to the exercise of riding a bicycle violently up Toft End 'bank' (hill) with empty stomach, on a warm evening in May. He did it badly – he was working as much with his mobile lips as with his legs – but he did it. As he approached the Foaming Quart he saw a man strolling upwards in front of him, and he shouted in an agonized voice:

'Mark!'

But the man did not hear, and Lawrence set his lips tighter, and frowned more fearfully, and bent lower over the handlebars, and forced the pace of the machine until he had lessened his distance from the man, and then he called louder:

'I say, Mark!'

The man, who by this time was within a few yards of Lawrence's temporary residence, a small, old-fashioned detached house nearly on the very pinnacle of Toft End, heard and stopped. Lawrence also stopped; indeed he fell off the bicycle.

'Steady on!' the other admonished him. 'I expected you at Knype,' he added.

'Yes, of course,' answered Lawrence, quite out of breath. 'But I couldn't get. I was kept at the office!'

And, Lawrence, having righted the bicycle, the brothers shook hands, each nervous.

Mark Ridware, though three years younger than Lawrence, looked older. He was taller and stouter; his face was larger and fuller, and he wore a closely trimmed black beard. Mark had gone to London at a susceptible age, the winner of a National Scholarship at what is now called the Royal College of Art, South Kensington. He had succeeded. His bearing had the touch of good-humoured arrogance which success so often gives. His arrivals in and his departures from the Five Towns were recorded in the *Staffordshire Signal*. His clothes were far better cut than Lawrence's and his collar was the antithesis of Lawrence's collar. In brief, he was a credit to the district, beamed on by the portly friends of his late father when he met them in the street, and a tremendous favourite with women, some of whom would cut his portrait out of illustrated papers. Yes, Mark had reached the illustrated papers; no small achievement for a painter. At thirty he had quarrelled with the Royal academy, most ingeniously quarrelled with the Royal academy. Only a mongoose who has persuaded an elephant to a formal encounter could appreciate the extreme difficulty of Mark's feat. He was a member of the International Society of Painters and Sculptors, and a pillar of the New English Art Club. The Royal Academy, deprived for ever of his pictures, struggled on without them. He painted extremely well. The sole question, when his name came up at the Chelsea Arts club or the Six Bells public-house near by, was whether he had genius or merely talent. He made almost no money by his pictures, though examples of them had been purchased by several European galleries. For his well-known 'Lamplight' in the Luxembourg, the French Republic had paid its customary price of twenty pounds. If Mark had depended upon his brush alone, he might have succeeded in Europe at large, but he would never have succeeded personally in the Five Towns; the older generation there would never have showered upon him its best cigars nor asked his opinion on its champagne; because he could not have afforded to dress for the part; the increasingly powerful race of local dandies would have outshone him and rendered his visits ridiculous. Fortunately Mark, in addition to his brush, had his eyes – those eyes, appealing and provocative, which no young woman of artistic aspirations could withstand. Mark lived on his painting classes, which were crowded with the most earnest of the sex. In particular his summer sketching classes at Barbizon, or in Brittany, were the rage of cultured Chelsea, and immensely remunerative. His income was perhaps four times Lawrence's income, and at least a fourth of that of many a first-class grocer.

The two brothers were deeply attached to one another. Save once, when Lawrence aged ten had kicked Mark aged seven out of bed in the middle of the night, no slightest misunderstanding nor coldness had ever sullied their relations. On matters of literature, painting and music they agreed; on most other subjects they held opposing ideas. But they seldom argued. And they were certainly not intimate. So little were they intimate that when they met, as they did about twice a year, the conversation invariably flagged if they were alone together, unless some topic of urgency happened to present itself. And in the first hour of meeting they were positively self-conscious. Yet their mutual affection was probably the strongest human instinct in both of them.

Lawrence had telegraphed that morning to Mark to come down and see him without fail that evening, and Mark had come, supposing a sudden crisis of supreme importance. But as to the nature of the assumed crisis he could form no guess. He did not, however, explode upon Lawrence with questions, nor did Lawrence pour out a tale. Each, while Lawrence wiped his brows, waited diffidently for the other to begin.

'So you biked up after me?' said Mark.

'I had to. I borrowed this jigger from the office-boy. I quite meant to –'

Lawrence stopped. The front door of his house had opened and a woman stood on the steps. 'Look here,' he went on breathlessly, and very hurriedly. 'I've not telegraphed for you. *You've* come down to see *me,* on business of your own. Understand? There's Phil at the door.'

Mark nodded comprehension. Like all favourites of women he readily sympathized with any policy of keeping them in the dark.

'I'll talk to you afterwards,' muttered Lawrence, in a conspirator's whisper.

'Right!' muttered Mark.

'Why, what is the meaning of this?' cried Phyllis Ridware from the house gate.

Mark raised his hat, and stepped forward to greet her, smiling. All under his eyes the skin wrinkled up when he smiled, and the minute network of lines caused by this continual wrinkling had become a permanent feature of his face. The smile produced in every woman the illusion that she and none other could have made the bachelor Mark happy.

'Wouldn't you like to know?' he chaffed her.

Then, taking her hand over the gate and growing suddenly very grave, he glanced at her with an air that said: 'With you I must be absolutely candid and sincere,' and he murmured,

'No. The fact is I've been getting myself into a legal mess, and Lawrence has got to get me out of it.'

Phyllis Ridware gazed at her brother-in-law questioningly, piercingly. And she dropped his hand.

She was nearly as dark in colour as the brothers, a woman of middle height, with the least possible tendency to plumpness, dressed in black. Her years were thirty, and she had been married at twenty-four. She had a very beautiful face, beautiful in its contours and in its pale olive complexion, but with the beauty that appeals to painters more than to common persons. The vast majority of people in Bursley would not have called her beautiful. And Mark's enthusiasm for her face had always been surprising even to Lawrence, who was compelled to admit in the privacy of his soul that Mark had first taught him to enjoy more perfectly the rare curves of mouth and nostrils and the severe purity of that classic oval. For the rest, she was one of those women whose faces afforded little information – and that chiefly misleading – about their thoughts, one of those women who seem to be always communing with nature's inmost secret and never to be giving you quite the whole of their attention, one of those women who have no true appreciation of facts and yet appear to possess the very essence of all wisdom. Perhaps they do; perhaps they do not. No man will ever know.

'And your luggage?' she questioned, opening the gate.

'Haven't got any, except a tooth-brush. Must go back first train in the morning.'

'Must you?' Lawrence demanded, evidently disappointed, with emphasis.

'Yes.' said Mark, tapping the nail of his thumb against his teeth. 'I must.'

Phyllis glanced at her husband.

'You're in a nice state,' she observed.

'Yes,' he said, after a little pause, 'I meant to meet Mark at Knype.' (Knype is the main-line station for all the Five Towns, and the radiating centre of the local lines.) 'But I couldn't. So I jumped on this thing and tried to meet him at Bleakridge Station. I was too late for that too, and so I bicycled up here after him as quick as I could.'

'I see,' said Phyllis mysteriously.

They entered the house.

Phyllis shut the door, called the servant to wheel the bicycle out of the way, and told her briefly to lay another cover for supper. She then went into the drawing-room, humming an air, and Mark, after he had taken off his hat and coat, followed her. She sat down to the piano, perching herself sideways on the stool. Mark approached the window.

'Ye gods!' he exclaimed. 'These sunsets alone are worth the rent you pay for this place.'

Phyllis began to play.

'What's that you're playing?' he asked, going to the piano.

'Aren't you coming up to wash?' said Lawrence awkwardly, putting his head into the room.

Mark looked up from Phyllis's fingers.

'Not I!' he said. 'You know I always wash in the express, between Sneyd and Knype. It saves time, and it's something to do. Isn't my hair straight?'

'Perfectly,' said Phyllis. 'Play this duet with me.'

Lawrence silently disappeared. Mark piled some bound music on to a chair, dragged the chair to the paino, and sat down by Phyllis's left side.

'Five sharps?' he complained, 'I shall never be able to read it. And Schumann at that!'

'Stuff!' said Phyllis.

His visits usually started abruptly in this way, with music.

When they went into the dining-room which was on the other side of the small hall, Lawrence was already seated at table. The supper (for it was not dinner, and was not termed dinner) had been agreeably and even enticingly spread, and a suspended lamp, with an orange-tinted shade, hung low over its white cloth and crystal and blue china. Phyllis seemed never to interest herself for more than a minute at a time in her household, but she could apparently choose precisely the minutes when guidance would be valuable. She despised the domestic craft, while thoroughly understanding it. The house had been taken furnished by Lawrence from an acquaintance on very advantageous terms, and she had transformed it with the minimum of labour from a furnished house into a home.

Nevertheless she was not one of those feminine creatures who with half a yard of cretonne, several photographs, and a right-about-face of the piano insist on giving the 'woman's touch' to a room previously habitable. She cared not for frills. I doubt if she had the 'sentiment of the interior.' When, six months before, Lawrence had allowed himself to be recalled to England after four years spent in Glasgow, and Lawrence as usual had been unable to decide exactly what to do it was she who had without a pang suggested the storing of their furniture in Glasgow until such time as Lawrence should have communed with his soul and learnt whether the residence in the Five Towns was to be permanent or merely temporary.

Lawrence sat with his back to the window, Phyllis opposite to him with her back to the sideboard, and Mark between them, facing the fireplace. The room was full. Lawrence, with an effort, asked Mark if he had seen a certain new edition of Robert Greene. Their common ground was mainly literature, in which domain Lawrence was indeed capable of taking the superior place proper to an elder brother. Mark might cut a figure in the great world; he might lay down the law to Lawrence upon the graphic arts; he might flatter himself upon being exceptionally well read, upon his genuine passion for reading; but he could not pretend to be Lawrence's equal in the realms of printed matter. Lawrence lived for books; he could only live among books; the little house at Toft End bulged with books, but there were also stored many cases of them in Glasgow. Lawrence did not write, did not attempt to write; he could not waste time in writing. He read. In a word, he was a bookman.

Mark had not seen the new edition of Robert Greene, and said so, and a dismal, disquieting silence followed the host's forlorn attempt to make conversation. Mark perceived, and not too soon, that the atmosphere was disturbed. He saw suddenly that he ought to have accepted Lawrence's invitation to go upstairs in order to chat privately, if only for a few moments. Why had he not gone upstairs? He was of course exceedingly curious to know what had led Lawrence to summon him from London. It must have been the attraction of Phyllis's personality, and of her face, which had kept him in the drawing-room. He was fond of examining himself, of prying scientifically into his heart, and he told himself with judicial severity that in Phyllis lay the explanation of his error of tactics.

Had Lawrence quarrelled with Phyllis? No! Impossible! Had some financial trouble supervened and was Lawrence hiding it and was Phyllis suspecting him of hiding it? Did Lawrence, to put it crudely, want money? Impossible! Then –

At any rate, Mark could know nothing until the meal was over, and in his quality of man of the larger world he thought that it was the duty of every one to live through the meal with tranquil pleasantness. He therefore remarked, in a tone pleasantly tranquil:

'Well, have you folks decided yet whether you mean to stay here or go back to Glasgow?'

There was no immediate answer, and he proceeded, obstinately cheerful.

'I suppose you won't keep living in a furnished house for ever?'

'No,' said Lawrence.

'Fearns wants you to stick by him, I expect?'

'I don't know. He may have a chance of another partner,' said Lawrence.

Phyllis meanwhile had contributed nothing but the enigma of her vague smile.

'Do you like Glasgow, Phil?' Mark demanded of her. 'I forget.'

She paused with a lightly laden fork. 'There's more "go" there,' she said, pointedly.

'Women are cautions!' thought Mark, the expert. 'No one would guess it, but she's having a dig at poor old Lawrence's general lack of enterprise.'

Another pause ensued.

'I saw the great Charlie the other night,' Mark presently resumed.

'What, Fearns?' Lawrence asked.

'Yes. In the promenade at the Empire. It's all very well, you know, but Master Charlie does go the pace. He'll be getting himself into the Divorce Court one of these days. And then what a sensation for the Five Towns!'

And Mark was astounded to observe that both Lawrence and Phyllis were confused to the point of blushing. He was astounded because for years he had been accustomed to talk with very considerable freedom in the presence of Phyllis. Phyllis was afraid of neither ideas nor words. Indeed her imperturbability under a fire of straight talking had more than once surprised him. And what had he said now? . . . Well, he gave women up, and decided that Lawrence must be yielding to the reactionary influences of old age. What *had* he said? Surely the reputation of Charlie Fearns was sufficiently notorious! Surely it wasn't sacred! . . . Perhaps the mysterious secret was connected with Fearns. But how –

Phyllis had retreated to the mantelpiece, in order to ring the bell. She returned with a face perfectly re-composed. And then the servant came in with a tray and coffee. As soon as the girl had gone, Mark, with characteristic pertinacity, made one more opening in the pleasantly tranquil vein.

'I see you've got a new servant since Christmas,' he said. 'What's become of Lottie?'

Lawrence appeared to mumble something.

'What?' Mark demanded.

'Married,' said Lawrence, in a hoarse and trembling voice.

And again husband and wife were blushing! Mark abandoned the affair. He owned himself defeated, utterly at a loss. After all, he reflected, you can only be a man of the world *in* the world. This was not the first time that he had tried to be a man of the world in the Five Towns and had not succeeded.

The meal was a failure. It ended by being a torture and an agony. Lawrence's condition grew more and more deplorable. Phyllis stared fixedly at her coffee. The tension was such that Mark dared not even produce his cigar-case and light a cigar. He was on the very point of audaciously snapping the cord by a curt appeal: 'Look here, you two – I wish you'd tell me what's the matter, instead of going on like this,' when Phyllis suddenly jumped up and held out her hand to him with a smile of the most absolute placidity.

'Good night!' she said, in the gentlest and serenest accents, just as though her supper had been a unique conversational triumph.

'You aren't going to bed?'

'Yes, I've got a bad headache. I must look after your bed for you, and I won't come down again. Good night.'

'Well –' He opened the door for her

'Besides, you have to consult Lawrence,' she said airily, with a strange intonation, as she slipped out of the room.

Giving women up anew, and this time with a renunciation more complete than ever, Mark shut the door and strode back to the table.

'Perhaps you'll tell me what's the *row!*' he addressed Lawrence, violently flinging down his serviette.

'My wife's the row,' Lawrence replied, and he went to the morsel of fire that was burning and poked it, and continued to poke it, staring up the chimney as if he expected to discover something unusual there. His voice was tragically desolate; surcharged with woe, with disgust, and with the asperity of disillusion. And as Mark's eyes rested upon the thin stooping figure with the nervous heavy hands and the slightly soiled wristbands in the confined stuffy little room full of other people's furniture, a wave of terrible painful sympathy with Lawrence flowed up from his heart to his throat; and to control himself he made involuntarily the motion of swallowing and was startled to find how dry his mouth was. He knew not what was the matter between Lawrence and Phyllis, but the quality of his brother's voice warned him that during the meal he had blundered among primary, elemental things without guessing it, and that he must make amends by rising to the supremacy of the occasion.

He could not speak, this man of the world.

'Pass me a match,' said Lawrence, who had taken an armchair by the fire and was filling his pipe. Mark leaned forward and put a box of matches on the edge of the table nearest the fire.

'Well?' he managed to say at length gruffly.

Lawrence puffed at his pipe.

'She's been playing about with another man,' said Lawrence between two puffs.

'You don't mean to say she's –' Mark could not bring himself to finish the sentence.

'Yes I do,' said Lawrence, throwing the match into the fire, and sticking his chin out.

Mark felt the blood colouring his cheeks. He was extremely
uncomfortable. In the common phrase, he did not know where
to look. It was as though he had been suddenly made guilty of
some crime. He had collected in his career various comforting
theories of the sexual relation; he was strongly in favour of
recognizing the facts of nature and of marking conventions
down to their real value; in other words he was an enlightened
and large-minded person. But these handsome bold theories
ran away like cowards before his brother's concrete case. As for
the supper, it seemed monstrous, nightmarish, incredible, that
the supper should have occurred at all.

'Who's the chap?' he asked.

'Greatbatch,' said Lawrence, gazing hard into Mark's eyes.

There are hundreds of Greatbatches in the Five Towns, but
Mark did not put any further question. Phyllis had once been
engaged to Emery Greatbatch, an under-master of the Middle
School at Oldcastle. He and Lawrence and Mark had been boys
together at that same school.

'Well, of course you've simply staggered me, that's all!' said
Mark at length.

'Yes,' said Lawrence. 'It's pretty staggering.'

'But –'

The 'but' was merely the expression of Mark's inferiority to
the situation, the embryo of a protest against the manner in
which the situation had shaken his confidence in himself.
Frankly, he had not so much as suspected that Lawrence and
Phyllis were on other than terms of mutual confidence.
Frankly, he had envied Lawrence, and during the supper he had
not ceased to envy Lawrence, saying to himself that domestic
storms and even battles added zest to existence, and that
anything was preferable to the eternal void of the bachelor's
life. Thus, as a philosopher and observer, had he reflected,
blind as a child to the fearful reality into which he had stepped.
It was mortifying.

'But what?' Lawrence puffed.

'Nothing,' said Mark. 'Tell me about it.'

'There isn't much to tell,' Lawrence replied. 'I got that this
morning.'

He drew a folded letter from his pocket and pitched it to
Mark. The letter was inscribed in characters to imitate print,

and ran: 'Dear Sir, Why don't you look after your wife and Emery Greatbatch? This is a hint from yours truly, A friend.'

'The classic anonymous letter,' Mark commented.

'The classic anonymous letter,' Lawrence agreed. 'Everybody is against anonymous letters in theory; every one says they ought to be ignored and the writers thrashed. But in actual practice – well, it's different. The average conventional man would say that I ought to have shown that letter to Phyllis, or burnt it and forgotten it. I couldn't do either. And the average conventional man wouldn't have done either. I telegraphed for you. I thought I'd just talk it over with you.'

'Know who it's from?' asked Mark, gradually recovering himself, and determined to show Lawrence that a younger brother might be relied on as a fount of practical sagacity. 'You've kept the envelope? What was the post mark?'

'Wait a bit, wait a bit,' said Lawrence testily. 'That's not all.'

'No, I don't suppose it is.' Mark put in quickly. 'You wouldn't hang a dog on that.'

'The post mark is Hanbridge Central. So that's no guide. However, I don't care twopence who sent it! I want to tell you about something else. Last August I saw Phyllis and that swine walking together out of St. Enoch's Station.'

'Glasgow?'

'Yes. They didn't see me. It was an accident. When I got home in the evening Phyllis said nothing about having met him. And I didn't tell her I'd seen them. I wished I had done, the next morning, but it was too late then.'

'Why too late?'

'Simply because I couldn't have done it naturally, then. Don't you see? Well, I thought it might have been a chance meeting. I thought that Phyllis hadn't cared to mention it to me out of a certain shyness, you see, as she'd been engaged to the fellow when she was a young girl. That would be natural enough, wouldn't it? Then I thought all sorts of other things. The damned thing stuck in my mind. The fact is, one minute I suspected the worst and another minute I said the mere notion of anything being wrong was grotesque. I used to get up earlier in the mornings to see the letters first, but I never came across anything peculiar.'

'But I always thought you and Phyllis got on awfully well together!' cried Mark naïvely.

'Did you?' snarled Lawrence, in a tone so dry, sarcastic and acrid that not another word was needed to indicate to Mark the disaster that his brother's married life must have been.

'I certainly thought so,' he repeated weakly.

'My wife has been nothing to me for four years,' Lawrence proceeded. 'She hates me. I believe that woman positively hates me, and I –'

'But she's so –'

'My dear fellow, you know nothing about women.'

Mark smiled sheepishly. (But his soul said: 'Oh! don't I?')

'I meant to meet you at Knype this evening, and I thought we'd go somewhere and talk it over. That was why I telegraphed you to be sure to catch the three ten express. And just as I was leaving the blessed office who should walk in but Lottie!'

'Your old servant?'

'Yes. I told her I couldn't stop, but she said I must. I never saw a girl more changed than she has in four months. She's as sharp as a needle, and neat, you wouldn't believe! She wouldn't let me go till I'd taken her into my room – said she'd come all the way over from Stafford on purpose and wasn't going back without talking to me. Well, she told me that Phyllis had seen Greatbatch several times at a house in Manifold where he had been lodging during his Easter holidays. You know the school is closed for a week, then. And again once at Whitsuntide – beginning of last week!' Lawrence paused. 'Last week!' he repeated angrily.

'How did Lottie know, if she lives at Stafford?'

'She knew because the house belongs to an aunt of hers, who lets rooms for the fishing, you know. It's just one of those coincidences that *do* give the show away. I expect Phyllis thought she was perfectly safe. Walk down the other side of the hill here to Stockley, take the train to Manifold, come back in the afternoon, and there you are! Phyllis didn't know who the aunt was, and the aunt didn't know who Phyllis was. But last week Lottie's mother pays a visit to her sister and sees Phyllis and Greatbatch leaving together. There you are! The mother tells Lottie. Lottie says she shall tell me. The mother says she mustn't and that no good comes of interfering with other people's business. But Lottie sticks to it she shall. And she does. And there you are. There you are! Nothing simpler!'

Lawrence was now standing up, very excited, and he kept repeating under his breath: 'There you are!' between puffs of his pipe; and at each puff his thin, fine lips closed tightly on the pipe.

At that moment Lottie's successor came into the room.

'What do you want?' Lawrence frowned on her savagely.

'I – I came to clear the things away, sir,' she stammered.

'Clear yourself away! Don't come worrying here now!' cried Lawrence, apparently furious. Mark scarcely recognized his brother, so changed was his manner. The servant fled before the tempest, another victim of human injustice. She left the door ajar, and Mark shut it.

'Look here, my boy,' said Mark. 'You'd better sit down.'

'Why?'

'Because I want you to, if you don't mind.'

Lawrence obeyed. Enheartened by this proof of his authority, Mark at last cut and lighted a cigar. Then he too sat down. He spread out his knees, fixed the cigar in the corner of his mouth, put his hands in his pockets, and smoked himself into a cloud.

'Why did Lottie leave here?' he asked.

'She left to get married.'

'But she was only eighteen.'

'What's that got to do with it? It seemed to me this afternoon that she knew a lot more about life than I did.'

'She doesn't like Phyllis?'

'I don't know. She likes me – always did.'

'H'm! And how did Phyllis explain her visits to Manifold to you? Or didn't she explain them?'

'She's got a wonderful dressmaker there. Cheaper and better than anything in the Five Towns, she always says. And you may be sure that she's never been to Manifold without calling at her dressmaker's. You may be sure of that! Trust her!'

Mark hesitated before he asked:

'She never spent a night there?'

'Yes, by God, she did! On Easter Sunday! She gave the servant a holiday.'

'But where were you?'

'Wasn't I in London with you, man?'

'Of course,' said Mark. 'I was forgetting. I remember she wrote me she didn't feel equal to London.'

'I should say she didn't!' Lawrence muttered, and went on: 'Oh! there's no *doubt* about it! Even apart from Easter Sunday night, there's no doubt about it. . . . If you'd heard Lottie, my dear fellow. By the way, Lottie's aunt must be a regular landlady – misses nothing. And women have no sense of decency. You don't know! The things Lottie told me without turning a hair made me feel deuced awkward.'

'Fancy Lottie!' murmured Mark.

Lawrence sighed. 'I've brought you down from London for nothing,' he said in a calmer tone. 'I wanted to discuss with you what I ought to do about that anonymous letter – give it me here! – but that's of no importance now. Still I'm awfully glad you came.'

'So am I,' said Mark, handing him the letter. 'But why in thunder didn't you tell me about all this before supper? I hadn't a notion.'

'My dear chap,' Lawrence protested crossly, 'how could I? I couldn't get to Knype, and I couldn't get to Bleakridge. I only caught you at the house-door. I asked you to come upstairs but you wouldn't.'

'You ought to have insisted.'

'Oh! that's all very well,' Lawrence complained. 'You were with Phyllis.'

'The situation was impossible!' said Mark. 'Impossible! Imagine that supper!'

'I know,' Lawrence concurred. 'But what was I to do?'

Mark was silent. He said to himself that he had never encountered a more glaring instance of Lawrence's fatal lack of enterprise and initiative. Because he could not decide upon any definite course of action, because he was incapable of taking circumstances by the neck, Lawrence had submitted to the appalling humiliation of the supper!

'The question is, what you're going to do,' said Mark positively. 'What are you going to do tonight, for instance?'

'I don't know,' answered Lawrence. 'I only know I'm not going to sleep here. You must tell her I've been told everything. She's no idea.'

'Oh, hasn't she!' Mark exclaimed. 'I bet you what you like she has! Didn't you notice her face when I mentioned Lottie?'

'No!' said Lawrence surprised.

'Why, she blushed like anything!'

'I never noticed it. I didn't see her,' said Lawrence feebly.

'In some way or other she must have smelt danger – that I'll stake my life on!'

'In any case she's got to be formally told,' Lawrence persisted. 'And I shall be much obliged to you if you'll go upstairs and tell her.'

'All right!' said Mark, crossing his legs nervously. 'Now?'

'Yes.'

'Then you'll put 'em in the Divorce Court at once?'

'I – I suppose so,' said Lawrence.

'Well – *won't* you!'

'I suppose there's nothing for it,' said Lawrence uneasily, tapping his pipe.

'I should think there *was* nothing else for it!' Mark retorted wrathful. 'It's the only decent thing to do. I can't understand your hesitating. What alternative is there?'

'My dear chap, I'm not hesitating,' Lawrence defended himself hotly. 'I shall tell Fearns about it first thing in the morning and get the petition out at once.' And he stamped his foot.

'Oh, well, all serene then!' Mark soothed him.

He was ashamed of having shown even the slightest irritation. Lawrence was not responsible for the limitations of his own character. Lawrence acted as he could, as his individuality would allow him to act, not as he would. Lawrence could not be expected to be a combination of Lawrence and of him, Mark. The general fineness of Lawrence's perceptions, the almost invariable distinction of his attitude towards life, – these qualities in Lawrence presented themselves for Mark's admiration and seemed to atone for defects which perhaps necessarily sprang from them. It was ineffably tragic to Mark that Lawrence, spiritually so delicate in organization, should have been selected by destiny to suffer

this coarse disaster, this disaster which overthrew his nicely
poised balance and showed him at his worst.

'Yes,' thought Mark, 'it is a tragedy at which I am assisting.
And I may never get nearer to the heart of life than I am at this
moment!'

His mind swept back to their school-days. Greatbatch and
he were in the Lower Sixth and Lawrence was head of the
school, a Titan of exact learning. And they all imagined
themselves such big boys, while in fact they were quite little!
And the innocence of those days, the immaculate purity of
those days, appeared to him marvellous, ideal, infinitely
beautiful! Greatbatch used to be a delightful fellow, and now,
what a change! Ah! this repugnant, vile process of growing
up, this soilure of the most perfect physical purity the world
contained, this commerce with women, women to whom
nature had denied physical purity! It was lamentable, hateful,
nauseous. One moment they were all innocent schoolboys
together, and the next, lo! the Divorce Court. A chance
spying at a railway station, two lines of a letter, a few words
from a girl who only the other day must have been a child in a
board school, and the full crisis was achieved! And what secret
shames had made the crisis possible, what misunderstandings,
what lyings and deceptions, what miseries, what
mortifications, what anguish, what debasement!

It was nothing! It was the most ordinary thing on earth!
Two people had cared for each other and had ceased to care for
each other, and a third person had come between them. Why
not, since they had ceased to care? What was love? A contact,
of souls or bodies or both. What was the Divorce Court but an
administrative machine of the State? . . . It was nothing. And
yet it was everything! He could not look at Lawrence without
feeling profoundly that it was everything. Poor tragic figure!
Aged thirty-eight! An unromantic age, an age not calculated
to attract sympathy from an unreflective world. But now in
need of sympathy! Youth gone, innocence gone, enthusiasms
gone, illusions gone, bodily powers waning! Only the tail-end
of existence to look forward to! And Lawrence had never
succeeded. He had never, after leaving school, sparkled in the
sunlight, never emerged from the shadow. His was the
common grey career. Mark's love for Lawrence, as he

furtively watched him smoking Navy Cut there by the fire, wellnigh burst the bonds of his heart. It was intolerable, more than Mark could bear. If English brothers kissed, he would have rushed to him and kissed his brother. He would have enveloped him in an atmosphere of tenderness. He would have consoled him by caresses for all his pain. This being out of the question, Mark pretended that the wick of the lamp was too high and turned it down somewhat.

'Look here, my boy,' said Lawrence with false calm, 'instead of fiddling with that lamp I wish you'd go upstairs and speak to Phyllis at once. We must get it over. I'll go out while you do it. You can ask her to come in to the drawing-room.

'Very well,' said Mark, and rose. He flattered himself on being pre-eminently a man of action. Lawrence rose also.

But when Mark opened the door, his heart beating with timorous excited anticipation of the ordeal that lay before him, he saw Phyllis in the passage. She was dressed for walking, and wore a black hat and jacket, and her gloved hands were in the act of drawing a veil over her mouth.

She looked at him fixedly, and dropped her hands, in one of which Mark noticed a small purse. Mark, entirely at a loss what to do, shuffled under her calm gaze, uneasily.

'Mayn't I come in, then?' she demanded, with a low but intensely clear and precise articulation; and, the phrase achieved, her lips closed resolutely into a firm line.

'Oh, I beg your pardon!' he exclaimed and drew aside in nervous haste to let her pass.

She entered the room, bringing into it with the soft murmur of her skirts a strange and troubling effluence. And she glanced around. Neither of the brothers spoke. Mark had placed himself against the wall, next to the mahogany sideboard, and he was close to her, seeing her face in profile. Lawrence stared, at first blankly and then angrily, putting his hand to his pipe but not removing it from his mouth. Mark, though he wished, could not break the dreadful silence. He too was reduced to staring impotently at the apparition that had captured their masculine fortress. Her face was beautiful beneath the veil, beautiful! He noted the graduations of that rare complexion, flushed now, and the exquisite grace of all the contours. The dark eye – he could see but one – was soft and humid. The breast heaved quickly and scarce perceptibly. This was the immortal soul with whom a few short hours previously he had been playing the piano. She was then as she was now! Nothing had since happened save comment on a situation already existing. And yet all was changed! At supper Lawrence could eat with her. And now her mere presence affected him with paralysis, simply because in the meantime he had put her offence into words.

'I've heard a good deal of what you've been saying,' said Phyllis, and her mellow tones descended on the room and its occupants like an even fall of snow. 'You needn't trouble any further. I'm going.'

No shame for her eavesdropping! Rather a pride in it! And no trace of feeling in her voice! She might have been ordering cakes at a confectioner's. Were her eyes afraid or defiant, innocent or guilty, cruel or compassionate? Mark could not tell. An enigma! A woman absolutely enigmatic! And yet, he reflected, perhaps not more so than any other woman in her stead would have been! The wonder of women was eternal, indestructible, universal. One was not more wondrous than another. . . . She hated Lawrence, this Phyllis! But who could have guessed it? She was impure! Who could have guessed it? Her beauty and her charm were unimpaired! They were triumphant. The pity was that they had been wasted on Lawrence, that they had meant nothing to him. What an incomparable mistress, thought Mark! What a minister of love! What a jewel to light the leisure of a busy, creative career! And then he thought of Greatbatch as a gay, fresh schoolboy. Life was really too complex.

Lawrence at last turned deliberately to the fire, and putting his elbows on the mantelpiece set his eyes doggedly on a picture over the fireplace.

'Yes, you may turn,' said Phyllis quietly and gently, with that maddening clearness of articulation. 'You may turn. Supposing I were to ask you about Annunciata Fearns!'

She retreated, deliberately. Lawrence did not stir, but a faint distressing smile came over his pallid features. Mark experienced again the same excessive discomfort as he had felt when

Lawrence began his recital. . . . Annunciata Fearns? What did the introduction of that name import?

But Phyllis was leaving. On the doormat she paused, and twisting her head she addressed Lawrence for the third time, quite ignoring Mark.

'Why you can't let the servant do her work and go to bed I can't imagine!' she said. 'You've already made the poor girl cry with your rough words! However . . .'

She spoke with a cold, measured censure, and she departed. Mark saw her prepare to open the front door, every movement full of instinctive grace. The effort which she made, with one free, slender gloved hand, to pull aside the old-fashioned brass knob was too much for him. He rushed to her. But she had accomplished it.

'Where are you going to – at this hour of the night?' he asked her solicitously.

Her nostrils twitched.

'Is that any business of yours?' she asked icily.

And they had always been great friends! He was shocked.

The next thing was the banging of the door – not a loud bang at all, as soft a bang as the mechanism of the door permitted.

When Mark went into the dining-room, Lawrence turned towards him from the mantelpiece and gave a short dry laugh, and Mark lowered the corner of his lips to indicate to Lawrence his opinion that women were a race apart. But both men had a shame-faced look. In some incomprehensible, impossible way, she had put them in the wrong. She had left them as a schoolmaster might have left a couple of young sinners. In vain they made faces behind her back. It was mere bravado, and each knew it. Each was intellectually aware of his absolute innocence, and yet each felt guilty. Of what? Of something that never has and probably never will be defined.

Lawrence scorned to tell Mark that her insinuation concerning Fearns' daughter was a baseless insult to Annunciata and to himself. He was sure that Mark did not need to be told. Yet he could not prevent his vocal organs from uttering the words:

'What she was driving at about Annunciata Fearns I'm dashed if I know!'

His brother's sole answer was to emit a sound blowing all that away.

Mark then, in silence, crossed the hall to the drawing-room and lit the lamp there. The man of action in him was now thoroughly aroused, and very brave in the absence of danger.

'What are you doing?' asked Lawrence, following him.

'Lighting the lamp,' said Mark. 'Come in here. Poke that fire up.'

And he proceeded to the kitchen door.

'What's-your-name,' he said very kindly to the little servant, who sprang up from a rush-bottomed chair, 'Mr Ridware wants you to clear the things away at once. You can then go to bed. Better leave the washing-up till tomorrow. But we shall want breakfast early.'

'Yes, sir.'

'Your mistress won't come back tonight.'

'No, sir.'

He quitted the frightened girl. Lawrence, who seemed able to do nothing but follow him to and fro, had stood in the hall to listen to him.

'Then you mean to catch that early train?' Lawrence complained, in the drawing-room.

'I must,' said Mark. 'I'll come down again in a day or two if you like, but I've got an appointment at one o'clock tomorrow I simply can't miss. What are you going to do about living?'

'About living? How?'

'About *living*,' Mark insisted. 'Are you going to stay here? Or what? As a matter of fact you can't stay here alone with that servant.'

'I can get Cousin Sarah to come, till something else is fixed up.'

'Yes. Well, you'd better go and see her tomorrow morning,' Mark advised.

'All right.'

'Don't forget it.'

'No, I shan't forget. Of course I shan't forget.'

Suddenly they heard the rattling of plates in the dining-room. Mark shut the door hastily, and then they sat silent for a long while.

'Where will Phyllis have gone to?' Mark asked.

Lawrence shook his head.

'That's more than I know,' he said. And without warning or explanation he walked quickly out of the drawing-room, and Mark heard the front door open. Mark made an aimless perambulation of the room, and picked up the newspaper from the piano, and read through the money-article, which had neither interest nor meaning for him.

There was a knock at the door, which Lawrence had left open.

'I'm going to bed now, sir,' said the servant.

'Very well,' said Mark benevolently. 'What is your name?'

'Maggie, sir'

'Well, Maggie here.' And he extended his hand and gave her a shilling. 'You'll remember to be up early in the morning, won't you? We must have breakfast at eight, not a second later.'

'Oh, thank you, sir. Yes, sir. Eight o'clock, sir. Good night sir.'

'Good night, Maggie.'

As Lawrence did not return, Mark decided to go outside to find him. A wild thought that Lawrence might be seeking to commit suicide shot through his brain and was gone. It would be ridiculous to commit suicide for a woman who for years had been nothing to you, and who hated you! Besides, they were Ridwares! Nevertheless, the perception that they had reached that evening the far-off emotional plane on which suicide becomes conceivable startled him.

Outside, the night was mild and strangely tranquil. In the vast deep purple canopy of the sky, stretching in one mighty unbroken sweep from horizon to horizon, all the uncountable stars glittered according to their magnitudes and their colours, calm, cold, and subjugating. The distant hills formed a circle whose uneven rim was plainly outlined against the borders of heaven. Here and there, in the direction of Dun Cow, and over towards Sneyd, the reddish furnace fires of earth put out the lower stars. And, down below, the illuminated towers and spires of town halls and churches kept their nocturnal watch over the Five Towns silent and reposeful in sleep. Not a sound disturbed the immense stillness, save an occasional dull roar from the inferno of Cauldon Bar Ironworks.

And leaning against the field-fence across the road was the solitary figure of Lawrence, hatless. Down that road Phyllis had lately vanished, to lose herself amid the sleeping hosts of the valley.

'Lawrence!' Mark called in a low voice. There was no reply. 'How terrible life is!' thought Mark, shuddering, while the beauty that spread before him made the tears start to his eyes. And he called again: 'Lawrence!'

'I'm coming,' came his brother's voice gruffly from the road. And Lawrence sauntered into the house.

'Better go to bed, eh?' Mark suggested.

'What's the use of going to bed? I shan't sleep.'

'Take a sedative.'

'Haven't got a sedative.'

'No. But I have.'

'What are you doing with sedatives?'

'I went up to Edinburgh last week by the night train, and I always take a sedative when I travel at night. The tabloids have been in this pocket ever since.' He produced a small phial from his waistcoat pocket.

'No thanks,' said Lawrence. 'I don't deal in sedatives.'

Mark paused.

'Well, shut the door, anyway. . . . Is there any milk in the house?'

'I don't know. I'll have a look if you like.'

They lighted a candle and blundered side by side into the unfamiliar region of the kitchen. They had the ground-floor of the house to themselves; there was no woman spying to laugh at their grotesque efforts to find that milk in the shadowed and mysterious kitchen. They looked high and low, in cupboards and on dressers, and they found everything from lamp oil to cold tea, but no milk. Ultimately Mark was happily inspired to search the larder, and in the whitewashed larder, on a deal shelf, amid cold beef and pieces of bread and eggs and butter and half a tart, they discovered a jug containing milk.

'Now where are the saucepans?' Mark demanded.

And their eyes ranged over the walls in quest of saucepans.

'Enamelled,' said Mark.

The enamelled saucepan was secured, and with a tumbler, the milk-jug and the saucepan, the brothers formed an absurd and forlorn procession through the woman-deserted house to the drawing-room, where Mark with various precautions put the milk to boil.

'It'll boil over before you know where you are,' said Lawrence.

'It won't,' said Mark. 'Do you suppose I can't boil milk?'

And it did not. Mark neatly caught it in the very act of bubbling and lifted it off.

'These things are always better if you drink hot milk after them,' said Mark.

'What things?'

'These tabloids.' He produced the tabloids.

'You're going to take some?' Lawrence questioned, with a slightly sarcastic air.

'Yes, and so are you, my boy! Where on earth is the sense of having a sleepless night if you can avoid it? You're so confoundedly conventional in your notions. You're like some people I know who won't play cards at all for fear the habit should grow on them. Here! Chew up these three quick, and drink half the milk.'

With a gesture of protest, Lawrence complied. And standing in the drawing-room they solemnly masticated the tabloids and drank what milk they did not spill on the hearth.

Then they went upstairs, with one candle, having extinguished the lights. In Lawrence's bedroom was an extra bed, which Phyllis had prepared. The clothes were turned down, and a night-shirt of Lawrence's spread out.

'Want anything to read?' Lawrence asked, as they were undressing.

'What have you got?'

'Oh, I don't know,' said Lawrence. There were many books in the room. 'Seen that?' He picked up a volume from a chair, *A Book for a Rainy Day*, and handed it to Mark.

'What's this?' Mark glanced at the title-page.

'You don't know about it?' Lawrence seemed loftily surprised. 'Have a look at it. What puzzles me is why it's only just been reprinted. It ought to have been reprinted years ago. Dip into it anywhere. It's a bed-book.'

At the head of each bed was a candle in a socket. Both Lawrence and Mark had read in bed every night of their lives for a quarter of a century, and the candles were so devised that they could be blown out without raising the head from the pillow.

And presently, after Mark had carefully folded his trousers in their original creases and put them under the mattress to press, these two men, aged thirty-eight and thirty-five, one rather gross and the other with greying hair, lay side by side in their beds each with a book and a candle, amorphous masses of humanity under the clothes. Not perhaps a spectacle of ideal romantic loveliness! But there is something about them that touches me profoundly. And first Mark blew out his candle, which burnt red an instant and expired, and then Lawrence did the same. And there was a vague shuffling, and then silence in the darkness.

CHAPTER II

ROGUES' ALLEY

Thanks to Mark's obstinacy, Lawrence had six and a half hours' sleep that night, and in the morning the relentless Mark forced him to acknowledge that he had done well to take the sedative. He found himself in the stern managerial hands of Mark, whose instinct towards being practical seemed only to have been sharpened by the sedative. Mark arose early, and Mark called the servant, and Mark superintended the preprandial labours of the servant, and Mark composed the menu of the breakfast with one eye on the larder and the other on the progress of the kitchen fire. Unhappily, owing to the nocturnal orgy of milk, the menu had to be composed without milk, for the milkman did not arrive in those altitudes until after eight o'clock. Mark told Lawrence exactly when he must get up; his organizing skill did not disdain to scheme the due cleaning of boots; and when breakfast was over he took out his watch and informed Lawrence that they must be ready to start in five minutes.

By such precautions there was no undignified hurry, no unhealthy haste. They walked in comfort down the long hillside to Bleakridge Station. And Lawrence perceived that a new day had dawned over Five Towns, and the calm indifference of nature struck him like a revelation. It seemed a year since the previous morning, but the sun had counted only his usual twenty-four hours, and was refusing, pleasantly yet firmly, to admit that anything worthy of special notice had occurred. And they got into the Loop Line train for Knype, Mark having booked and found an empty compartment. They scarcely talked at all; each appeared to be meditative, and even shy; they were tongue-tied; and moreover there was nothing really useful to say. So they sat face to face, yawning

29

occasionally from the effects of the sedative. Then the train threw them out on to the Knype platform at nine-twenty.

Knype is no mean railway station. It is the headquarters of a local railway company with a capital of over ten millions of money, a gross income of nearly a million, and a permanent way of two hundred miles – a steady four per cent line. Over two hundred trains a day pass through Knype, and between five and six thousand passengers; not one train offers to the Five Towns the insult of not stopping there. These facts speak. And the Five Towns always observe with haughty satisfaction that the local company takes its place among the 'principal' companies of the United Kingdom. Now the lordly up platform of Knype is at its best between nine-twenty and nine-forty in the morning, for at the latter instant of time the Manchester to London corridor express, having paused five minutes alongside, steams out while porters cry proudly: 'Next stop Euston!' The worlds of pleasure and of business meet on that platform to await the great train with its two engines. The spacious pavement is crowded with the correctness of travelling suits and suit-cases; it is alive with the spurious calm of those who are about to travel and to whom travelling is an everyday trifle. 'Going up to the village?' the wits ask, and are answered by nods in a fashion to indicate that going up to the village is a supreme bore. And yet beneath all this weary satiety there lurks in each demeanour a suppressed anticipatory eagerness, a consciousness of vast enterprise, that would not be unsuitable if the London train were a caravan setting forth to Baghdad. You can see Baghdad written on the foreheads of even those weary second-class season-ticket holders who go first-class by arrangement with the Grand Vizier of the train, and, bridge-despisers, play solo whist for a hundred and forty-six miles.

Into this crowd Lawrence descended with the illusion that everybody was staring at him curiously. He blushed when acquaintances addressed him, and replied gruffly, almost fiercely. Mark had to behave otherwise. Mark, though far from being the richest, was the most distinguished person on the platform. Mark felt it, and the broader-minded people felt it. Consequently Mark had to practise all his natural affability, as much to commercial travellers who had been his

schoolfellows as to magnates who could have given him a
thousand guineas for a portrait without incommoding themselves in the least. At the same time, he had to avoid making a
companion for the journey, for he was exceedingly fastidious
in the choice of travelling companions. His rôle demanded the
nicest tact; but he was equal to it. The brothers stuck close
together, full of Lawrence's woe and of their unspoken
affection, and after Mark had flung down a penny for the
Manchester Guardian, they began to discuss the contents of
Smith's bookstall with the enlightened severity of genuine
bookmen and impassioned readers, and in this pleasing
exercise of exact valuation they grew quite talkative and were
surprised when the express rolled grandiosely in.

'Well, you'll send me a line, eh?' said Mark, as they
struggled through the prosperous mob assaulting the train.

'Yes,' said Lawrence.

'Might send a line tonight – if anything happens. Let me
hear, anyhow.'

'All right,' said Lawrence.

'And look here – I'll come down again at the weekend.'

'I wish to God you would!' Lawrence replied earnestly,
shaking hands.

'I will. Saturday afternoon. Ta ta.'

Mark climbed up into a carriage, and stood there, slightly
conscious of his distinction, with the *Manchester Guardian* and
A Book for a Rainy Day under his arm. And the train gradually
swallowed up the élite of the crowd.

'Going to lunch on board?' asked Lawrence.

'No. I'm lunching at the Continental at one,' Mark answered.

It was the first hint he had given to explain the absolute
necessity of his departure by that train. After a moment he
winked. Lawrence, however, ignored the wink. Mark's tact
had failed him.

'I'll give you that book if you like,' said Lawrence, moved
by a sudden impulse.

'I'm enchanted. Well –' He waved a gloved hand.

They nodded to each other sternly, without a smile, as the
carriage began to glide away.

At Knype the train leaves behind its tail, which grows a new
head like the fabled snake, and rushes off to Birmingham with

a minor grandiosity of its own. Just as Lawrence was slowly quitting the station he saw a woman hurry out of the booking-office and across the platform – a well-dressed woman of forty or so, rather stout, obviously the mother of a family, with a kind, melancholy, sensible, maternal face. She got into the Birmingham train and sat down breathless, and then rose again to arrange her skirts. Lawrence, after hesitating, went to the carriage window.

'Good morning, Mrs Fearns,' he attracted her attention, saluting. 'Are you all right? Can I do anything for you?'

She turned quickly, and the maternal face, beaming, broke into a beautiful smile.

'Oh! Mr Ridware!' she exclaimed. 'It's very good of you. I think I'm all right, thanks.'

'Travelling alone?'

'Yes, and I do so hate it. I'm going to see my sister in Birmingham. She's ill!'

'Nothing serious?'

'I don't know,' said Mrs Fearns gravely. 'That's what I have to find out.'

The guard whistled and waved.

'Let's hope not,' said Lawrence.

'Yes. Good morning! And thanks so much for looking after me.'

She bowed twice, and he uncovered, with a deprecating gesture. In a few seconds the platform was deserted.

It was astonishing how this banal dialogue remained in his sick and tortured mind, like something gracious, healing, and divine. He admired Mrs Fearns very much. Her personality seemed always to radiate kindliness, her face denied the very existence of evil and transformed the world. As what Midas touched was turned to gold, so what her honest eyes dwelt on was turned to good. Such women exist. Lawrence reflected for the thousandth time that Fearns was unworthy of his wife. Fearns' conduct, indeed, was inexplicable – simply inexplicable – for Fearns was not a fool, nor a brute. If he, Lawrence, could have had such a wife, instead of Phyllis, how he would have cherished and enfolded her and made her existence heaven itself! An infinite regret surged over him.

And as he walked slowly up the broad Knype road to
Hanbridge, past the new park and the cemetery, and past the
houses of the comfortable and the aristocratic earthenware
manufactories with names of worldwide celebrity across their
gates (in one of them his father had fulfilled an honourable
commercial destiny), and while electric cars shot to and fro,
and carts cheerfully rattled and heavy wagons groaned, and
the populace went its ways, his bitter thoughts began to range
over the years of his marriage like lost spirits over a field of
disaster.

He had heard of Phyllis for a year or two before he met her
by accident in London in the studio of a friend of Mark's. She
was the daughter of an architect at Hanbridge, and when quite
young had acquired a vague reputation for being out of the
common. She had become a schoolmistress because she had
theories about education, not in order to earn her living.
Then, on the slightest resources, she had gone to London to
study education. In the studio she had impressed Lawrence at
once. She was well-dressed in a bluish-green colour and she
had a bluish-green parasol exactly to match. She was very
self-possessed; she had her strange mysterious smile; she put
Lawrence at his ease in the difficult studio; she listened to him
with attention. It seemed extraordinary to Lawrence that she
should be a product of the Five Towns. He quitted the studio
with regret. Then Mark raved of her beauty and Mark said she
was a remarkable woman. Then Lawrence, thus encouraged,
defined to himself the feeling that lay in the depth of his mind.
He put it: 'I've never met a girl like that before.' What he
meant was: 'There is something about that girl which makes
her unique among her sex.' He honestly believed that he had
been regarding Phyllis with a clear, cold, unprejudiced eye,
and that nature had indeed singled her out to be the recipient
of supreme feminine qualities. He was convinced that the first
celibate great poet or musician who happened on Phyllis
would carry her off and marry her. Then he returned to the
Five Towns. He did not expect to see her again, and he saw
her again within a fortnight in Hanbridge. Her father had died;
she had come home to be a daughter to her mother. She was in
mourning, seriously cheerful, quite self-possessed, equal to
the occasion with the mysterious smile more wondrous than

ever under her black hat. She asked him to call and see her; she said she was sure her mother would be delighted to see him. He did not, perhaps, care for her quite so much at that interview in the street; infinitesimal traces of the Five Towns showed themselves in her; but he still admired her enormously.

He called, with a peculiar mixture of reluctance and eagerness. He liked Mrs Capewell. He liked Phyllis's way of serving the tea. The scheme of marrying Phyllis appeared inconceivable. She was destined for great poets. She would never . . . no!

One day Mrs Capewell, talking to him with delightful intimacy, told him that Phyllis had once been engaged to Greatbatch, and that the breaking-off of the match was one of poor Phyllis's reasons for going to London. Lawrence, characteristically, had contrived to live in the Five Towns during those years without hearing a word of such an engagement. It shocked him; Phyllis had kissed Greatbatch! He recovered; she helped him. The scheme of marrying her seemed now just wildly conceivable. He spent a year in resolving to propose to her. He was ill with excitement for two days before he did it, and could neither sleep nor assimilate his food. She asked him gently what was the matter with him, and he informed her, nearly fainting. He was that sort of man. He also informed her of the secret history of his parents, as related to him by his father long after his mother's death. Mrs Capewell and Mark were quite foolishly joyous over the engagement, and the fact of its existence put a strain on Lawrence's powers of belief. Why should this astounding happiness have occurred to him? There was only one Phyllis in the world, and he had got her! Luck, undeserved luck! In brief, Lawrence's case did not differ in any material way from that of the lover in the average English romantic engagement.

They were married.

Lawrence had no experience whatever of women, and all the innumerable books he had read had taught him nothing. He married as a child picks up a razor. The first thing that startled him was the tone in which Phyllis said that her mother should not live with them. Though Lawrence himself was quite prepared to admit Mrs Capewell to their household, and though he was somewhat surprised at Phyllis's objection, he perfectly recognised her right of veto; what startled him was the suddenly hard, curt voice that exercised the veto. That voice showed him another Phyllis in a single flash. In three months he perceived with dismay that the ecstasy of the honeymoon was dissipated – he knew not how! He was capable of being bored by Phyllis. Then they had a quarrel. It was about nothing; its pettiness humiliated Lawrence; but the thing happened one morning on waking up, when Lawrence's nerves were in a delicate condition; he was a bad sleeper; Phyllis slept like a log. He went to the office and did no work at all, his mind preoccupied by this terrible schism. Undoubtedly right was on his side; he knew it; and he had a passion for justice, also considerable self-respect. By the time he returned home he had arranged all the arguments by which he should convince Phyllis that her conduct had not been entirely justifiable; he had a persuasive answer to anything she could possibly say. During supper he broke the silence which had begun before breakfast. She flew at him. She strangled his sentences. Instead of artfully indicating a compromise, she consolidated her position and made a reconciliation doubly difficult. The way that woman ignored the common rules and decencies of debate shocked Lawrence, and he learned more concerning women in ten minutes than all his previous life had taught him. She had no sense of logic nor of justice; she misquoted him; she misrepresented him; she dragged in a thousand matters quite irrelevant to the subject in hand. Lawrence recovered from his shock and became really angry. When roused he was himself alarming. He beat down her defences one by one; by dint of repeating the same phrase fifty times he forced her into a muteness which was at any rate not a denial of the truth. Then perceiving his advantage, he grew magnificently calm; he adopted a firmer attitude, and swore in his heart that she should express to him some sort of regret; after all, he could manage a woman. At length, with the most tactful precautions, he let out the word 'regret'. And in an instant he had lost everything, and was obliged to start again. That he did start again was a tribute to his chin. A second time he beat down her defences, new and original defences; and a second time he was loosing the word 'regret' when suddenly in the very middle of one of her own bitter, cruel, scowling responses, she stopped short, and, putting out her hand across the table, touched his.

'Great stupid!' she said in a voice utterly winning and adorable, and with the pristine mysterious charm and her old smile. It was not the same woman! The quarrel was over.

The quarrel was over, but the question had not been settled according to the rules of debate. Justice had not triumphed; reason had not triumphed. Lawrence felt that he had been taken by surprise. He was much relieved to have peace, and yet he was conscious of a moral cowardice in not offering a final calm, kindly statement of his case. The sense of humiliation did not leave him, nor a certain resentment against Phyllis, even in kissing her. As for Phyllis, in a quarter of an hour she seemed to have completely forgotten the quarrel. Gradually Lawrence resumed the dominion of his soul. He too endeavoured to forget the quarrel, and he did forget it. He became philosophic and was thankful for the lessons it had taught him. He knew now exactly how to treat Phyllis, and how to avoid future quarrels. The secret lay in one's tone, he said. Phyllis was decidedly an inferior creature (though often delightful), and she must be treated as such. Useless to appeal to her reason, to her sense of justice! Useless even to appeal to her good nature! She was not good-natured – this was the dreadful pill he had to swallow. She must be humoured. Yes, he now thoroughly understood women. They were a disappointment – but what would you have? Life is life. People are born as they are born. Etcetera.

(And she had had theories on education, she! Why, she possessed no exact knowledge about anything! She had no sense of perspective! She could not co-ordinate facts! Her taste was capricious and unreliable. Sometimes she talked very cleverly. But that could not justify her staggering audacity in having dared to pose about education.)

One of the thousand extraneous matters which Phyllis had imported into the quarrel was an accusation against Lawrence of lack of enterprise. Soon afterwards she suggested to him, very delicately, that he ought to employ his small fortune in buying a partnership in some firm of solicitors. She had previously mentioned the idea, as a possibility, during their honeymoon. On the first occasion he had merely heard it and forgotten; it did not penetrate to the seat of his brain. On the second occasion he had realized the advisability of treating what Phyllis said with circumspection and at least an outward deference. He therefore replied that the idea struck him as one worth considering. And it did. He would have considered it till doomsday. He had not guessed, then, that Phyllis's accusation of lack of enterprise was perfectly well-founded. He thought the charge absurd. He mistook vacillation for prudence, and an exaggerated estimate of risks for business acumen. He was incapable of initiative, a dreamer, a meditator, with a soul too fine for ambition. Whereas the key to Phyllis's character was ambition. She had meant to perform miracles with Lawrence, once she had got him, but she had counted without his chin. She was a disappointed woman. Her scheme for buying a partnership was an excellent one. Lawrence ought certainly to have adopted it. But his nature would not let him do so. Ten locomotives could not have forced him up the hill of the undertaking. His wheels slipped round in meditation and he did not move.

Several times, apropos of several subjects, he had caught the sudden sinister change in Phyllis's voice which heralded a quarrel, and by a lavish use of tact based upon his complete knowledge of women he had avoided a quarrel. And then one day, in response to something she said in that changed voice, something inexcusable, he found himself speaking in the very tone which he knew he must not employ. In spite of himself he was defying his own maxims. The experience was most curious and disagreeable, as it were unreal. If he was angry, it was with a cold anger; he was decidedly not carried away by temper. A profound instinct rose up in him and deliberately challenged Phyllis. In two seconds the quarrel existed vigorously. It was never decently settled and dispatched. It died a natural death, and became like diseased meat of which they had both eaten and which was poisoning them. After a time they spoke to each other as usual; they had moments of placid gaiety. But in Lawrence was the sick consciousness that things could never be the same again, and that their mutual life was a pretence.

He could not imagine what he had ever seen in Phyllis to attract him. The faults of her character were so glaring to him that he accused himself of stupidity for not having perceived them at the first glance at her. Where was the strange charm which once had seduced him? Well, occasionally, when he had a glimpse of her unexpectedly at a distance in the street, he recaptured that strange charm – in her gesture, her attitude – and in an instant it was gone!

He made the best of his life. He had vast intellectual and artistic resources. He drew on them, and not in vain. Temperamentally cold, he accustomed himself to the secret estrangement which followed on a third quarrel caused by her tongue. He was a man of the finest honour, and he honourably did his best to render her existence tolerable. He yielded in disputes far more often than his sense of justice could approve. But he forgot that she, the creature whom he could not treat as an equal, had not his interior resources, and it did not occur to him that she was not temperamentally cold. He never so much as suspected that he had innocently ruined her life. So they became superfluous to each other.

Such, in brief outline, was the history of the birth and death of the divine illusion called love in their hearts.

The monstrous revelation of the last twenty-four hours nauseated, wounded, and appalled Lawrence. He was by no means a conventional person, and yet he could not regard Phyllis's conduct in other than a conventional light. He could not go behind the words impure, disloyal, deceitful. He could not attempt an impartial inquiry into her defection. He could not seek an explanation of it in the notorious weakness of human nature. Even to think of it gave him ineffable torture. He was one great bleeding resentment, that thrust instinctively away the horrible cause of its injury. He hated and loathed Phyllis with an intensity surpassing ten-fold the intensity of any feeling he had ever before experienced. His love for her had been nothing to this hate, this loathing, this rancorous and ruthless contempt. He spat out a 'Bah!' in a voice that might have blasted her like lightning. On Greatbatch his mind did not dwell. Greatbatch was a dog to kick soundly and to dismiss. But Phyllis, his wife . . .! He wondered how her poor mother would survive the daughter's infamy.

Long before he wished to be there he had arrived in Holborn, the principal thoroughfare of Hanbridge, that local metropolis which has amused itself by imitating London in the nomenclature of its noisy streets. At the corner of Holborn and Chancery Lane, where strangely enough are to be found legal offices, money-lending offices, and insurance offices, stands the shop of Brough the bookseller, stationer, and artist's colourman. Brough called himself principally a bookseller, but his business in literature was almost negligible, the demand for books in the Five Towns being inferior to any other demand whatsoever. Lawrence generally had a volume on order at Brough's, and Brough respected him deeply, in that his regular custom, though barely profitable, gave dignity to Brough and to the shop. While Lawrence patronised Brough's it could not and should not be said that the Five Towns was unliterary. A book was due for Lawrence that morning. Should he enter and get it? Like all bookmen, he suffered keenly from unsatisfied desire between the moment of ordering a book and the moment of handling it. Nevertheless it seemed uncanny to him that he should desire so trifling a thing as a book that morning; it seemed sacreligious. He was still unaware that books had become his life, his unique and overmastering passion; he was still unaware of the tremendous formative influence of habitual indulgence. He went into the shop, which was fresh from its daily toilette, and which, with its elaborate crowded display of sentimental coloured prints in gilt frames, almanacs, pocket-books, ladies' purses, picture-postcards, fountain pens, india-rubber rings, playing-cards, writing-paper, drawing-pins, and colour tubes, bore testimony to the high state of luxurious civilization in the Five Towns. Mr Brough, a white-haired man with a thin pale face, delicate trembling hands, and a narrow black necktie, stood behind the counter undoing a parcel which contained ten copies of Meiklejohn's School Geography, a small Wages Reckoner, and a two-shilling reprint of *The Little Flowers of Saint Francis*. He pushed the last across the counter to Lawrence with a proud smile, as if to say: 'There! you see how you may rely on me to satisfy by return of post even your most singular caprices!'

'Good!' said Lawrence, with unconscious eagerness, examining the book.

And Mr Brough continued to disengage examples of Meiklejohn from the parcel, staring the while mildly and sadly through the glass door into the street. He could have performed no matter what feat while staring through the glass door.

Lawrence placed half-a-crown on the counter, and Mr Brough with his slow precise movements offered the half-crown to the cash register, which rang and yielded sixpence in change.

'Thanks,' said Lawrence, taking up the sixpence.

'Thank *you*, Mr Ridware,' said Brough courteously, and he emerged from behind the counter as Lawrence was putting the book into his pocket. 'How is your dear wife?' he added.

'My wife!' stammered Lawrence.

'It is quite a long time since I had the pleasure of seeing her,' proceeded Mr Brough, with even blandness. 'She used to call here now and then. She is quite well, I hope?'

'Yes, thanks,' stammered Lawrence. 'Quite well.' He was blushing.

'You might give her my kind regards,' Mr Brough smiled, opening the glass door. 'Her father and I were old friends. Tell her I say she has forsaken me. Will you?'

'Yes,' said Lawrence. 'Certainly. I'll tell her.'

He slipped out, pretending to be in a hurry. Oh! The shame, the misery, the anguish of such a trivial incident! To old Brough Phyllis was no doubt an ideal figure, standing for youth, beauty, distinction, goodness, and the unattainable. Old Brough had perhaps nursed her on his knee. Why had he not cried out to Brough the odious and fearful truth, instead of lying? With a noise in his ears he hastened up Chancery Lane to the office.

Chancery Lane, Hanbridge, the Lincoln's Inn Fields of the Five Towns, and known locally as Rogues' Alley, is a sinister little street. On one side of it is the blank dark red wall of an old-fashioned manufactory, and on the other, tightly packed together, are mysterious little houses which once were homes and which are now kennels where lurks that last uncompromising descendant of the Medes and Persians, the 'legal mind.' In the very midst of its length are the County Court Office and the local Registry of the High Court of Justice – dread names, names of fear! The houses, since they ceased to be homes, have not been structurally altered, but in certain cases swing-doors have been added within the old front doors, heaven knows why. The front doors, from nine to six, are kept invitingly open, and drab panels lettered in black, or black panels lettered in white, afford dim clues to the mysteries that may be seen within. You cross ragged mats, and climb sombre, narrow, naked, soiled stairs, and push tremblingly against portals of ground glass, and find yourself confronted by one or two young men with short shiny sleeves, who regard you suspiciously from behind a screen and ink-stained desks, and demand your name, and write your name in a book, and write it on a piece of paper, and disappear with the piece of paper, and reappear, and with a peculiar expression ask you to sit down. You obey this behest on a piece of wood, or on nothing encircled by ends of cane; and when your eyes have become accustomed to the obscurity you observe through the interstices of the screen a fireplace that was once a hearth, and probably a window that was once the object of a housewife's pride. In due season you are told to get up and walk, and you are led through passages to another room, equally shabby, bare, dusty, and forbidding, and there, at a vast desk, in an armchair that revolves like the earth on its axis, surrounded by all the evidences of poverty and decay, sits a human being who probably owns a beautiful house and beautiful children in some other street and boasts a pretty taste in Chippendale. You are in the presence of an incarnation of the 'legal mind.' So it was – and so it is today. Step out of Holborn (Hanbridge) into Chancery Lane (Hanbridge), and you step into the Middle Ages. There are offices in Chancery Lane where the typewriter clicks not nor rings its bell, because the typewriter is 'unprofessional'. Above all things Chancery Lane is 'professional.' Situated in the heart of a district inhabited by a population of a quarter of a million which gibes openly at the House of Lords, it preserves with holy and rigorous zeal the sanctity of tradition.

The establishment of Charles Fearns comprised the first floor of a typical house in Chancery Lane, three rooms in all, of which the largest was divided into two by a wooden partition, one portion forming the outer or inquiry office and the other the articled-clerks' office; the next room was Law-

rence's, and the third belonged to the principal. Except for its
cleanliness, a somewhat damp cleanliness in the early morning, it resembled a dozen other establishments in the street.
Charles Fearns had a passion for cleanliness. He in fact liked
comfort, and had he not been overawed by the toryism of the
street he would have followed the fashion recently set up in
the more modern solicitors' offices in the Old Town Hall, and
treated himself to a Turkey carpet! As things were, he had
stopped short at speaking-tubes and a typewriter. The
practice, which had been started by his father in the late fifties,
was a sufficiently flourishing affair, miscellaneous in character.
Charles, in common with most solicitors, imagined himself to
be extremely business-like, and in common with most
solicitors he was extremely unbusiness-like. He had immense
energy, good judgement, tact, a talent for diplomacy, and
some forensic skill, but business-like he was not. He frequently persuaded himself that his office was run with the
precison and exactitude of a battleship; perhaps he thought
that occasional irate outbursts of passion for efficiency
constituted discipline.

Lawrence arrived at the office at ten minutes past ten,
twenty-five minutes late. The office-boy, Gater, who was
supposed to begin at nine-thirty, was only just opening the
letter-files to start his preliminary duty of letter-filing. The
shorthand and engrossing clerk, a middle-aged fat man named
Clowes, was reading a creased and dirty copy of the *Athletic
News*. These two inhabited the outer office.

'Mr Fearns come?' demanded Lawrence.

'No sir,' said Gater.

And Clowes folded up the *Athletic News* with a deliberation
meant to indicate that if Lawrence supposed that Clowes was
afraid of *him,* Lawrence was mistaken.

Lawrence passed through the outer room to the articled
clerks' room, in order to reach his own. There were two
articled clerks, and they represented the two great divisions of
their caste, the division which pays and the division which is
paid. Mr Arthur Sillitoe, of the gilded youth, had paid a
premium of two hundred guineas in order to sit in Fearns'
office; he received no salary, and his view of the seriousness of
life and law varied with his distance from an examination. Mr

Paul Pennington had paid no premium, and he received a salary of a pound a week. Pennington came from Oldcastle, which, though contiguous with, is not part of, the Five Towns. He had won a series of scholarships up to the age of seventeen, and afterwards, in eight years of assorted clerkships, had saved enough money to pay the eighty pound stamp on his articles, his examination fees, and the cost of his law books. Fearns 'gave him his articles' as the phrase is, on the clear condition that he should work. And he did work. He was one of those young men of the people, all vigour and integrity and no humour, who rise with the irrepressibleness of a tide to a certain height and then gradually sink because they are without imagination. In a year Paul Pennington had terrorized the office; even Fearns went morally in secret fear of him. For Pennington was business-like. He discovered the crass inefficiency of the office. He coldly pointed out that the indexing of the letter-book was always in arrear, that neither Fearns nor Lawrence wrote up his professional diary fully and properly, that the bills of costs were not delivered with regularity, and that the system of book-keeping was simply a complete lack of system. He was relentless, and the mighty force of right was behind him. He meant to reform the office. He engaged single-handed in a warfare against the temperaments of Fearns, Lawrence, and Sillitoe. He had far less brains than any of them, but he fought and defeated them every day. Out of sheer enthusiasm for order and efficiency, he undertook, in addition to his ordinary work, the whole of the book-keeping and the superintendence of the costs. He put perhaps a couple of hundred per annum into Fearns' pocket, and Fearns resented it. He never arrived late, and he never left early. He was terrific, a prodigy. He would never earn more than a hundred and fifty a year.

'Good morning,' he said drily to Lawrence, looking up from a Kean ledger. He was alone; Sillitoe's chair was empty. His black hair shone; he was wearing his office coat.

'Good morning,' said Lawrence, trying to slip through the room.

'Will you let me have your attendances in Wilcox v. Wilcox today?'

'I'll try,' said Lawrence, 'I've got –'

'You promised me them the day before yesterday,' Pennington stated, as he bent to the ledger.

'Well, I can't do everything,' snapped Lawrence. Pennington's writing-master way of holding a pen irritated him.

'As you please,' said Pennington suavely. 'I merely mention the matter, Mr Ridware.'

He was always like that, invincible and calm. He always left it to your conscience. Considering his age, he was an inhuman exaggeration of righteousness.

Lawrence went to his own room and sat down with his hat on.

It was quite a small room, furnished with an old flat kneehole desk, a large tall cabinet of newly stained wood comprising closed pigeon-holes lettered in black from A to Z, two old chairs, a covered washstand, and a legal almanac. The floor was bare. Behind the door hung an old coat. A fire was laid but not lighted in the tiny fireplace, and on the mantelpiece were a few law-books and a towel. The desk bore a Hudson and Kearns blotting-pad, an enormously thick Legal Diary, with a page for every day in the year (except Sundays) and immense quantities of miscellaneous information; also several shallow wicker-baskets containing bundles of papers tied with pink tape (not red tape) or buckled in a sort of worsted strap; some of these bundles were thick with dust; an Isobath inkstand and two pens completed the treasures of the desk. The geography of the room was such that when Lawrence sat at the desk he had his back to the window and his face to the door; nobody had ever been clever enough to arrange the room differently; but some daring and ingenious person had carried an indiarubber pipe from the gas chandelier in the centre of the ceiling to a movable lamp, which could be placed on the desk when necessary, mingling its tube with the speaking-tubes. In this apartment Lawrence spent nearly a third of his life.

The unique and terrible Pennington had evidently been before him in the room that morning, on a mission of efficiency, for the bundle of papers in Wilcox v. Wilcox was propped up in a prominent position against one of the baskets so that his eye could not miss it. There were also on the blotting-pad some letters for his attention. He stared at these things with a fixed determination to ignore them; he had no conscience whatever for his duties. For as he had climbed the stairs he had suddenly and tremendously resolved that he would plunge into the matter of the divorce at once, that he would not palter with it, nor hesitate. And this resolution was like a new resolution. He had definitely promised Mark last night that he would commence proceedings instantly. But that promise seemed to be unreal, not authentic nor binding, a mere form of words, one of those promises which Lawrence too frequently made to himself or to other people, and broke, having known always that he would break them. The present resolution was different. It was among the few genuine resolutions of his life. It possessed, absorbed, and frightened him, as his resolution to propose marriage to Phyllis had once possessed, absorbed, and frightened him. He would be capable of nothing else until the vow had been fulfilled.

He had settled precisely the order of the steps which he would take. Immediately on the arrival of Mr Fearns he would go into Fearns' office and tell him, and ask his advice, and he would then go to the articled-clerks' room and inform Pennington and Sillitoe of the sensation that awaited them, in a voice so loud that Clowes and Gater would hear. Thus the entire staff would learn the news, and he could draw breath, for something would have been accomplished.

And now Fearns was late at the office! And Lawrence was forced to undergo the ordeal of inaction. He gazed at the covered washstand and at the old coat. . . . Astonishing, was it not, that Mark had not seen through Phyllis? He suspected that Mark still thought Phyllis a damned fine woman. Well, let Mark live with her for a month and try her voice, her egotism, her grumbling, and especially her nagging voice! Let him try it! It was infamous, infamous, infamous, what she had done! No excuse, no possible excuse! Why hadn't she told him straight that –? She must have spent the night at her mother's! Of course she might have run off direct to Greatbatch! No, she would not do that. He reckoned he knew her well enough to be sure that she would not do that. She was at her mother's. She was therefore not very far away from him at that moment. She existed at that moment! She was doing something at that moment. They both lived and moved as they had lived and moved yesterday, just as though nothing had happened. It was the same Phyllis, the same Lawrence! Strange and disconcerting thought! Was it not like her, like her unscrupulousness, like her unfairness, to drag in the name of Annunciata? Why drag in the name of Annunciata? Never before had she mentioned that name. Scarcely even had he mentioned it to her. Certainly he admired Annunciata, that image of the pure, fresh young girl. He had not concealed the fact. Was that it? Was that the explanation? Had he once by chance spoken of Annunciata to Phyllis in a tone that that vile woman, with a woman's capricious stupidity, had misinterpreted? Annunciata was a surprising daughter for such a man as Fearns to have. But then he seemed to have heard that such men as Fearns often had such daughters as Annunciata. Yes he *did* like Annunciata. He recalled a walk with her from Hanbridge to Bursley a year ago. In fact he had not forgotten that walk. And certain Sunday afternoons in Mrs Fearns' drawing-room, Annunciata pouring out tea! A pure girl! Not beautiful, perhaps! But that quality of purity! Her mother had it. He liked mother and daughter equally. Astonishing that Phyllis should go and hit Annunciata in that manner. It was as if she had hit a nail full on the head with a hammer by accident in the dark. But that was just what women were always doing. They were always being right and always wrong. What would Mrs Capewell say when she knew of the affair? How shameful of Phyllis to shock the old lady!

He heard Fearns' quick neat footsteps along the passage! The moment had arrived, – the second great decisive, dramatic moment of his life, it seemed to him! He rose, with a heart wildly beating. Fearns had gone into his own room and shut the door hurriedly. He struggled into the articled-clerks' room and escaped by the door into the passage. Pennington did not look up. He went to Fearns' door, and stood there a few seconds. No, no! Useless to postpone! The words must be uttered at once! He had sworn; he had sworn; the oath must be kept, the appalling step taken! He pulled out his handkerchief and blew his nose violently, and then he knocked and pushed himself into the room.

Fearns was already at his desk: a tall well-made man of forty-five, but looking decidedly younger, with very dark brown hair, and a strong moustache showing a first faint hint of grey; his nose was big, like his white hands; his eyes bluish-black; at a distance he seemed to be in the perfection of physical health, but on a nearer view one saw fatigue in the eyes and the lips, and the skin, though rosy, would not bear inspection; a powerful, handsome creature, one would say, audacious, proud, rather gross, and generally equal to the occasion; a man who would refuse to grow old. He glanced at Lawrence, raising his eyes from a letter which he had just torn from its envelope.

'Ah! Ridware! I want you,' he said curtly.

'I came to speak to you, Mr Fearns,' Lawrence said timidly, shutting the door. His emotion was really grotesque in its intensity; even to himself it appeared ridiculous.

'What about?' Fearns fired the words at him like a bullet.

'About – a matter of my own.' His voice was husky.

'Well, that'll wait a bit, I reckon. Look here. Here's the title deeds of Nevinshaw's manufactory. I've been there this morning. The mortgage is arranged, and it's got to go through as smart as possible. I've promised Tommy Nevinshaw. I want you to make the Abstract of Title at once, and give the draft to Clowes to copy sheet by sheet as you do it. I'll see Hollins Brothers some time today. I shall tell them they will have the Abstract tomorrow first post and ask 'em to examine deeds on Monday. We can complete on Thursday, perhaps.'

He pushed a great parcel of deeds towards Lawrence.

'Understand, don't you! Title's clear enough. But don't err on the side of brevity all the same. It may save trouble in the end. You never know. See?'

And Lawrence said meekly: 'Yes.' And he left the room, taking the deeds.

When he reached his own room he cursed in whispers. He could not sit down. Why had he allowed Fearns to sweep him like that off his feet? What was a mortgage, compared to *his* affair? He stood by the window, holding the deeds and staring blankly into a small backyard. Now he would have to begin again, nerve himself again, suffer the torture again. And if he had only been obstinate and courageous, Fearns would at that moment have already heard the facts, and the worst would have been over. He cursed himself to hell, and threw the parcel of deeds savagely to the floor.

He would return to Fearns instantly. He would insist. Yes, instantly! . . . Phyllis was the cause of all this. . . . Thoughtfully he picked up the parcel. Should he go to Fearns instantly, or should he wait to recover himself? He heard the whistle of a speaking-tube somewhere and then the feet of Gater leading a client along the passage to Fearns' room. He could not go now. He must wait.

And then Fearns and the client went out together, talking and laughing loudly. The client was the Mayor of Hanbridge; he recognized the voice.

He sank into his chair.

He could not make that Abstract of Title. He simply could not. And Fearns was relying on it.

Jumping up, he took the deeds in to Pennington. Sillitoe had not yet come.

'I say, Pennington,' he said hurriedly, 'I wish you'd oblige me by abstracting this Nevinshaw title at once. The governor wants it done quick. He's told me to do it, and I can't. The fact is, I'm not well at all.'

'I'm sorry to hear that,' answered Pennington kindly. 'What's the matter?'

'I'm upset.' He wished to tell him the truth, but he could not.

Pennington eyed Lawrence furtively, and began to open the parcel.

'Certainly,' said Pennington. 'I'll do it as quickly as I can.' He was quite sympathetic.

'Give it to Clowes to copy sheet by sheet, so as to save time, will you?'

'Yes.' He put a piece of blotting paper geometrically in his ledger, shut it, and secured it in a drawer; took out some blue draft paper from another drawer; creased it longitudinally in several places so as to give the different margins necessary for an Abstract of Title; and then unfolded the topmost deed. He was an invaluable machine.

Lawrence retired. After all Pennington was a decent chap.

Once again in his room, the prospective petitioner to the justice of England sat down and resumed his bitter sullen stare at the washstand and the old coat. He could recall, he could hear, the very tones, hard, loud, and exasperating in which Phyllis used to maintain her unscrupulous arguments with him; he could remember precisely her words. And his heart glowed with fierce, merciless resentment. Such women as Phyllis . . . Why, even Pennington was decent. Phyllis was not *decent;* in her composition there was no basis of kindliness. He went suddenly, with a new resolve, into Fearns' room, and opened the glass doors of the bookcase. Hung on the wall on either side of the bookcase were framed photographs of a charming child dressed up in a judge's wig and robes, and imitating with delightful archness the ponderous didactic gestures of some judge of the Supreme Court of Judicature. Fearns had bought them from a touting commission agent. They appealed to something in Fearns' inmost soul, and certainly they were the only things in the place that ministered to the human sense and the sense of beauty. But Lawrence hated them in that moment; they offended him as photographs of a child imitating the gestures of a torturer or an executioner might have offended him. They seemed to him to be an outrage on good taste. He saw the odious ordeal and climax of the divorce proceedings in a vision, and the vague, vast thought of all the distress and misery that lay between him and the distant end of those proceedings settled on his mind like a nightmare.

Presently he found the object of his search through the shelves of the bookcase, Dixon's *Law and Practice in Divorce and other Matrimonial Causes,* a shabby large volume bound in black. It was an old edition, probably bought second-hand at a sale, not for its immediate usefulness, but because it might prove useful some day, because it was one of those books without which no solicitor's library is complete. The dust was thick on its top edge, for no divorce case had ever been known in the annals of the Fearns' business. There are over sixteen thousand solicitors in England and only a few hundred divorce cases a year. Now at last the famous Dixon was to be useful in the office; it would perhaps even be necessary to buy the latest edition of the famous Dixon! And for him, Lawrence, for just

him! Out of a quarter of a million people in the Five Towns *he*
had been chosen by destiny for this disgraceful renown. Often
he had caught sight of Dixon on the shelves, and Dixon had
been nothing to him but a text-book. Whereas today . . . Life
was incredible, incredible.

He carried the book away to his lair. He must study it. He
must get it up! In the seventeen years which had passed
(seventeen years ago he was beginning his career – and what a
career, he reflected sardonically!) since his final examination
for admittance as a solicitor, he had almost completely
forgotten the law of divorce, and the details of the practice he
had forgotten utterly. He began to read the book, to swallow
its contents with the facile rapidity of the expert reader and
student. It was a horrible book; it was decidedly the most
horrible book in the world. It was Chinese in its laconic,
impassive indifference to the possibilities of emotion. It went
across the whole naked field of human suffering like a
steamplough. On every page were terse sentences that ripped
the tissues of the heart. 'Bad language. Evidence of, is useful
where it leads up to personal violence. *Dysart v.* D., 3 N.C.
343.' He thanked heaven that he had never reached bad
language – to a woman! Personal violence! Good God! What
vistas of abasement! Or: 'The husband's conduct. Inattention
to his wife's conduct is not connivance at her adultery. He
must have been privy to it, or have led her into it. *Rix v. R.* 3
Hagg. E.R. 74' Connivance! The unspeakable, ignominious,
polluting word was all over the page. It was even printed in
capitals! And Dixon was good enough to assure him, the
husband inattentive, that his inattention was not connivance!
Thanks, oh Dixon!

When he had gulped down the whole book, he turned back
to the chapter entitled 'The Petitioner's Case,' and mechanically took up some memorandum sheets in order to make
rough notes. These memorandum sheets consisted of
discarded office notepaper, bearing the legend, 'Fearns &
Thomas,' instead of 'Charles Fearns.' They were one of the
few traces of Fearns' brief partnership with the dead Thomas.
And Lawrence somehow saw that partnership name in a new
light, in a light so strange and sad that the moisture glistened
for a moment in his eyes. He had occupied that room for

years. And then he had made way for young Thomas, and
Thomas had occupied it for a little space; and now he had
come back, and Thomas was dead and buried, his memorial a
quire or so of discarded notepaper! The sea of existence rolled
deep over young Thomas! And he, Lawrence, had descended
to the Divorce Court! What a world was this world!

There were footsteps outside the door. Like a guilty lad he
shut Dixon and covered him quickly with paper, and leaned
back in his chair.

'I'm going out to dinner,' said Pennington, standing
gravely at the door. 'I've done quite half of that thing.'

'Have you? I'm awfully obliged to you.' Lawrence
blushed.

'Not at all. Are you all right? Can I get you anything?'

'No, thanks,' said Lawrence. 'I'm all right.'

'Why don't you go home?'

'I'm just as well here.'

'Very good!' Pennington agreed, coldly and discreetly
incurious. And left, closing the door.

Lawrence looked at his watch. It was past one. Fearns
would now surely not return before two o'clock at the
earliest. He was proud of his industry. At any rate he was not
wasting time; he was not hesitating in his distasteful,
sickening enterprise. He was on the contrary, showing
energy. And he reopened Dixon. At half-past one he felt
hungry. The morning had slipped away. The activity of the
office had gone on as usual, Pennington writing, Clowes
doggedly copying, Gater busy in nothings, Sillitoe no doubt
bending indolently to the law from the lofty platform of the
gilded youth! Usually Lawrence brought with him a packet
of sandwiches and a flask for his lunch, for the distance to
Toft End was nearly two miles; but today he had never once
thought of his lunch. And now he was very hungry indeed.
He went to the outer office, where he knew Gater would be
sitting in solitary charge of the establishment, and told the
boy to go and buy a pork-pie from the Coffee House.

'By the way, Gater,' he said, 'I'll bring you your bicycle
tomorrow.'

'Thank you, sir. I suppose you found the gear high, sir. It's
over ninety.'

'Terrible,' said Lawrence.

And Gater ran off, flattered by this tribute to his high gear.

Lawrence took his place in the outer office as guardian, and glanced idly at the Call Book. Eight people had called during the morning. Pennington must certainly have taken measures to prevent Lawrence from being disturbed! Extraordinary, how thoughtful Pennington was!

A dirty ragged old woman came tremblingly in, after having knocked twice and been twice summoned to enter. She curtsied.

'I've brought th' rent,' she said in a hoarse voice. She was a tenant of one of the hundred or more cottages belonging to this or that mortgaged estate administerd by Fearns on behalf of mortgagees – his clients.

'Where's your book?' Lawrence asked. Rent-collecting was a branch of the business with which he had nothing to do.

The old, bent, bareheaded woman handed up a filthy rentbook and with it a greasy half-crown that was offensive to the touch. The odour of rum permeated the air.

'But look here,' said Lawrence, examining the book, and adopting the firm tone which he knew to be necessary. 'It's just three weeks since you paid anything and now you come with half-a-crown!'

'Us canna' help it.' The old woman whined, rubbing her eyes with an apron made of sacking. 'My son's pleeing (playing – not working) three days a wik, – and four childer! And th' house inna fit for live in –'

'That's all very well,' said Lawrence. 'But we shall have to –' He stopped.

'Bums!' exclaimed the old woman. 'Nay, nay, mester! Dunna say that. I bin i' that house thirty-four year.'

He initialled the book, and gave it to her, trying to look stern. And just as she was leaving, with another curtsey, Fearns himself burst in. And she curtsied lower to him.

'Mother Podmore!' he greeted her with gay familiarity.

'Eh, Mester Charles!' she replied obsequiously.

'You've been drinking.'

'Not a drop!' the old woman swore.

'Well,' said Fearns. 'Here's sixpence for you. Be off. I won't inquire about your rent – not this time.'

She blessed him, and assured him that beyond doubt he was a true gentleman, and then she departed, mumbling her appreciation of this splendid and generous male all the way down the stairs.

'Where's Gater?' Fearns demanded of Lawrence, suddenly dropping into a cold, almost savage tone, and when Lawrence had informed him he said, in the same tone, 'You're getting on with that Abstract, eh?'

'It's more than half done,' Lawrence replied evasively. He could not begin his explanations to Fearns in the middle.

Fearns, apparently preoccupied, hastened without another word to his room. He had been preoccupied and curt for several days past. It was remarkable, thought Lawrence, how he had softened to the old woman Podmore, just for a few instants. Fearns was one of those men who do not distinguish between women. The mere presence of Woman, even if she is worn out and wears a coal sack and poisons the air, changes them, challenges them to please.

'Put it on my desk,' said Lawrence to Gater, when Gater brought the pork-pie. And without giving himself a moment to think he went straight to Fearns' room, knocked, and entered.

Fearns, with his hat on, was drumming against the window pane.

'I want to speak to you, Mr Fearns,' Lawrence began.

'I haven't had lunch yet,' Fearns complained, as he turned to face Lawrence.

'It's about a divorce case,' said Lawrence, ignoring the remark. And, having uttered the fatal word, he felt calmer. 'After all,' he said to himself, breathing like one who has just come through a peril, 'I'm only talking to him. There's nothing to be afraid of or ashamed of.'

'What divorce case?'

'My divorce case,' said Lawrence boldly.

'You've left the door ajar. Better close it,' said Fearns. Lawrence, with a startled jump, obeyed the suggestion. And then Fearns, looking at him steadily, continued: 'You don't mean to say that *you've* been making a fool of yourself, Ridware?'

'I propose to bring an action against my wife,' Lawrence told him with singular quietude. 'And the co-respondent will be Emery Greatbatch, B.A.'

Fearns sat down in his revolving chair, and put his hat with a bang on the desk. He had certainly gone pale.

'Ridware,' he murmured. 'You shock me! You shock me!'

Lawrence took the chair on the opposite side of the great desk.

'Yes, I dare say,' he said angrily. 'But I've been a great deal more shocked than you are.' He saw quite plainly that Fearns was affected as Mark had been affected. The first movement of Fearns' heart was clearly one of sympathy for Phyllis. Why? How was it that these men had got it into their heads the idea that Phyllis was the pearl of her sex? Let them live with her! Let them live with her! Fearns was gazing at him as though he ought to be ashamed of having brought such a charge against such a woman.

'Has your wife confessed?' Fearns asked.

'Confessed!' Lawrence sneered, and he was surprised at his own freedom in handling the interview which he had so much dreaded. He knew his demeanour was rapidly losing its accustomed restraint, and he rejoiced. 'I should think she hasn't confessed!'

'Then how do you know – what proofs have you –'

'I'll tell you in two minutes what proofs I have,' Lawrence responded. 'I expect you didn't see that woman who called here last night?'

'No,' said Fearns stiffly. 'What woman?'

And Lawrence described to him in detail what he had learnt from Lottie.

There was a pause.

'A discharged servant!' Fearns exclaimed at length and his voice was full of insinuation.

'Not in the least a discharged servant!' cried Lawrence, growing angrier.

'My dear fellow, don't talk so loud,' Fearns expostulated. 'You'll do yourself no good by losing your temper, you know.'

'I won't lose my temper,' said Lawrence in a low tone. He leaned back in the chair and threw out his legs. 'All I say is, she isn't a discharged servant. It's not that kind of thing at all. And there can be no doubt whatever of the facts! Moreover, my wife has already left me.'

'When was that?'

'Last night.' And he proceeded further with his recital, repeating more than once what he had previously stated.

'And you are determined to bring an action?'

'Absolutely.'

'It's a pity you've no one to consult.'

'But I'm consulting you!'

'I mean your own people – relatives.'

'I've consulted my brother Mark. He came down specially from London last night to see me.'

'Oh! Mark!' Fearns muttered the name queerly, and hesitated. 'And what does he say?'

'Why, of course he agrees with me that I must commence proceedings at once!' Lawrence felt as though for the last twenty hours he had been burning to bring an action and had been hindered by his friends. 'What *else* is there to do?'

'Certainly, certainly,' Fearns concurred. 'Your wife's not likely to let it go undefended I suppose? Anyhow, Greatbatch isn't. It will ruin his career – him, a schoolmaster!'

'A good thing too!' said Lawrence, once more startled and pleased by his own fierceness.

'You'll have to give security for your wife's costs,' said Fearns warningly.

'Yes, I know,' Lawrence replied. 'It's a scandalous thing, this is.'

'It isn't a scandalous thing at all,' said Fearns crossly. 'It's perfectly just.'

'My wife has a small private income.'

'That's nothing to do with it. The law was made to meet the average case.'

'Well, I shall give security for my wife's costs.' Lawrence said, with acerbity. 'There will be no difficulty about that. I shall give security.'

'And I take it you want me to act?'

Lawrence nodded.

'Very well,' said Fearns reluctantly, 'if you are decided. Begin when you like. You know quite as much about the procedure as I do. You've got to make sure of your witnesses. The lodging-house keeper at Manifold is the first person to see.'

'I don't want to conduct the thing myself, sir,' Lawrence said sharply. 'You'll appreciate that.'

Fearns seemed puzzled, taken aback. 'Well, then,' he said, 'give it to Sillitoe. It will be experience for him.' And he rose and picked up his hat.

'Sillitoe? Do you think he's equal –'

'Well, Pennington if you prefer. As you please.'

'I was hoping that you would keep an eye on it yourself, sir,' said Lawrence, suddenly and inexplicably grown timid.

'I shall naturally do that,' Fearns replied icily. 'I try to keep an eye on everything in this office. I'm going out to lunch now.'

And he departed, nervous, disturbed, irritated, as it were with a grievance against a trusted employee with whom he was ordinarily on terms of amiable if occasionally brusque familiarity.

Lawrence ate the pork-pie with appetite and drank a glass of water. He was in a peculiarly uplifted state. The misery, the disquiet, the hot resentment still dominated his heart; the sense of appalling and undeserved injury remained always there. But he now somehow exulted in calamity. He was conscious of a strange momentary energy, and of a desire to talk about his affairs to all the world. He actually had an impulse to go and tell Gater; he did not, however, yield to it. He meant to be philosophical, in a rather cynical way. He was determined to be surprised at nothing; for instance, he was determined not to be surprised at Fearns' remarkable attitude in face of his disclosure. Fearns had seemed to be upset by the mere idea of divorce, of anybody's divorce; it had seemed to trouble him. . . . Well, one must not be surprised at anything, nowadays, from human nature, said Lawrence to himself loftily.

He resumed his study of Dixon. At half-past three he boasted that he had mastered the law and practice of divorce. The pepper in the pork-pie had made him very thirsty. He put on his hat and with a certain swagger went into the articled-clerks' room. Sillitoe's chair remained consistently empty.

'I shall have done in half an hour,' said Pennington.

'Good!' said Lawrence. 'When you are free I want a private chat with you, old man. I've something to tell you that will surprise you.' His hands were deep in his pockets, his hat at the back of his head. And he had called Pennington 'old man'! Assuredly he was a changed Lawrence.

'Really!' murmured Pennington, unmoved.

'Yes. I'm just going out to get a drink. Back directly. Hasn't young Sillitoe turned up at all today?'

'Oh, yes,' said Pennington. 'But he went out a minute since.'

Lawrence strolled to the Turk's Head in Crown Square.

The old Turk's Head was not the most magnificent hotel in Hanbridge; it was not magnificent at all. Nevertheless its series of bars and parlours and smoke-rooms, with different levels of tiled floors, and grimy ceilings, mazily confusing to the stranger but simplicity itself to the habitué, were frequented by the governing classes of Hanbridge, and history was made in them. The Turk's Head, in a superlative degree, was what is known among experts as 'a good house.' Magnetized by the irresistible attraction of a reliable whisky (young men with a tendency to sweep said it was the only whisky in the Five Towns that could be differentiated from poison), reassured by traditions of impeccable respectability, and by that air of being an institution which the Turk's Head had, town councillors, justices of the peace, officials, journalists, actors, and men of mark professionally and commercially, would 'drop in' from morn to night for half an hour's relaxation and fellowship. It was emphatically a resort of persons 'in the know.' It was a spot where hypocrisy was abandoned and make-believes put aside, where the gullibility of the public was deplored and laughed at, where men talked sincerely about many things – and especially about women. The most dreadful truths were accepted as the commonplaces of human nature at the Turk's Head. Less stiff and stuffy than the Conservative Club, and infinitely more solid and influential than the Liberal Club, it united all parties except the Temperance and the extreme religious. Decidedly there were important men in Hanbridge who would never have dreamed of entering the Turk's Head, but they were not of the kind that is prepared to make allowances for the excessive humanity of human nature. In brief, the Turk's Head was a hotel calculated to support the doctrine that the world is not such a bad world after all, a large and lovable inn. Such organisms can only flourish in the provinces, and in a certain way they illustrate roughly the most agreeable and satisfactory aspects of the national character.

The licensee was a widow. She wore black alpaca in the morning and black silk later in the day, tightly stretched over her generous form. And as her customers were experts on women so was she an expert on men; she knew; she could hold her own on County Court day and market days; also on Shrove Tuesday, when the entire clientèle called to eat her adorable pancakes. Her domain had a grimy look, but what could one expect in the middle of a town like Hanbridge? And the fixtures were not in the first blush of a vigorous youth. But everything had the comfortableness or the accepted uncomfortableness of long, long use, and each bit of brass was polished daily. There were two barmaids. Emmie was a young thing, and nothing more; while Miss Parratt was the peeress of the widow, and knew the separate eccentricities of some scores of customers. Better even than the widow she knew where to draw the line. No one under the rank of a magistrate was allowed to get too mellow in the Turk's Head. With a magistrate, where are you?

Lawrence was not a frequenter of the hotel. And he went in with the defiant shyness of a stranger, lighting a cigarette to hide his embarrassment as he passed to the smoke-room by the narrow place where the private bar was installed. The Mayor and Bob Cyples were holding small glasses to each other at the private bar, and Miss Parratt (Lawrence did not even know her famous name) was doing sums in a ledger. Cyples nodded affably to Lawrence, and the Mayor nodded.

Bob Cyples was one of Hanbridge's familiar figures, and a member of the Town Council. He was a tall and very quiet stout man of fifty-five, with grey hair and a short bushy beard. Although he happened to be a sober individual and a regular liver, time was measured at the Turk's Head by Bob Cyples' drinks. This was the hour of his second drink; his third would occur at a quarter to six, his fourth at eight-thirty, and his fifth at five minutes to eleven. In theory Cyples was a clerk in the legal firm of Bradwell, Breeze, Robinson & Willan, a really large firm of solicitors, one of the most

important in the Midlands, with an immense conveyancing
and general practice; there were seven admitted solicitors in
Bradwells. Cyples was not 'admitted'; he had never been
through an examination; he had no right to practise; he was
just an unadmitted clerk. Nevertheless, in fact, Cyples was the
head, the heart and the brain of the firm. Old Bradwell openly
treated him with the respect due to an equal, and the other six
admitted men, including the junior partners, simply took
Cyples' orders. He had property in various parts of the town,
and he lived the spacious life of a wealthy bachelor. The
situation was a genuine mystery. Some said that, in order to
keep within the statutes of the Incorporated Law Society,
Bradwells paid him a fixed salary of fifteen hundred a year;
others, that the statutes of the Law Society were secretly
traversed and that Cyples was a partner in the firm. His
astounding knack of getting business, his wonderful talent for
conducting it when got, his surpassing influence over his
fellow men – these qualities in Cyples were denied by none.
Yet his knowledge of law was quite elementary.

   He was as great in pleasure as in business; a jolly fat man,
with a perfect stomach. Habitually he drank little, but he
could drink a lot with impunity. He enjoyed life; he enjoyed
his meals; he enjoyed his cigars and his whisky and his wine;
he probably enjoyed the gusts of temper with which he
occasionally gave variety to the course of existence inside
Bradwells. He was a very good billiard-player, and a finished
card-player. Solo whist was his passion, and he frequently
won several sovereigns at it in an evening. But he would not
play at poker, which he called 'gambling.' Bridge he scorned.
He knew nearly all the good stories on earth; only now and
then could an actor in a musical-comedy touring company or
an exceptionally experienced commercial traveller add to his
stock. He told his tales – and he had tales for every occasion –
in a rich, vibrating, hearty voice and with a deep though
restrained appreciation of them. He spent all his waking hours
in offices, committee-rooms, hotels, and clubs; and in his own
world he had no superior. He was inimical to fads and
movements; his perceptions were not very subtle; he had no
feeling for art; he could not possibly be called refined; his
interests stopped short in various directions in a most disap-

pointing manner. But his was a remarkable and powerful individuality, and he knew it. He was born to lead. He did lead. He would not have changed places with a Prime Minister.

In the smoke-room Lawrence discovered Sillitoe alone, and he was very glad to discover Sillitoe. Sillitoe supervened as a friend in a foreign land, and asked him what he would have, and generally did the honours of the place. Sillitoe, aged twenty-three, was an orphan with too much money, a fair, stout, dandiacal youth whose boyish face was already beginning to coarsen, a weak soul doomed from the first to destruction, a person of no importance. Lawrence despised and pitied him. And yet, over a glass of beer, he told Sillitoe in a few words of the forthcoming divorce case, and Sillitoe was much flattered to learn that no one save himself and Mr Fearns yet knew of the affair. He said he should be delighted to do all he could in the matter. Never before had Sillitoe been conscious of a sincere interest in Mr Fearns' business. Lawrence suggested that he might search the office stock for forms for petition, citation, praecipe, etcetera. And Sillitoe, having insisted on paying for Lawrence's beer, hurried back to the office full of the urgency of his mission, and left Lawrence solitary in the smoke-room. He promised to tell Pennington. It had been Lawrence's intention to speak first to Pennington, but he altered his plan in obedience to the hazard of this meeting.

Then he heard the voice of Cyples saying to the Mayor, 'One moment and I am with you,' and Cyples came into the smoke-room with his easy alert tread, carrying lightly that vast bulk.

'How do you do, Ridware?' he greeted Lawrence with marked seriousness and deference, and drawing forward a chair he sat down and put his expressive, sagacious face close to Lawrence's

'I needn't tell you how pained I am about – you know what,' said he in a confidential whisper. And ere Lawrence could utter a word he added, 'Mrs Ridware has instructed us.'

Lawrence was taken absolutely by surprise. 'What? My wife?' he stammered, blushing. 'She's been to see you already?'

'Her mother brought her to see me this morning,' said Cyples.

'Oh, very well! Very well!' Lawrence haughtily responded.

'Of course we will accept service,' Cyples said.

'You can't,' said Lawrence shortly.

'Oh! Must it be personal? I forget,' Cyples urbanely murmured.

'And Greatbatch? What about him?' demanded Lawrence, nodding.

'I know nothing about Mr Greatbatch,' said Cyples, still in a whisper. 'Good day.'

And with a smile almost genial, he left to rejoin the Mayor.

The fact that the formidable Cyples was arrayed against him frightened Lawrence. How rapidly events matured! The action seemed already to have begun! Well, he was in for it! It was like Phyllis to go straight to Cyples! And with her mother! He felt that he must see Mrs Capewell.

Later, in the office, he talked much, and with a freedom that continually astonished him, to Pennington and Sillitoe. And except a fruitless search in the form cupboard for divorce forms, nothing in the way of office routine was accomplished until Fearns telephoned some instructions about correspondence, with a message that he should not return that evening. And gradually the hour of closing approached. Lawrence dictated some miscellaneous letters, and glanced at the Abstract of Title. Sillitoe left at a quarter to six, Clowes and Pennington at six precisely. Gater was busily copying letters in the press, and addressing and stamping envelopes and entering up the Postage Book. It was Gater's hour of importance. At a quarter-past six Gater inquired whether he might go, and, having received permission, deposited the keys with Lawrence and went, his hands full of letters in virgin white envelopes of various sizes. Lawrence sat meditative as the sun descended. Another day of his life was gone. What a day! What changes! It seemed to be years since the fact of his wife's deception had reached him. He was a man marked and labelled, a petitioner in the Divorce Court. And Cyples was against him. All Hanbridge would buzz tomorrow; the bars of the Turk's Head would tinkle to the luscious gossip. He rose dully and sardonically, and passed out of the offices. At the

end of the street an electric car flashed down populous
Holborn.

And his worries had scarcely begun! The inquiries, the
collection of evidence, the innumerable annoyances of a
tedious and complex litigation . . .! Suddenly it struck him
that he had entirely forgotten to see Cousin Sarah about
coming to stay with him at Toft End, – entirely forgotten!

CHAPTER III

ANNUNCIATA

The two little Fearns boys, Frank and Sep, aged six and five, were playing at a game invented by Frank called 'Seashore,' in a nondescript space of ground which extended between the large garden at the front of the house at Bleakridge and the paved yard at the back, and which was overlooked by the kitchen and scullery windows. It was about six o'clock in the afternoon of the day on which Mrs Fearns had suddenly gone to Birmingham. Several loads of fine gravel, deposited that morning and intended for the reparation of the garden paths, were the basis of the game, constituting a beach, while the great oval lawn, of which the garden principally consisted, was the rolling sea. The intrepid adventurers, with the sleeves of their tiny blue jerseys rolled up, had their Llandudno spades and buckets, and were building a castle in the sea, or rather on it. They did not go into the sea, from a prudent fear of getting their sandalled brown feet wet, but they stood bravely at the very edge of the waves and flung spadefuls of gravel as far as they could, and a fine castle was gradually rising from the deep. In the two essentials of a maximum of innocent joy to the players and a maximum of unintended exasperating inconvenience to the adult world, it was a game not easily to be surpassed.

Annunciata Fearns was in the kitchen, wearing a pink pinafore apron over her white frock, and busy in cake-making at the dresser under the open window. Annunciata's age was twenty. Like many girls of twenty she had the seriousness of Methusaleh. Her mother being absent she had voluntarily taken upon her shoulders the crushing burden of the entire establishment, including a wayward father, 'the children,' a French nursery-governess, a cook, a house-parlourmaid, a

scullery-maid, a gardener, two cats, two reception-rooms, a
hall, seven bedrooms, a greenhouse and a garden. In addition
to her piano practice, her French lesson, and her reading, she
had already during that industrious day accomplished long
letters to a brother and sister away at school, and she had met
the telegraph-boy at the gate, and opened a reassuring telegram from her mother about her aunt, and composed a reply
in twelve words and paid sixpence for it from her own privy
purse, and she had said 'Certainly' with dignity when Mademoiselle had expressed a desire to go out alone for two hours
and leave the children to her care; and now she was making
cakes, and getting fuller and fuller of the conviction that life
was an affair of heavy responsibilities.

When she had finished as much of the cake-making as she
considered too delicate for the skill of the cook, she looked at
the kitchen clock.

'What are you doing out there?' she called through the open
window. She could see the sandy beach but not the mighty
ocean.

There was no answer. A first faint suspicion had entered the
heads of the castle-builders that perhaps after all their
operations were not void of offence.

'Do you hear what I say, Frank?'

'We're playing,' cried Frank shrilly at length.

'Well, you must play off to bed,' said Annunciata, like
doom.

'But Mamzelle hasn't come home.' Frank argued. 'There's
no one to give us our baf,' Sep supported him.

They both waited anxiously, spade in hand, to hear the
result of these unanswerable objections to the proposal of
going to bed,

'I'll give you your bath myself,' said Annunciata, who saw a
method at once of adding to the responsibilities of life and of
silently showing to Mademoiselle that Mademoiselle had not
kept her word.

'That's not fair,' Frank piped. 'Muvver never gives us our
baf.'

It was a smart thrust on Frankie's part, this insinuation that
to be more motherly than mother was cheating, but
Annunciata pretended not to feel it.

'I'm coming to catch you,' she smiled persuasively.

She threw off the pinafore apron, and ran, resuming her childhood for a moment, through the side-passage and hall to the front door, meaning to startle Frank and Sep from an ambush. At the front door she paused, knowing not why, and began to think about she knew not what. She had these fits. She stood there looking vaguely at the lawn with the croquet hoops, and at the row of small houses that could be discerned through the hedge in the street beyond. She was that exquisite, unique, inscrutable thing, a young girl opening pure eyes upon the world. Slim, even thin, with long limbs, she had the delicious gawky gracefulness of her years. Her pale face was not beautiful, the nose being insignificant, but its complexion was adorable, and the blood ran faintly beneath the delicate skin in restless emotional tides. And she had bright yellow hair, done up very tightly; and on her finger was an opal ring which her father had given to her, and round her slender neck an old gold necklace that had been her grandmother's. And she herself was the jewel of that red house which her grandfather had built, and which her father had enlarged despite the fact that it was being gradually hemmed in by mean streets. She was its most precious treasure, guarded passionately by her parents, loved, worshipped, brooded over, dreamt of. It was as if all the ancestors of the Fearns family and of the Leigh family had descended one from another in two converging lines solely in order to meet at last in Annunciata, their final expression and justification. The house existed round Annunciata; it was her frame. And she was so touching in her *naïveté,* her simplicity, her seriousness, her sincerity, her wonder, her capriciousness, her sensitiveness, her gawky grace, her enchanting alternations between childishness and womanliness, – she was so touching that even to watch her, or to catch her in a characteristic attitude, would sometimes bring tears into the eyes of one who had eyes to see. Why? Heaven knows! She was not at all extraordinary. There are thousands and thousands like her, tens of thousands of these strange disturbing mysterious vitalities. And yet, frequency cannot cheapen them. Each is the supreme excuse for the universe, a miraculous vase from which the pure fluid of life itself seems to gush forth.

'You're walking on the sea! You're walking on the sea!' Frank and Sep shoutingly protested when they saw Annunciata creeping towards them along the edge of the lawn.

'Am I?' She good-naturedly lifted up her skirts and pretended to splash about in the foam.

'You'll get drowned!' they warned her.

'Oh! You naughty, naughty little things!' Annunciata exploded when the castle caught her eye.

'What?'

'Martin will be back from his tea in a minute, and *then* what will he say? I'm very cross with you indeed. Come to bed now, or I shall be really angry.'

'No, no, no!' the sinners protested. 'Mamzelle hasn't come, and muvver never gives us our baf!'

And they ran madly off across the sea, which had suddenly changed into dry land, and Annunciata after them. And, always precariously balanced, they fell over each other, and their clumsy little limbs mingled, and their ridiculous jerseys worked up from the waist and disclosed their little shirts and braces. And then Annunciata was bending over them, sweet and yet formidable, and tickling them in all their most ticklish places, and whimperings became shrieks. This enormous sister of five feet picked them up, one under each Titanic arm, wriggling and giggling, and marched them away. Sep was upside down with his sandals in her eyes and his head near the placket-hole of her frock, so that as he was being carried towards the house he had a topsy-turvy view of the garden-gates.

'Mamzelle!' he shouted frantically. 'There's Mamzelle!'

Whereupon Annunciata turned, allowed the boys to slip to the ground, and composed herself to be prim.

'She's got another one of her beggars!' Frank remarked with loud contempt,

'Hush, Frankie!' Annunciata admonished him.

Mademoiselle Renée Souchon came quickly and demurely to the house; a ragged cringing old man was standing near the gates. Renée smiled benevolently, and with a certain preoccupation, at the youthful group on the doorstep.

'I will be ready in one moment,' she said in her precise, clear English, as she passed them. 'One little moment,' she repeated, hastening upstairs, as if on a mysterious, holy errand. In a little moment she came neatly out again, and with no further word of explanantion, tripped to the old man, and the man gratefully took something from the gloved hand with its curved fingers, and made an obeisance and departed, while Renée meticulously and gently shut the gates.

Annunciata did not approve of Renée Souchon. Her disapproval was calm and restrained, and she imparted it to nobody at all, but it was very genuine. You see, Annunciata was such a serious girl. She read what she could; and she thought tremendously. The whole spectacle of life offered itself for her criticism; and she criticized it, with much freedom, and much seriousness, and no humour whatever. She gazed at it as though it had never been gazed at before, and made the most singular discoveries. Thus she had discovered that servants are exactly as human as we are, and have the same right to wear jewellery and pretty hats and to discuss men as we have; to force servants into a uniform was immoral because tyrannous; still she couldn't imagine herself waited on at table by a crimson blouse, and the question of servants' clothing was one of the few great human questions to which in the privacy of her own mind she had no solution to offer. She believed in herself intensely, and once she had thoroughly pondered upon a subject, her conclusions were sacred to her. The notion that they could be wrong, and that she was not indeed fully equipped for her rôle as constructive critic, did not even occur to her. People who happened to engage her in serious conversation were astonished at the range and gravity of her thoughts. It is so with innumerable young girls.

The advent of Renée Souchon nearly a year ago had raised mighty issues in the breast of Annunciata. Renée was an outcome of the sad fact that Charles Fearns, junior, had twice failed in French at the Cambridge Local Examination. Mr and Mrs Fearns had put their heads together and decided that at any rate Frank and Sep should not fail in French. The children had to have a nursery-governess, and therefore they should have a French nursery-governess, who should also give lessons to Annunciata in that language so essential to modern English culture. Really, in these days everyone spoke French. And like all British parents in a similar predicament Mr and

Mrs Fearns were very anxious that when Frank and Sep spoke French in such a manner as to be mistaken for Frenchmen, Frank and Sep should be mistaken only for Parisians. They insisted on the 'good accent.' The thought of Frank and Sep being one day mistaken in France for natives of Lyons or Bordeaux was painful to Mr and Mrs Fearns. Hence Renée Souchon, a guaranteed Parisienne with a guaranteed accent and truly excellent testimonials, had come into Bursley out of the void, conjured there by a governess agency in London. Renée was somewhat of an innovation in Bursley. Bursley approved. The progress in French was not quite as wonderful as had been expected; Annunciata declined to attempt to talk French outside her French lesson, and Frank and Sep, despite their tender years, had sufficient personal force to stipulate that French should cease to be the sole medium of communication at one-thirty p.m., when their dinner finished. Still, in three months the children could understand whatever Renée said to them, and other children's parents were not unimpressed. And neither Mr nor Mrs Fearns suspected that Annunciata, guided by lofty general principles, disapproved. For of course she would not have ventured openly to criticize her parents.

Annunciata was very English. It had been vouchsafed to her that the English race was the master-stroke of the eternal powers. The very defects of the English were good qualities. All other races were inferior; the thing was obvious. And if there was one other race that Annunciata in especial contemned, that race was the French. The French were not serious; they were not moral; they were frivolous. *You could not rely on them.* Their women were dolls; their men were wicked, besides being paltry and grotesque to the eye. Germany had humiliated them – catch Germany trying to humiliate England! – and there they were enjoying themselves and 'going on' as though nothing had happened. She had read that Parisian theatres were often crowded during the siege of Paris. That settled the French, so far as Annunciata was concerned.

And her parents had summoned into her English home a living representative of the dangerous and despicable spirit! They had undertaken this hazardous experiment for the trifling end of teaching a language to two little boys! It seemed to Annunciata unwise, and also unnecessary. She knew why Charlie had failed in French – simply because he hated French as she did. He could have passed it if he had tried. He decidedly had not failed because he had had no French governess in infancy. Wherein was the reasonableness of this craze for French? If one wanted to travel there were always hotels with English-speaking waiters. And the French had no Dickens, no Thackeray, no Scott, no Tennyson. They had Racine and Corneille, and Annunciata did not opine that it was worth while to learn French in order to read Racine and Corneille.

In short, while determined to be scrupulously just, even to the point of generosity, in adding up the French governess, Annunciata had had an inward conviction that she would not like her. And she did not. She did not like her corsets, which she more than once by accident saw. Renée was blonde and somewhat stout, and not very tall; neither ugly nor pretty; and her age was quite thirty. She used powder. Annunciata had never anticipated that the day would come when she would inhabit the same house with a woman who used powder. But it had come. Her dressing-table was a sight! How could a woman who used powder and wore those scandalous corsets be the prim and religious woman that Renée pretended to be? Annunciata, having lately been attracted towards the creed of Christian Science, was all for religious liberty. But Renée was a Roman Catholic. She went to low mass, and high mass. And she positively went to confession. Annunciata did not care to think of the private life of her home being exposed to Father Hurley. Roman Catholicism was not a sincere religion, like other religions.

Then there was the question of Renée's charities. Annunciata was obliged to admit that the Fearns household did not expend much of its energy in charity, perhaps rather neglected that duty, in fact, *did* neglect it. But she did not wish to be reminded of duty by Renée Souchon. Moreover, charity ought to be a pleasure, not a duty. Renée made of charity a regular occupation. She had her days for rummaging among the Catholic poor of the town; she would recount her adventures sadly at the dinner-table, and, without a single direct word against England or the country or the district, she would tacitly formulate a terrible indictment of our social organism. Apparently matters were quite different in France; apparently France was civilized, whereas England was just emerging from a sort of Viking barbarism: such was the implication, unexpressed of course. Annunciata's Saxon blood raged impotently within her. Annunciata was sure that the high pulpit from which Renée silently preached did not cost the preacher in money more than a shilling a week; and she detested Renée's queenly condescending compassionate gesture in giving a halfpenny to a mendicant. She was absolutely convinced that Renée with her impeccable demeanour, her frigid and changeless propriety, and her manifold Christian virtues, was a two-faced creature. She dreamed occasionally of Jesuits! And this woman was in their home, part of their home, and influencing from morn to night the impressionable characters of Frank and Sep! Annunciata's blind, bland parents were oblivious of the evil that was being wrought! And Annunciata could not interfere.

What annoyed Annunciata more than anything else was the instinctive knowledge that Renée regarded her as a raw young girl whom a very little diplomatic skill could manage. She hated to admit to herself that Renée was a vastly cleverer and subtler person than herself, but there were times when she did admit it.

And with it all Annunciata in the secrecy of her kind little heart felt ineffably sorry for the poor French governess. Annunciata's pity was sometimes almost too painful to be borne, and she would turn away from the contemplation of Renée's plight as one turns away from the spectacle of a miserable outcast in the street on a wintry night, when one drives by enveloped in furs. For Renée was a solitary. Renée had no kindred to love her, no home, no ties, nothing to cling to. She was a wanderer. She existed in the Fearns house essentially a stranger, familiar but not intimate. She could not enter into its joys and sorrows; she was not expected to do so. They all tried to be good to her, and to give her the illusion of being at home. But she merely camped among them, as she might have camped in the desert of Sahara. Often in the evenings she would retire early, and her retirement was a

relief! What irony, then, was their goodness! Renée's lamp
burned very late. Once Annunciata had gone into her room,
and found her sitting up in bed, wrapped in a dressing-gown,
with her pillows at her back, reading *The Heir of Redclyffe*; it
was in January; she had steadfastly refused a fire, but after that
Annunciata had insisted, passionately, that a gas-stove should
be fixed in the room, and evening after evening had lighted it
herself, until at length Renée promised without fail to use it.
The picture of the woman reading there in thick folds of
woollen, lonely, withdrawn, proud, with the lamp rays falling
on the bed and the rest of the room in obscurity, had lacerated
the tender soul of Annunciata. . . . And Renée's life would
always be like that, if not in their house then in some other,
perhaps in some house less kindly than theirs! And she would
grow old and grey. And people would not want her. And then
what? Then what? Annunciata thanked her scientifically-
conceived gods that she was not a governess.

She followed the procession of children and governess
upstairs, and went to her own room to prepare for dinner.
There could be no doubt about the fact that Mademoiselle was
extremely skilful in her profession. Annunciata was sure that
Frank and Sep did not adore Mademoiselle, but they obeyed
her without hating her. And she was never flurried, never
angry; she never even raised her voice. Mrs Fearns could
control her tumultuous offspring pretty well, yet even
Annunciata would not have asserted that the mother had
nothing to learn from the governess in this matter. A
conspicuous instance of Mademoiselle's extraordinary powers
occurred when the procession arrived in the bathroom. She
turned on the taps of the bath, and then told Frank to begin
undressing and put his clothes on one chair and Sep to begin
undressing and put his clothes on another chair; and then she
imperturbably left them in order to remove her own hat and
jacket and don an apron. It was a feat of apparent bravado,
such as the lion-tamer accomplishes when he sticks his head
between the lion's jaws. If Annunciata had dared to attempt it
the result would have been disastrous – waste-plug pulled out,
the bath probably full of clothes, and both lavatory taps turned
on to overflow the lavatory basin. But Mademoiselle went
unhasting back to the bathroom in full confidence that the

children would have withstood the terrible temptations which she had set before them; and the confidence was justified.

Presently Annunciata from the window saw her father coming into the house. And she hurried her toilette. In the absence of her mother she considered she had to be more than a daughter to her father, that she had to be more grown up, more like her mother to him. She must watch over him, hover round him, distract him, conduct herself so that her mother was missed as little as possible. She heard the front door bang loudly; her father always banged the front door. He would be coming upstairs directly. The door of her own room was carelessly left wide open; the bathroom door also was open, and there reached her from the bathroom the splendid miscellaneous splashings and shoutings which Mademoiselle permitted each night to her charges. The children were now shouting for father; they too had heard the thunderous banging of the front door. Mademoiselle was being exhorted to go and fetch father to see a wonderful wound on Sep's knee. Annunciata pushed her door nearly to, and from sheer girlishness peeped through the inch-wide space which she had left. She meant to call out to her father concerning the telegram as he passed to his bedroom. She saw Mademoiselle's aproned figure as it descended the three steps from the bathroom to the level of the passage. At the same moment her father appeared up the stairs. The two encountered one another on the dusky landing at the head of the stairs.

'The children would like to see you,' said Mademoiselle.

Then Annunciata saw her father glance round and raise his hand and caressingly pat Mademoiselle's cheek. The gesture was an affair of half a second. Mademoiselle's face seemed to protest against the imprudence of the act. But she smiled in a way quite novel to the watcher behind the door. Annunciata could not see her father's face at the instant of the caress.

'Very well,' said Mr Fearns.

And they disappeared into the bathroom.

Annunciata, with crimson cheeks and neck, and heart wildly thumping, moved from her door to the window. In her gentle and rather self-satisfied progress from birth towards death she had suddenly received a staggering, dizzying blow – she who had been used to nothing worse than glimpses of real

pain – and some minutes elapsed before she could resume her
shaken faculties and think. She loved and admired her father;
she was proud of him. She found him handsome, and she was
delighted when people said he looked young enough to be her
brother. He was dashing, gallant, generally gay, and he
spoiled her – there could not be two opinions about that. He
had a kind heart, like hers. But it would have been too much
to expect that even her father should pass wholly unimpeached
before the ruthless tribunal of her young judgment; only her
mother could do that. She privately censured him for a certain
lightness, a lack of seriousness, also for leaving her mother too
frequently alone in the evening; and she objected to his playing
cards for money. His occasional short, sharp, unreasonable
outbursts of wrath she was ready to excuse as an inevitable
part of the unreasonable masculine temperament, but she
could not in her terrific honesty excuse the other things. She
forgave them constantly; so that her attitude towards her
father was often a little maternal and angelically grieved.

And her father had done something really very wrong
indeed. She was sure that it was very wrong and utterly
inexcusable for the master of the house to pat a governess on
the cheek. She did not need to be told that. Supposing a
servant had seen them! And it was the last indiscretion of
which she would have deemed her father capable, because he
was always so dignified and correct, especially with women.
He might neglect her mother, but his mere behaviour to her
was almost invariably what it ought to be. He was in fact at his
best with women, so thoughtful, so courteous, so
appreciative! And losing his own self-respect and robbing her
of hers! A pat on the cheek, said Annunciata, was nothing,
regarded as a pat. But such a thing ought not to be. It was not
a bit nice. It was odious. An indiscretion, yes, but there were
indiscretions that were worse than crimes! She would have
infinitely preferred to convict her father of getting drunk and
knocking a man down than to convict him of that pat.

And her mother absent too! That appeared, in some way
that was mysterious to Annunciata, to make the indiscretion
more indiscreet.

As for Renée, Annunciata's intellect blamed her less than it
blamed the man, but Annunciata's heart blamed her a great

deal more. She was astounded at Renée's conduct. Renée ought to have – ought to have done what? Screamed? Walked straight out of the house? Told her employer that his behaviour was infamous? . . . Annunciata could not exactly decide what Renée ought to have done. But she ought to have done anything rather than smile. Anyhow, Annunciata had always been convinced that Renée was two-faced, and now she had the proof. And yet the proof astounded her!

She knew nothing of her father's reputation in the world where men talk. Though by no means ignorant, she was as ignorant as a girl can be who has been to school, and glanced occasionally at the newspapers, and assisted distantly at the birth of babies, and reached the age of twenty. And by nature it was excessively difficult for her to think impurely. If to have a very weak sexual instinct is to be pure, Annunciata was pure. Her purity was not shocked by what she had seen, for the reason that she had simply not seen it in a sexual aspect at all. It had not occurred to her to regard that caressing pat as a symptom, as one act in a series of acts. She regarded it by itself, as an unpleasant but isolated indiscretion.

And what was she to do with the secret of which she had unwittingly become possessed? Ought she to tell her mother? Or rather, could she bring herself to tell her mother? Could she tell her father that she had seen him, and express to him her respectful but uncompromising disapproval? Or could she give Renée a private hint that would lead to the voluntary departure of Renée? In the midst of all her pain, confusion and outraged propriety, Annunciata was conscious of a strong desire to act wisely, prudently, for the best. She wanted to prove to herself that she was equal to the situation, that she was no ordinary girl. The feeling, however, that she was quite unequal to the situation unfortunately dominated her. She did not know what to do. And her mother seemed so far away.

She sat a long time on the bed, hot, quivering, suffering, shamed. She wished she had never been born. She thought she could never look anyone in the face again. The life of the house proceeded as usual. Her father came out of the bathroom and passed to his bedroom and then went downstairs. The children padded from the bathroom to the nursery, chattering. Doors closed and opened. The light began to fail. She heard the explosion of the gas as a servant lighted it in the hall. A gong sounded. '*Faites dodo,*' she heard Renée say, shutting the door of the nursery. And then suddenly she sprang up, and bathed her eyes, and went haughtily downstairs. She had taken refuge in an immense pride. She summoned all her powers of duplicity – and like most women of her temperament she was in this respect richly endowed – to hoodwink her father and Renée. On entering the dining-room she first gave an order to Louisa the parlourmaid, in a rather curt, preoccupied voice, as though the cares of the household still weighed heavily upon her. She meant to produce this impression on her father, and she succeeded perfectly. He was standing on the hearthrug, waiting.

'Now Tommy,' he said, indicating that he desired his dinner.

She looked him fairly in the face and smiled guardedly, as if to warn him that she was mistress of the house today, and he must be careful how he used his disrespectful pet name for her.

'Any news from your mother?' he demanded.

'Yes, dad,' she replied, and took the telegram from her pocket and gave it to him.

'What's this writing on the back?' he inquired.

'That's a copy of my reply to mother,' she said.

Meanwhile she was moving her cover from its ordinary position to the empty place which was her mother's.

'Good!' murmured her father, putting the crumpled telegram on the mantelpiece. 'What are you doing, Tommy?'

'I'm going to sit opposite you,' said Annunciata calmly, sitting down and pushing the flower vases into new latitudes.

Mademoiselle came into the room, and dinner began. How Mademoiselle could have the audacity to come and take her seat as though nothing had happened, Annunciata could not imagine. The governess's air was absolutely demure, as usual. She looked down at her plate over the beetling precipice of her corsage just as usual. She talked just as usual; Mr Fearns also; yes, and Annunciata also. If these two could dissemble, so could she. If these two were a man and a woman who had seen the world, and she was a little thing who knew nothing, nevertheless she would match them at their own game. And she did. The pat grew unreal, impossible; the pat of a dream. Should she tell her mother? Or should she try to forget? Her gaze wandered round the heavy oak solidity of the dining-room and she felt the thick Turkey carpet under her feet. Everything was real, homely, unchanged; and yet by moments, just as the memory of the past seemed a dream, so the very house seemed insubstantial and illusory.

Towards the end of the dinner there was a peculiar noise outside the door.

'What's that?' Fearns exclaimed.

'I'm afraid it's Master Frank and Master Sep, sir,' answered the servant, smiling faintly.

And those two imps, in nothing but their nightshirts, plunged into the room, crying that father had promised them chocolates and had forgotten. As a matter of fact, their father's visit to the bathroom had unduly excited them, encouraged them to a deed which was rash even for them. But in their father's presence they never had any fear of Mademoiselle.

Both women sprang up together with exclamations of horror.

'Mademoiselle,' said Fearns, with awful solemnity, 'is this the way you bring up my boys?'

But the boys were not to be misled by mock-heroics. They were already pulling at his knees, inarticulate, joyous, triumphantly grinning. The knees were sanctuary from Mad-emoiselle, who glanced at them undecided what to do.

'This is what comes of your mother being away,' said Fearns. 'But she shall be told. She shall be told.' And he reached forward to the silver dish in the middle of the table containing chocolates.

'Mr Fearns!' Mademoiselle protested.

'Well, I did promise them, you know,' said Fearns, as he put one chocolate into each mouth. 'Now hook it!' he shouted. 'Hook it! Or by the beard of the prophet, I'll –'

They ran off delighted with themselves. Mademoiselle made as if to follow.

'I'll go,' said Annunciata. 'I'll look after them.'

'Oh, no,' said the governess. 'Not at all –'

'I'll go,' Annunciata repeated firmly.

And she did go. And upstairs, because Sep did not instantly get into bed, she smacked him and he cried, and she said it served him right. And gloom descended upon the nursery.

She went downstairs very quietly and entered the dining-room with suddenness, fearing what she might see; her father sat there alone.

'Where's Mademoiselle?' she asked him.

'Don't know. Drawing-room, I expect. Children all right?'

She nodded, and began to eat an apple.

The sound of the piano came from the drawing-room.

'Have some fruit, dad?' She smiled at him.

'No, thanks,' he said, and lit a cigar.

'What are you going to do tonight?' she asked.

'What do you want to know for?'

'I thought perhaps you might like to take me to the theatre to see *Patience*.'

'No, thanks,' he said drily. She was hurt. 'I'm going to the club in a minute,' he added.

She was extremely hurt by his tone, but she would not show it. She went into the drawing-room and sat down. Mademoiselle continued to play the piano, some waltzes by Waldteufel. The front door banged. Annunciata rang the bell.

'Is father gone out?' she demanded of Louisa sharply.

'Yes, miss.'

Annunciata looked through *The Girl's Realm* from the first page to the last, comprehending not a word. The house was strangely and disturbingly empty without her mother. She felt it more than ever now.

'Good night,' said Renée abruptly, rising and leaving.

Five minutes later Annunciata went to the kitchen to give final orders for the night, and she too ascended to bed. It was scarcely nine o'clock.

Annunciata's bedroom was spacious; it occupied a corner of the first storey, and had two windows, one overlooking the front garden. The bed also was spacious, for during the school vacations she was obliged to share it with Emily, a chit of fifteen. Emily referred to the bedroom as 'ours,' but Annunciata obstinately regarded her as a guest in that room. Annunciata had chosen the wall-paper and the blue eiderdown on the bed, and the rug by the side of the bed. And she had caused the furniture, originally of a Regent Street green, to be enamelled white. Most of Annunciata's books were ranged in a small hanging bookcase, bought with her own money, over a microscopic writing-bureau given to her by her mother. The photogravures on the walls were every one Annunciata's private property; there were two Maude Goodmans, a Virgin and Child wrongly attributed by Annunciata and the authorities of the Louvre to Botticelli, Burne-Jones's 'Golden Stairs,' two Orchardsons, and some minor items with interesting personal associations. On the night-table by the bed were about a dozen books and a silk-covered photograph frame containing portraits of her father and mother. Hung above the table was another and more imposing portrait of her mother, signed. Photographs and knick-knacks abounded everywhere in the chamber; a few of the photographs had already begun to fade, showing that even Annunciata was not as young as she had been. This history of her life and opinions was written at large in the bedroom. It was the expression of herself; and she was intensely proud of it, and intensely jealous for its sanctity. The servants were allowed only to make the bed and sweep the carpet; the dusting was done by Annunciata. She was not a very orderly girl, but in that apartment she had a place for everything, to the tiniest trifle, and if by accident a servant deranged a pin-cushion or a china slipper, there was the very deuce to pay. She entered the room as she might have entered a fortress; when she shut the door she sighed with satisfaction, shutting it on all the world.

That night she meant to find moral help in a book; but she could not read. Then, having put on a dressing-gown, she thought she would write to her mother, on the chance of her mother not being able to return on the morrow; but she could not write, though she had no intention of referring to the pat in her letter. She could not control her mind. At length she turned down the gas to a speck and got into bed, and gave her mind free play. Should she tell her mother? Or should she swear to herself to forget what she had seen? All at once a method of solving the question occurred to her. She must put herself on one side, and act as her mother would wish her to act. It seemed to her that her mother would certainly not wish to be kept in ignorance of the incident. Therefore she must tell, at no matter what personal pain. And she suddenly decided to tell. But she would begin by extracting from her mother a promise of absolute secrecy. She could not have borne that her father should know of her knowledge. Yes, she would say to her mother: 'Mother, I've got something to tell you, but you must promise me not to say anything to anyone about it.' And then she would go to the window or look at a picture while she told her mother. Her one desire now was for her mother's speedy return, so that she might finish with the affair. At this point she went to sleep, lying on her back, whereas she usually slept on her left side.

She woke up with a start. Rain was beating on the window nearest the bed. Perhaps it was the rain that had wakened her. She was wide awake. She rose out of bed, and as she did so the clock in the hall struck twelve. She went to the front window, and lifted the blind an inch or so and looked out. Through the low trees that screened the garden from Lawton Street she could see a light here and there in windows of the small houses opposite. She could hear the thunder of the electric tram in Trafalgar Road. Then the garden gates clicked and she descried a mysterious form crossing the garden. It was her father, returned from the club. He had no umbrella, and his head was bent and his hands apparently in the pockets of his overcoat. She heard the closing of the front door. . . . What obscure instinct made her creep to her own door and listen? She listened a long time. Not a sound, her father must have gone straight to the dining-room. At last he came upstairs, in his slippers, deliberately, calmly; he paused an instant to lower the gas on the landing, and went by her door to his own room. Then after an interval, a door closed softly; then utter silence in the house. The clock in the hall struck half-past twelve.

The first-floor corridors formed a right angle at Annunciata's door. When she stood at her open door she looked down the corridor leading to the head of the principal stairs, and the flight of stairs from the first floor to the second floor ran parallel with this corridor, the stairs beginning just opposite her door. On the left of the corridor were two doors, of a small, spare bedroom and of the day-nursery, and finally the recess leading to the bathroom. The other corridor was

broader and more important; it cut through the main part of
the house and ended in a window. Starting from this corner,
there were, first Annunciata's door, then the door of her
mother's bedroom, and then that of her father's bedroom. Her
parents' bedrooms communicated one with the other, and
indeed, the door giving access to her mother's room from the
corridor was always locked, her mother entering and leaving
by her father's room, which was a corner room corresponding
to Annunciata's. On the opposite side of the corridor were
two doors, of the night nursery and of Renée's bedroom.
These two rooms also intercommunicated, and at night the
door between them was left open so that Renée might have
cognizance of anything unusual in the nursery; the unusual
often happened in that nursery. The door between the
corridor and Renée's bedroom was exactly opposite Mr
Fearns' door.

The idea of the proximity of those two doors seized the pure
girl and as it were gripped her by the throat. There in the
night, all was changed; the simplest things became sinister; the
most innocent things became vile. She wanted her mother's
presence more than she had ever wanted anything in all her
life. She could hear nothing whatever, and yet the strange
mysterious instinct to go out into the corridor was very
strong. The caressing pat grew immense with a terrible
significance; it pointed to a past, now, and it pointed to a
future; it no longer stood by itself. Why had her father spoken
to her so curtly after dinner? Why had Renée left the dinner-
table with such abruptness and gone to play the piano in the
drawing-room? Renée never played the piano in the evening,
and she nearly always lingered at the dinner-table eating nuts,
of which she was very fond. Annunciata had no clear
conjectures; she could formulate no definite surmise. But her
soul was filled with a vague and incomprehensible horror. She
loathed herself as she recalled Renée's smile, Renée's rich
curves. And the recollection of Renée reclining against two
pillows with the lamplight on her blonde face and hair, a
recollection once pathetic enough to rouse her keen sympathy,
now shocked and repelled her.

She crept into bed and put her head under the clothes,
desolate, miserable, and agonized. Heavy was the account she

had then against her dashing, chivalrous father! She felt that in a moment of criminal indiscretion he had changed the whole of her life for her. Her head gradually emerged from the clothes and she lay staring with burning, blinking eyes at the blackness of the ceiling. And the clock struck once or twice.

Then she sat up, as if stabbed. Had she or had she not heard a sound? Was it a door shutting, or the creak of a floor under a footstep? Or had she fancied it? She could not be sure. But now some force, apparently external, took hold of her. She slipped cautiously out of bed, groped for her dressing-gown, and put it on. She tip-toed to the door, unlocked it with infinite careful slowness, and inch by inch opened it; and listened. There was no sound of any kind except the ticking of the clock in the hall. The gas-jet on the wall between the servants' staircase and the door of the night nursery burnt low. It was never turned completely out at night lest Renée might have need of it for the children. Annunciata took courage and stood boldly on her mat, and as her eyes grew accustomed to the twilight she examined each door, leaning forward. The door of the night nursery had been left slightly open, as usual. Renée's door was also ajar; her father's was shut. Annunciata was sure that when she came to bed Renée's door had been a little less ajar.

The awful force not herself (or was it the profoundest part of herself?) impelled her across the corridor to the door of the night nursery, which she pushed open. In that room too a gas jet was burning blue. She hesitated for a long time, listening, and then she raised the gas. Side by side in their cots, Frank and Sep were sleeping with the exquisite soft sleep of infancy. Their chubby hands were clenched, and their little red pouting lips apart. On Sep's flushed cheeks were the marks of the tears that his hard-hearted sister had made him shed. And the repose of these two irrepressible organisms was so perfect that it was almost impossible to detect their breathing. The door between the nursery and Renée's bedroom was wide open. Annunciata coughed discreetly. Then she stole into the bedroom. The gas from the nursery illuminated it sufficiently for Annunciata to make sure that it was empty. The bed had been occupied; Renée's clothes, including the famous corset, were scattered about.

The perspiration stood on Annunciata's forehead; currents of electricity seemed to course through her flowing hair. Her heart beat like a hammer. She tried to listen, but she could hear nothing but her heart. She had not conceived the possibility of such suffering as she then endured. After a moment she returned to the nursery, lowered the light, and with a thousand precautions regained her own room. And, arrived there, she fixed the door so as to leave a crack of a quarter of an inch, and she placed her eye to that crack, thus commanding the whole corridor. And with the tremendous, bitter, ruthless patience of a woman mortally injured, she waited.

And shortly after the clock had struck two, when the first inception of the dawn had already changed the black opacity of the corridor window to a pale grey, the door of her father's bedroom slowly opened, and she saw Renée, a dishevelled and obscene figure, pass swiftly across the corridor and disappear.

Charles Fearns had lived one hour too long. For twenty-five years, in obedience to the ever-growing tyranny of concupiscence, he had carried on a series of intrigues of all kinds. Year by year his power over women and his skill in chicane had increased. Year by year his sense of honour and of shame had dwindled, until he was in a way to become nothing but the embodiment of one overmastering and lawless instinct. And as the drunkard cannot measure the depths to which he has sunk, so Charles Fearns could not measure his degradation. He was capable of committing enormities without realizing that they were enormities. He had successfully survived several minor disasters. He had come to believe utterly in his luck and his adroitness. But now the supreme disaster had happened. The bomb had burst. A moment's indiscretion, a moment's folly at the top of a staircase, had nullified the amazing and elaborate ingenuity in deceit of a quarter of a century. Charles Fearns the tight-rope dancer had fallen, and crushed the tender and delicate creature whom alone he purely loved.

CHAPTER IV

MOTHER AND DAUGHTER

The actual disintegration of the fabric of family existence was begun by Annunciata herself, unconsciously, the next morning. Acting under the sway of an urgent instinct whose propriety seemed to her to be above argument, she rose very early, and, with as many precautions as she had used in the night, crept out of her room, across the corridor, and into the nursery. The door between the nursery and Mademoiselle's bedroom was now shut. The little boys slept, their postures unchanged. She did not hesitate a moment. Putting her arms under Sep first, because he was the younger and because of the tear-stains on his flushed soft cheek, she picked him gently up and carried him, all warm and limp, to her own chamber. Then it was Frank's turn; and a third time she came for their garments, and for the sacred indispensable toys which diverted their owners up to breakfast. She closed her door, relieved, and breathless from nervous excitement. The sleeping boys were side by side in her great bed, unexpectant of the immense surprise that awaited them. Only once had the floor of the corridor creaked.

She dressed noiselessly, with frequent glances at the bed, and as she was fixing the final comb in her tight-bound hair, Sep awoke. She sprang to him, and stifled with a kiss his amazement at seeing her.

'Ssh!' she whispered, smiling sadly into his limpid eyes, which were close to hers. 'You're in my bed. I've brought you, and Frankie too. It is a secret. Here's your grey horse.'

He had exactly his father's eyes, naughty-twinkling, and irresistible; and he had his father's heavy under lip. The possibilities, nay, the certainties that peeped forth out of the innocence of that baby afflicted Annunciata. She saw the

83

whole generation of babies, boys and girls, of Sep's age, and
she thought of what they must come to, and a gust of angry
protest against the very march of nature swept through her.

Sep put his brown fists into his eyes, sleepily inspected the
new environment, and then yawned.

'I don't want my grey horse,' he said. 'It's my elephant
morning.'

This aroused Frank. As Annunciata leaned her long body
across them both, kissing them, cuddling them, mumbling
tender words with her lips on theirs, calming with her hand
their tumultuous legs and arms, she was like a cook who has
to keep watch on two saucepans at once lest either should boil
over. If one child cried, the other would cry, and the whole
household would instantly be acquainted with the facts.

Their astonishment was short-lived. They accepted
Annunciata's bed and Annunciata's room with the philosophic
fatalism of their years.

'Does Mamzelle know?' Frank cautiously asked, pulling at
the fine lace of a pillow.

'Don't!' Annunciata entreated. 'No; she doesn't. You
mustn't talk so loud. Haven't I told you it's a secret? I'm going
to take you for a walk.'

'Where to?' demanded Frank.

'Where would you like?'

'Pond,' said Sep with firmness.

'He means the pond in the Park,' Frank explained.

'Swan,' said Sep. 'And two teeny tiny baby swans.'

'Very well,' Annunciata agreed. 'We'll go to the Park. But
you must get up very quietly, both of you, do you hear? Who
will get up first?'

'It's my turn,' Frank answered gloomily. He would have
preferred to get up last, so that he might play with the
combined toys for a few moments; but he had a passion for
truth which victimized him as often as it defended his rights.

He slipped out of bed, and Annunciata found his shirt.

'My socks,' he corrected her, pained. Annunciata's
ignorance of the elementary fact that he put on his socks
before removing his night attire astounded him. He could not
get over it. So the dressing proceeded, with many false starts
and setbacks, Annunciata's spine being always bent, and her

face red, and her thin fingers accommodating themselves with
a strange clumsiness to unaccustomed tasks. And long ere Sep
was clad and upright, it was as if the angel of confusion had
passed through the scrupulously kept room. A battle might
have raged in the space between the bed and the washstand.
She sighed at the sight of Frank pretending that her embroidered nightdress case, which had travelled under the bed, was
a white bear. And she did no more than sigh when Sep, his
feet entangled in a wet towel, subsided on his stomach and
broke a tortoiseshell comb. But at length they were definitely
dressed.

'Now you can sit on the sill and look out of the window,'
she said, 'while I write a note. Then we'll go.'

She went to the little writing-desk, and wrote on a let-
tercard:

'Please leave the house as quickly as possible. I am looking
after the children. Annunciata Fearns.'

The next minute she had put on her hat and opened her
door. The letter was between her teeth, Frank under her right
arm, and Sep under her left. Frank clutched a pair of her
gloves. She reached the ground-floor with her burdens safely,
despite an accident with the two cats, who were reposing on
the top step but one of the stairs. She relinquished the
children, who now, having taken a fancy to be conspirators,
were behaving precisely according to her wishes. Sunshine
was slanting into the hall through the open door of the
drawing-room, the beam crowded with large motes from a
disturbed mat. The clock ticked as if nothing had happened.
The morning newspaper had already been pushed under the
side-door. She led her babes through the kitchen, where the
cook, new and unsympathetic, was blackleading the range, to
the larder, where she fed them on bread and milk.

'Please take this note up to Mademoiselle's room and give it
to her,' she said to the cook.

'What, now? As I am, miss?' the cook questioned.

'Please.'

'Well,' said the cook's back, leaving the kitchen, 'I've been
in some queer houses –'

Outside, in Trafalgar Road, Annunciata breathed largely
and freely. She let the children run loose while she put on her

gloves, and then she took their hands. At Grange House, a little way down on the right, there was a tap on a pane. Annunciata looked up, startled and blushing. Her friend Helen Pierpoint was at her bedroom window, half hidden by a curtain. Helen' face expressed much wonder and curiosity, but Annunciata only smiled, shamefast, and shook her head and went on. The Hanbridge car, crammed with workmen and workwomen, rushed with a roar and a swish up the slope. The pavements were dotted with hurrying, noisy-footed, preoccupied people, who seemed to ignore the singular and pretty sight of the white girl leading two blue boys whose little legs took two steps to their sister's one.

Annunciata prayed that she might meet nobody she knew. She could not imagine herself once again speaking naturally to a friend.

Up in the town the new terra-cotta post-office had not opened its absurd portal. The town-hall clock showed half-past seven. She stopped.

'Pond,' said Sep.

'Anny', Frank inquired, after a calm inspection of her, 'why are your eyes black?'

She was examining the notice in the window of the post-office.

'And you never made us say our prayers either,' he added.

'Pond,' Sep repeated insistently.

She took them, protesting, for a walk in the direction of Turnhill, along a road from which the town park was clearly visible, like a promised land, on the right. And at eight o'clock she led them back to the post-office, which was just unbarred, and they pushed valiantly at the swing-door for her and fell over a broom that a woman was wielding in the vestibule. Annunciata had never in her life sent a telegram from a post-office. But a kind fate guided her to the dark corner provided for the public writing of telegrams, and with a stumpy pencil, heavily fettered, she composed a telegram to her mother: 'Come home at once, Annunciata.'

'What's this name, please?' demanded a girl behind the broad, ink-stained counter.

And Annunciata had to spell her name letter by letter.

'Sixpence, please,'

A telegraph instrument was clicking the whole time behind a screen, and the boys, overcome by the height of the counter and the unprecedented mysterious clicking, whispered solemnly to each other. Annunciata affixed the stamps to the form and summoned the boys, who pattered in her wake. She felt that she had done all that could be done. And suddenly she was very frightened, almost dumbfounded, by what she had dared to do. Consequences began to shape themselves vaguely and horribly before her.

At half-past ten she returned home with her brothers. The boys were tired, tired of swans, of little brown swans, of flowers, of gravel pies, and even of chocolate from the slot-machines in the park shelters. And Annunciata was exhausted utterly. She had tasted nothing but bits of chocolate, which had nauseated her in the hot morning sun. The scullery-maid was cleaning the front steps. It was quite wrong that the scullery-maid should have been cleaning the front steps at such an hour, but Annunciata was glad to see her in the porch, because Martha had been an inmate of the house much longer than the other servants, and had something of the faithful bondslave in her ungainly fat body.

'Eh, Miss,' she observed. 'You're that pale!' And she kept the boys off her clean steps with smiling protests and gestures of her red arms.

'Has father gone?' Annunciata asked.

'Yes, Miss. He come downstairs, and drank his coffee, and hasted off quicker nor ever like.'

Mr Fearns was of those incurable persons who prefer bed to breakfast. To catch him of a morning between his bedroom door and the front door needed the eye of a lynx and the pounce of a cat; one moment he was, and the next he was not.

'Where is Mademoiselle?' Annunciata's heart beat.

'She ain't stirred, Miss,' replied Martha. And Annunciata seemed to detect a peculiar intonation in the girl's voice.

'Well, that's a nice thing!' Frankie remarked. 'Who's going to look after us? Nobody can teach us our lessons but Mamzelle.'

Annunciata recovered herself. 'You won't have any lessons this morning. Martha shall play with you in the nursery. Take them, will you, Martha? Put on a white apron. Now you must be good, or else I shan't take you out any more.'

'Rum!' said Frank. 'Come on, Sep.'

Sep was smiling to himself. He was not an impassioned talker. They carefully left four footmarks on the white steps.

'And ask cook to make me some tea,' Annunciata called out, 'and to bring it to me in the drawing-room.'

She tried to convince herself that the domestic organism showed no signs of the night's horror. But the very aspect of the senseless chairs straddling on the drawing-room carpet seemed to cry aloud that all was changed, and that they were no longer the same chairs. The cook brought in the tea with an expression to indicate that she was not a woman to be easily deceived and that she had witnessed strange matters aforetime and could hear a thunderstorm a hundred miles off. And Annunciata's thoughts ran: 'I have done this. I have done all this, without consulting anybody.' And then she would ask: 'All what?' So she drank her tea.

At twelve o'clock, as Mademoiselle had not appeared, she formed the extraordinary resolution to visit the governess in her bedroom and command her to depart. The idea at the back of her mind was that Renée must on no account meet her mother. She ran with mad, quivering courage upstairs, and burst into Renée's room. And it was empty and strange. Renée's two trunks were strapped and labelled at the foot of the bed. Renée, then, had gone, leaving her trunks to follow. Annunciata took breath.

After all, the night had not been an awful dream. Renée fleeing secretly at the instance of that brief note penned while the boys played on the window-sill, had admitted her guilt. Annunciata went into the garden and questioned the gardener. Yes, he had seen Mademoiselle leave the house at a quarter-past ten. She was carrying a small bag, and appeared to be in a hurry.

To avoid meeting her father at lunch, Annunciata determined to be unwell. But, just as she re-entered the house the telephone rang its imperious bell. By force of habit she answered the call. It was her father's voice she heard, cold, grave, haughty.

'Who's there!' he demanded.

'Me,' her lips trembled.

'What? Annunciata?'

'Yes, father.' Somehow she felt ashamed and guilty, as though she, and not her father, had sinned.

'I have to go to Liverpool, on business. I shan't be in for lunch. I don't know if I shall be back tonight.'

And he rang off, curtly, without another word.

She was stunned by the rush of events. In a vision she seemed to see Renée creeping into her father's room, and to hear her say: 'Look at this note that your fine daughter has sent me!' And then the feverish discussion of what the note implied and how they should act.

Bradshaw always lay on the ledge under the telephone next to the list of telephone subscribers. She tried to discover the times of trains from Birmingham, but with no success. She could not decipher the figures on the page, much less hit on the right pages. With an admirable sense of her needs at that moment she issued an ordinance that Frank and Sep should have lunch with her in the dining-room.

It was towards the end of the perilous meal that the door of the dining-room opened swiftly, and her mother stood there, a little dishevelled and heated from the journey.

'My dear!' asked her mother abruptly, but in a low restrained tone, 'whatever is the matter?'

Annunciata could not speak, though she tried to form some words. And the boys stopped eating and gazed at her with open mouths, not even greeting their mother. Her mother's presence choked her. The terribleness of what she had done, of her own initiative, its irremediability, its audacity, struck her now with overwhelming force. Had she remained quiescent, the household would have been revolving as usual. But her action had devastated it like an internal fire, and what remained was the shell, to deceive onlookers, and them only for a little space.

'Dearest!' exclaimed her mother, approaching her with uplifted, importunate hands.

No! She could not speak. She could not begin. She could not control her muscles. And yet all the morning she had fancied that she was so calm, perfectly mistress of herself. She turned away her dizzy head with a supreme gesture of impotence, and the last thing she saw was a patch of egg-yolk on Sep's bib.

When she recovered her senses, she was lying on her back on the couch in the drawing-room, her face towards the door, and a faint smell of ammonia in her nostrils. The three servants were grouped at the door, with alarmed, foolish faces. Her mother stood by her side, fanning her with a Japanese fan taken from the mantelpiece. There came from the hall a sudden shrill sound of Sep crying.

'Martha,' said her mother, 'take them into the garden and keep them good. That will do, thank you, she is better now.'

Her mother waved away the servants, shut the door on them and on Sep's weeping, and returned to the couch.

Annunciata stared mournfully, and seized her hand in a limp clasp.

'This is a nice home-coming!' murmured her mother quietly, smiling. 'What is it, dear? It seems that Mademoiselle has gone,'

'Oh mother,' said Annunciata, in a languid, imploring, invalid's voice. 'I was obliged to telegraph for you.' She spoke now without difficulty, as if in a dream.

'But why?'

'Because of Mademoiselle – and father.' The last syllables melted into soft tears.

Her mother dropped her hand, and put the fan on the mantelpiece.

'Your father?' Mrs Fearns questioned sharply, moving from the sofa.

Annunciata had to say it, and she said it. She had to look her mother in the face, and she looked her in the face. And the face was drawn, pinched, pallid, like the face of a dead mother.

'They were together, last night,' she said, ceasing to cry.

'Together, Annunciata?' her mother repeated in a hissing voice. 'Annunciata, what do you mean?' The woman crossed the hearthrug in three rapid steps.

'Mother –'

'I know what you mean, my poor child!' cried Mrs Fearns. 'I know! I know!' she reiterated in slow, expiring tones, and sank on to a chair, the muscles of her spine rigid. 'So that is why you telegraphed! God forgive him! God forgive him!'

The make-believe was at an end. Unlike the majority of girls, Annunciata had not had to wait until she was married

and expecting a baby, for her mother's explicit recognition of
the fact that she had ceased to be a child and had looked on
existence and understood. Never till then had a word passed
between them to compromise, to breathe a stain upon, the
assumed purity of Annunciata's mind. Never had the sacred
doors of convention been boldly unbarred that Annunciata
might glance, were it for an instant, on the central disquieting
mystery and secret cause of life's continuance. But now fate had
broken down the barriers, and mother and daughter gazed eye
to eye on the most shocking sight that even the wife of Charles
Fearns had ever seen, and neither pretended that Annunciata
was blind or incapable of comprehension. Annunciata was
extremely surprised to find how simple and natural in its
profound grief was the avowal. And she was astonished too,
that, without assistance, without reflection, by mere instinct,
she had understood so much and so immediately. In a single day
the theoretical initiation had been begun and completed, and
accepted by the last person in the world likely to accept it.

'Tell me,' said her mother. 'Not here? Not in this house?'

Annunciata nodded, and with a weak hand pointed to the
ceiling. The bedrooms of her father and mother were over the
drawing-room.

'Surely not!' Mrs Fearns whispered in accents made solemn
by the sense of outrage. She put her chin in her plump hand, and
rested her elbow on the arm of the chair, staring at the carpet.
'Surely not!'

Annunciata did not insist. She pushed back her hair with a
fatigued, worried movement, and waited. She felt herself to be
in the midst of a unique crisis, a crisis than which she could
conceive nothing more thrilling and dreadful. And mingled
with her great distress was a strange, timorous pride – that she
stood for once on an equality with her mother. Annunciata
knew herself to be inferior to her mother both in intellect and in
force of character; she knew that this would always be so, that
no development on her part would ever change their relative
positions. She had loved and admired her father, but an
immense respect was the basis of her sentiments towards her
mother, whom in her secret soul she had from her earliest years
recognized, with the sure, impartial judgment of infancy, as the
strongest individuality in the house.

'How came you to know anything of this, Annunciata?' asked Mrs Fearns, after a silence.

The girl turned to lie on her left side, and looked her mother candidly in the face, and Mrs Fearns raised her eyes and met the glance.

'Am I to tell you all about it, mamma?' Here spoke the mother's equal, the young woman of the world.

Their mutual glance was prolonged.

'Yes.'

And Annunciata, in a tired, drawling voice, related the whole episode from the moment of the pat on Renée's cheek. She spoke naturally, without self-consciousness, without even a blush. She was amazed at her own serenity, amazed that she could relate the awful thing in a manner so cold-blooded. It may appear incredible, but it is nevertheless a fact, that, while she told it, her father's monstrous obliquity seemed to her less a crime than a vagary. She did not in truth know what she was talking about.

'You sent that note up by the cook?'

'Yes, mamma. Then I took the children out instantly.'

'And did your father see her before he went to the office?'

'I don't know.'

Mrs Fearns rose from her chair, and put up her hands to take the pins from her hat.

'Did your father say anything else when he telephoned?' she demanded, a hat-pin between her teeth.

'Oh, no, mother – he spoke very crossly.'

The notion gradually formed in Annunciata's mind that her mother had exhibited rather less than the utmost degree of surprise at the disastrous news. The girl was not deceived by her mother's calm. She had a little expected her to remain calm. But there was something subtle and unseizable in her mother's manner that implied, if not a faint premonition, at any rate a previous foreboding fear, born of past experience. And Annunciata saw her father's charming way with women in a new and sinister light. Had he then always been one of those wicked rakes that . . .? And had her mother always known and suffered? And had her parents lived always a double existence under her unsuspecting eyes?

She was filled with a fierce and dangerous curiosity, which almost compelled her to say to her mother: 'Mother, you do not seem very surprised.'

But she dared not. Happily her awe of her mother was stronger than the impulse.

There was a screeching yell from the garden, then a silence, then a series of yells, crescendo and diminuendo; which phenomena could only mean that Sep had fallen flat on some stony substance and really hurt himself.

'If you're quite recovered dear,' said Mrs Fearns in a cold and even tone, 'do go and look after those boys, and send Martha in. By the way, your aunt is better.'

It was a singular close to the interview.

During the afternoon Mrs Fearns disappeared from view. Annunciata conscientiously occupied herself with the boys. She played with them, she gave them a lesson and their supper, and she put them to bed, early. And then the desire to see her mother again overcame her. She went quietly into her father's bedroom, whose perfect orderliness showed no trace of the night's history, and through the open door leading to the inner room she saw a form seated on the edge of the bed there. The pale green blind was drawn and the chamber in shadow. She advanced on tip-toe, with beating heart.

'Mother!' she cried aloud, and flung her arms round that soft neck, and pressed her girlish bosom against the rich breasts that once had fed her. Her mother, with dry eyes, was sobbing painfully. Annunciata kissed her eyes with a wild spiritual abandonment, and they wept together in a close and ecstatic embrace.

'Mother!' the girl whispered through her tears, 'you've been here all by yourself for hours and hours!'

And Mrs Fearns nodded, drawing breath hysterically through her nostrils.

'Mother, dearest! I did right, didn't I? I couldn't let her touch Frank and Sep again, could I?'

'You did quite right, my darling.'

There was a knock at the outer door.

'Go and see,' said Mrs Fearns.

A telegram had come from the master of the house to the effect that he could not return that night. Annunciata, having read it first, offered it to her mother in silence.

'Mother,' she said, 'you need someone to talk to, to consult.'

'Who is there I can talk to?' asked Mrs Fearns, with apparently a touch of cynicism.

'There is Mr Ridware.'

'Oh, no! I can't bother Mr Ridware with my troubles.'

'You ought to have someone, mamma,' Annunciata persisted.

CHAPTER V

AFTERNOON AND NIGHT

The same afternoon Lawrence Ridware returned from midday dinner to the office on Gater's high-geared bicycle. He had forgotten it in the morning. At the corner of Holborn and Chancery Lane he passed Paul Pennington, carrying his indispensable little shiny black bag; and there was a look of prim and temperate satisfaction on Pennington's face which caused Lawrence's heart to sink. It was the energy of Pennington, his passion for doing things instantly which had to be done, that disturbed Lawrence. An action for divorce having been decided upon, Pennington took it in hand at once. That very morning Pennington had told him there was no reason why the petition should not be heard early in the Michaelmas Sittings. Pennington had asked him for the address of the landlady at Manifold, and also for a photograph of his wife. Lawrence had replied with a certain unreasonable relish that Pennington would have to wait for a photograph till the afternoon. But Pennington reminded him that a photograph of some lady had been lying about Lawrence's room for years – it had survived even the brief reign of the later Thomas – and was now probably in one of the drawers of his desk. Was not that the portrait of Mrs Ridware? It was. Pennington himself found it in a lower drawer, together with a forgotten volume of Rétif de la Bretonne and a number of the *Bibliophile*. Pennington dusted it, and put it in an envelope and pocketed it. 'I can just catch the 10.33 for Manifold,' Pennington had said, hastening away. Why could not Pennington have waited a few days? This dispatch annoyed Lawrence; but he could not protest; he could only thank Pennington for being so assiduous.

And now Pennington was returning from his mission.

Lawrence carried the bicycle upstairs with a rush, so that he might be ready to receive Pennington calmly in his own room. He felt himself to be very nervous. He swore at himself for being thus nervous on no pretext whatever. But his profanity worked no cure. Fortunately, only Gater was in the office, and Gater was too interested in the reappearance of his bicycle to notice the rider. With a word of thanks for the loan, Lawrence went straight to his room and sat down. Through the half-open door he saw Pennington come into the articled-clerk's office, put down his bag, change his coat, and sheathe his cuffs in notepaper. Pennington then made an entry in the petty cash book (which he kept), unlocked a drawer, put some money into it, and locked it. No doubt he was dealing with the expenses of the journey to Manifold. Pennington's precise manner of manipulating a bunch of keys was always irritating to Lawrence. To see the young man turn a key with a snap, withdraw the bunch, and drop it into his pocket, would sometimes make Lawrence grind his teeth. It reminded him, in some preposterous way, of the Scribes and Sadducees.

Pennington took a paper out of his bag and entered Lawrence's room, shutting the door.

'Well,' he said, 'I've got everything.' He did not smile. He had the fitting gravity of an undertaker.

'You have?' Lawrence exclaimed flushing.

'Yes. She wouldn't talk at first.'

'Who wouldn't?'

'Mrs Malkin, the landlady. Your wife – Mrs Ridware – had evidently made a most favourable impression on her.'

'Indeed!' said Lawrence. There it was again – another instance of Phyllis's skill in imposing on people.

'But I soon made her see reason. I told her that anyway she would be subpoenaed and have to go to London. And I also pointed out to her that if it transpired at the trial that she was an unwilling witness, that very fact would give her house a bad reputation, because every one would say that she had connived. I told her that the only way for her to save the reputation of her house, was to do everything she could to help us to get at the truth.'

Pennington paused for admiration of this diplomacy.

'Very good,' said Lawrence, looking up at him as he stood correct and virtuous behind the desk.

'She's a regular landlady. That knocked her. I got everything out of her, and what's more, I made her sign a note of her evidence.'

'Did you? What does she say?'

'I'll read it to you.'

Lawrence wanted to say: 'No, let me read it myself.' But he could not bring himself to do so. And Pennington read:

' "My name is Mary Malkin. I keep a boarding house at No. 3, Ilam Terrace, Manifold. Mr Emery Greatbatch has frequently stayed in my house at holiday times for several years past. He has a large bed-sitting-room. On the Thursday before last Good Friday he came in the morning, by arrangement. He then told me a lady would come to take tea with him on Good Friday, and I was to get something nice for tea. The lady came. She was veiled. But I took the tea up myself and saw her. The photograph shown to me this morning is her portrait. She left about nine o'clock. They neither of them left the room during that time. Mr Greatbatch did not accompany her when she went." '

Pennington coughed, glancing up from the paper.

'As a matter of fact,' he said, 'I asked her if there were any signs of disorder in the room when she came up to clear the tea-things away afterwards. But she said it was too dark to see. She stuck to that for sometime, and then she admitted that the bed might have been unmade and re-made. I saw the room. It contains a large bed and a sofa and many other things. However, that doesn't matter. The inference is sufficiently strong, and besides there's a lot more evidence. She goes on: "The lady came again for tea on Easter Sunday. Mr Greatbatch didn't ring afterwards, and the servant didn't go up to clear the things away. I asked the servant at ten o'clock if the lady had gone, and she said she didn't know. I went upstairs quietly and listened outside the door, and heard talking, but there was no light in the room. It was a man and a woman talking, very low. I then went to bed. I had a made-up bed in the front parlour, it being holiday time. I stayed awake till two o'clock, and will swear that no one left the house before two o'clock, because the parlour opens on to the lobby

and the door was ajar. At four o'clock I was wakened by the
front door banging. The next morning Mr Greatbatch rang
for his breakfast to be brought up to him at eight o'clock, and
there was no one in the room but him. The servant had got up
at six. Therefore the lady in question must have left the house
between two o'clock and six. I –'' '

'That's enough,' Lawrence murmured, his sensibilities
utterly outraged. He was so ashamed and distressed that he
had no emotion left to be angry.

'Yes, isn't it?' said Pennington, with calm satisfaction. 'But
there's more: "I do not remember exactly –'''

'Please don't read any more,' Lawrence requested in a
trembling voice.

Pennington gazed at him over the edge of the paper,
apparently astonished. But it did not take Pennington more
than five minutes to grasp a situation. He flattered himself on
his perspicacity.

Abruptly he folded up the paper.

'I'll write to agent's by tonight's post,' he said in a low tone,
'with this. They do everything, you know, in matrimonial
cases. We shall have the petition down by return. As for the
affidavit in support – by the way, here's that photograph, shall
you keep it?'

He left the room, closing the door very gently, as though he
had been leaving a sick-room. With all his virtues, he had his
moments of humanity.

A few minutes later Lawrence, in a forlorn effort to induce
himself to work, rose and went into Mr Fearn's office in
search of several bundles of papers and Prideaux's
Conveyancing. As he passed through Pennington's room he
had a glimpse of Pennington, whose penholder slanted
inwards from right to left in a manner distressingly pedagogic,
writing his attendances for the morning. And he could read on
the blue draft paper: 'P.D.A. Division, Ridware *v*. R. and
Greatbatch. Journey to Manifold and attending Mrs Malkin.'
It seemed to Lawrence, so rapid was the apparent march of
events, that he was already in the midst of the Divorce Court,
already entangled in the undergrowth of procedure; and yet
the action had not even been commenced. In his principal's
room, instead of looking for papers, he dropped into his

principal's pivoted armchair and laid his arms on the desk. He was sick, weary, disgusted. The evidence which Pennington had collected revolted him. Phyllis defiling herself in a lodging-house, with all the miserable accompaniments of secrecy, shame, deceit, and genteel squalor! Had Phyllis been some other man's wife, he would have been more philosophical. He would have put conventional morality in its proper place, neither too low nor too high. He would probably have said that everyone concerned was to be pitied, and that to distribute blame was inept. He might gently have asked what it mattered after all, since sorrow was the very woof of life. For Lawrence was capable of sitting on a throne with renowned poets and sages. But because Phyllis happened to be his, he suffered cruelly. His instincts rose up and inflicted on his intellect the worst defeat his intellect had ever known. And yet he had not loved Phyllis for years. Now he hated her bitterly.

There was a rush along the passage, and Charles Fearns, a surprising figure, took the room as it were by assault. Fearns was supposed to have gone to Liverpool two hours before on business of which the staff knew nothing.

'Stopped at last moment!' he growled angrily. 'Missed train. Get out of my way, please. What are you doing here, Ridware?'

'I'm looking for papers,' said Lawrence, haughtily, but quitting the chair in haste.

'Here! Send Gater out to cash me this cheque, will you?'

And Fearns pulled a cheque-book from a drawer, filled it in for twenty pounds, and gave it to Lawrence.

'You haven't endorsed it.'

'Oh! Hell!' the principal exclaimed, savage. 'Tell him to run. I must catch the three train at Knype.'

Fearns fumed at the threshold of his room for five minutes, awaiting Gater's return, and at last went out to meet the boy on the stairs, after which he was no more seen. When Gater came in, breathless, Gater winked at Clowes, and Clowes winked at Gater. Of the entire staff, Pennington alone did an honest afternoon's work.

When Lawrence reached home in the evening, it was Cousin Sarah Ridware who opened the door for him, and the old woman had a peculiar expression of triumph on her face.

Addressed as cousin by the brothers, Sarah Ridware was more correctly the cousin of their father. She was one of those needy and undistinguished relations of which a family indomitably ascending in the social scale has almost the right to be ashamed. She stood at the level of Lawrence's grandfather, a potter's fireman of thrifty habits, who died in 1862. And, with the brothers, she was all that remained of the blood. She had obstinately refused to rise with Lawrence's father, who had become a traveller and, just before his death, manager, for the historic potting firm of Boones. To be even an errand boy at Boones conferred respectability in the seventies. And when Ridware senior passed away he had half a column in the *Signal*. But Sarah, who never married, was as unambitious as she was unsusceptible to the spirt of change. She had a mind of incredible narrowness, and her independence was ferocious. At sixty she lived in two rooms of a cottage between Hanbridge and Knype, and supported herself by a needle that was indefatigable. She had conserved the simple customs of her uncle the fireman. She was astoundingly proud, especially on the way to church in black silk. She would not accept presents of money from her nephews. She would not call on Lawrence. But she expected Lawrence to call on her from time to time and praise her tea, which, somehow, was invariably stewed. Mark also dared not forget her during his sojourns in the district. She sniffed at the grandeur of the brothers, yet her own importance by some ingenuity fed itself therefrom. Her attitude said: 'Look at the splendour of what I scorn!' Phyllis had paid her one visit, of state, and had absolutely declined to renew the experience. Sarah's unique comment was that she, Sarah, was not fine enough for some folks – with their airs.

Lawrence had gone to her on the previous evening. She had been shocked, desolated, and delighted by his news, and enormously flattered by his request that she should temporarily keep his house. She had made her consent a great favour, but she had gone with him nearly at once, he carrying a tiny tin trunk of hers with a most uncomfortably thin handle. As a fact, she loved Lawrence, though her love was of a highly singular kind. In a museum of affections it would have agitated expert amorists, as a specimen of a plant presumed to be extinct will agitate botanists.

That night she had spoken no word to the servant, Maggie, but she had vouchsafed to Lawrence that she could not abide wenches! The tin trunk contained chiefly clean white aprons, one of which she had donned immediately on arrival. Before retiring to bed she had read a chapter of the Bible aloud to Lawrence. She was tall and flat with wiry grey hair and blue eyes, and she did not wear spectacles.

'Well,' she began in her thin voice, having opened the door to Lawrence on the second evening. 'Here's a nice how d'ye do! Her's sent a man with a cart up for her things. I pretty soon packed him off about his business. I can tell you.'

'Who has sent?'

'Her! I told him to come again when the master was at home.'

'When did the messenger come!'

'He has but just gone.'

'No note or anything?'

'Yes. A note to the *servant,* if you please, tellin' what things her wanted – in the wardrobe, and in th' chest o' drawers, and a fan, and a dress-basket.'

'Is the man coming back?'

'He said as he should. He's no doubt at the public down yonder, swilling.'

'I'd better tell Maggie to put the things together at once.' Cousin Sarah paused.

'Maggie's gone,' she said, shortly and firmly.

'Gone? What for?'

'I told ye I was none for wenches, lad. Her's gone home. I'd liefer do the work myself, big as th' house is, than stand by and see a trollop dallying round.'

Lawrence made no answer. He shut the front door, hung up his hat, and stifled a sigh.

'Supper ready?' he asked.

'It will be by the time you are,' said Cousin Sarah. 'I'm toasting a bit of cheese.'

The supper comprised toasted cheese, the fleshy remains of dinner, thick bread-and-butter, part of a fruit-pie and tea, which Cousin Sarah had succeeded in stewing; all the courses were served simultaneously. It was a repast of her father's infancy, distributed by Sarah's bony and needle-blackened

hands with their bitten finger-nails. Lawrence ate parts of it
without comment. Like most narrow-minded people, Cousin
Sarah dwelt happily in the absolute conviction of being right
upon every subject on which she put herself to the trouble of
forming an opinion. The mere expression on her face was a
proof of her certitude that the meal was an ideal meal. She was
never disturbed by doubts, either concerning the ultimate
destiny of the universe or the best manner of making tea.
Lawrence therefore determined to abandon the tenancy of the
the house and to find lodgings as soon as possible.

'Eh, lad,' she observed in the middle of a desert of silence. 'I
never thought as a Ridware would ha' come to this! I never
thought it!' Which remark was honestly meant to comfort him
in his marital misfortune.

The return of Phyllis's messenger diverted him from the
fruit-pie. He went dully upstairs, and began to put in to the
dress-basket the various things which his wife had demanded.
Cousin Sarah helped him, criticizing Mrs Ridware's linen and
dresses by means of facial contortions. Then there was a ring
at the door.

'Bless us!' said Cousin Sarah.

'I'll go,' said Lawrence. Phyllis's messenger was waiting in
the hall, a self-conscious young man who twirled his cap in his
hands under the hall lamp.

Lawrence opened to Annunciata Fearns. She stood there,
tall, slim, pale, distinguished, with the aspect of a heavenly
visitant, of some creature fragile and angelic, exquisitely and
marvellously different from Cousin Sarah, and so young, so
touching in her youth. She was a sight to startle Lawrence at
such an hour, and he jumped with apprehension. He thought
of what Phyllis had shamefully said, and how strange were the
hazards of life.

'Good evening, Mr Ridware,' she spoke quickly and nervously, 'I'm sorry to trouble you, but mother would be very
glad if you would go and see her.'

'Why, of course!' he replied. 'Do come in, Miss Fearns.'

'No, thank you,' she murmured. 'I won't come in. I
mustn't stay.'

'Your mother wants to see me tonight?'

'If it isn't troubling you too much.'

'Can you wait five minutes? I'll come with you now,' he said.

'I won't wait,' she answered. 'I'll go on, thank you, and tell mother you're coming.'

And she departed, with no more words, very mysteriously.

'What's up?' he thought, frightened. And he ran upstairs. 'Cousin Sarah,' he said, 'I've got to go down to Fearns' immediately. You can finish with those things. The man will carry the basket downstairs. I'll be back soon.'

He hurried after Annunciata, without listening to Sarah's response. In a moment he saw the girl's white figure before him in the dark road, hastening downwards towards the lights of Bleakridge and Bursley. His first impulse was to overtake her. But some shyness, some fear, held him back, and at a distance of fifty yards he followed her under a starry sky all the way to Bleakridge. At Fearns' garden gate he hesitated, and then went forward. Annunciata herself answered his ring, as he had answered hers.

'You have been quick,' she smiled faintly. 'It's very kind of you. Mother's in the drawing room – this way.'

He hung up his hat.

'Nothing wrong, I hope,' he ventured.

She lifted her eyebrows, opened the door of the drawing-room and vanished.

Alma Fearns was leaning against the mantelpiece when Lawrence went into the room. She wore a cream-coloured dress, with a broad waistband of creased silk curving to upper and lower points in front. The lace-finished sleeves were rather short, showing her plump forearms. She looked pre-eminently a comfortable woman, with a certain elegance in her embonpoint; and the graciousness of her heart expressed itself in her face. The permanent cast of her features showed an attitude of mind, which, while not unhappy, was calmly and contentedly melancholy, with the melancholy that comes less from expectation having been disappointed than from expectation having been restrained by the force of reason. She was mature; she knew what human nature was; she had suffered; she had had seven children. Her girlhood was behind the mist of time. And yet now and then she would make some gesture, or some naïve glance would flash in her brown eyes, that rolled away the years, and left her for an instant as girlish as Annunciata. She had in particular an unconscious habit of throwing back her head after putting a question, a habit that was most curiously agreeable. Strangers thought her stiff and chilly, but if acquaintance ripened they were soon amazed that they could ever have thought so, for her illimitable sympathy was really the most salient thing about her.

She welcomed Lawrence, and thanked him, with all the generous warmth of her dispostion. She pulled a chair into position for him with her strong arm, and gave him a cigarette, and struck a match and held it with a jewelled hand. He felt as though he was an invalid and she was spoiling him as an invalid has a right to be spoilt. A *morceau de salon* of Chaminade's stood on the open piano, and lying on a small table was a reprint of Alexander Smith's *Dreamthorp*. Not in Lawrence's house would such examples of the brilliant second-rate have been found conspicuous, and his highly sensitive taste recoiled from them. Nevertheless, he said to himself that Mrs Fearns' sheer goodness and the personal distinction that she exhaled were worth more than all the artistic taste in the world. He would, at that instant, have sacrificed his whole intellectual and aesthetic equipment in exchange for the assurance of passing the rest of his life in the atmosphere that he was breathing then. Mrs Fearns had good blood and a kind heart; the two things that Phyllis lacked. And he, the grandson of a potter's fireman, possessed emphatically the aristocratic temper. When he was differentiating between a masterpiece and an imitation of a masterpiece, you could see that he had the nostrils of an aristocrat.

'I'm going to do something very unusual,' said Mrs Fearns, sitting down in the middle of the sofa.

'Are you?' he returned, full of apprehension.

'Yes. I'm going to ask you to let me talk to you about an extremely delicate matter.'

'Either Fearns has spoken to her,' he reflected, 'or Phyllis has been here and made an appeal for interference.'

All the way down from Toft End, he had fancied something of the sort and now he was sure. He resigned himself. If he could tolerate interference from anybody he could tolerate it from Mrs Fearns.

He was, moreover, convinced of his power to persuade her that divorce was the sole possible course. He knew her common sense, her openness of mind. Still, he regretted that her quick kindliness should have misled her into a futile enterprise. It grieved him to disappoint her. He wondered, as he had often wondered, whether her mother, dead a dozen years, had ever told her the strictly concealed history of his birth – that strange contradictory passage in his virtuous father's career – and if so, whether herein was the origin of Mrs Fearns' special sympathetic goodness to himself. For old Mrs Leigh had been the only individual in the Five Towns cognizant of that affair. He rather hoped that Mrs Leigh had indeed confided in Alma Fearns.

As he said nothing, Mrs Fearns proceeded:

'It was Annunciata who suggested sending for you. I said "No." But she insisted and I gave way. And do you know, I wish I had not given way, now.' She smiled timidly.

'So do I!' thought Lawrence. 'Annunciata discussing my divorce!' He blushed with shame.

'Tomorrow,' said Mrs Fearns, and then paused, 'I am leaving this house.'

Her tone, and the faint tremor in her voice on the first word, seemed to convict him suddenly of the most stupid blindness. He stirred uneasily as his mind groped about for new bearings.

'With my children,' Mrs Fearns added.

'You are leaving Mr Fearns?' he asked, on a note of the extremest astonishment.

She leaned forward to him, with her elbows on her knees, the forearms horizontal and the hands restlessly clasping each other.

'Surely you aren't so very surprised?' she said quietly.

'Well –' he temporized.

'Are you?' she insisted.

'No,' he bluntly answered. 'At least, I am, and I am not.'

'You mean, I suppose,' she remarked coldly, sitting up straight, 'that as I have lived here so long, I might have stayed a little longer.'

'That's not quite what I mean, but it's near enough. I'm very sorry to hear this.'

'Was Charlie's manner at all strange in the office today?'
she demanded.

'I thought he was excited,' said Lawrence, 'just before he
went to Liverpool. He's not coming back, then, tonight?'

Mrs Fearns shook her head. 'If he were, I should not be
here now.'

'I'm very sorry,' he repeated. He could think of nothing
else to say. He had a feeling of profound and contemptuous
anger against Fearns, but he could not express that to Fearns'
wife. For the rest, he was puzzling to discover what might
have been the last and worst of his employer's iniquities.

'You see,' said Mrs Fearns, 'I know Charlie. Nobody
knows him as I do. I expect many people think I'm blind,
and say "Poor thing!" He has nearly always been very nice to
me, though he has often made me suffer frightfully. I liked
him. I was comfortable with him. When I came into a room
and he was there, I had a feeling of pleasure. I understand
him. I know his faults, perhaps better than I do my own. I
knew he used to go after other women. When I first realized
that, it almost killed me. But I got accustomed to it. You
may think I'm a very strange woman, and perhaps I am, but
yet I don't think I am. Yes, I got accustomed to it. You see, I
have had a comfortable feeling with Charlie. I can't explain
it. It's love, I suppose. I was sure he admired me tremendously. You know, Mr Ridware' – her voice became
exquisitely soft – 'one can't have everything in this world.
One has to make the best of it. So I got accustomed to it.
What could I have done? He couldn't be cured, you know.
He's incurable. I used to wait for him to come back to me.
He always did.'

'But now?'

She bit her lip, and looked at the fire-screen. 'Charlie has
ceased to be a gentleman. I trusted him absolutely. But I was
wrong. I see now that men like my poor Charles can't be
expected to remain gentlemen for ever. . . . I went away
from the house to see my sister in Birmingham with the
most perfect confidence. And in my absence, Mr Ridware,
my husband makes love to the governess, here, in my house,
and he is so clumsy, or careless, or callous – call it what you
like – that the person who has the task of telling me about it

when I come home is my own daughter. What can one do?'
She was tapping with her foot on the carpet.

'It is terrible!' Lawrence exclaimed in a low voice. 'I had
no idea –' His face was working and there was a slight haze
before his eyes. The world seemed to be full of odious and
revolting sensuality and of its victims. Life stank. And here
was this soft and delicate, forgiving creature outraged to
such a point that she could forgive no more! And upstairs,
hidden away somewhere, there cowered a young girl, who
should surely be deemed as much a martyr as her mother.
He did not forget his own woes. He added these others to
them.

'I'm telling you all this,' said Mrs Fearns, gazing at him
again. 'I don't know why I should. I hope you don't mind. Of
course, you're in Charlie's office, and it might make
difficulties between you and him, if he knew – I ought to have
thought of that.'

'Please don't think of that for a moment,' Lawrence urged
fiercely. 'Not for a moment! In the first place, Mr Fearns isn't
the sort of man to be mean; and in the second place, I
shouldn't care a pin if it did make difficulties.'

'I really couldn't think of anyone whom I could talk to as
well as you. I have some woman-friends from whom I could
be sure of sympathy, but I wanted more than sympathy
tonight. And besides, I would sooner talk to a man. Now you
think I ought to leave, don't you? After what has occurred, we
could never live here again on those terms. Imagine
Annunciata! Isn't it awful?'

'She – do you mean to say that, supposing you brought
an action against Mr Fearns, she would have to give evidence?'

Mrs Fearns nodded. 'I feel just as if it wasn't real,' she said
with a shiver. 'But it is real. It is real. And do you know, I
ought to have foreseen it. That's where I was wrong. I was a
simpleton. At the bottom of my soul, I'm not at all surprised
that it's occurred.'

'Aren't you?' he said sympathetically. And quite suddenly
the interview seemed to shift to a much more intimate plane,
and his constraint vanished.

'No,' she asserted stoutly. 'Not at all.'

'Well,' he said, 'you are certainly quite right to go, and to take your children. In fact, that is the only thing you can do.'

'I'm relieved you think so. But it's past arguing. I would do almost anything for Charlie, and I can't tell you how sorry I am there's no way out of it. But after all, it isn't my fault. And I have my children to think of, especially, Annunciata. Suppose I did pass this over, for the sake of – Oh, no! no! no!' She made a wild gesture with her hands. 'The idea is ridiculous. Our married life is ended. Poor Charlie has finished it. Now, will you tell me a good solicitor I can go to?'

'For the divorce?'

'It won't be divorce, will it?' she asked. 'I don't understand these things. But I thought it would only be judicial separation. I was under the impression that for a wife to get a divorce she had to prove cruelty or desertion.'

'That is so.'

'What a shame!' She jumped up from the sofa in the swift heat of her protest.

'Yes, it's a shame,' Lawrence agreed. 'But there's "legal" cruelty. And I think – I'm not sure – that adultery in the household is legal cruelty.'

He stumbled over the phrase; he had the usual masculine cowardice about crystallizing a shameful thing in a definite form of words.

'It ought to be,' said Mrs Fearns. 'I hope it is. A judicial separation is neither one thing nor the other. What I need for the sake of my children is a real and final separation, a divorce. I did not think I could get it, but if I can, so much the better. Now what about a solicitor?'

'Oh!' Lawrence answered. 'You must go to Bradwells, and see Cyples.'

'Cyples? Yes, he's very good, isn't he?'

'He's the best in this district. But if you are going away, perhaps you'd prefer a complete stranger. Where do you mean to go to?'

'I thought of Folkestone or Sandgate. Emily is at school at Folkestone. Annunciata suggested Llandudno. But in another six or eight weeks half Bursley will be at Llandudno. We must be by ourselves for a long time.'

'Exactly,' he agreed.

'And I've lived in Trafalgar Road, here, all my life!' she said. In silence he put the end of his cigarette in an ashtray by the side of *Dreamthorp*.

'Then perhaps you'd like the name of a good solicitor in Folkestone?'

'No,' she said. 'It would be the same as going to a strange doctor. I think I should prefer Bradwells. Indeed, I believe old Mr Bradwell used to act for my father up to the time when I married Charlie. Then what business there was went to Charlie. We can meet somewhere, no doubt, they and I.'

'Anyhow, Folkestone will be handy for London. Their London agents will attend to things, you know.'

There was a silence. Mrs Fearns stood on the hearthrug, leaning slightly forward. Lawrence tried to think of some way of helping her, of expressing his sympathy by more than words. But he could not. She appeared so equal to the emergency, so conversant with her own mind, so capable, and so fearless, that to offer aid would have had the air of an impertinence.

'I suppose the governess has gone,' he said.

'Yes,' replied Mrs Fearns absently, 'she had the grace to leave us.' And in this sentence he fancied he could detect a faint but bitter touch of scorn. She dropped her arms heavily. 'Oh,' she burst out, 'it's the trial! It's the trial that I dread. I don't feel this – No, really, I don't seem to feel it yet. I only feel tired. But when I think of the trial, I feel sick. Still, we are in for it, and it has to be gone through. It will be just as bad for Charlie. Worse, indeed!'

'The wisest thing,' observed Lawrence, 'is not to think in advance. Tomorrow you are going away. Think only of that. Don't look further than Folkestone. What train are you taking? Have you considered the trains?'

'Yes,' she said calmly. 'I shall take the noon train to London, and we shall just catch the 4.23 at Charing Cross. You see, I've done it several times with Emily.'

'And when would you like to see Mr Cyples? Because I think I know where he can be found tonight, and I could hunt him up and arrange an interview.'

'That's very nice of you,' she said. 'I wish you would. Would he come here?'

'Of course.'

'Ask him to be here by ten o'clock tomorrow morning. Annunciata and I will do all the packing tonight. We shall leave the house at eleven. I want to leave as soon as possible – in case Charlie might be coming back. He won't be back before lunch.'

'He will go to the office first,' said Lawrence.

'Yes,' she concurred, 'he's sure to go to the office first. And I want you to tell him. Will you?'

Lawrence started, diffident as ever in front of any enterprise.

'That you have gone? You aren't writing to him, then?'

'No,' she cried with sudden emphasis. 'I can't write, and I won't. I am just going – that's all – with my children, and Martha, the youngest maid. I shall leave him his house, and the other servants, and he will do as he pleases. He will find everything in order. But I can't bring myself to write to him. There are some things one can't do.'

She resumed her seat on the sofa.

'Yes, I will tell him certainly.'

'Thank you,' she said.

'He knows you know?'

'I should be very much surprised if he didn't. Oh, he must know. They must have seen each other, after she knew that Annunciata had seen. Oh, she went like a lamb, so it appears. She didn't come to the office?'

'The governess? No.'

'Then probably they made their plans before either of them left the house. Was this journey to Liverpool arranged beforehand?'

'No. No one in the office knew anything about it.'

'But there is business in Liverpool?'

'Yes. There are one or two things that he might have gone to Liverpool for.'

'I thought so,' said Mrs Fearns. 'Trust Charlie to have a good excuse! He went to Liverpool to be out of the way when I returned, and he's sent her to London.'

'Why do you say London?'

'Because of the labels on the trunks she has left to be forwarded. I wonder what they mean to do?'

'He will get rid of her,' said Lawrence with savage curtness. He could not prevent himself from saying it, nor could he control his tone. The explosion gave him relief. For the instant he didn't care whether he shocked Mrs Fearns or not.

She mused.

'Tell him,' she said, in a tender and dissolving voice, 'that I said there was nothing else to be done. And so I'm doing it. I shall never see him again.' Then her accent changed. 'Except at the trial. And yet, yesterday, we were happy enough, all of us, in this house.'

Lawrence rose.

'Goodbye,' he said. 'It's awful, awful!'

'Oh!' she protested, with sweet mildness, 'one has to accept what comes.'

With a shake of his head, he in his turn protested against her philosophy. 'I'll go and see Cyples at once,' he said. They stood close together.

'Thank you,' she murmured, taking his hand and looking into his face. 'You know, Mr Ridware, you have considerable influence over Charlie.'

'I!' He was astounded.

'Yes, he's afraid of your bad opinion.'

'Well, I never guessed it.' said Lawrence, flattered.

'Oh, but he is. So if he talks to you, don't hesitate to talk back.'

'I won't. Goodbye.'

She came out with him into the tiled hall, where the gas burnt steady and solitary in an atmosphere quite different from that of the drawing-room, an atmosphere of suspense and mystery. The clock drawled its eternal tick-tack. Mats lay brooding before the closed solemnity of empty rooms. Shadows clad the angle where the side-passage led to the kitchen – apparently far off. The stairs slanted strangely upwards into black gloom. And there was the disturbing sense of human life, hiding out of sight behind the veils.

They trod softly.

'Good night, Mrs Fearns,' he whispered. He could scarcely speak.

She pulled the stiff latch of the heavy front door and swung it open.

'Why,' she said kindly, 'you take it harder than I do.'

'No I don't,' he answered hastily. 'But all the same, I'm just going into the divorce court myself. My wife has left me no alternative. I'm fixed like you are. So I understand.'

He escaped like a criminal through the doorway, and hurried down the dark garden, ignoring her exclamation. Outside the gate he stayed for a moment in the shade of the gatepost. Then he heard the low clang of the front door shutting.

Striking the blue sparks at regular intervals on its aerial wire, the Hanbridge car came noisily up out of Bursley along Trafalgar Road, that thoroughfare which, under one alias or another traverses the Five Towns from end to end. It staggered across the rough points opposite the King's Head Hotel and waited on the loop for the Bursley car to pass. Lawrence boarded it, nodding to the conductor and taking the seat on the rear platform. In the interior, ornamented with advertisements of soap and boots, and exhortations to respect the floor, were two shawled, bare-headed women, half asleep, the only passengers. Lawrence lit his pipe and smoked stolidly as the vast vehicle, so typical of the Five Towns, resumed its jerky and deafening pilgrimage to Hanbridge, past the hoardings, the churches and chapels, the little manufactories, the little shops, and the little Indian-red houses. This was the inmost heart of the Five Towns, and nothing was altered in it. And yet Lawrence had a foolish feeling of astonishment that everything was not altered. Although he had heard many and many a startling lascivious story of the district, although he knew that in Hanbridge alone five hundred frail ones served the Goddess by night, he had never till now realized that human nature was the same within as without the Five Towns, and it was as if some change had occurred therein, and as if the dark frontages of the very street itself ought to speak of it. He too, in his time, had lived in Trafalgar Road. He could hear Mrs Fearns' voice, rich with sorrow and resignation, saying: 'And I've lived in Trafalgar Road all my life!' And in the sad and passionate enthusiasm of the moment, he told himself that a pure, intelligent and courageous woman, who has kept warm the fires of a kind heart, was the superior of all other created beings. His soul melted with sympathy for those two hapless creatures trailing on the morrow with a couple of children and a servant and luggage from Bursley to a vague destination in Folkestone, driven out with shame and lashes from all that was theirs.

The car breasted the hill into Hanbridge, screeched round sharp curves, and drew up with a spasm beneath the electric globes of Crown Square. Other cars were absorbing crowds of revellers from the theatre and music-hall; and the publichouses had just dismissed their jolly customers full of the pride of life, and their taciturn customers full of philosophy which they never imparted to the world. Lawrence got off the car and directed his steps to the Conservative Club, where he knew that Cyples generally finished the evening.

CHAPTER VI

RENÉE

On the beautiful morning when Annunciata took her young brothers out for an early walk, Annunciata's father left his house hurriedly, and rather late, to go to the office. He had had, as usual, very little breakfast, but on the other hand he had foregone no detail of that sacred rite, his bath, and he looked and felt himself to be in splendid physical health. As he passed with firm, rapid gait up Trafalgar Road in the direction of Hanbridge, he could not, even in smiling, avoid a sigh of relief. Certainly he had committed indiscretions in the house before, but many years ago, and quite minor indiscretions compared to the supreme indiscretion of the previous night. He was bound to admit that he had been uncommonly foolish. He almost shivered when he thought of the risks he had run. And his smile had the inane, braggart quality of one who has just crossed with false leisureliness in front of an oncoming train and is beginning to realize the danger escaped. From the first, every instinct of prudence had counselled him to leave Renée alone. But circumstances and Renée had been too much for prudence. He recalled the morning after breakfast when she had happened to come into the hall while he was brushing his hat, and had spoken to him with a curious languor, and how the idea that she was desirable and not impregnable had pierced his brain suddenly like a little dart of a revelation. Similar ideas concerning women invariably struck him in that way. It was as if he were inoculated with a minute drop of virus which spread through his system, despite all his efforts, until there was only one cure. He had never, unaided, fought successfully against the poison of the virus. But in the special case of Renée he had most decidedly not meant to yield. Indeed, he had pretended that the little dart had not pierced

114

him, that the wound was only imaginary. Renée must be
respected. Even he must draw a line somewhere. And it
seemed as if he actually had arrested the progress of the
poison, when one trifling thing after another occurred to
weaken his resolution. He had accidentally touched her.
Chance had left them alone together more than once. And
when Alma had gone away! Alma had gone away! And Renée,
with her sleeves turned up, had met him at the head of the
stairs, and he had patted her on the cheek, and she had not
protested. A tremendous force had lifted his hand and
compelled him to pat her on the cheek; a force, however,
which he thought he could have resisted if her sleeves had not
been turned up. And then, at the end of dinner, owing to the
naughtiness of the children, matters had so fallen out that he
and Renée were again alone together. He had struggled
terribly not to lean over the corner of the table and kiss her.
But the tremendous force had conquered him and he had
kissed her. She had looked down, smiled vaguely and left the
room. . . . Why had he not accepted Annunciata's suggestion
to go to the theatre? That might have saved him. But no, he
could not. And throughout the whole evening at the club he
had suffered as he did suffer from time to time: an ignominious agony. And he had come home in the rain, and the
night air had calmed him. And already, going to bed, he was
despising his enemy, when lo! he had noticed that Renée's
door was not quite shut. The tremendous force had insisted
that he should push it open and glance within. He had fought,
he had struggled (and half a second was like hours), but in
vain. He had pushed the door open and glanced within, and
she was sitting up in bed, reading! A violent and exquisite
shudder had shaken him from head to foot. Instantly he had
perceived that she must come to his room, and with a habitual
gesture, he had invited her. . . .

Madness! Yes, he agreed that it had been madness, the
madness of a boy, not of a man of immense experience! He
must take himself in hand. However, the danger, though
terrific, was safely past, and it must not be allowed to recur.
The affair was finished. He could manage Renée. He knew
exactly how to manage her. When the descent became
advisable, he had reconducted dozens of women from the

116   WHOM GOD HATH JOINED

pinnacle of emotion down to the everyday level. Still, Renée
was not a mere numeral in the catalogue of dozens. How
many times, driven by relentless prurience, had he not
besieged women who did not attract him, simply because they
seemed vulnerable! How many times had he not loathed that
which he possessed, and spent days in self-disgust until his
invincible passions had recovered from the blow and seized
him again! Renée could not be classed in that section of the
catalogue. Renée was an astounding creature, a creature apart.
He said the affair was finished. He said he must take himself in
hand. Yet already before he got to Hanbridge, he was
dreaming of Renée, no longer governess in his household, but
discreetly established in some not-too-distant spot where he
could visit her and pass idyllic hours. A wild, impossible
dream, but it brought a luscious smile to his coarse, handsome
face. There was no hope for Charles Fearns.

At the office he read his letters, and while he was reading
them, the magnitude of the risk he had run and the danger he
had escaped impressed him more and more, so preoccupying
him that he was obliged to read some of his letters twice
through in order to grasp their meaning. 'Well, anyhow, it's
safely over!' he murmured, impatient with himself. Still, he
had a slight misgiving as to whether, if his wife returned home
that day, he would be capable of behaving at dinner in a
manner absolutely natural. He rang the bell. Clowes came in,
shorthand notebook in hand.

'Tell Mr Pennington I want him.'

'He's gone out, sir.'

'Gone out? Where?'

'To Manifold, sir.'

'What for? Do you know?'

'I think it's in that matter of Mr Ridware's, sir,' said the
thick-set Clowes with a significant intonation and a self-
conscious look.

Fearns was angry. He objected to Ridware introducing a
divorce case, and his own divorce case, into the office at that
juncture. The objection was infantile, indefensible, but he held
it. The very word 'divorce' made him feel queer. It touched
him too nearly. It gave him to think most unpleasantly. He
was in such a state that even the greatest master of diplomacy

could not have handled the case of Ridware *v*. Ridware in a style to satisfy him. Certainly he had said that Pennington should, under his supervision, assume charge of the case, but Pennington had no right to go running off to Manifold without notice and without permission. Pennington took too much upon himself. Was the entire business of the office to be dislocated because Ridware, who was an unpractical fool, chose to rush into the divorce court? He strove to master his resentment.

'Take down these letters,' he commanded abruptly.

'Yes, sir,' said Clowes with servile alacrity, sitting down, and taking a pencil from behind his ear. The telephone bell rang outside.

'Gentlemen. Mayor and Corporation of Hanbridge *v*. Clarke. I am in receipt of your letter of yesterday and observe. Yours truly.'

There were mornings when he snapped out his letters curt and brief, like that, without a dispensable word. He was just giving the names of the addressees when Gater entered.

'You're wanted on the telephone, sir,' said Gater, with the casualness of an office-boy who knows the supply of officeboys is unequal to the demand.

'Who is it wants me?'

'I don't know, sir.'

'Well, go, and see, you stupid fellow!' Fearns grumbled with increasing irritation, and continued to dictate.

'They say it's a lady, sir,' said Gater, coming back. 'No name, sir.'

And Fearns felt a sudden and dreadful sinking of the heart. Some intuition warned him then of the calamity that was overtaking him; and he rose and went to the telephone in silence, with a physical sense of nausea. The telephone was in a corner of the corridor.

'Who's there?' he asked, trying to find jauntiness in the hope that it was his wife in Birmingham, or Annunciata bent on the satisfaction of some girlish caprice.

'*C'est moi!*' came the reply.

He recognized the voice, and he understood a little French. What had happened? What did she want? She had him at her mercy at the end of the wire: so he apprehended.

'Where are you?' he asked.

'At the post-office.'

'What post-office?' He stared blankly at the soiled card hung by the side of the little desk of the telephone.

'Hanbridge. I must see you.' Her tones, rendered metallic and unearthly in transmission, assailed his ears, against which the long-handled twin discs were pressed, like a horrid menace. She was within a couple of hundred yards of him!

'I'll come to you,' he replied, low; and still lower: 'Be on the pavement.' He dared not argue. And he rang off.

'I shall be back in a few minutes,' he said gruffly to Clowes, seizing his hat from behind the door of his room, and walked slowly downstairs, his hands in his pockets. He really had not thought that Renée would play feminine tricks on him, would attempt to take a silly advantage of their intimacy. He had supposed her a woman of extraordinary good sense, capable of conducting herself with a sagacity perfectly adapted to the situation created by the event of the night, and of estimating that event at its proper value. Her behaviour under his caresses had seemed to him little less than a miracle of fitness. It had enchanted him. It had differentiated her from all the other women who had ever sinned with him. And here she was within twelve hours amply proving that she was, after all, no less fatuously incalculable than the rest. He savagely cursed her.

In two minutes he had passed the Town Hall and was approaching the post-office. He saw her coming rather quickly towards him. She was very plainly dressed in grey, and she carried an umbrella and a handbag. As they met and stopped, he raised his hat, against his will. Her face was grave but composed.

'What is it?' he questioned her, with a swift, shamed glance. 'Walk along with me this way.' And he led her down Spode Street, which is a fairly quiet residential thoroughfare, marred only by the branch tram-line that runs to Sneyd Vale.

She opened up her gloved hand, and disclosed a letter folded up very small.

'Read that, my friend,' she said. 'The cook brought it to my bedroom.'

And he read Annunciata's note.

'My God!' he exclaimed. There was the true tragic in his voice then. For a moment he felt as though he had been through a fearful surgical operation and had lost his stomach. He perspired. He trembled. Nemesis had leapt upon him. The worst, the unthinkable had occurred.

She looked up at him through her veil.

'What can that mean?' he asked feebly.

'It means that she knows,' said Renée.

'But she can't know!' he protested. 'How can she know?'

'She knows,' Renée repeated coldly. 'Perhaps she heard you kiss me after dinner, and had suspicions and watched at night.' She shrugged her shoulders. 'I do not say. But she knows. The proof? When I got up, the little boys were not in bed. She had taken them away.'

'We can't talk here,' he muttered, gazing about in alarm. 'What have you done?'

'I have left, my friend, *tout simplement*. I have packed my trunks and left.'

'You ought not to have done that,' he cried. 'That puts us in the wrong at once. That gives the damned show away. Why did you do that?'

'I had no intention to have a scene with your daughter,' said Renée 'She knows. That is enough.'

'Why didn't you tell me before I left the house?' he asked, exasperated by her calmness.

'I tried to tell you. It was dangerous. I came into your bedroom. You were in the bathroom. Martha came up to clean the corridor. I had scarcely time to fly back. And she was always there, cleaning. I could not come out. You saw her? Then, when she had gone, you had gone also.'

'Of course you could have come out!' he protested. 'You could have waited for me in the dining-room. You could have done fifty things.'

'Do not blame me,' she urged tranquilly. 'It is shameful.'

In his heart he told himself he must behave like an Englishman to this Frenchwoman. He must not be a cad. And he searched frantically for a plan. They could not hold passionate discussions in Spode Street, under the scrutiny of a hundred bow-windows. He must demonstrate to her his masculinity. The Sneyd Vale car appeared.

'Take this tram,' he said. 'Get off at the canal bridge, and walk by the canal side. I'll follow you in a minute or so. Go along, please.'

She obeyed, hailing the driver, and Fearns raised his hat with a painful smile, and turned back towards the centre of the town, so as to avoid suspicion. He passed by the front of the Town Hall again, nodding to one or two acquaintances with exaggerated cordiality, for he had to maintain to himself his reputation for sangfroid in a crisis; this was by no means his first crisis. And he kept exhorting himself to be steady, not to be flurried. The device of sending Renée in advance down to Sneyd Vale seemed to him pretty good for a man called upon to invent something on the very instant. They could talk by the canal side; it was one of the few spots in the Five Towns where they could talk. The difficulties in the path of a famous rake in a district such as the Five Towns are prodigious and demand prodigious qualities. He was content with the Sneyd Vale idea; he nourished his self-respect on the Vale idea, until suddenly he thought of an infinitely better one, the obvious solution. He ought to have walked boldly with Renée to the cab-stand in Crown Square and there taken a cab to Longshaw. They would have had more than half an hour of absolute privacy in the cab; they could have called at some shop in Longshaw and then driven back, and the keenest noses in Hanbridge would have missed the scent. The Sneyd Vale idea was now utterly discredited; its clumsiness and the peril of it became apparent.

For a moment he dreamed of suicide. The spirit was beaten out of him. How he loathed himself! How black was his desperation! It was incredible that he should have been such a fool last night! And for what? What was it worth, this brief commerce with women? Nothing! Less than nothing! He shuddered with disgust at the mere thought of sexual pleasure. Could a sane man risk an hour's peace of mind in order to obtain it! He remembered the Arab proverb that fireworks last seven minutes, love seven seconds, and sorrow the rest of life. What was the strange intoxication that came over him at sight of a woman? It was a delusion. He could conquer it. He would conquer it. Once out of this mess – and he could get out of it, he would assuredly get out of it – he would never again leave the domestic hearth. He had learnt his lesson, he said.

He went through the empty cattle-market, and down by a
narrow road running parallel with Spode Street. Yes, he must
send Renée away; that was the preliminary. And then he must
deal with his wife and Annunciata. Boldly he said that he
could persuade them of his innocence. But Annunciata, whom
he had kept in the background of his mind by force, sprang
forward now. No, the thought of Annunciata being
concerned in the affair was awful! It was so awful that he could
scarcely conceive it. Like all rakes, he was extremely
sentimental, especially in seasons of remorse, and he had the
prettiest ideas of womanly purity. And even if he had not been
Annunciata's father, even if in a mood of romantic expansion
he had not chosen from a book Annunciata's name at her
birth, the thought of her knowledge of his crime might
justifiably have cowed him into despair. In a moment he had
lost all hope, energy, and initiative. So his temper alternated as
he descended the hill towards the vale.

He turned into Spode Street at the bottom, after the houses
have come to an end and where the sooty market-gardens
begin. A quarter of a mile further on, the tram-car, having
been to Sneyd Valley, was crossing the canal bridge on its
homeward journey. He went slackly forward, and the car,
empty save for the driver and conductor, passed him. He
stood on the canal bridge and glanced guiltily from right to
left along the black towing-path of the canal. There was not a
sign of Renée. Then he went down the steep steps cut in the
embankment of the road, and reached the level of the canal,
which for all its foulness glinted in the sunshine. She was
there, in the deep shadow under the bridge. The towing-path
was hard and dry except under the bridge, where mud
abounded, and she was holding her skirts nattily out of the
mud. She had raised her veil. She gazed at him sadly, and, so it
seemed to him, humbly, as he came near.

'What have you decided?' she asked in a stricken, appealing
voice.

He felt at once the peculiar, voluptuous charm of the voice.
It was the same voice, full of languor, which had fallen on his
ear that morning in the hall of his house while he was brushing
his hat. Renée was very much shorter than he. And he looked
down on her form, looked down on those rounded curves,

that trim waist, those folds of the skirt that her hands clutched. And if his situation had not been so desperate, the magic would have enslaved his senses yet again. He could have almost run away with her, and counted the world well lost for the sake of a few lustful months. But the vision of an outraged Annunciata checked the poison in his veins. Moreover, Renée herself wore an expression which he had not seen before on her piquant face.

'Nothing,' he said, with a gesture of defeat. 'What is there to decide? You've left the house. That's the difficulty.'

'Ah!' she murmured rapidly. 'How I was wrong! Why did I go into your room last night? You were wrong. But men . . . I was more wrong. We were both mad. I must leave you. That is all I can do. She will help you to persuade Annunciata that there was nothing.'

'Do you think so?' he replied gloomily.

But the gloominess was deliberate deceit on his part. Renée had suggested an idea which appeared to him really practical. He saw in it his salvation, unhoped for, miraculous, wondrously beneficent. Yes, he must enlist his wife's aid against Annunciata; that was the plan. Alma was extremely clever, and had tremendous influence over her daughter. Alma was also an angel, capable of forgiveness to an indefinite extent. He would appeal to her; he could not appeal in vain, for the future of the children was at stake. He would confess to Alma, and then persuade her of the necessity of convincing Annunciata that, whatever the girl had seen or had not seen, her conclusions were wrong. The matter would require the nicest delicacy, coupled with firmness, but Alma would succeed. Of course his relations with his wife, while remaining normal on the surface, would for a long time be secretly painful. But he could win her back. He was sure that he could prove to her that at last he had learnt his lesson.

And it was Renée who had hit on the scheme! Women certainly did know how to deal with women. Men were children compared to them. But he did not mean to let her see that she had saved him, that he was drowning when she had stretched out a hand. That would have impaired his masculine dignity. Hence he had replied to her with false gloom. Nevertheless he appreciated her.

And he excused himself to himself by the help of the basic
axiom of the rake's philosophy – that women exist for men
and fulfil themselves only in serving men. Renée was an
agreeable little thing; she was much more than an agreeable
little thing; but she had no rights as against him.

'I will go now,' she said. 'Then you will be free to act.'

'But where shall you go?' he demanded, striving to show an
interest in her fate, and to hide his relief.

'That is not your affair,' said she. 'Only let me leave you.
Do not make it difficult for me. I have been wicked to your
wife. And as for that poor Annunciata –!'

'Where shall you go?' he repeated. He could do no less than
be firm. Her femininity was a challenge to his chivalry.

'To London. Perhaps to Paris. There are many English
families in Paris. I can place myself.' Her tone was sweetly and
resignedly cheerful.

'Not without testimonials, you can't,' he said. 'I will
give you a testimonial. I will write you the best character
you can possibly want, and then perhaps you will be all
right.'

She thanked him with a modest, grateful glance, as though
he had offered something beyond her hopes or deserts. It was
wonderful to him how she had changed by calamity. This was
not the same woman that he had held in his arms and fondled
and kissed, and who had repaid his caresses with her own.
This was a serious, good little woman. Her nature evidently
had two sides. He felt a brute. Still, women were amazing.
There was no other word.

She gave him the address of a home for French governesses
in Kensington, and he wrote it down. Then she sighed.

'You will do what I say?' she breathed.

'What?'

'Ask your wife to forgive you, and me. And to help you
with poor Annunciata.'

'I can't help imagine how Annunciata suspected –' he burst
out, reflective. 'What did she –?'

'Never mind that. You will do what I say?'

She was solemnly staring up at him, her lips parted.

'I'll try it,' he said, permitting his voice to show a faint
hope. 'I'll try it. I had a note from my wife this morning to

say she would come home tomorrow by the half-past twelve train. I'll meet her at Knype, before Annunciata sees her.'

'But if Annunciata writes to her?'

'What does that matter?' he said, with an accent of superior wisdom. 'My wife must know, anyhow. The only important thing is that I should see her before anyone else does.'

She nodded meekly. 'How I pity you, my friend!'

'Oh!' he said curtly. 'What is done is done. We must make the best of it. All I can say is, I'm awfully sorry I've got you into this hole.'

She shook her head. 'It is myself I blame. For me there is no excuse.' And she whispered: 'I am not sorry for myself. For myself I am glad. I do not regret for myself. It is for you and your wife and poor Annunciata that I regret.' She gazed up at him tragically. He was touched, and at the same time he suddenly felt very self-conscious.

'Well – ' he stammered, not knowing what to say.

She broke in, evidently preoccupied by the dangers that beset him: 'But tonight? Your wife will not be in the house. And you will be obliged to meet Annunciata! How shall you –?'

'I shan't do any such thing,' he replied. 'I've thought of all that. I shall have business in Liverpool this afternoon, and I shan't return till tomorrow evening.'

'What time shall you go to Liverpool?' she demanded.

He drew from his pocket the local time-table which is carried by every business man in the Five Towns. 'Twelve thirty-eight at Knype,' he said, and added: 'By the way, you know there's an express to London at twelve eleven? You might catch it.'

'Yes.' she agreed softly.

She was acquiescence itself.

'Take my bag a little second, will you?' she asked him. He took her bag, and also the umbrella, which she held out to him, letting her skirts fall. He wondered what she was going to do. She glanced downwards with a charming coquettish instinct, to be sure that her skirt had escaped a puddle, and then she raised her small gloved hands and arranged his necktie. 'T'es ficelé comme quat' sous,' she murmured. He did not comprehend the phrase. Then she picked a bit of fluff off his breast. He said to himself that such was the nature of women, and that these attentions must be borne stoically. His spirits were mounting now. Hope shone like a star before him. He saw the time when he could look Annunciata in the face. Lastly Renée lowered her veil.

At the same moment there was a wild, stertorous snorting and tramp of hoofs, and round the bend of the canal a horse suddenly entered the tunnel of the bridge, straining at a taut rope. The rope wrenched his forequarters in the direction of the water, so that he walked a little askew. Fearns dragged his mistress to the wall, and the animal struggled on, his legs raking forward like the masts of a ship. Each time he lifted a hoof out of the viscid mud there was a sound like a smothered Titanic kiss.

'Oh! The brute!' Renée exclaimed. 'I was frightened.'

And Fearns smiled with indulgence. Presently the long, narrow boat appeared. A man was steering, and the water rippled off the rudder, which he held firmly to port. Smoke ascended from the cabin. A woman was nursing a baby at the cabin door. The inhabitants of the boat did not give a second glance at Fearns and Renée. They spent their lives in surprising couples under bridges. The cortège passed from view.

Then a car rumbled overhead, shaking the earth.

'What time is it?' Renée asked.

'Twenty-five past eleven. That is the car going to Sneyd Vale. The other will be along in five minutes. If you take it and then get a cab, you will just have time.'

'I will do that,' she said.

'Have you enough money?' he questioned her. She nodded. 'Let me give you some.'

She shook her head. And he saw two tears in her eyes. He had wounded her. 'No, no,' she muttered, with a kind of horror. He regretted that he had mentioned money. And yet he could not have let her go without mentioning it.

'*Adieu!*' she said, resuming her bag and umbrella.

'Goodbye,' he responded, and in giving her the bag, he tried to squeeze her hand; it was the least he could do. However, her hand was occupied with the umbrella, and he only succeeded in squeezing her thumb. He felt foolish.

'You go first,' she entreated him. 'We cannot leave together.'

'No,' he said, 'I will stay till you are safely off.'

'I wish to be the last in this place,' she begged.

'Don't be silly,' he spoke with kind firmness. 'You'll miss your car.'

She yielded submissively, and went from under the bridge. Then she stopped, and hesitated, and came back to him. And as she did so, she lifted her veil with one hand. She raised her sad, set face to his with a mute appeal. He blushed, bent down and kissed her cheek, and she kissed his cheek.

'Goodbye, little girl,' he said, and his voice broke. It was the facile emotion of the Lovelace that had overtaken him unawares.

She said nothing; but put her lips together, lowered her veil, seized her skirt and shook it, and hastened from his sight. Immediately afterwards the bridge vibrated to the passage of the Hanbridge car.

The words that he uttered as the echoes of the car died away, had they been heard, would perhaps have deprived him of the last shred of human sympathy. But they were not to be construed in a too literal sense. They were in part the mere bravado of one who, having been well frightened, is getting over his alarm and scorning the man he was a moment before. And in any case they expressed only a small fraction of his feelings. He exclaimed: 'Good riddance!'

He tapped nervously with his stick against the brick wall, frowning at it. She was a mysterious creature. After all he wondered if she had not been performing a comedy with masterly skill. His opinion of women was now very high, now very low. She was gone, the chapter closed, the leaf turned.

She was gone. Never would he see her again. And the final interview had occurred more smoothly than he could have dared to hope. He had now to face the situation with his wife and Annunciata. It dismayed him horribly. But, thanks to Renée he had emerged somewhat from the sick despair of half an hour ago.

Inextricably mixed up with the tumult of his thoughts concerning that situation was a thread of regret for certain

qualities in Renée. He could not dismiss from his mind the
haunting conviction that she was the finest mistress he had
ever had.

He hastened back to the office, this time walking boldly up
Spode Steet. There could be no further danger now, no matter
who saw him. The notion of departing instantly to Liverpool
appealed to him very strongly. He felt the need of movement,
the need to get away out of the atmosphere of the Five Towns,
which seemed to choke him. At Liverpool he would be
capable of continuous thought, and could carefully consider
how he should approach his wife. For the moment he had the
idea of going to Birmingham, instead of to Liverpool, and
meeting his wife at once. But when he remembered the sort of
house in which his wife's sister lived, and the fact that it would
be completely upset by illness, he saw that a private and
lengthy interview in the house would be impossible. And
certainly he could not take his wife for a walk and explain to
her his sin and his remorse in the streets. Moreover, he had the
coward's preference for tomorrow. It seemed to him that
Annunciata might write to her mother and tell her . . . No!
Impossible! The child would never do that. She would never
dare even to hint on paper . . . There would be something
about such an action that would appal a modest girl. Still, he
was dimly aware that Annunciata had in her character a streak
of the fanatic, of the martyr. He had glimpsed that streak more
than once. After all, she might write to her mother; it was just
conceivable. Then the brilliant scheme of writing to Mrs
Fearns himself came into his mind, and he was enchanted with
it. He would go to Liverpool and he would write to her in his
best style – and he could write a letter to a woman, he said, if
any man could! – and smooth the pathway for the interview.

   In his office, a client who had an appointment, and whom
he had entirely forgotten, was waiting to see him. He
apologized to the client, gave him a cigar, and told him he
could spare him exactly five minutes. He said that during the
last day or two he had not been able to call his soul his own.
Unexpected interruptions had followed one another in a
series, and now he was absolutely compelled to rush off to
Liverpool at a moment's notice ('A quarter of an hour ago I

was kissing her,' his thoughts persistently ran, 'A quarter of an hour ago I was kissing her.' And in memory the scene under the bridge seemed fantastic.) He talked seriously with the client for a minute or two, and then rang for Ridware, to whom he specially commended the client's affairs. And to show the client that he regarded him as no ordinary client, he spoke briefly to Ridware, in his presence, of other business, and informed Ridware that he was off to Liverpool.

'I'm going out,' he said, as his client rose, and they left his room together, each smoking. Fearns saw the telephone.

'Half a second,' he demanded of the client, the cigar between his teeth. 'I'll just telephone to my daughter. The wife's away.'

And he rang, and gave the number to the Exchange.

When Annunciata answered his call, he put his cigar on the desk, but so clumsily that it fell to the ground. Her 'Yes, father,' frightened him. He knew he was afraid of her. And as a criminal endeavours to anticipate his fate from the judge's preliminary tones, so he endeavoured to read the future in Annunciata's voice. But he could not succeed in the divination. He delivered his message in the sharp, curt tone of a busy preoccupied man.

'There! That's done!' he exclaimed, picking up the cigar and dusting it.'

'Soon done!' the client observed.

'Well, good morning. I must hurry,' he said outside. 'What time do you make it, exactly? I know you've always got Greenwich.'

They compared watches, shook hands, and left. Fearns had the good fortune to catch a Knype car at the end of the street.

Bob Cyples was on the rear platform of the car, smoking. He and Fearns were somewhat less than cronies and somewhat more than business friends; though neither ever enjoyed the other's hospitality, except in bars, restaurants, and clubs; a sort of fellowship, which had never been put to any test, existed between them. They were familiar rather than intimate, but there was liking and a certain amount of respect at the bottom of their friendship. Fearns did not wish to talk to anybody just then. However, as he hesitated to throw away his newly-lit cigar immediately, he was obliged to accept the situation and remain on the platform. Such sacrifices must be made at once if they are to be made at all.

Cyples was very cordial, as usual, and the exchanges were of the lightest nature until the conductor went inside to collect the fares. Then Cyples altered his tone.

'You're going on with the matter, I suppose?' he said cautiously.

'What matter?'

'R. *v*. R.,' said Cyples.

'R. *v*. R.?' Fearns repeated, at a loss.

'Ridware,' Cyples breathed the word very low. If he had called it out aloud no one but Fearns could possibly have heard it above the rattle of the car, but in business Cyples' name was prudence.

'Oh! Ridware!' Fearns exclaimed. 'Why? You aren't against us, are you?'

'Yes,' said Cyples. 'I told R. Didn't he tell you? The lady came to us immediately after the rupture.' And Cyples seemed to convey that not every lady would have been so wise as not to wait for the actual commencement of proceedings before consulting her lawyers.

'The devil she did!' responded Fearns. 'No, Ridware didn't tell me. Fact is, I haven't had a chance to speak to him about it today. Why do you ask if we're going on. Of course, we're going on. You simply won't have a look in, my boy.'

Cyples smiled in a manner to indicate that, on that point, he had his own opinion. Between friends who were professionally enemies, unofficial conversation as to the *casus belli* could not with due regard to etiquette be carried much further. Moreover, the conductor returned to the platform.

'I only mentioned it because I've just heard that G. is seriously ill,' said Cyples.

'G?'

'Yes you know.'

Fearns nodded. 'Ah! What's up with him?'

'Don't know.'

There was a pause.

'Where are you off to?' Cyples resumed in a normal tone.

'Liverpool,'

'Long?'

'No. Come back tonight or tomorrow morning.'

Shortly afterwards, Cyples dropped off the car opposite Boone's manufactory. Fearns was glad to be alone. It was astonishing how the mere mention of a divorce case distressed him. But he assured himself that he had shown no sign of perturbation to Cyples.

Just as there is a right and a wrong pavement of Piccadilly, so, at large railway stations, there is always one platform which is modish beyond the others, and this platform is usually the main up-platform. Such was the case at Knype. The main down-platform, though it pointed to Manchester, Liverpool and Scotland, and though the greatest expresses halted their magnificence before it, could never – no, not on the morning of the Grand National! – compete in social distinction with its rival. That day happened to be Thursday, the half-holiday of the shop-keepers, and the down-platform was crowded with a miscellaneous assortment of trippers – good, modest people, capable of asking for an excursion-ticket without shame, and of sitting five-a-side and laying open their souls to fellow-mortals without an introduction. The down-platform was therefore even less fashionable than usual. Charles Fearns found himself delayed at every corner. There was a score of persons in front of him at the booking-office; the approaches to the subway were encumbered, and by the time he arrived on the platform, the train was overdue. He had the scorn for Thursday people which invariably animates the breasts of those who take holiday on Saturday, for it is accepted that to be idle on Saturday is more correct than to be idle on Thursday. He was out of breath, and hot and very thirsty, and his thirst reminded him that he had omitted lunch from his programme of arrangements. He cared, however, nothing for lunch, but his parched throat was rather peremptory in its demand, and it depressed and angered him to think that he could not drink earlier than Crewe. He discovered from a porter that an economical railway company had, by merely taking thought and by no other process, transformed the twelve thirty-eight ordinary to Crewe and Liverpool into an excursion train, and that first-class passengers would accordingly suffer. Taller than most of the crowd, and not recognizing a single individual in it, he regarded the simple faces with resentful disdain, refusing to yield to excited plebeian elbows and shoulders, and swallowing his thirst as best he could.

'Stand back, please! Crewe and Liverpool train,' cried several porters.

The train slowly entered the reverberating station, and carriage doors opened like fins along the length of its smooth flank. By chance a first-class compartment came to a stop precisely in front of Fearns. In a mechanical manner he read on a board at the top of the coach – 'Birmingham and Liverpool. Through carriage.' His fingers were on the handle of the door when he perceived a woman inside. She stooped over a bag, and her face was hidden from him. His heart gave a jump. It was his wife that he had seen, and already, having apparently fastened the bag, she was turning to alight. Instinctively, wihout reflection, he pushed violently backwards into the crowd and forced a passage to the open space between the edge of the crowd and the wall of a waiting-room. What should he do? With cruel suddenness he was called upon to decide a course of action, and he dared not decide.

His wife descended, and for the moment was lost to view. Annunciata, then, must have telegraphed to her mother. What had Annunciata telegraphed? And the monstrous question of what Annunciata knew, what Annunciata had seen, presented itself to him with desolating effect. He had caught a glimpse of his wife's face, and he thought it displayed extreme pain and anxiety. Surely Annunciata had not telegraphed the naked fact! No! Even the clumsy inexperience of a girl whose feelings had been utterly outraged would not have committed the folly of telegraphing the naked fact! The idea could not be conceived. There was, then, yet time. By the merest chance he was yet in a position, by the exercise of all his vaunted tact and persuasive skill, to save the situation. He must go up to his wife instantly and begin upon the dreadful business. He must grasp the nettle without pusillanimity and without shrinking. Perhaps Annunciata had not telegraphed. Perhaps the recovery of Alma's sister had progressed so rapidly that his wife had resolved to come home a day earlier. There was hope. Already the multitude on the platform was thinning. And, behind the Crewe train, the loop-line train, which would take his wife to Bleakridge, had crept up. He could see her now, moving towards it. He must not hesitate. There was not a second to lose.

He counted himself a man, but as the alternative courses dictated by courageous prudence and by imbecile cowardice offered themselves to him, the manhood left him. It was not for nothing that for twenty years he had devoted his life to carnal indulgence. The fibre of his character had been eaten away, and now for the first time he realized with horror that this was so. He did not doubt that his fate and the fate of his family depended on his action during the next minute. He could not think of a single argument in favour of delaying the encounter with his wife. Nevertheless he could not approach her. His legs would not carry him in her direction. He was no longer to deal with logic, but with instinct. And the instinct which had forced him away from the carriage door forbade him to follow Alma to the loop-line train. He was powerless. He was conscious of an abject fear of his wife. He knew that he could not meet her eyes.

And so he slipped again like a thief towards the Liverpool train. 'It will be better to write,' he murmured in his heart, and knew well the while that it would not be better to write. 'Annunciata has not compromised me, and she will not compromise me,' he said, and sought to find an illusory solace in the obvious lie. Then he felt a touch on his shoulder. He ignored it, and the touch was repeated. He turned. Renée was at his side.

He was so taken aback that he could not utter a sound.

'I must speak to you,' she said, and she seemed to lean her body towards him. Her veil was raised. Her face, with its melting eyes, invited and implored him to accept her.

'What?' he muttered in a strange voice.

'I must speak to you.'

He could have struck her and killed her without a qualm.

'But you can't,' he said. 'My wife's on the platform. She'll see us.'

And he gazed fearfully around, lest anyone should have heard their colloquy.

'I must speak to you,' she reiterated; 'come to the waiting-room. Come.' She appeared to ignore the news of his wife's presence, or not to have heard it.

He was trapped and helpless. At once it seemed to him that if she had not sprung herself upon him, he would, after all, have had the courage to go to his wife. And now Renée was audacious enough to seize his coat. She was bent on his ruin; he could see that, and he anathematized her with the savage sincerity of desperation. But he followed her; he might not do otherwise. She led him, blindly and swiftly, to the ladies' first-class waiting-room. There was no other person in the waiting-room, a large, lofty, and obscure apartment, with an empty fire-place, cushioned benches running round the walls, and a massive table in the centre; on the table lay Renée's bag and umbrella. He placed himself against the wall between the window and the door. The lower panes of the window were of ground-glass, but he could look over them and survey the platform. Dividing his frightened glances between the platform and the woman, he gasped:

'What do you want?'

'I missed the train,' she stammered, boldly clutching at the lapels of his coat. And then, abandoning herself to emotion, she cried aloud. 'No, no! I did not miss it. I could not leave you, *chéri!* Forgive me! I could not leave you. I have waited for you.' And she sobbed as freely as if they had been locked up in some secret chamber, secure from any possible interruption.

He was furious with anger at her deceit, at the calculated comedy she had played under the canal bridge. He was sure it was comedy that she had played. And this too, though real tears rolled from her eyes – this too, was comedy. She did not mean to lose. She had got him, and no scruples would prevent her from keeping him. 'Ah!' he thought wildly, 'Will you? Will you? Damn you! We will see if I am the man to be caught like this! You hoodwinked me under the canal bridge, but not twice, my girl!' Her charm, her intention, were as voluptuous as ever, but she had ceased to enchant him. They stared at each other.

'Oh! *Mon Charles!*' she murmured. 'Have pity on me!'

'You must be mad,' he replied, repulsing her, 'to go on in this way, here!'

'Yes,' she said, 'I am mad. I thought I could leave you, but I cannot.'

He looked at the platform. It was nearly empty. The train had gradually absorbed the excursionists, and there was a banging of doors, a waving of a green flag, and two whistles. He could see his wife approaching the waiting-room.

'My wife's coming in here,' he cried, at his wits' end. 'Let me go!'

'*Charles!*'

'Good God!' he muttered, and then ferociously: 'If you don't let me go, you devil –'

The Liverpool train passed out of view, and immediately the loop-line train came up and took its place, waiting the appointed minute of departure. He saw his wife get into a first-class compartment, and shut the door, and then lean from the window, idly scanning the platform. And as he drew his head into the shelter of the wall, the sense of his gigantic folly, the sense of all that he had risked and all that he was forfeiting, swept though him and overwhelmed him. If only he could have rushed to the calm and heavenly creature outside and cast himself at her feet, and humbled himself, and entreated her to listen to none but him – if only he could have done that! But Renée had him. Renée and he were one in that moment! And the seconds ticked away on the clock above the vast fire-place, and then there was another whistle, and the loop-line train slid from the station, and, except for porters and the bookstall clerk, the platform was quite empty. Alma had irretrievably gone to Annunciata.

Renée poured out broken words.

'Look here, my girl,' he addressed her bitterly, forcing her hand anew off his coat. 'You can't come these games over me. So don't think it. I don't suppose I'm the first that you've hooked, not by a long sight. You've got to go, and you may as well understand it. Do you hear? You've got to go. Do your worst. If it's blackmail do your worst. You must take me for a confounded fool. But I'm not. I'm not! I may be ruined, but I'm not an absolute mug. Do you hear?'

'Yes,' she answered, stifling her sobs.

'That's good. Did you get your ticket for London?'

'No, I had no money.'

'Then why in God's name did you tell me you had money?'
he demanded with uncontrolled passion.

She shrank away. 'I was too proud,' she said.

'That be damned! That be damned!' he shouted. He did not
care who heard him. He made one step to the table, pounced
on her bag, opened it, and put a lot of gold and silver into it,
all the money he had, save for one sovereign which he kept in
his hand.

'Here! Take it!' he ordered her. And she submissively took
the bag. 'And this, too!' And she took the umbrella. 'Now
come along with me!'

He hurried her out of the waiting-room, and through the
subway to the booking-hall on the up-platform.

'Second single to Euston,' he said laconically to the
booking-clerk, depositing the sovereign. 'There's a train to
Stafford at one three, isn't there?'

'Yes, sir,' said the clerk.

He handed the ticket to Renée, and made her sit down in the
booking-hall, while he planted himself under the archway
leading to the platform. It was already one o'clock.

'You change at Stafford,' he said, as he put her into the
train. 'You won't have long to wait. The Euston train comes
in from Crewe. I'll send you the testimonial.'

He did not say goodbye, and since leaving the waiting-room
she had been silent. The train departed.

He almost ran into the refreshment-room.

'Bottle of Bass, miss.' He drank the Bass in three gulps, and
smacked his lips.

'Curse her!' he thought. 'Curse her! But I took the blasted
Frenchiness out of her. A nice thing!' And deep in his paternal
mind was an indignant protest that French governesses, with
their Catholic ways, could thus worm themselves into decent
families and play hell with domestic peace. He knew he had
been disgracefully brutal. He did not attempt to disguise from
himself that he had behaved to her infamously, even granting
to the full her unscrupulous duplicity. But he did not care. He
said he would do the same again under the same circumstances. Yes, a hundred times!

He returned to his office to obtain some more money.

The next morning, Charles Fearns, back again in the Five

Towns, jumped off the car at Lawton Street, Bleakridge, and
turned with hurried steps to resume possession of his house
and his family. Superficially he had the same air of the
conquering, jaunty, powerful male that always distinguished
him. It seemed as if nothing could destroy the elasticity of that
stride nor dull the fire of that eye, nor blanch that cheek, nor
derange the hat's cavalier poise.

Moreover, he had desperate reason to wear the mask of
victory, if by so doing he could enhearten himself to win. But
he was nevertheless really in a state of approaching collapse,
nearer even than he feared, to the end of his forces. He had
spent a pitiable evening and night at Liverpool. No sooner had
he arrived there than he began, with reason, to ask why he had
gone thither. What purpose was he serving? What conceivable
excuse had the journey? For four hours he divided his time
between the streets and the smoking-room of the Adelphi
Hotel. Twice he essayed a letter to his wife, and found the task
beyond him. But he telegraphed to say that he should not
return that night. At length, just before the post left, he did
scribble a note to her; it was a ridiculously inadequate example
of his skill, vague and perhaps scarcely comprehensible; it did
nothing but request her to suspend her judgment; it
incriminated him, and he felt that it incriminated him. But he
sent it. Having sent it, he conceived the scheme of returning to
Bursley that night and preceding the letter. However, this
project demanded more resolution and courage than he could
furnish for it. He drank a couple of whiskies and retired to bed
about ten o'clock. During most of the night he remained
awake, reviling himself in the most abject and violent manner,
and ceaselessly tormented by the gnawing question: what did
Annunciata know, what had she seen? He was wide awake at
six o'clock. But at eight, to his extreme surprise, he woke up
out of a heavy sleep. He was calmer then, if not less sticken;
his faculties were a little restored. He rang for Bradshaw and
tea; he sent a messenger to buy a clean collar, he had a cold
bath, making an inordinate splash; he visited the barber, and
then walked to Lime Street and took the first available train
home. He had at last come to a decision. He would see Alma
face to face at the earliest possible instant, and he would accept
the risk of having to see Annunciata. Instead of going on to

Knype, and, having changed there for Hanbridge, calling at the office to attend to pressing business, he left the train at Shawport and caught a car up to Bleakridge; he thus saved over an hour. He was mad to go through the interview with his wife, so eager, and withal so afraid and tremulous – with his assertive stride – that he would not, or dared not, cogitate upon the interview in advance. He formulated no plan of campaign. He did not prepare for possible dangers. He hastened on, as one who can neither fence nor shoot hastens to a duel, irrationally and spasmodically hoping for the best.

As he approached his garden-gate, he saw Martin coming up Lawton Street in the opposite direction. Martin was wearing his green apron and wheeling a large, flat, empty barrow. And Martin's master flinched, at the moment scarcely appreciating why he flinched. The principal use of that large, flat barrow was to transport heavy luggage to Bleakridge Station, when the family, or sections of the family, went away for a holiday. And Lawton Street led to Bleakridge Station. Surely his wife had not gone already? No! She could not have acted with such precipitation! No, she had not gone! He had written that he should return not later than lunch, and she was awaiting him. It must be so.

He ignored Martin, who was still several score yards off, and passed into the garden. The front of the house looked exactly as usual. Annunciata's front window was open and one of the white curtains bellied outwards in the breeze, a common phenomenon. The lily was magnificently blooming in the drawing-room window. Smoke ascended from the kitchen chimney to the left. He had a glimpse of clothes drying on a line in the yard behind. A hoop that he remembered buying for Sep lay on the damp grass. And yet he thought the house seemed lifeless. It appeared merely to simulate life. The front door was open. On the hall table was a small pile of letters; the topmost bore no stamp and was addressed to him in his wife's hand. He dropped his stick with a rattle into the umbrella-stand, and pushed his hat to the back of his head. Then he picked up the envelope, and nervously ripped it open with fingers that visibly trembled. The ink was pale, had only just been blotted. The note bore no date, and began with no form of address. It ran: 'Your letter came by the second delivery. We are just leaving. I shall take the children to Folkestone. You cannot expect me to stay. I have consulted a solicitor (Mr Cyples). He will attend to things. Of course, the servants know nothing. I take Martha with me. A.F.'

As his eyes absorbed the letter he heard the wheel of Martin's barrow crunching the gravel, and with astonishing bravado he came out to the porch and spoke to Martin.

'They caught the train all right?'

'Oh, yes, sir. Missis was that nervous of missing it, us got there twenty minutes afore time.' Martin smiled as one man may to another in discussing a woman.

'Good, so long as you caught it.' Fearns' demeanour was unsuspicious and uninquiring.

He was unconsciously crushing the letter in his hand. Of course she had left the house early in order to minimize the chance of meeting him.

He glanced into the drawing-room – it was empty; into the dining-room – it was empty. The house was like an echoing, deserted palace, where history crouches in the corners. Then his ear distinguished the distant sound of a servant singing, in a rude and vulgar voice, fragments of a music-hall song. He surmised that it must be the new cook, whom he had scarcely seen. The household machine, under his wife's control, never creaked in his hearing; he never had any curiosity as to the works, and his wife never displayed them to him.

So she was gone! Of all the husbands in the Five Towns, this indignity had happened to him! Incredible! Insupportable! She must come back! The children must come back! It was all a mistake. He would see Cyples. Consulted Cyples, had she? Well, Cyples or no Cyples, she must come back! And all the time he knew with certainty that not he nor forty thousand such as he, could persuade Alma to abandon a course of action, once she had decided that it was her duty to follow it. She would yield to him in everything until her conscience was aroused, and then she would be adamant. Always he had more or less mildly tyrannized over her, imposed his will upon her, taken advantage of her sweet acquiescence, and yet he was profoundly aware that hers was the stronger spirit. He felt that if she had gone she had irrevocably gone.

Sick and ashamed, he went upstairs and wandered about. He could hear the singing more plainly now. It proceeded from the second-floor, where the servants' bedrooms were. In his own bedroom nothing was abnormal. Nor was there any sign of untidiness in his wife's room. He hastened feverishly to her wardrobe. It was empty. He stared blankly into its emptiness. and in the corner to the right of the wardrobe, where her boots and shoes were wont to be arranged in a row, there was nothing.

'Well, of course she's gone!' he muttered savagely, as he saw himself, with his hat at the back of his head, reflected in the pier-glass. 'What the hell do you expect? Did you expect her to send for the governess and kiss her? They're all gone. So there you are!'

He wandered into Annunciata's room, which was littered with newspapers and empty cardboard boxes. He was not very well acquainted with Annunciata's room, and he examined it with inquisitive misery. This, then, was the retreat of the mysterious creature, his daughter. He thought that he had never known his daughter. How disturbing it was that children should grow up under the gaze of their parents, and yet be utter strangers to their parents! Imagine it! Annunciata had ruined him. It seemed only yesterday that Annunciata was small enough to be put in the corner, and now she had come between him and Alma and pushed them into the Divorce Court. The little Annunciata!

Was it the Divorce Court? he wondered. Yes, Alma would be capable of suing for divorce. The perception of his wife's moral courage chilled him in the region of the spine. Unless he could alter her notion of her duty he was done for. All the Five Towns would laugh at him, revile him, say that he had got what he deserved, and sympathize with her. He scanned the letter. 'Mr Cyples – he will attend to things!' What could that mean, if not divorce? It might mean that Cyples had merely been asked to look after her private income; she had four hundred and fifty a year. Perhaps it was that. He tried to believe that she did not intend divorce, but he scarcely succeeded.

He kicked a newspaper lying on the floor, as he moved about the room; an odd glove was concealed under it. That was like Annunciata's untidiness. She had probably gone to the station with only one glove. His eye roved. There was dust on the night-table, showing clearly where books had been. And above the table he noticed an oblong patch of the wallpaper that was lighter in tone than the rest. A picture had hung over that patch. He puzzled his brain to think what the picture could be, for none of the other pictures had been moved. And at length he remembered. It was her mother's portrait that Annunciata had taken away with her. He put his hands deep in his pockets, and sat down heavily on the unmade bed, amid the litter. And he heard the faint rubbing of the curtain against the window-sash, and the coarse singing of the servant; and he stared at the oblong patch on the wall and wept. He had not sufficient volition left to keep the tears from spilling.

There was a scampering tread up the servant's staircase.

'Martin says master's come.' He heard the rapid whisper.

'Well, what be that?' It was assuredly the new cook who had replied.

One or other of the girls might at any moment surprise him sitting there like a fool on the bed. He wiped his eyes with his hand and went downstairs into the dining-room with a step of exaggerated firmness, leaving his hat in the hall. The clock showed half-past twelve. He was astounded to discover that he had been in the house nearly an hour.

Two minutes later the parlour-maid entered with a white tablecloth.

'Good morning, sir,' she said, flouncing her skirt.

'Good morning,' he answered, and looked steadily out of the window.

'Missis said I was to say there was cold beef and a rabbit pie, and would you like scrambled eggs first sir?' Her tone was decidedly peculiar.

He coughed. 'No eggs,' he murmured, and tried hard to make his voice easy and natural.

'Yes, sir.'

And when the lunch was served he stood and beheld it, a little archipelago of dishes in the middle of the great table. His loneliness overcame him. For more than twenty years he had been the petted and pampered god of the household. His wife or his daughter, or both, were continually thinking of his convenience and satisfaction. Never did he eat alone. 'Some one must be in to keep father company.' It was all father, father. They lived for him. As the state of the tide is always at the back of a mariner's mind, so were his moods at the back of their minds. And now they had gone. They had fled. Their pure and delicious influence, which used to spread through the house like a universal ether, had vanished. He had the place to himself, and it was no longer a home; it was a strange and inhospitable tenement, a furnished lodging. 'Yes,' he growled, gazing at the embroidered napkin-ring which Annunciata had stitched for his birthday years ago, 'and it's my damned lechery that's brought me to this!'

He thought of all the scandal and the gossip; a few hours, and the condition of his domestic affairs would be common knowledge.

CHAPTER VII

PHYLLIS

One afternoon a telegraph-boy brought a telegram for Phyllis Ridware to her mother's little house in Sproston Street, behind the Mechanics' Institute. She opened it and read a message from Emery Greatbatch asking her to go and see him at once. Since the day when she parted from her husband, she had had no communication of any kind from Emery, though she had written to him three letters which imperatively demanded replies. The request in the telegram surprised her; for, the strictest prudence having been enjoined by Mr Cyples, and old Mrs Capewell having implored her in the same sense with tears, she had in her letters to Emery emphasised the necessity for extreme discretion. And yet, now, after an incomprehensible silence, he was asking her to visit him at his rooms in Oldcastle!

She went upstairs, and somewhat elaborately made ready to depart; and as she moved about the small bedroom which her mother had placed at her disposal, her lips were firmly pressed together and her eyes scintillating. She stuck the pins into her hat, and tied her veil behind, with cold leisurely exactitude, but as she put on a pair of nearly new gloves her gestures began to be less calm. She picked up a tiny satchel and her parasol almost feverishly, and she ran downstairs. At that instant there was a rat-tat at the door.

'I'll attend to the door, mother,' she cried, 'I'm just going out.' The old lady was resting.

Paul Pennington was at the door. He was dressed in his usual neat, modest, dark-grey suit, with the bowler hat, and he carried his usual little black bag. And he stood very upright and stiff.

'Good afternoon, Mrs Ridware,' said he, quietly saluting. 'May I speak to you?'

'Certainly, Mr Pennington,' she answered icily.

'May I step inside a moment?' he suggested, as she gave no sign of letting him in.

She stood away from the door, and he entered the narrow lobby.

'Well, Mr Pennington?'

He unfastened his black bag, having deposited his hat carefully on a chair, and handed her two papers.

'I have to serve you with these,' he said.

She took them. 'Is that all?' she replied with a scornful smile.

'Yes, thank you,' said Pennington, and hurried away, forgetting even to say 'Good afternoon.' Beneath that impassive exterior he had been excessively nervous.

Phyllis glanced at the papers. One was marked 'Citation,' and the other 'Petition,' and both of them commenced with the formidable phrase, 'In the High Court of Justice.' She saw her own name, and her husband's name, and the name of Emery Greatbatch, and in several places the word 'adultery.' Then, without trying to comprehend them she stuffed the documents into her satchel.

'What is it?' old Mrs Capewell asked, appearing at the sitting-room door.

'Nothing, mother,' Phyllis shouted; her mother had latterly grown deaf.

Mrs Capewell's face was anxious. She obviously did not credit her daughter with speaking the truth. The next moment Phyllis was gone, without another word.

She took the Oldcastle car, and in less than half an hour she was in the prim red market-place of the exalted borough which draws its skirts away from the grimy contact of the Five Towns, and employs its vast leisure in brooding upon an ancient and exciting past. Oldcastle has the best schools, bookshops, and pastry-cooks in the northern half of the county. It is not industrial; it never will be. It stands for history, and carefully conserves its Georgian mansions and that air of distinguished respectability which makes it the secret envy of the Five Towns. Phyllis was so little familiar with Oldcastle that she was compelled to ask her way to the street at the lower end of the town where Emery Greatbatch resided. But on the rare occasions when she went into it, the aspect of Oldcastle always particularly appealed to her. She would have liked to live there. Even a divorce case in Oldcastle would carry with it a certain decent refinement.

Greatbatch lived in lodgings – two medium-sized rooms on the ground-floor, separated by folding-doors. But by means of personally-acquired furniture he had given to his abode some semblance of a home, and he was very well cared for by a good-natured landlady. There are some men who have the gift of inspiring devotion in landladies, and Emery was one of them. It was not, however, the landlady who answered Phyllis's ring. It was Emery himself. At the first glance at her lover, Phyllis gave a little gasp of amazement, and her cheek paled. Then, realizing that her demeanour was affecting him, she summoned her extraordinary faculty of courageous self-possession and pretended that she noticed nothing strange. Less than three weeks before, she had left him a florid, powerful and somewhat obese man, with huge unwieldy shoulders to match his height, and a general appearance which indicated dogged force. She now saw him wasted, if not absolutely emaciated, with a wrinkled and dried skin of peculiar tint, and a fatigued, apprehensive look in his eyes; and she thought, in despair, 'Can our misfortune have brought him to this?' He was no longer the same man. His clothes hung loose on him.

She tripped lightly up the two stone steps leading to the house, and, closing her sunshade, entered in silence. Emery shut the door and with febrile abruptness folded her in his arms; and as he took her, and as she abandoned herself, brief though the caress was, there stole over them both that profound and noble satisfaction which only genuine passion can induce, and which no disasters can entirely mar. The whole of Phyllis's bearing was changed in his presence. Her beauty grew softer, and lost its enigmatic quality. Her mouth and eyes ceased their disturbing and challenging mockery. She seemed to submit gladly, humbly, unreservedly, with a sort of splendid and complete honesty. Emery might indeed boast that Phyllis was one woman to him and a different woman to the rest of the world

'You're ill, my poor boy,' she murmured; 'why didn't you write to me at my mother's as I told you?'

'I only got your letters this morning,' he replied. 'Yes, I've been ill.'

'Then didn't you know till this morning that Lawrence had –'

'No,' he smiled sadly. He put a hand on her shoulder to steady himself, and she clutched it warmly.

'You aren't so weak as all that?' she demanded.

He nodded. 'Come and sit down,' he said. 'The old woman's out, won't be back for a couple of hours. I've sent her out.'

They passed into the sitting-room. A large sofa occupied the space between the curtained window and the door, opposite the chimney-piece, and the arrangement of cushions showed that Emery had been lying there. He allowed her to persuade him gently to resume his place; he scarce protested when she lifted his legs on to the sofa. Then he made space for her to sit by him, and, gazing at him, she removed her gloves and hat.

'Well, child,' he said, 'I've got you into a nice mess.'

'Don't talk about that yet,' she answered gravely. 'Tell me about your illness; what is it?'

Before answering, he glanced long into the humid eyes of the creature who had ruined his life, and whose life he had ruined. When these two had first loved, they were young enough and proud enough to quarrel. The altercation had sprung from his strong sense of justice and from her perfect lack of that sense. She had been in the wrong; she had scarcely denied it. But she would not yield. She sincerely imagined that it was his place to yield, and he would have yielded, had not the yielding presented itself to him as a violation of the elementary principles of justice. Her attitude had shocked him, as, later, her attitude had shocked her husband; but while Emery was capable of a mighty and terrible passion, Lawrence was not. From the date of their quarrel to the hour when, Phyllis being a married woman, they had met by mere accident in Glasgow, Emery had never spoken to her, had not even seen her more than once or twice. The love which was to destroy them had slept like a damped fire, and then ten words of greeting had shown them their hearts, and in an instant of time they were lapped from head to foot in the living flame.

There were no explanations, no apologies, no reluctances, no shames. The past was consumed. They both realized what lay in front of them, of misery in bliss, and they went forward. In a week the irremediable had happened, and, accepting each other candidly, embracing with gladness each other's imperfections, they launched without regret into an existence of deceit and dishonour. They had no alternative. And what an existence! To what subterfuges were they reduced! Why, for his letters to her, they created a post-office in a bricked-up mouth of an old pit-shaft on the Toft End slope, and he would deposit his missives therein at dusk, walking the four miles to Oldcastle afterwards!

'You remember,' he began weakly, 'I told you I was going to Manchester as usual this year with the entries for the Sports to get the handicapping done. I always come back the same night, because old Markyate can generally finish his job in about three or four hours. But he was unwell, and there were fifty per cent. more entries than usual, and he said he couldn't guarantee to finish 'em that day. It was a Saturday, and the Carl Rosa were doing *Tristan* at Prince's, so I thought I'd stay overnight and see that, and come back Sunday afternoon. When I woke up the next morning in the hotel, I couldn't make out what was the matter with me. Something with my left eye – I couldn't see out of it, and I was so feeble, I just managed to get as far as a doctor's. The doctor said I'd had a haemorrhage into my retina while I was asleep.'

'A haemorrhage!' she replied. 'But how came you to have a haemorrhage like that?'

'How can I tell?' Emery said, after a pause. 'The doctor looked after me a bit. I fancied I was good enough to go to the handicapper's and I did go. I got into the house, but I couldn't leave it, and those people have been looking after me till this blessed day. You wouldn't believe how kind they were!'

'His wife?'

'No, he's a widower – his two daughters. I had to have an oculist at last. I couldn't sleep, and he enucleated the eye, as the term is. Then I was easier.'

'And now it's quite better?'

'You don't notice anything do you?'

She examined the eye. 'No,' she said, 'but how it's pulled you to pieces, my poor boy!'

'Well, you know, a haemorrhage! What can you expect?'

'It's horribly strange,' she muttered.

'It is strange,' he agreed. 'However, it's all over now.'

'And I never knew! Emery, why didn't you . . .'

'How could I?' he protested. 'Mallows, the classical master, came over to see me. But how could I let you know, child? I found your letters here this morning when I arrived. The old woman was in a pretty state, you may guess. I had the greatest trouble in the world to get her out of the house. She thought I was dying, whereas the fact is I'm lots better.'

'Really better?'

'My God! If you'd seen me last week!'

She bent her face to his, and put her arms round his neck, and kissed him with slow, deliberate kisses.

'Emery!' she said. 'I'm not satisfied. I shall fetch a doctor here.'

'Much better fetch a lawyer,' he replied curtly and feebly, and then sighed. 'Phil, what the devil are we to do! How did he find out?'

'What's "enucleated"?' she asked, putting a hand on his forehead.

'Oh!' he said. 'Just cleaning out, straightening up.'

'Did it hurt you?'

'No, very little. You say you've gone to Bradwell's, eh?'

Leaving the topic of his illness, she began to tell him in minute detail all that had happened during his absence. She related her impression of the evening when Mark Ridware fell into the house at Toft End like a bolt from the blue; and how she had left the brothers and gone to her mother, calling on the way at the pit's mouth to see if by chance there was a letter for her; and how she had denied her guilt to her mother while admitting a perfectly innocent, desultory friendship with Emery for the sake of old times; and how her mother had eagerly and passionately believed her, asserting that she had never really liked Ridware; and how they had paid a visit to Cyples together, because Cyples had been a friend of her father's.

'I don't think Mr Cyples quite believed me,' said Phyllis calmly. 'But he pretended to and he talked to mother in exactly the right tone. Wasn't it fortunate I overheard what Lawrence told Mark? That gave me my line. I explained that night at Easter, and I've carefully remembered exactly what I said. I said you were ill, and you *were*, you know, a little. And now your being ill again like this! It fits in, doesn't it? . . . What's the matter?'

'Nothing,' said he.

'You look so queer.' She sighed. 'I did the best I could. I couldn't see you, and so I did the best I could without you. Emery, if it hadn't been for your prospects and all that, I would have told them straight out that it was every bit true and they could get as many divorces as they chose, for all we cared. Dearest, what *are* we to do?'

'There isn't much to do,' he replied. 'We'll fight, of course, but it's all up.'

'If it's all up,' she said stiffly, 'why fight? Why not go away at once? Go to Canada or somewhere? I don't mind. Anywhere. It can be done. It's been done lots of times.' A dark flush overspread her cheeks.

He gave an inarticulate murmur.

'Why, my darling boy, you're crying!' she exclaimed, an immense astonishment in her voice.

He could not speak. The tears flowed slowly from his eyes, and she gazed at him, alarmed by this extraordinary symptom of his physical condition.

Just then there was a sharp ring at the door. Phyllis rose.

'I'll go,' Emery managed to say, lifting his head, and grimacing to control himself.

'You will stay where you are,' she slowly ordered him.

'But you can't possibly be seen here, answering my door!' he argued.

'Can't I!' she said indignantly. 'And you ill like that! If it's all up, I'm here to nurse you, and I won't leave you.'

The ring was repeated.

'Really,' she murmured. 'They're in a hurry!' Her nostrils were dilated, and she left the room with a gesture of impetuous enterprise.

In vain he called after her: 'Look through the window and see who it is first.'

She opened the front door. And Paul Pennington confronted

her for the second time that afternoon. Of the two, Paul was
the far more disconcerted. His face gradually reddened, and he
could scarcely look at her. She waited haughtily for him to
speak.

'Mrs Ridware!' he began lamely, 'I came . . . is this Mr
Greatbatch's?'

'Yes.'

'Is he in? Can I see him?' He unconsciously brought his
black bag into prominence.

'Mr Greatbatch can't be seen,' said Phyllis, staring out into
the street.

'I'm sorry. If he's at home . . . one moment . . . I . . .'

'Perhaps you had better come in.' Phyllis changed her mind,
speaking in a resigned tone. 'Please walk this way. Mr
Greatbatch is lying down.' She boldly preceded him into the
sitting-room, and pointing to the form on the sofa: 'That is
Mr Greatbatch.' And she added in a different tone to Emery:
'Here is some one who wants to see you. No, do not move,
please.'

'Are you Mr Emery Greatbatch?' Pennington inquired.

'Yes,' said Emery, entirely bewildered, but with a defiant
expression.

Pennington deposited his hat on a chair, opened his bag, and
produced two documents. 'I have to serve you with these,' he
said, handing the long narrow papers to Emery, who accepted
them limply. 'Thank you. That is all. I'm sorry to trouble
you.'

Paul Pennington hastened off, like a criminal seen in the act.

'What else could I have done, my poor boy?' cried Phyllis,
sitting down on the sofa when they were alone again. 'He saw
me at the door. I've had those papers, too. It's the – the case.'

'When did you have them?'

'This afternoon. Just before I came. What do they say?'

She craned her neck to look at one of the documents as he
read, with a forced note of amusement in his voice: '"In the
High Court of Justice, Probate Divorce and Admiralty
Division (Divorce). Edward by the Grace of God . . . hum
. . . hum . . . To Emery Greatbatch of Oldcastle in the
County of Staffordshire. Whereas Lawrence Ridware of
Bursley in the said County, claiming to be lawfully married to

Phyllis Ridware, has filed his petition against her in the
Divorce Registry of our said Court, praying for a dissolution
of marriage, wherein he alleges that you have been guilty of
adultery with her. Now this is to command you that within
eight days after service hereof on you . . . hum . . . hum . . .
hum . . . you do appear in our said court then and there to
make answer to the said petition, a copy whereof, sealed with
the seal of our said Court, is herewith served upon you. And
take notice that in default of your so doing, our said Court will
proceed to hear the said charge proved in due course of law,
and to pronounce sentence therein, your absence notwith-
standing. And take further notice that for the purpose
aforesaid, you are to attend in person, or by your solicitor . . .
hum . . . hum . . . enter an appearance in a book provided for
that purpose, without which you will not be allowed to
address the Court . . . hum . . . hum . . . Dated at London
. . . hum . . . hum . . . and in the second year of our reign."
My stars, what a thumping seal!'

The sight and fingering of these papers, hers and his, which
were, however, nothing but common glazed foolscap forms,
filled in by shabby copying-clerks and perfunctorily sealed in
stuffy official bureaus, seemed to startle the lovers. In spite of
themselves, their very voices were altered. They strove to
affect that these papers left them unmoved, but they did not
succeed. And as for Emery Greatbatch, he could feel his
mistress's heart beating against his breast. The first rays of the
terrifying lamp which justice holds aloft had suddenly touched
them, displaying their deeds in a new and eerie light. And
when they read together, in the sealed copy of Lawrence's
petition, the precise details of their adultery, with the day of
the month, and the names of the town and the street, the
black-and-white of the recital in some curious way
communicated to them a sense of guilt and of shame such as
they had not before experienced. Phyllis began to talk,
repeating her previous explanations in the same words; and
he, in order to be more sure than sure, repeated previous
questions, well knowing the answers he would receive. And
they were soon in the midst of one of those immense and
formless conversations in which a complex subject is discussed
without order interminably, and without apparent result, until

there comes a moment when the speakers perceive that all the ground has been many times covered and that it is no longer possible to say anything that has not already been said; and pauses occur, and the unavoidable conclusion emerges and shapes itself and imperiously demands acceptance. And while Emery's mind had room for a shameful sympathy with his old friend Lawrence, while Phyllis could only think of Lawrence with an almost virulent hate, the conclusion here was that this Lawrence, that distant and threatening figure, once so mild, once so ignored and flouted, would inevitably crush them in the battle that was to ensue. They saw that they must either flee, or else fall with an indomitable but futile lie on their lips.

There was silence in the room.

Phyllis broke it. 'What are you thinking about?' she murmured, and gently took the papers from his hand and put them on the table.

'I was wondering what I could do for you?' he answered, turning a little on his side in order to follow her movements with his eyes.

'My poor boy,' she said. 'As soon as you are better we must collect what money we can, and leave, mustn't we? It isn't for me, it's because you won't possibly be able to stay on at the school.'

'But you've denied everything to your mother and Mr Cyples. Our going would –'

'Does that matter?' she exclaimed impatiently. 'That was only a precaution. What do I care?' She was standing over him now, and her hand caressed his shoulder. Could Lawrence have seen the persuasive smile on her face, it would have recalled to him the sweet forgotten marvels of their early acquaintance, whose memory had been washed out of his heart by the bitterness of later years.

Emery glanced up at her, with a sickly and self-conscious grin – which he meant to be a smile – on his shrunken features.

'Ah!' he muttered shortly, and closed his lips, and then looked meditatively at the wall.

'Emery!' she cried in renewed alarm. 'I'm sure you aren't telling me everything. I've felt it all along. What is there that you haven't told me?'

'Child!' he said and drew her to him with his arms. 'It's nearly finished so far as I'm concerned. Do you understand? It's nearly finished so far as I'm concerned.'

'So far as you're concerned? Why –'

'That's why I telegraphed you to come here. I knew just as well as you that it was indiscreet. I wouldn't have done it if the thing hadn't been serious. You understand, don't you?'

They gazed at each other, and Phyllis moved away from him.

'No!' she said faintly, and in her soul she asked bitterly of fate: 'Can I be more unfortunate than I have been?'

'Yes,' he insisted. 'You do – this haemorrhage –'

Her face became the colour of milk, and her eyes blazed darkly in the pallor of that oval.

'It isn't – serious?' she demanded. That was the strongest word she could induce herself to employ.

He nodded. 'It's the first symptom of acute diabetes,' he said, sitting up, but adverting his gaze. 'I'm unfortunately too young to have diabetes in a mild form. I've had the first seizure. The second will finish me. It may be next month, or it may be delayed for six months, but it isn't likely to be much later than that. And in the meantime I shall get a little better. That's the way of it, my dear girl.'

She made as if to come near him again, and then hesitated.

'Oh, but Emery! Surely –' she whispered.

'Now, my dear girl,' he protested gently, picking at one of the cushions. 'You mustn't try to pretend it isn't so. It is so. You've got lots of pluck, or I wouldn't have told you – like that. And by God, you'll need all the pluck you have! It's you that will suffer. It isn't me. I shall have done with it all long before you have. It isn't sure even that I shall have the extreme pleasure of hearing the trial of our case.' He shot a timid momentary look at her.

'Was it the doctor told you all this?' she asked.

'The doctor told me in five minutes that I'd got diabetes. It was partly from what he carefully didn't say, and partly from what I've read up since, that I discovered where I stood. And yet only two months ago I never suspected that there was anything the matter with me at all! It's just how things happen, that is.'

From her knowledge of him she could not but believe him.

'And you knew all this!' she said, awed. 'And you travelled here by yourself from Manchester – and then found my letters! Oh, Emery, why didn't I know? I could have spared you a little!'

'That's how things happen,' he repeated mechanically.

'It's no use you saying it is so, it is so,' she said. 'You! So ill as that! I can't credit it.' And after surveying him with a long glance, she threw herself on the sofa, sobbing.

'I simply can't,' she wailed. And now it was he who soothed her, as an hour before she had soothed him.

Her sobs gradually ceased. 'Why didn't you tell me when I came?' she complained pitifully. 'What was the use of us talking about the case?'

'I couldn't,' he said, 'I couldn't begin to tell you.'

'But I knew something was wrong. Oh! I was certain something was wrong.'

'Kiss me,' he entreated her.

She put her lips to his. And with their faces together she murmured: 'Emery, listen. When I wrote to you time after time, and you didn't reply, do you know what I thought?'

'No,' he replied, scarcely audible, 'what did you think?'

'I'm bound to tell you. I thought – I began to think – that you meant to end it.'

'End what?'

'Our relationship. I did not think that for long together. But I suspected you sometimes. And now I know that you were ill there in Manchester – it makes me – Emery!' She burst out into wild sobbing. 'You forgive me?'

He kissed her again and smiled. 'Nonsense!' he cajoled her. 'There's nothing to forgive.'

'You must say you forgive me,' she persisted hysterically. 'Say it!'

'If it will please you,' he agreed, and putting his mouth to her ear, he breathed into it some words. 'What a child it is!' he added louder. 'With its fancies!'

She lay calm on the sofa, clasping him tightly with both hands. And as she lay there, all the prospect of suffering which had appalled her before Emery explained his condition, suddenly became beautiful and desirable. To desolate her mother,

to quit the Five Towns stealthily amid circumstances of utter
disgrace, to be known for a liar and an adulteress, to creep
under a false name into some new and infinitely remote town
in another land and to settle there in continual fear lest the
rumour of shame should follow and overtake, to know
poverty and to endure hardship, to struggle, to try to forget
and never to be able to forget, to have nothing worth having
but the constant companionship of Emery, and to grow old –
all that seemed the most exquisite future that the fates could
have offered her. There was not one detail of it that she would
have wished to alter. She saw vague visions, formed from
conventional notions about far colonies, of herself and Emery
together on rich autumn evenings outside a bare house with
wide verandahs, gazing in ecstasy at a horizon of magnificent
mountains and the oncoming of darkness, and the patting of
dogs, and the withdrawal into closed rooms, and the lighting
of lamps, and the long, long, changeless intimacy of two
persons who possessed only each other. The beauty of
melancholy and renunciation took hold of her as she clung to
Emery, and intoxicated her. She had an illusion that by
gripping him tight with her frail and convulsive fingers she
could keep him alive for ever, that he could not die while she
cleaved to him.

Death was the sole terror; and it was terrible to such a point
that her mind could not conceive it. The coat that he was
wearing, whose texture was so thrillingly masculine to her
touch – was it possible that in a few weeks or months it would
be folded away because there was no one to wear it? That
seemed the saddest, cruellest thing in all the universe. She
remembered once, years ago, watching him on the breaking-
up day of the Middle School, in the cricket-field, surrounded
by a mob of boys. And she recalled every slow, easy,
muscular movement of his burly frame, and how he swung a
cricket bat as though it had been a cane, and how, as he moved
to and fro, the boys followed him, admiring, noisy pigmies
encircling a giant. And in that recollected scene there was so
much of youth and strength, so much of the very essence of
pure physical life, that the idea of death grew monstrous,
wanton, and obscene. Was he to lie under the ground while
boys still played and shouted in the cricket-field? Was he never

again to go out among them and talk to them and teach them,
and understand them as only he could? . . . And she saw a
funeral, and she could not imagine anyone but herself at that
funeral. She had never met a relative of Emery's. And, more
poignant still, she saw herself returning solitary from the
funeral, having left *it* behind in its everlasting repose. And
then she saw herself, dressed in widow's weeds – yes, widow's
weeds – standing up in the witness box in the High Court of
Justice and answering questions. She could not hear what she
said, but she was very positive, queenly, and sorrowful. And
her tremendous and impassive grief weighed on the whole
court like a pall. And all the time that she was answering
questions in the witness-box, she could see *it* lying forlorn and
lonely in the cemetery.

'And so I missed the Oldcastle Sports,' she heard him say.
'Never been known to happen before. In fact they very nearly
didn't get the handicaps.'

The sound of his voice, so natural and familiar, with its faint
trace of humour, awoke her out of what might have been a
trance. Her powers of clear thought and cool enterprise
seemed to return to her like spirits that had wandered awhile.
And she reflected, 'How foolish and weak I am, to dream that
he is already dead! He lives. There is no reason why he should
die. He's an invalid and he has fancies, and here I am listening
to them as though they were facts. He needs to be looked
after; that is all. And I will look after him.'

She slid from the sofa and stood up, smoothing her ruffled
hair. She felt herself equal to no matter what situation.

'What is diabetes?' she inquired; 'I never knew that it was
really dangerous.'

'Diabetes,' he answered, 'is a disease in which grape sugar is
secreted in the fluids of the body. The pancreas doesn't work
properly.'

'Who is your doctor in Oldcastle?'

'Haven't got one. Never wanted one.'

'But surely you are going to send for one at once?'

'I expect I ought to have one,' was the languid reply, 'but
it'll be no use.'

'How tiresome you are, Emery!' she chided him. 'I shall
fetch one myself, instantly. I'm perfectly certain that all you

need is proper treatment. If diabetes was as bad as you think, I should have known about it; I'm sure I should.'

He said nothing for a moment! Then, without meeting her eye: 'Which doctor shall you fetch?'

The honoured name of the foremost physician in the district, an old man who was an authority throughout England on diseases connected with the local manufacture, and who resided in Oldcastle itself, flashed across her mind. In walking down the market-place, she had even that afternoon chanced to see his worn but glittering brass plate on the door of a large house.

'I shall fetch Dr Thatcher,' she said. 'At least I shall ask him to come sometime before night.'

Emery remained silent. She put on her hat and gloves, and then, bending her head, she offered her mouth, very quietly and primly. He kissed her.

'It will seem rather queer you going to old Thatcher's,' he murmured, 'and asking him to come to me. He'll wonder what the dickens you have to do with it.'

She protested against such notions with a gesture. 'Nothing seems queer when it's a case of illness,' she said. 'Besides . . .'

And with a tranquil smile she left him, enjoining him to rest until she came back.

As she emerged into the street her features had resumed their old enigmatic quality. It was on the steps of the house that she encountered a thin, middle-aged woman with a key in her bony hand.

'Why!' she said to the woman, with an extraordinary warmth of geniality, 'you must be Mrs Oliver, aren't you?'

'Yes, mum. Was you . . .'

'Mr Greatbatch has often mentioned you. He says you are very, very kind to him. I'm an old friend of his. So is my mother.' She lowered her voice. 'You've noticed how unwell he is?'

'Eh, miss!' said Mrs Oliver. 'Never in all my life have I seed . . .'

'I'm just going to Dr Thatcher's to ask him to come as soon as possible. I'm so glad Mr Greatbatch is with you. Because he'll need looking after, and he won't look after himself, you know.'

'Not he, miss! Eh, when he come in this morning, I stared at him like a stuck pig, I was that took aback!'

'Well, as soon as Dr Thatcher has been, we shall know what we ought to do. I shan't be away long, Mrs Oliver. He is lying down on the sofa now.'

Phyllis nodded and went.

'So he's got a young woman, after all!' the sagacious Mrs Oliver decided. 'That's why he would have me out of the house. Her's a handsome wench, too! Eh, poor things! Poor things!'

CHAPTER VIII

DEATH

On the day after August Bank Holiday, Charles Fearns opened for a few hours in the morning; and the whole staff, with the exception of Sillitoe, who had gone to Llandudno, was formally present, though only Pennington behaved as if the morning was quite an ordinary morning. Shortly after noon Pennington stepped gently into Lawrence Ridware's room with a bundle of papers most neatly tied up in pink tape, a number of loose sheets of blue draft on which the ink was scarcely dry, and between his teeth an ivory penholder. The weather was very warm, and through the open window came the strident sounds of steam-whistles and steam-orchestras in Crown Square, where the great annual Wakes, that prodigious revelry, wassail, and debauch of a rude and vigorous people, was beginning its third day with little sign of fatigue.

'It will perhaps be as well if you glance through these things,' said Pennington, putting the bundle in front of Lawrence. The latter was engaged in preparing a codicil to the will of an aged client who amused his final years by varying his testamentary dispositions every few months and by speculating in public-house property.

'Oh!' murmured Lawrence stiffly, when he saw the bundle, which was entitled, 'Ridware *v*. Ridware and Greatbatch.' Pennington, having perceived long since that Lawrence wished to stand aloof from the proceedings, had conducted them with that air of a responsible autocrat which he always assumed when a matter had been left definitely in his hands.

'I'm just drawing the brief,' said Pennington, holding out the blue sheets.

'Drawing the brief?' Lawrence repeated apparently surprised.

158

'Yes. I didn't see why agents should draw it.' In the technical vocabulary of the provincial solicitor, 'agents' means the firm of London solicitors who represent him and act for him in affairs demanding the frequentation of courts and offices in London. London solicitors refer to their professional clients in the provinces still more vaguely as 'the country.'

'Certainly not,' Lawrence agreed. 'But it's going along awfully quickly, isn't it? I scarcely thought –'

'N – no,' answered Pennington judicially. 'About the average time. You see, it's so simple. I had a letter from agents this morning to say that they had the Registrar's certificate that the case was in order for trial, and would be set down at once.'

'So much the better,' said Lawrence.

He untied the bundle with leisurely fingers. That bundle, which was less than an inch in thickness, displayed at once to the expert the extreme ordinariness of the Five Towns *cause célèbre* – afterwards to become famous in legal circles in the same manner as a strange variation of a malady becomes famous in medical circles. At the top of the bundle was a minor and shorter bundle of letters from agents and from Bradwells, Phyllis's solicitors; and as Lawrence lifted this it disclosed a whitish oblong on the grey surface of the topmost large paper, as a picture removed from a wall leaves its trace behind. The black dust of the Five Towns had already begun to settle on the early stages of Ridware *v*. Ridware. Lawrence idly turned over, one by one, the citation, the petition, the answer of Phyllis denying the allegations and her affidavit in support; the answer of Emery Greatbatch also in denial, and his affidavit; Phyllis's petition of alimony *pendentelite;* his own answer to that petition with an affidavit; the order commanding Lawrence to pay her a pound a week during the continuance of the proceedings; Phyllis's authority to Bradwells to receive this money on her behalf; an opinion of Counsel on the whole case, with a marked fee of one pound three and sixpence; a note of the evidence of the landlady and of her servant; a note of his own evidence; a copy of his marriage certificate; and a few other papers. There were no summonses to amend, or for further particulars – none of those indications of carelessness or of perversity on the one side or the other, which too frequently disfigure the records of such cases. The essential excellence of the principles which govern contentious proceedings in English law stood plainly revealed. To Lawrence's trained eye the simplicity and the dispatch which distinguished the affair were almost startling. Hitherto unfamiliar with the working of the matrimonial courts, he too, in common with the laity, had vaguely imagined that a divorce could not be obtained without an exaggerated expenditure of time, patience, and money. But Pennington had informed him, with the weightiness of authority which was Pennington's that the decree *nisi* would follow within six months of the petition, and that the total cost would probably not exceed fifty pounds.

He could have wished the period longer; the mere thought of the trial itself made his heart beat.

'Here's the draft brief,' said Pennington, depositing the blue sheets, and recapturing the contents of the bundle, which he carefully tied up in their original order. 'You might just see if I've missed a point.'

That Pennington should have missed a point was a wild, mad supposition; but he was not the man to leave the least loophole for inimical chance. Moreover, the fear of Cyples was before him, despite the manifest impossibility of even Cyples himself doing anything with such a case. So Lawrence perused anew the curt and artless annals of his domestic misfortune.

'That's all right, I think,' he observed.

Pennington smiled confidently.

'I can't imagine why they should waste their money in fighting,' said Pennington. 'Unless of course Greatbatch hopes somehow to save his face at the school. But anyhow he's bound to lose his situation.'

'Yes.'

'I wonder he hasn't been asked to resign already,' Pennington continued. 'By the way, I shall tell agents not to mark the brief more than three guineas and a guinea for conference. A case like this conducts itself, don't you think?'

'Certainly,' Lawrence concurred absently. He was conceiving all the odiousness of the trial, and the remarks which would be made to him in the Five Towns upon his return from it. So far, by extraordinary good fortune, not a single acquaintance had so much as referred even in the most casual and distant way to his calamity. But then, the case was still obscure. When the Press Association had telegraphed down a verbatim report of the hearing, to be published in the extraspecial of the enterprising *Signal* and read by the entire population of the Five Towns, he might expect to be a man doomed to hear personal comments.

In the outer office, Gater, who had surreptitiously visited the street to buy a copy of the early edition of the *Signal* was searching the newspaper for an item which peculiarly interested him. Gater, stricken down in the first flush of youth, by the fever of photography, had decided to sell his high-geared bicycle in order that he might become the possessor of a Brownie camera before his holiday commenced in the following week; and he had accordingly sent an advertisement of the bicycle to the *Signal*. He examined in vain the serried columns of private advertisements on page two of the only daily organ published in the Five Towns. His renowned bicycle was decidedly not among the articles for sale or exchange. Then, at last, he traced it in the unclassified 'late' advertisements on the news-page, side by side with the 'stop-press' blank space. He passed the paper to Clowes and demanded the opinion of Clowes as to the comparative efficacy of the news-page and the regular advertisement page in the selling of second-hand bicycles. Clowes, the day being the slack morrow of Bank Holiday, took the opportunity to read all the news in detail.

'What ho!' Clowes dramatically murmured, after a time, and his eye rested on a particular spot.

'Well?' demanded Gater, perceiving that Clowes had encountered something of uncommon piquancy.

'What'st think of this?' said Clowes, pointing with a thick and inky finger. 'No; not that. The next paragraph.'

And, Gater, having read, whistled cautiously.

Clowes fidgeted for a few seconds. Lawrence and Pennington could be heard talking through half-open doors.

'Should you go and tell them?' Clowes ventured. It ill becomes a man of forty-five to ask advice of a boy, and Clowes did not often ask advice of Gater. That he should have done so now, showed that he was agitated out of his usual self.

'Ay!' said Gater.

And Clowes, swollen with the importance of that which he had discovered, and absolutely unable to postpone for another moment the pleasure of communicating it to his superiors, marched with false nonchalance to Lawrence's room, tapped at the door, and entered. The solicitor and the articled clerk ceased talking as Clowes glanced from one to the other.

'Perhaps you haven't seen this,' he said gruffly, handing the paper to Pennington and indicating the item. Pennington read.

'Well, well!' Pennington coughed, and gave the paper to Lawrence.

Lawrence read: 'We regret to hear of the sudden decease of Mr Emery Greatbatch, science master at the Oldcastle Middle School. Mr Greatbatch, who we understand had been in indifferent health for some time, succumbed to a haemorrhage in the base of the brain on Sunday last.'

Clowes, his effect duly made, left the room again, abandoning the newspaper. Lawrence remained silent.

'Why!' said Pennington. 'I scarcely knew he was ill.'

Lawrence swung round on his chair, and, resting his chin on one hand, stared out of the window.

'Oh, yes,' said he quietly. 'I knew he was ill. At least I'd heard so.'

'Well,' Pennington added, 'it makes no difference to us.' He hurried away, and in an instant returned with the indispensable Dixon.

'Yes,' he said in his cold, calm, assured voice, when he had consulted the index. 'Here it is. Page 110. We've simply got to apply to have his name struck out; that's all.'

And he shut the book with a snap, as though he was shutting the lid on Emery Greatbatch's coffin, and blotting him out for ever from the recollection of men. When Pennington had a case in hand, a death or so was not to be allowed to interfere with its normal course.

'I'll write to agents at once,' said Pennington, and he did write to agents at once.

Lawrence stared a long time through the dusty window at the brown wall of the manufactory opposite, and the sound of the Wakes increased in his unheeding ears. Clowes departed

for the day, and then Pennington – with a shutting of drawers
and rattling of keys. And then Lawrence heard a voice saying
sharply to Gater:

'Is Mr Ridware still here?'

It was the voice of Charles Fearns.

'Yes, sir,' said Gater.

'Well, if you've copied your letters and done everything,
you can go. I'll lock up, or Mr Ridware will.'

'Thank you, sir,' in astonished tones from Gater, who did
not delay two seconds.

Charles Fearns came into Lawrence's room, carrying a
bundle of papers. The two men glanced at each other, not
with hostility, but yet suspiciously.

'Oh! You're here, Ridware. I want to have a chat with
you.'

Fearns shut the door, and stood where Pennington had
stood, at the back of the desk, ignoring the chair upon which
sat such clients as Lawrence had to interview. He had not
much changed during the mysterious weeks that had elapsed
since the flight of his family. It is rarely that suffering other
than physical alters the appearance, especially in a man; and
Fearns bore himself well. His health was always excellent. But
his eye and his demeanour were not as they once were. He
had become both defiant and sullen at the same time.
Everybody noticed it, and everybody drew conclusions.
Exactly what had happened, no one knew, and particularly no
one in Fearns' own office. The sole authorized information
was that Mrs. Fearns and the children were spending the
summer at Sandgate, and that Fearns was living at home with
one servant and the gardener. Rumour stated that an action
for divorce was in progress against him, but Fearns' clerks
had no knowledge of such an action. And Bradwell's clerks –
Cyples was understood to be acting for Mrs. Fearns – did not
satisfactorily respond to curious catechists. The towns of
Hanbridge and Bursley were greatly perplexed and pleasantly
excited by the prospect of disclosures. Meanwhile Fearns
attended to his practice with unprecedented diligence. Occasionally he went to the Turk's Head, or to his club, and
played cards, or talked with a new, reserved air. He and
Cyples seemed to be as friendly as usual.

'Yes?' said Lawrence.

'Yes,' Fearns said, 'I want to have a talk with you. Look at that.'

He violently pitched the bundle of papers on to Lawrence's desk. Lawrence, without moving, read the endorsement: 'Fearns *v*. Fearns. Copy petition for divorce.' The facts were that an action had been commenced by Mrs. Fearns immediately after her departure, that the correspondence between Fearns and his London agents had been entirely written from, and addressed to, his private house, and that Fearns had arranged with Cyples to maintain an absolute secrecy.

'I see,' said Lawrence, nodding his head and lowering the corners of his mouth to express a proud scorn of his employer. Never had the matter been mentioned between them. He had heard nothing whatever from Mrs. Fearns, and though he had by no means forgotten her entreaty to him to talk sense to Fearns, he had not even attempted to broach the subject; latterly, preoccupied by his own affairs, he had ceased to think about other people's troubles and interests.

'Read the petition, will you?' Fearns requested, moving his feet nervously on the bare floor, but otherwise showing no sign of confusion.

Lawrence obeyed, glancing also at other documents, and for the first time knew precisely what had occurred in the Fearns' household on the night before Mrs. Fearns sent for him. He had vaguely guessed the truth, but nevertheless the detailed revelation of it shocked, offended, and disgusted him. After the perusal he could not persuade himself to look Fearns in the face, and he kept his eyes on the desk, blushing.

'You grasp the situation?' Fearns demanded.

'Yes,' said Lawrence gruffly.

'Now, you went and saw my wife before she left?'

'Who told you that?' Lawrence challenged his employer in a voice suddenly angry and menacing. He did not care a fig for Fearns, and Fearns might be as furious as he chose. Fearns, however, replied with easy diplomatic self-control.

'Cyples told me. I only mention it because my wife likes you. She has a great belief in your opinion, and the proof of it is that she sent for you that night.'

'I don't agree with you, Mr Fearns,' said Lawrence coldly. 'But supposing she has? What then?'

'Ridware, this action can't go on!' Fearns cried. 'It can't go on. It has got to be stopped. I'll do anything – anything. But it's got to be stopped.' He spoke passionately, and Lawrence, startled into gazing up at him, saw that his mouth was twisted out of its usual shape, and that there was a white patch, from which the blood had been forced, across the bridge of his nose.

'It's bound to go on,' Lawrence answered.

'Don't say that, man! I know all you can tell me. I don't mean to offer any excuses of any sort. Nobody on this earth can explain to me anything that I don't feel. I'm speaking to you now with perfect freedom, remember. I respect you. You're a decent fellow. I meant to come to you a long time ago, but I couldn't make up my mind. For one thing, I couldn't believe that my wife would persist in the action.'

'But what else – ' Lawrence began.

'I know – I know,' Fearns stopped him imperiously. 'You're going to ask me what else can she do. Well, she *can* do something else. She can stop it, and come back to me.'

'That's not argument.'

'To hell with argument!' Fearns shouted, and then he continued in a low, controlled voice. 'Just think of the trial, man! I needn't put the dots on the i's. Think of the scandal. Think of what our lives will be afterwards.'

Lawrence, while hating himself for it, could not resist the obvious: 'You ought to have thought of that before, Mr Fearns.'

'Yes, I know,' snapped Fearns. There was a pause.

'Why don't you go and see your wife?' Lawrence inquired.

Fearns approached closer to the desk, and looked down at Lawrence, who met his gaze with a chill stare. 'Because I daren't. I haven't got the pluck. And Cyples won't do anything. Now look here, Ridware. My wife likes you very much. So do I. She'll listen to you if she'll listen to anybody. I want you to go down and see her, and explain things to her. Make her understand that the action really can't go on. I know you can succeed if you try. And listen! I want a partner in this business. If you'll go down and see Alma, I'll give you a partnership.'

Lawrence was momentarily frightened by his terrible earnestness, and he pushed back his chair so as to be a little further from Fearns' face. Fearns also drew away.

'You are mad,' Lawrence muttered in a melancholy, hopeless tone.

'Then you won't?'

'Do you want my opinion?'

'That's just what I do want.'

'Well, I think your wife is quite right and that you are quite wrong. Why shouldn't the action go on? It will be awful, of course. But it will not be so awful as your wife's return to you would be. As to the scandal, that is nothing. Anyhow, it won't touch your wife. Your wife's return is impossible. I thoroughly agree with everything she said to me. I'm sorry for you, in a way – that I must say – but not very much. And the trial, after all, is a very little thing. It won't last more than half an hour or an hour. Of course it isn't certain that your wife will get a divorce, but it's certain that she'll get at least a judicial separation. Then everything will be over and done with. You'll each of you know where you stand, and the scandal will soon die down.'

'I'm thinking of my daughter,' said Fearns solemnly.

'I know you are,' said Lawrence, 'and do you suppose that your wife hasn't also thought of your daughter? Do you suppose you are the only person who thinks of your daughter? Bad as the trial will be, it will be better than anything else, even for your daughter.'

'Then you won't go?'

'I will not.'

A long silence followed. Then Fearns gathered up his papers and disappeared. Soon afterwards Lawrence, who had resumed his gaze at the window, heard him leave the building.

Lawrence sat still for many minutes, and then, having shut the window and covered his desk with its dust-sheet, he made a circuit of the deserted rooms, found the outer keys on their hook, and departed, and soon found himself in the multitudinous turmoil of the Wakes. The fair made no impression on him whatever, beyond a vague assault on his ears. He moved through the crowds without noticing them, a heavy and preoccupying weight on his heart, and presently he turned into the Coffee House for lunch. He had given up his house and his singular cousin at Toft End, discovering them both to be intolerable, and had taken rooms at Cauldon, a suburb of Hanbridge and Knype. Thither he had transported his books, which lay unshelved in forlorn mountain ranges on the floors. While he consumed a tasteless meal off a marble-topped table in the Coffee House, served by a bouncing, red-skinned, and fluffy creature with heavy gestures, there moved over the depths of his mind trifling cloudlets of thought concerning this passage with Fearns. If he had been in Fearns' room, instead of Fearns in his, the interview might have been less summary; he was much more at home in his own room, entrenched in his own chair behind his own desk. Fearns was a fool: Fearns had proved that. He must have been at his wits' end. Fancy his offering a partnership! Fancy his hoping that Lawrence could be tempted by such an offer to perform any social act which he would not otherwise have performed! The idea was comic to Lawrence. Fearns had been immensely excited; he could understand that. And yet, despite the circumstances, to see Fearns an excited and pathetic suppliant was sufficiently astounding.

He flattered himself that he had duly appreciated the conversation with Fearns, and Fearns' bearing; but he had not. He had merely assisted at the episode in a kind of dream, all his essential faculties of emotion being monopolized by the news of the death of Emery Greatbatch. It was in the far-reaching sentimental consequences of that death that his mind was, half unconsciously, absorbed. A tremendous and irrational pity, a pity that was at once splendid and futile, rolled into his heart like a flood and took possession of it. For the first time during months he did not feel bitter. Under the urgent guidance of an instinct which he could not explain and which intellectually he resented, he left the Coffee House pretending that he was going home to his rooms, but fully aware that he should go to quite a different house. The awful music of the Wakes crashed down upon him from a dozen round-abouts; two feathered girls squirted water into his ear to prove that carnival reigned; the odour of all things that would be eaten last by men dying on a raft arrived at his nostrils from the stalls that lined the packed pavements. He went along Holborn unnoticing, colliding with people, giving bumps and receiving them. And, having reached a certain corner, he escaped out of the turmoil into a street which led to Sproston Street. And Sproston Street, with its little neat houses, and its view of the dignified, sombre back of the Mechanics' Institute, was prim and silent as a cathedral close.

He assured himself that he was a fool, as big a fool as Fearns; but the pity in his heart, awakened by the power of his imagination, drove him forward. At length he knocked on a grained front door numbered 16 in old-fashioned green letters.

A very young, blithe unfinished servant-maid answered his faint summons.

'Is Mrs Ridware in?' he asked in a murmur.

'Oh, yes, sir,' said the maid cordially. 'Will you step in?'

He stepped into the narrow hall, with its empty hatstand of varnished pitch pine and its reproductions of Sir Edwin Landseer.

'In the sitting-room, sir,' the maid said. She was fresh from a neighbouring colliery village, and her sole object was to be agreeable in her new exalted sphere. Her ignorance of her calling was magnificent. She roughly pushed open the door of the sitting-room, and, with a hospitable smile to Lawrence, announced loudly: 'A gentleman, mum.'

Lawrence entered the room, which, with its horse-hair, convex mahogany, wax-flowers, and window-vases, had not apparently altered since he entered it years and years ago to woo Phyllis. Phyllis and her mother were seated near together at a table, sewing at something black. At any rate, Phyllis was sewing; he saw the thimble on her finger; Mrs Capewell held a large pair of scissors.

Both women looked at him, and he looked at them and not a word was said. Phyllis appeared to be in good health, and her face had that mysterious expression which once he had understood but understood no more. She was like a strange woman to him.

'I was very sorry,' he began. But he did not know what he had meant to say. As a fact, he had never defined his intention.

Mrs Capewell's winking eyes dropped tears behind her gold-rimmed spectacles. 'I'd better leave you,' the old lady muttered, rising.

'Stay where you are, mother. Do, please!' Phyllis commanded her sharply. 'What do you want, Lawrence? What have you come for?' Her voice was frigid, scornful, acrimonious; a voice he knew well, out of several voices which she possessed. He cursed himself.

'I read about the death,' he recommenced, crestfallen, striving to conceal his anger.

'Do you think I want your sympathy?' Phyllis asked, and her tones were clear and terrible against the background of her mother's smothered sobbing. 'Do you think I want your sympathy, now? You've slandered me. And you've slandered Emery Greatbatch. And now he's dead you think you'll get me back, do you? What if it was you that really killed him? Why didn't you ask me plainly if I was guilty before you sent for Mark? Go on with your precious divorce case, and you'll see. But I don't want your sympathy.'

'Then there's nothing more to be said,' he replied with forced bravado. He was blushing.

'I should think there wasn't. Mother; do stop crying, please.'

He retreated. It had been an enterprise utterly disastrous. Why had he undertaken it? Had he not reason to know that always she would be incalculable and inhuman? She could not be otherwise. When he emerged again into the street, there was nothing in his heart but hot shame and bitterness.

CHAPTER IX

MATRIMONIAL DIVISION

Lawrence did not greatly love London. It appealed to his imagination, but in a sinister way. To him it was the city of vast and restless melancholy. And though there was nothing of the sentimental in his compositon, and he despised the facile trick of fancy which attributes to cities, heroically, the joys and griefs of the unheroic individuals composing them, London did nevertheless impress him painfully as an environment peculiarly favourable to the intensification of sorrow. Whenever he went to London it seemed to him to be the home of a race sad, hurried, and preoccupied; the streets were filled with people who had not a moment to spare, and whose thoughts were turned inwards upon their own anxious solicitudes, people who must inevitably die before they had begun to live, and to whom the possession of their souls in contemplation would always be an impossibility. The unique and poetic grandeur of the theatre which the character of this race had created for the scene of woes, only added to the situation the poignancy of visual beauty. Instead of lightening it increased the burden.

On a Tuesday in November, Lawrence was walking down Chancery Lane at about a quarter to ten. The arctic dusk which broods continually over London days from October to March was neither brighter nor darker than it usually is on such a damp, muddy morning. In response to a telegram received on the previous evening, Lawrence had arrived at Euston at five a.m. by a mail train, conveying the landlady from Manifold, with her indispensable testimony, and the landlady's servant. These he had deposited in a bedroom at Anderton's Hotel in Fleet Street, classic resort of witnesses under subpoena; and, relieved of them, he had spent the

170

miserable hours before dawn in dozing, reading, and drinking
tea. He had been in Holywell Street when the bookshops
opened, and had there lost for a few minutes the spleen which
had prevented him from rushing directly to Mark's studio in
Chelsea for breakfast. He had walked several miles, but he felt
no fatigue, nor was he sleepy. His brain whirled in the
growing activity of apprehension and suspense. At the huge
antique gateway which leads westwards out of Chancery Lane
into the warrens of the law, he hesitated, partly from a
provincial's geographical uncertainty, but more from his
instinctive reluctance to take a decisive step. He looked again
at Chancery Lane, and suddenly perceived that London,
which he had just seen dead, was fully awake; he had watched
the first omnibus of all the omnibuses pass swingingly along
the twilight of the Strand, a strangely moving spectacle, and
lo! now the streets were full of omnibuses. Then he went into
the gateway.

Instantly he was in a different world, a world like nothing
else. Here, hidden away in ten thousand lairs behind a chaotic
jumble of façades in all styles, from venerable Tudor to the
ludicrous terra-cotta of late nineteenth century, the least
productive and yet the most necessary of professions practised
its mysteries, flourishing on the imperfections of humanity,
taking and never giving, destroying and never creating,
concerned with neither beauty nor intellect, eternally busy
with nothing but the altercations of dishonesty and avarice,
the apportionment of gain, the division of amassed property,
the pilgrimages of money, and the neat conclusion of disasters
in proper form. Round about lawns and fountained gardens,
trim alleys, spacious squares, and obscure courtyards, this
singular profession, which mankind has united to curse, to
revile, and to honour, laboured amid dirt and old usages, often
in bizarre and foolish raiment, at operations sometimes useful,
sometimes of an inconceivable fatuity, but invariably attended
by rite and ceremony. From Chancery Lane to Sardinia Street,
from Holborn to the Embankment, justice, a commodity
unknown to nature, was retailed with astonishing results.
Precedent reigned; and the whole population was engaged in a
desperate battle for the sacred legal principle that that which
has been must continue to be, no matter what the cost.

But Lawrence, who saw law like a lawyer, experienced merely the sensations of a country solicitor who is on the border of Lincoln's Inn Fields.

Before No. 2 of a terrace of houses newly-built in stone, he stopped and examined the medley of names which were painted on either side of the main doorway. A score of separate but similar activities performed their functions in the house and there were nearly a score of houses in the terrace, and many scores of such terraces, courts and squares in that mysterious and formidable quarter of London. At last his eye encountered the words: 'Basement. Messrs. Apreece and Co.: Solicitors. Commissioners for Oaths.' And he descended by means of a dark flight of steps under the porch to the cellarage. At the end of a long passage an electric light was burning at an open door, and he read: 'Messrs. Apreece and Co. Inquiries.' He went forward, feeling, as he had known he should feel when the moment arrived, extremely self-conscious. He was the traditional figure of ridicule, the deceived husband, and he could not for his life behave as if nothing had happened to him. He entered the inquiry office; it was untenanted; but Lawrence perceived at once, from its size, from the number of desks, and the countless rows of letter-files and copy-letter-books on the walls, that the business of Messrs. Apreece and Company, though transacted in a cellar, was on a scale quite different from that of Charles Fearns. Apreeces had only recently become agents to Fearns; they happened to be connections of his deceased partner, and little was known of them in the office at Hanbridge, except that they were sharp and reliable people who delivered their annual bill of costs with disconcerting promptitude.

Two sallow-faced youths, strolled simultaneously into the inquiry office through another door. One of them was sheathing his wristbands in cream-laid note-paper; and they both seemed to regard Lawrence with a certain frigidity of indifference.

'My name is Ridware,' said Lawrence aggressively. 'I'm from Mr Fearns. Will you please tell whoever is looking after Ridware *v*. Ridware that I'm here.'

The two clerks looked at each other vaguely.

'Ridware *v*. Ridware,' one of them repeated dreamily, and turned to obey. At that moment a tall, full-bodied, youngish man, wearing a frock-coat and a blue Melton overcoat, with a silk hat far at the back of his head, rushed into the room like an incarnation of energy.

'Look here, Collins!' he addressed the clerk who was leaving. 'You've done a nice, useful sort of thing. You've arranged two conferences for me at ten o'clock. How the devil can I be at both of them?'

'This is Mr Ridware, sir,' replied Collins unmoved.

'Ah! Very glad to meet you, Mr Ridware; will you come into my room?'

And the man shook hands with Lawrence in high, honest, good humour, smiling and benevolent. His age was apparently about thirty. He was clearly one of those persons who, having a good digestion, simple tastes, and no idle curiosity concerning the secret nature of things, are never afflicted by inexplicable melancholy.

'Run round and get the conference with Gardner altered to ten-thirty, if you can, there's a good fellow,' said he to the younger clerk.

'Yes, Mr Bowes.'

Lawrence passed in the wake of Mr Bowes along another electric-lit corridor full of doors open or closed, with glimpses now and then of solid, rather shabby interiors. Mr Bowes' room was large, and seemed to contain more furniture than the whole of Charles Fearns' establishment. No less than twelve leather-covered chairs were ranged round its walls. There were three bookcases, two desks, and a toilette-stand half hidden by a screen, some dozens of lettered tin boxes, and a cabinet with pigeon-holes for documents. The carpet was in holes under the principal desk, and the fire-irons could not have cost more than half a crown; the black and brass coal-box was also of the cheapest description, and very old; but the best coal fizzed generously in the grate, and a new Turkey hearthrug flanked the steel fender. All the lights were lit. Outside, a smooth lawn sloped gently up from two French windows, and an aged keeper of the gardens, dressed in an eighteenth-century uniform, was pacing to and fro with the solemnity of a peacock.

'Sit down,' said Bowes. 'Make yourself comfortable. Have

a cigarette? It's pleasant enough here in summer, but in winter it's a bit off, I must admit.' He had taken his seat at a desk, and was fingering bundles of documents. And in a moment the two were smoking, and Bowes was directing attention to two legal caricatures from *Vanity Fair* which hung over the mantelpiece; he said he had subscribed to *Vanity Fair* ever since he was married, seven years ago, and that he had all the cartoons in a portfolio which he had made himself, but that these two were the gems of the collection.

'Everything's in order, I think,' he went on in the same tone, untying a bundle of papers. 'You've got your witnesses here, of course?'

'Oh, yes,' Lawrence replied.

'Well, I've briefed Wray. I told you I should. He's about the best junior there is. I've marked him five guineas. Couldn't mark him less.'

'That's all right,' said Lawrence hastily.

'It's ten to ten now.' Bowes closed a silver hunter with a snap. 'Suppose we toddle along to his chambers. They're in New Square. I've got a conference for you at ten.' He spoke with a certain amiable casualness, as though there was nothing in the least unusual in Lawrence's position; nevertheless, Lawrence thought he could detect beneath his amiability a faintly condescending commiseration, and this hurt him. But he considered himself fortunate in Mr Bowes.

They climbed up out of the earth, Bowes throwing a word loudly into the inquiry office as they passed, and then bore southwards through a maze of alleys and courts. Bowes stopped under a Tudor archway, where the cause-lists of the day were exposed beneath glass.

'You see we're third,' said he, pointing.

And Lawrence read:

Probate   Divorce and Admiralty Division (Divorce).

        Before the President (without a jury).

Carr *v*.   Carr, Isaacsohn, and Dove (part heard).
        Simpson *v*. Simpson.
        Ridware *v*. Ridware
        Smalls *v*. Smalls and Jackson

'I see,' said Lawrence.

The sight of his name, printed there and hung under the archway for the world to peruse, made him blush. And Bowes, noticing this, avoided his eyes, and said in gay accents: 'This way to Wray,' and hurried on.

'Have many divorce cases?' Lawrence asked.

'No,' said Bowes. 'Not many. I think I've had two, not counting yours, since I've been at Apreece's. I'm their Chancery clerk, you know. At this present time I've got fifty-seven Chancery actions all a-blowing and a-growing.'

'The dickens you have!' Lawrence exclaimed, impressed.

'Yes. Not bad, is it? The fact is, you men in the country don't know what work is.' He laughed easily, and remarked, beaming, that he seldom got to his wife and children in Fulham Park Gardens before seven-thirty of a night.

They ascended a corkscrew staircase, and discovered Mr Wray adjusting his wig before a cracked shaving-glass in a small, shabby room overlooking the ancient square which has been called 'New' for a couple of centuries or more. The barrister did not turn round; he recognised Bowes through the glass.

'Bowes,' he said in a high-pitched voice with a slight Cockney accent, 'you're always three minutes too early. What in the name of God do you mean by it?'

He was a small, thin, middle-aged man, with a slight, mud-coloured moustache and greying hair. He had a big nose and large eyes, and had he been sufficiently famous he would have made an excellent subject for the caricaturist of *Vanity Fair*. But Mr Wray was not famous outside the Law Courts. He had never 'taken silk,' and he never would take it, for the reason that he dared not accept the risk which would be involved in abandoning his existing humble practice and beginning anew on the loftier and more perilous plane of a King's Counsel. At fifty he remained a junior; he worked hard, and was well liked by solicitors; but many cases at five guineas apiece are required in order to arrive at a respectable income. And Mr Wray's face bore the mark of decades of financial worry.

'Sorry sir,' said Bowes, and introduced Lawrence.

Mr Wray nodded, and, leaving the glass, picked up his brief, which was lying open on a desk. It was heavily scored in blue pencil. He neither sat down himself nor asked the others to sit down.

'Let me see, Mr Ridware,' he remarked, adjusting his eyeglasses. 'You're a lawyer, aren't you?'

'I am,' said Lawrence.

'Well, that's something,' he laughed. 'You're sure of your witnesses – this landlady, now?'

'Oh, yes,' said Lawrence.

'Becuase she seems to have been pretty friendly with what's-his-name – Greatbatch.'

He stared hard at Lawrence.

'She was,' Lawrence admitted. 'But her evidence is perfectly clear.'

'Her evidence *looks* clear. The question is, Is she a willing witness? All landladies are – ' he used an inconvenient word. 'That's my experience. I know the race. Is she a willing witness?'

'I believe so,' said Lawrence.

'She's your case, this landlady,' proceeded Mr Wray. 'Who's against us, Bowes?'

'Knight,' said Bowes.

'It might have been worse,' was Mr Wray's comment. 'He was drunk last evening. He'll be waspish, but I can deal with him. Still, if he shakes the landlady –'

'I don't see how he can,' Lawrence ventured.

'Suppose she wants to be shaken?'

'But there can't possibly be any *doubt*,' said Lawrence simply.

'In the divorce Court,' Mr Wray replied, 'there is always a doubt. Besides, Greatbatch's death may have affected the landlady.'

The idea that he was not absolutely sure to win entered Lawrence's mind for the first time.

'It's a devilish odd case,' said Mr Wray.

Lawrence began to be afraid. Surely it was impossible that he should fail! He had had many apprehensions, but the apprehension of failure was not one of them.

'They're all devilish odd,' said Mr Wray. 'I never had a divorce case that wasn't. Has your wife ever come near confessing to you, Mr Ridware?' He put this question in such a matter-of-fact tone that the last remnant of Lawrence's self-consciousness momentarily disappeared as he gave a negative.

Mr Wray seized his gown from a chair and put it on.

'How long is it since you were on good terms with her?' he demanded suddenly, struggling with the gown.

'Good terms?'

'Yes. Damn it! When did you last sleep together?' He spoke with impatience, gathering together his papers. 'Now, my dear, good sir, don't get startled. That's nothing to what Knight may ask you.'

'It's some years ago,' Lawrence replied. It was as if he was at the dentist's merely to have his teeth scaled, and the dentist had informed him that a molar must be extracted. He abandoned himself to the prospect of utter humiliation.

'You never refused intercourse?'

'No.'

'There's no allegation of conduct conducing to adultery in the respondent's answer,' Bowes put in.

'I am aware of that,' said the barrister coldly. 'But the court won't rule it out if it comes up, you may bet your life. You have to remember, my young friends, that in the matrimonial courts the odds are always on the respondent. Divorces aren't given away in this country. They're dragged out of an unwilling Court by main force. And when you've got your bone, there's no knowing if the King's Proctor won't stroll up and take it off you. Now, Mr Ridware, when you're in the box, keep calm. Leave yourself in my hands. And don't let Knight get your dander up. We'll see what we can do. Sanders!' He yelled for his clerk. 'I must be off. I'm in Carr *v*. Carr. You may possibly come on after lunch. If I have time for a chat with your precious landlady, I'll take a look at her. Good morning for the present.'

'He's always like that,' said Bowes, outside on the pavement. 'The thing's all right.'

'Of course,' Lawrence murmured. Nevertheless, he was perturbed by Wray's remark, 'We'll see what we can do!' An hour ago he had been so sure of success that the trial had presented itself to him as a mere unpleasant formality. But now the solid ground seemed to be slipping from under his feet.

At the corner of Carey Street he parted from Bowes, who had several other appointments. Bowes appeared to juggle with conferences, hearings, and proceedings in chambers, as a juggler with balls. It was arranged where Lawrence might find him in case of necessity.

'You'd better round up your witnesses first,' said Bowes, 'and then go into Court and stick there. One never knows when a case won't fall to pieces and the next be called. Anyhow, I'll look you out before lunch.'

And Bowes hurried smiling away, papers under his arm and his hat far at the back of his head.

Lawrence went down to Anderton's and learned that his witnesses, doubtless urged by the eagerness of a pardonable excitement, had already gone to the field of encounter.

He entered the Royal Courts of Justice by the Carey Street portal, which is the professional entrance. He had never before examined the immense grey building which in its shapeless plan, its ill-balanced frontages, its unpretentious situation, and its curious fine distinction, illustrates so perfectly the English character. There is an elaborate and yet unaffected honesty about the aspect of the Law Courts which could not fail to inspire confidence. Lawrence felt it. With his exaggerated sensibility to influences that escape definition, he thought vaguely as he walked up the steps: 'After all, it is impossible that I should be wronged here.' And he was accordingly reassured. The official in sober blue who sits for ever in the gate, for no other reason than he has always sat there, glanced at Lawrence as he passed inwards, and his glance was so dignified and benignly stern that he seemed to represent in his own person the spirit of English justice. In spite of the rush of multitudes to and fro in the wide corridors – barristers, solicitors, clerks, suitors, witnesses, quidnuncs, and unemployed – the vast interior had somehow the hush and solemnity of a cathedral; and not the sight of a restaurant in the obscure distance, with white tables gleaming under Gothic shadows, could destroy this impression of a temple. The architect, an imperfect genius, had certainly conceived a temple, and had put into it the religion of his life. Every detail of the austere decoration was ecclesiastical in origin, and showed in its simple, passionate sincerity a horror of the theatrical and the meretricious. As Lawrence, ignorant of the position of the various courts, wandered at hazard through the interminable passages, knowing that he must ultimately arrive at his goal, the calm self-respect of the place produced in him an emotion which was almost awe. He went by court after court, each labelled in Gothic lettering, each protected from the noises of the corridor by double swing-doors, and though no sound whatever reached him from these mysterious retreats, he nevertheless felt in his most secret soul that justice was being administered therein with scales ineffably even. Stone walls and heavily-leaded glass could not prevent the effluence of those magnificent qualities which have earned for English justice the homage of the world. Here, he thought, is something pure; perhaps there is naught else so pure.

He had traversed three sides of a rectangle, and looked down from a gallery on the huge nave-like hall of waiting, when, after traversing another corner, he suddenly saw Cyples and a portly barrister in conversation with Phyllis. They were standing in an embrasure, and he was intensely glad that they did not observe him as he slipped past. The blood had flowed to his cheeks. His wife was dressed in mourning, and wore a black picture-hat and a black boa. She had smiled up at Cyples precisely at the moment when he caught sight of her. How well he knew that smile! His wife was an adulteress; but adultery seemed to make no difference to her; she was unchangeable. The two middle-aged, stout men, Cyples and the barrister, were most evidently pleased to be talking to her. If they knew!

A little further on was Mrs Capewell, sitting by herself, with folded hands, gazing at the stone floor. Her, too he passed successfully, and then he was in the midst of a miscellaneous crowd of persons who were talking in louder tones than he had yet heard. There were elegantly dressed women, sluts, even young girls in grey costumes, and various kinds of men, including a Catholic priest. They had some topic of extreme interest, and all appeared to be chattering at once. A couple of barristers and several solicitors' clerks surveyed them with affable and amused disdain. On the wall was painted the legend, 'Divorce Court No. 2.' He searched for the sister court, and, having achieved it, remembered that he must impound his witnesses; but he could not see them in any of the corridors. He came back to Divorce Court No. 1, and fronted the guardian of the swing doors.

'What case, sir?' the doorkeeper asked politely.

'Eh?' said Lawrence.

'What case, sir? What name? If you aren't a witness or a party, the entrance for the public is upstairs.'

Lawrence could not persuade himself to designate to the impassive dark-blue doorkeeper the name of his case.

'I'm a solicitor from the country,' he said gruffly.

'Beg pardon, sir.' The doorkeeper saluted with due respect and opened the door, and Lawrence entered. Before he had opened the second door a hand touched him on the shoulder. It was Mark's.

'Here I am!' said Mark.

They shook hands in silence.

'You aren't dressed for the part, my boy,' Mark whispered.

Mark wore strict afternoon dress, with a black-and-white necktie and new gloves, whereas Lawrence was in brown travelling costume, with a bowler hat.

'Oh, rot!' said Lawrence, somewhat loudly, as he pulled at the second door. He had not once thought of his dress.

'Hsh!' cried an official voice within the court.

Lawrence espied Mr Wray, who was addressing the judge in his cockney treble. There was room on the bench immediately behind him, and Lawrence slid into the longitudinal aperture of the bench, Mark following. Then he extracted his papers from the inner pocket of his overcoat and put them on the narrow desk. Wray, without pausing in his speech, moved his head a little in order to see who had so closely approached him.

The petitioner in Ridware *v.* Ridware gazed about him nervously. He was at last in the Divorce Court. There in front of him, high up, and entrenched behind an apparatus of carved oak and shaded electric lamps and calf-bound volumes and huge inkstands, was the celebrated President of the Divison, dominating the lofty and prelatical chamber. He was large and heavy; his face, though puffed, had the pallor which comes with long hours spent in foetid atmospheres, and the austere, glacial refinement of feature which comes perhaps from constantly dealing with niceties. He had the air of a distinguished man; he sat sideways in his chair like a distinguished man, and he even raised himself up from time to time in his chair, which was too high for him, like a distinguished man. He alone of all the people present seemed to be completely detached from the matter in hand; it was as if he were rapt in contemplation, and as if Mr Wray's words glanced off his reverie as arrows might glance off armour. But once, not shifting his gaze from a spot in the gigantic bookcase to his right, he ejaculated in that renowned aristocratic voice of his, masculine and yet delicate, with its amazing clearness of beautiful enunciation:

'You mean Philip Carr, not Andrew, do you not?'

'I beg your lordship's pardon. I should have said Philip,' Mr Wray corrected himself hastily.

The President was of a piece with his court – with its purple *portières*, its rich woodwork, its Gothic windows near the roof, its massive and stately furniture. He imparted his judicial majesty to the whole interior and the entire personnel. Below him were ranged, in a row, the clerk of papers, the judge's clerk, the official shorthand writer, and the clerk of lists; and in the centre of these, differentiated from them by his wig and gown, was the aged Associate. And all the men showed in all their gestures that they were accustomed to exist in dignified silence under the shadow of the great and trained intellect above them. The inane face of the black usher was magisterial in its inanity. In a corner to the judge's left, near the empty jury-box, was a many-armed hat stand of a design inconceivably banal: and even this importation from Tottenham Court Road could not impair the tremendous dignity of the court, and one felt that, were it loaded with the hats and coats of a jury gathered from all the suburbs of the town, even then it could have had no ill-effect on its proud environment.

In the well of the court, facing the Associate and his companions, sat a lady and a few solicitors. Behind these, rather higher, came the wrinkled faces of the King's Counsel, sprawling in their silk gowns in various attitudes before piles of papers. Some of them were conversing together in soundless whispers. Then came the juniors, of all ages. And

behind these two irregular rows of wigs were more solicitors
and clerks, and then the rabble of suitors, witnesses, and
persons interested. The gallery above was crowded and the
gangways were crowded, and the audience listened intently to
the utterly tedious remarks of Mr Wray concerning the
admissibility of certain evidence, for in the Divorce Court you
must miss nothing lest you miss something extremely
piquant.

And presently, Mr Wray having concluded his argument,
the judge said:

'I do not agree with you, Mr Wray, and I shall admit the
evidence.'

Mr Wray bowed blandly; he did not seem to care one tittle.

And a very old man was called into the witness-box and
began to give evidence as to what had occurred in a hotel. 'I
get up at six o'clock in the morning – always did,' said the old
man. 'And three times I saw him coming out of Mrs Carr's
room.' And he continued with details as to costume displaying
a kindly and yet cynical humour.

'And did you make any observation to him on these
occasions?' asked the examining King's Counsel.

'He made an observation to me.'

'What did he say?'

'He said, "Good *morning*".'The old man's eyes disappeared
in a smile.

'And did you offer any reply?'

'I said, "*Good* morning, Mr Isaacsohn" '

'Nothing else?'

'Nothing else.'

And the witness reproduced these two greetings with such
an appreciation of the comedy in them, he forced them to
carry so much of that naughtiness which passes between man
and man when a woman is in question, that everybody, except
the judge and Lawrence, laughed with delight. The whole
Court hugged itself in its joy at receiving this titbit.

And gradually the secret imperious attraction of the Divorce
Court grew clearer to the disgusted and frightened Lawrence
than it had ever done before. Here there was no pretence that
the sole genuine interest in life for the average person is not
that which it is. Here it was frankly admitted that a man is

always 'after' some woman, and that the woman is always running away while looking behind her, until she stumbles and is caught. Here the moves of the great, universal, splendid, odious game had to be described without reservation. Nothing could be left out. There was no Mrs Grundy. All the hidden shames were exposed to view, a feast for avid eyes. The animal in every individual could lick its chops and thrill with pleasure. All the animals could exchange candid glances and concede that they were animals. And the supreme satisfaction for the males was that the females were present, the females who had tempted and who had yielded and who had rolled voluptuously in the very mud. And they were obliged to listen, in their prim tight frocks, to the things which they had done dishevelled, and they were obliged to answer and to confess and to blush, and to utter dreadful things with a simper. The alluring quality of this wholesale debauch of exciting suggestiveness could never fail until desire failed. As an entertainment it was unique, appealing to the most vital instinct of the widest possible public. It had no troublesome beauty to tease the mind or disturb the sleeping soul. In short, it was faultless. And only the superhuman and commanding mien of the judge, who was capable of discussing the foulest embroidery of fornication as though it were the integral calculus, saved the scene from developing into something indescribable.

If Lawrence watched them, the hands of the clock would not move, but whenever he took his eyes off them they leapt. And so the time passed, and the case of Carr v. Carr grew into clearness under the eternal patience of the judge. Interest might vary in degree, but it was never less than lively, and the court became more and more crowded, for the caprices of Mrs Carr had been anything but commonplace; and yet no one could be quite sure whether, after all, Mr Carr had a genuine grievance. Lawrence gazed round the court at intervals; and he descried his landlady behind him; she was in irreproachable black silk. She recognized him with a smile, and by a gesture made him understand that the servant was waiting outside, the Divorce Court doubtless being in her opinion no place for the servant. He also saw Cyples, and nodded cordially, but Phyllis had not entered the court. He wondered whether Knight, the barrister who would oppose his petition, was present, and his eyes rang along the row of juniors to find Knight and sum him up in advance. Mark made sketches in a little book; he drew a delicious caricature of Mrs Carr, and was amusing himself pretty well until the black usher, having nothing better to do, crept round to him and whispered in a whisper of the deepest and most respectful consideration:

'Excuse me, sir. Perhaps you don't know that sketching is forbidden in court; also reading newspapers.'

'I'll stop,' said Mark.

'Thank you, sir,' said the usher, as though Mark was doing him a favour. Mark made a few more strokes, just to prove that he was an Englishman not to be intimidated, and then shut his book. And the stimulating and agreeable evidence continued, the name of God being invoked by the usher on behalf of each witness. And then, suddenly, the judge lifted himself out of his chair and disappeared like magic behind a curtain. It was the hour for luncheon. The court emptied as the theatre empties at the end of an act; only the official shorthand writer and the reporter of the Press Association remained behind to compare notes in the seats vacated by the august.

At the door Bowes was waiting.

'Not your turn yet,' he said to Lawrence.

'No.'

'Tasty little bit of stuff, Mrs Carr, eh?'

'Yes.'

'Well, I'll toddle round again after lunch, though I doubt if we shall be called today.'

'Who's that ass?' demanded Mark, who had been staring hard at Bowes. The brothers were in the corridor, which was crowded.

'He is rather a johnny, isn't he?' Lawrence agreed. 'But I like him. He's Apreece's clerk.'

'Well, don't let me deprive you of him.'

Mark suggested lunch at a chop-house in Fleet Street which was living on its reputation, and they walked down together. They had seen each other only once since the unforgettable night when Phyllis left the house at Toft End, Mark having spent the following weekend with Lawrence, according to his promise. But now, as usual, they had nothing to say to each other. They went to the chop-house in a silence which was unbroken save by a few remarks about the contents-bills of newspapers that they encountered. Lawrence was inclined to be cheerful because there was a chance that his case would not be heard that day. He fervently desired that Carr *v.* Carr and the next petition after it might endure for weeks. And though he knew this desire to be absurdly infantile, he could not get rid of it. Mark's mute companionship soothed him, and in spite of his hatred of sentimentality, he found comfort in the secret assurance which he had, that Mark, at no matter what personal loss and inconvenience, would not leave his side until the trial was over.

And in the expensive chop-house they seated themselves on hard benches, and kicked up real sand with their feet, and watched fat, perspiring men dressed in white handle lumps of raw flesh with their great greasy hands. And they listened to the frizzling of the raw flesh over an open fire, and saw it flung on to plates. And when the plates were brought to them they began to eat the flesh with gusto. And Mark, who knew, if anyone knew, said that a better steak could not be obtained within a four-mile radius. Then three men with whom Mark was acquainted strolled into the chop-house. Two were black-and-white draughtsmen and the third was a journalist. But they belonged to the higher ranks of their crafts. They were like Mark himself, bachelors who just contrived to make both ends meet on a thousand or fifteen hundred a year. Mark introduced Lawrence, and invited them to sit at his table. When they asked him what he had been doing with himself that morning, he replied that his brother was on a visit to London and they were spending the day together. Mark was now quite talkative, quite the man-of-the-world. One of the draughtsmen said that he had heard a good story, and he related the good story, and many other good stories followed, including several from Mark. They were all excellent, for the standard of good stories in such circles is very high. But they were monotonous; there was not one that did not touch a petticoat. Yet neither Mark nor his friends seemed to tire of them. Their interest in the subject was ingenuous and inexhaustible. At the stage of coffee it was just as fresh as it had been at the commencement of the repast. Lawrence, too, was a considerable amateur of such good stories, and his taste in them, if fastidious, was extremely catholic. But he could not savour them that day. It appeared to him that the whole silly world was obsessed by the petticoat, that symbol! As for him, he hated it. His ideas had come to be violently monastic.

The journalist mentioned a passage in *Là-Bas*.

'By the way,' said Mark, who wished to show his brother off, 'you were asking me about Huysmans' early novels the other day. Lawrence can tell you all about them.'

The journalist became deferential at once.

'Do you like Huysmans?' he demanded.

'Huysmans,' said Lawrence, 'is a test of literary taste. Of course I like him. Have you read *Les Soeurs Vâtard*?'

The journalist humbly admitted that he had not. The draughtsmen were soon struggling in water too deep for them, and they and Mark listened to Lawrence and the journalist. Mark was proud of Lawrence. For a few minutes Lawrence almost forgot that he had a wife.

The Court was sitting when Lawrence and Mark returned, and just as in the morning it had seemed that the judiciary spectacle, as Lawrence's gaze first caught it, had existed since everlasting, so now it seemed that there had been no break in its activity and that it would continue thus for ever. The judge lifted himself tranquilly from time to time in his chair; the officials beneath him maintained the old dignified and motionless silence; a witness exactly like all other witnesses was squirming in the witness-box; one grey wig stood aloft above the other wigs, nodding and offering conversational remarks to the judge and to the witness; the pencils of the shorthand writers flitted from line to line of their notebooks; and the eager, spellbound public listened with pristine intentness, despite the narcotic impurity of the exhausted afternoon air. But the downfall of Mrs Carr and the end of the agreeable case of Carr *v.* Carr, Isaacsohn, and Dove was at hand. Mr Dove, the second co-respondent, proved to be not quite clever enough in the witness-box. With a few clumsy admissions he ruined the edifice of innocence which Mrs Carr and the other co-respondent had so ingeniously erected. The junior Bar, all those acute, clean-shaven, sharp-featured faces, looked at each other with pained and chivalrous contempt of the cad Dove. Dove had given a woman away. Dove had not lied with sufficient conviction. Dove was unworthy of the name of man, and, if such an outburst had been permissible, the junior Bar would have expressed its disgust by hissing the wretch's performance. Within a few minutes the judge had granted a decree *nisi*, and the very next instant the black usher called loudly, Simpson *v*. Simpson. The case of Carr *v*. Carr, Isaacsohn, and Dove was finished, done with, and forgotten by judge, counsel, solicitors and public. It was like an old wife's tale.

Simpson *v*. Simpson was quite a different kind of case. The petitioner was praying for a declaration of nullity of marriage, and the arguments were purely legal and technical, having no connection whatever with nature. The stimulus of sex was curiously absent from Simpson *v*. Simpson. The issues raised had a higher and palpitating interest for the judicial mind, and the judge was obviously roused by them out of his inhuman calm; but the general audience melted away like snow under the forensic heat engendered. After two hours, when a couple of King's counsel and a couple of juniors had ended their altercations, a hush fell upon the Court. The Bar thought that the judge would reserve his decision. But no. He remained in brooding silence for a few minutes, which seemed like hours, and then he proceeded to deliver one of those judgements, clear, stylistic, penetrating, perfectly balanced, and unanswerable, which were the dazzling delight of lawyers and also of himself. The hour for the rising of the Court was already past, and Lawrence knew that his own action would be first on the list the next day.

He spent the evening with Mark in Mark's small private studio, which opened out of the large studio where he held his classes in London. This studio was richly furnished, and maintained the meticulous perfection of orderliness which only a bachelor may achieve. There was a grand piano in it. They were interrupted in the performance of the C Minor Symphony, arranged for four hands, by a ring at the door of the large studio. Mark answered the summons, and Lawrence heard in the distance the murmur of a girl's voice, and caught, through the gloom, the momentary sheen of yellow hair under a lamp. Then a door banged, and Mark returned to him, a little self-consciously. And to cover his self-consciousness Mark suddenly began to talk about the divorce.

'I can see you're awfully nervous, my boy,' said Mark. 'But really you oughtn't to be. There's simply nothing in it, you know, if you look at it in the right way. What is it, after all?'

Lawrence agreed that there was nothing in the ordeal, after all, and swore that he was not a bit nervous. And they talked late, discussing Lawrence's case from every possible point of view.

'Now all you've got to do is to treat it as the most ordinary thing in the world,' Mark insisted again, just as they were going into court the next morning. 'It will be over in no time,' he added, 'and you'll see – if you get that idea firmly into your head – you'll see there'll be simply nothing in it.'

Lawrence made no reply.

'But isn't it so?' said Mark, who was determined, as a man of the world, to do his duty by Lawrence.

'Oh, yes,' Lawrence agreed.

The court was not full, but it was quickly filling. All the officials were in their places, except the judge's clerk. One of the shorthand-writers was sharpening a pencil. Then the judge's clerk, a portly man in a blue reefer suit, appeared in front of the *portière* behind the President's great chair and drew the *portière* aside, and the President holding his robe in a fold with one hand, entered. The usher sprang up. Everybody rose and remained standing until the President, having acknow-ledged the existence of the rest of the world by a stately bow, assumed his seat.

'Ridware *versus* Ridware.'

The cry fell on Lawrence's ears like a knell. Nevertheless he was determined to treat the experience as the most ordinary thing in the world, and he winked at Mark. He was stationed immediately behind Mr Wray, as on the previous morning, and he had Mark on his left and Mr Bowes on his right. Further along, on the same bench, was Cyples. Lawrence was so little his usual self that he had forgotten to look among the crowd for his wife.

'Isn't *she* here?' he whispered to Mark, suddenly thinking of her.

Mark silently pointed with his finger. Phyllis was seated in the well of the court, almost precisely where Mrs Carr had been the previous day. He could not see her face, but he could see her hat, and the back of her head, and they were purity itself. Mrs Capewell was with her.

Mr Wray got on his legs. 'My lord,' he began, and opened the case in a casual conversational tone of his cockney voice. And while Lawrence studied the whiteness of his collar and the crimson of the nape of his neck, and a torn seam in his stuff gown, and thought what a ridiculous person he was, Mr Wray explained to his lordship that the case was of the utmost simplicity, and that he should not long detain his lordship; and in a moment he was launched on a smooth recital of the facts, hesitating sometimes for a word, but steering a straight course. And in another moment, so it seemed to Lawrence, the usher was calling out Lawrence's name, and Mr Bowes, with an encouraging smile, was making room for him to pass.

And then he was in the witness-box, and his large, reddish hands, presenting a strange contrast to his thin, pallid face, were playing nervously with the rail. 'There's nothing in it,' he said to himself boldly. 'All I have to do is to keep calm and answer questions.' And when the usher, a busy, officious individual, administered the oath to him, calling his name very loudly and clearly in the judge's direction, but mumbling the formula with slovenly haste, he stared coldly at the usher, and waited a second before kissing the book. From the witness-box the court had a different aspect. In the first place he could see the general public in the gallery; they were simply rows of dull, foolish faces, faces without features. The double rows of bewigged barristers appeared to ignore him. Some of them were whispering to each other. Only Mr Wray, raised above the rest, had an eye upon him, expectant and anxious. Phyllis had averted her face; he saw it in profile. The eternal, faint, enigmatic smile exasperated him. He was somewhat lonely, up there in the witness-box. But he was very close to the judge. In a furtive glance he could detect the lines on the judge's face.

Mr Wray opened his mouth, and then, interrupting himself, turned to Bowes, and asked something of Bowes and Bowes,

putting on a serious expression, answered. Lawrence, on the
rack of suspense, thought, as all litigants do, that Counsel was
being rather perfunctory.

'Your name is Lawrence Ridware?'

'Yes.'

'And you are a solicitor?'

'Yes.'

'You are the husband of Phyllis Ridware?'

'Yes.'

And he had to give the date of his marriage, and some other
details.

'When did you first suspect that your wife had secret
relations with the late Emery Greatbatch?'

'In August of last year, at Glasgow.' And he described the
episode at St Enoch's Station.

'You were then living in Glasgow?'

'Yes, I had my house there, at that time.'

The judge turned to look at him, somewhat abruptly.

'Are you a Scotchman?' the judge asked.

'No, my lord. My father was English, but my mother was
Scotch. I was born in England.'

Lawrence was perfectly calm, and he felt quite thankful to
Mark for having insisted to him that the trial, regarded
dispassionately in the light of detached common sense,
would be the most ordinary affair in the world, and
therefore supportable. His fears had been groundless. The
one thing that mattered was his dignity, and he felt now that
he should keep his dignity with ease. He knew that the judge
was a gentleman; and as for Knight, Phyllis's Counsel, he
did not care twopence for Knight. It was extremely fortunate
that his own evidence did not bear closely on his wife's
conduct.

Under Wray's guidance he informed the Court about the
anonymous letter, the visit of Lottie, and Phyllis's sudden
departure from his house, and Emery Greatbatch's death. And
after a few more questions Wray said: 'Thank you,' and sat
down. There was indeed nothing for Knight to cross-examine
him upon.

Then Knight rose, a stout, genial person, distantly
resembling Cyples, with a leisurely, quiet voice.

WHOM GOD HATH JOINED 191

'Now, Mr Ridware,' said the barrister amiably, consulting
his brief, 'when you saw your wife with the late Mr
Greatbatch at St Enoch's Station at Glasgow, why did you not
go up and speak to them?'

Lawrence could not think of an answer. 'I did not care to,' he
said lamely.

'You did not care to? But surely that would have been the
most natural thing to do! Greatbatch had been an old school-
friend of yours, had he not?'

'Yes.'

'And you had never quarrelled? You had nothing against
him except the fact that there had been a boy-and-girl
attachment between him and your wife?'

'An engagement,' corrected Lawrence.

'Well, call it an engagement.'

'It was an engagement,' said Lawrence stiffly. And then he
thought he saw Bowes making a discreet sign to him not to be
bellicose, and he restrained himself.

'So, that you considered you had a grievance against
Greatbatch because he had once been engaged to your wife?'

'Not at all.'

'But still you saw him with your wife in the street, and you
ignored him?'

'I was taken by surprise. I didn't know exactly what to do,
and I did nothing.'

'Did you tell your wife afterwards that you had seen them?'

'No.'

'Why not? You had had time to recover from your surprise.'

'My wife said nothing to me.'

'I'm not asking you what your wife did or did not do. I'm
asking you why you said nothing to her.'

'I do not know. I simply did not care to.'

'Do you consider that you acted wisely?'

'Yes.'

'Assuming that there had been something wrong between
your wife and Greatbatch, do you consider that you were wise
in pretending to her that you knew nothing of it? Would it not
have been better, as a prudent husband, jealous for his honour,
to have spoken to her plainly, and – er – nipped things in the
bud? Would not that have been fairer?'

'Perhaps,' said Lawrence.

'I really don't quite see what my friend is driving at,' said Wray, half rising.

'You will see directly,' Knight replied coldly. And he proceeded, to Lawrence: 'Then soon afterwards, you gave up your Glasgow house, and came to live in the Five Towns?'

'Yes.'

'Greatbatch lived in the Five Towns?'

'He lived at Oldcastle, just close to.'

'Just close to. Now at that time did you or did you not suspect your wife?'

'I don't know. It is difficult to say.'

'Difficult to say? Let me put it differently. Were you absolutely convinced of your wife's innocence?'

'I was not.'

'And yet in spite of the fact that you were not convinced of her innocence, you brought her back to live in the Five Towns, just close to Greatbatch? Was that the action of a prudent husband, careful for his wife's honour and his own?'

Lawrence blushed. What were Phyllis and Cyples and the abominable Knight attempting to prove? The insinuation was obvious.

'I had the offer of a better situation in England,' he stammered. 'With my old employer.'

'How much better?'

'A pound a week better.'

'So for the sake of a pound a week you were willing to risk the peril of – er – relations between your wife and Greatbatch?'

'Such an idea, of course, never entered my head,' said Lawrence hotly. No one could help him. He was there alone in the witness-box, and obliged to ward off the attacks as best he could. 'I may tell you,' he added proudly, 'that I did not mean to stay in Five Towns. I only came back to oblige my old employer for a period. And the proof is that I stored my furniture in Glasgow and took a furnished house in the Five Towns. And my furniture is still in Glasgow. I came back simply to oblige Mr Fearns, my employer.'

'Ah!' commented Knight. 'You used to quarrel with your wife a great deal?'

'We have had several quarrels.'

'About what?'

'Trifles. I can't remember.'

'They began soon after your marriage?'

'Yes.'

'You ceased to love her?'

A mad desire came over him to explain what sort of a creature Phyllis veritably was. But he merely said: 'Yes.'

'Since when have you ceased to live together as man and wife?'

'It is more than three years ago.'

'Did she ever refuse intercourse?'

'N – no. It was by mutual consent.'

'You spoke to her about it?'

'No. Nothing was said.'

'You will agree, I suppose, that when intercourse ceases and nothing is said, the responsibility rests with the husband, not with the wife?'

'Certainly,' Lawrence answered resentfully.

'Ah! Now during your quarrels, did you not once say to your wife that you would give all you had, and more, to be free of her?'

And Lawrence remembered that one night in Glasgow, after they had been to the Pavilion Music Hall together to see some Japanese jugglers, Phyllis had quarrelled with him about nothing – about a preposterous question of car tickets – and he had used some such phrase.

'I may have said that, when I was angry,' he admitted honestly, in a murmur.

'Then you did want to be rid of your wife?'

'I often wished that I had never married her,' Lawrence said haughtily. 'But that is not the same thing.'

'Would you say you did everything you could to keep her out of the hands of Greatbatch?'

'I will only say that I acted for the best.'

'Thank you.' Mr Knight sat down smiling, and Mr Wray jumped up.

'Did your wife ever mention to you that she had met Greatbatch in Glasgow?' Wray asked.

'Never.'

'Is there any foundation whatever for the suggestion that you wished her to fall into the hands of Greatbatch?'

'None. None! The suggestion is infamous, absolutely infamous.'

'Thank you, Mr Ridware.'

Lawrence left the box, full of shame and anger, and slowly made his way back to the seat behind Wray. What astonished him was that no one seemed to be in the least indignant on his behalf at the scandalous treatment he had received under cross-examination. The judge stared blandly about, rubbing the side of his nose occasionally, and lifting himself in his chair; but apparently the judge saw nothing improper in what had occurred.

'You're all right,' Bowes whispered kindly.

And Mark gave a gesture which in some way indicated to Lawrence that at any rate there was one thing to be satisfied about – the ordeal was over. And then Wray turned to him, and smilingly remarked in a benevolent style: 'Our friend evidently wasn't drunk *last* night. Pity we weren't heard yesterday morning. However' – and he waved his eyeglasses philosophically. During this interlude the judge manifested no impatience, but continued to stare blandly about, as though absorbed in some agreeable and not too deep meditation.

Then Mrs Mary Malkin, widow, who kept the lodging-house at No. 3, Ilam Terrace, Manifold, was called, and she waddled, in her rustling black silk and gold chains, from the back of the court to the witness-box. She refused the usher's Bible and produced her own. But the usher scored against her in the matter of her right-hand glove, which she had forgotten to take off. She lifted her veil as far as her upper lip and then put herself into an attitude to defy all comers.

She was a very strong witness, and impressive. And she did much for Lawrence's case by breaking into sobs when Mr Wray first mentioned the name of the dead Greatbatch. 'I ask your lordship to excuse me,' she said, wiping her eyes, and the judge nodded compassionately. This conduct proved that she was not hostile to the respondent's case, and lent value to what she said in support of Lawrence's.

'Mr Greatbatch always had that room,' she replied to a question, and added, 'It was a nice large bed-sitting-room with a large bed.'

'And one day Greatbatch received a lady?'

'Yes, he warned me that he should.'

'What date was that?' the judge demanded.

'Holy Thursday in the present year, my lord,' said Mrs Malkin. 'He received her on Good Friday.'

'What time?'

'For tea. She was veiled. I got them a nice tea.'

'Did you see the lady unveiled?'

'Oh yes. I took the tea up myself and saw her.'

'Do you see her in court now?'

'Yes – she's there,' and Mrs Malkin pointed to Phyllis.

'How long did she stay?'

'About five hours. Till nine o'clock.'

'During that time Greatbatch and Mrs Ridware were alone together in the bed-sitting-room?'

'Yes.'

'Did you go into the room afterwards?'

'Yes. I didn't like to disturb them while she was there. But I went up myself the moment the lady had gone, to clear the things away.'

'Did you notice anything peculiar?'

'Well – I noticed when I turned the bed down for the night that the top sheet wasn't under the bolster as I put it.'

'You inferred from that that the bed had been disturbed and re-made?'

'Yes.'

'Did the lady come again?'

'Yes. The next day but one. Easter Sunday.'

'Tell his lordhsip about that.'

And Mrs Malkin told.

'Will you swear that Mrs Ridware came at about four o'clock on Easter Sunday, that you overhead a man and a woman talking at ten o'clock, and that at two o'clock in the morning Mrs Ridware had not left Greatbatch's bed-sitting-room?'

'I will. I had not gone to sleep at two o'clock, but at four I was awakened by hearing the front door bang.' Mrs Malkin glared round the court and her gold chains rose and fell on her heaving bosom.

'Were your other lodgers all in the house the next morning?'

'They were. But the lady was gone.'

When Knight began to attack her, she proved herself invulnerable. Knight accused her of eaves-dropping: she said that as a landlady she was in duty bound to eavesdrop. He suggested that the talking she had heard was Greatbatch talking to himself, she smiled. He suggested that she had gone to sleep and that Phyllis might have left the house at an early hour unnoticed by her: she replied that she was in the witness-box to tell the truth and that she told it. And when Knight demanded why she had not gone or sent up to clear the tea-things away on the Sunday as she had done on the Friday, she burst into tears again and referred to poor Mr Greatbatch, and said that she had gone into the witness-box against her will, and that it was most painful to her to be forced to soil his memory, but that the reason why she had caused the tea-things to be left alone was that she did not wish to be mixed up in anything wrong, and that she was afraid to go into the room or even to knock at the door lest she should have the proof of something being wrong thrust upon her unwilling eyes or the eyes of her servant.

She more than satisfied the expectations of Lawrence and his friends. And when she descended from the box every one felt that Phyllis was a lost woman.

The servant gave evidence chiefly to show that Phyllis could only have left the house by the front door.

'That is my case, my lord,' said Mr Wray sharply.

'Soon afterwards Phyllis was called to give evidence. And immediately she entered the box, the emotional atmosphere of the court grew electric. Phyllis was immensely effective in black; it suited her pale olive complexion as no colour could have suited it. She was beautiful, grave, and distinguished, and the accident of Greatbatch's death had invested her figure with an undeniable tragic dignity. She no longer smiled. Her mien was that of sweet and proud resignation. Everybody was impressed as she slowly removed her glove and kissed the book. She let her glove hang over the rail of the box.

'Until I saw him by pure chance at St Enoch's Station,' she said in a clear and soft voice, in answer to Knight's question, 'I had not seen Emery Greatbatch since long before my marriage.'

'What passed between you?'

'Nothing except friendly talk. He told me that he was afflicted with an incurable disease, and that the doctors said he had scarcely a year to live, and that there was no one to look after him.'

'That aroused your sympathy?'

'Yes.'

'Why did you say nothing to your husband about the meeting?'

'Because I knew my husband to be of an exceedingly jealous and violent disposition, and I wished to keep the peace as much as possible.'

Lawrence jealous and violent! He raged with hate of her.

'And when did you see him next?'

'I did not see him again until just before Easter this year. I met him again by accident in Manifold, where I have a dressmaker. It was the Thursday before Good Friday. He told me his disease was gaining on him, and that he could not live much more than three months. He lived rather less than three months. He asked me to go and have tea with him the next day. I consented. I was wrong, I know. But I did consent. And I went. I arrived at four and left about nine.'

'And then afterwards?'

'My husband was away in London. He had left me in Bursley. I went again on the Sunday and nursed Mr Greatbatch. At least I tried to cheer him up.'

'How late did you stay?'

'I left about nine o'clock, as on Friday. I came downstairs, and seeing no one, I opened the front door and went out of the house. I was in a very nervous state, and I walked all the way home from Manifold to our house at Toft-End. Our house was empty. I had given the servant a holiday.'

'Is the landlady, Mrs Malkin mistaken in saying that she heard you and Mr Greatbatch talking at ten o'clock at night?'

'Absolutely. She could not have done so, because I was not there.'

'Did you commit adultery with Emery Greatbatch?'

'I did not. He was very ill and lonely, and once or twice I tried to be a friend to him, for the sake of old times. That was all.'

She wept softly, and then forced back her tears. The audience was moved.

'Thank you,' said Knight.

Wray was obviously somewhat timid in commencing his cross–examination.

'Now, Mrs Ridware,' he piped. 'Do you mean to state seriously that you have never given your husband just cause for suspicion? Is it not a curious thing that these visits to the late Emery Greatbatch, which you wish us to believe were perfectly innocent, took place exactly at the time when your husband was away in London?'

She made no reply.

Lawrence leaned forward and pulled Wray's arm. 'She said I left her alone in the house,' he whispered fiercely. 'The fact is she was asked to go to London and refused. My brother here can prove that. Get that out of her.'

Wray nodded, with a touch of impatience, and then put the question to Phyllis.

'Yes,' said Phyllis cautiously. 'He did leave me alone in the house. It was true that I was asked to go to London with him, but I did not feel well enough. I begged him not to go, but he went.'

'What an awful lie!' Lawrence murmured. 'She wasn't well enough to go to London, and yet she could walk ten miles home from Manifold.'

'As to just cause for suspicion,' Phyllis went on, not in response to a further question, 'in the relations between the sexes my husband was always extremely suspicious. You see he himself is an illegitimate child.' She spoke deliberately, in her low, clear voice, playing the while with the glove that hung on the rail. And she faintly smiled.

There was a rustle throughout the court, and everybody involuntarily stared to look at the illegitimate child. Lawrence was staggered. It seemed to him impossible that even Phyllis should have taken so mean and wanton a revenge on him, a revenge so futile and cruel. Honestly, in the early stages of their acquaintance, he had disclosed to her that guarded secret, which probably only Mark knew besides himself. He had trusted her implicitly. The blood surged to his head. He suffered perhaps the supreme agony of his life.

'Never mind,' Mark whispered. 'What does it matter, after all?'

Lawrence nodded; but there were tears of fury in his red eyes. He did not hear the remainder of the cross-examination. Presently Phyllis stepped down from the box, half ran to her mother, kissed her impulsively, and burst into tears. She had magnificently lied, from a pious and hysteric desire to shield the memory of her lover, and from a vindictive desire to thwart her husband. She had profoundly impressed a number of people in court; but not the experts.

'She's done herself no good,' Bowes whispered. 'She won't weigh against the landlady.' He obviously tried to speak to Lawrence in a perfectly natural tone, as if to convince him that he had ignored Phyllis' revelation about his illegitimacy as it deserved to be ignored. But he did not entirely succeed.

'Now or later,' said Wray to the judge, 'I will recall Mrs Malkin, with your lordship's permission.'

'Before going further,' the judge replied, looking, not at Wray, but at Knight, 'I will put a few questions to the petitioner.'

'Petitioner!' cried the usher.

All the lawyers were now suddenly and deeply interested. Wray glanced anxiously at Bowes.

'Have I got to go back to the box?' Lawrence asked with foolish blankness.

'Yes, yes. Quick. His lordship is waiting.'

And he stumbled back to the witness-box, half dead with shamed confusion, and utterly mystified.

'Is it true,' the judge demanded in a suave and courteous tone, 'that you were not born in wedlock?'

'Yes,' murmured Lawrence, and then in a louder, angry voice: 'The fact was naturally kept secret as much as possible. My parents were married immediately afterwards, and I cannot understand why my wife should have –'

'Yes, yes,' the judge stopped him. 'I quite comprehend your feelings. Your mother was Scotch, you have said, and your father English?'

'Yes, my lord.' A horrible fear came over the lawyer in Lawrence.

'Your mother had not, I presume, acquired an English

domicile before your birth? She could only have done that by marriage.'

'She came to England a few weeks before my birth and then went back to Glasgow.'

'You did not, last year, leave Glasgow with the definite intention of not returning?'

'No, my lord.'

'Your furniture, indeed, is still there?'

'Yes, my lord.'

'Thank you. That will do.'

Lawrence retired, with a feeling of acute nausea. Instead of going to his seat he remained standing near the usher, spellbound.

'My lord,' Knight resumed.

'I fear that I shall not have to trouble you further,' said the judge in measured accents. 'It appears to me that a question of jurisdiction has arisen. This Court has direct instructions from the Lord Chancellor to watch carefully and see that no divorces are granted except in cases where an English domicile is clearly established. The Scotch courts are, rightly, very jealous for their jurisdiction, and, as was decided in the leading case of Le Mesurier *v.* Le Mesurier, jurisdiction is given by domicile and not by residence. Now the domicile of origin of a legitimate child is that of his father, but the domicile of origin of an illegitimate child is that of his mother. The petitioner's domicile of origin is therefore Scotch. He certainly, by long residence in England acquired an English domicile, but when he went to live in Glasgow his domicile of origin reverted. The domicile of origin is always the stronger, and easily reverts. Since then, has he definitely re-acquired an English domicile? Obviously not. To acquire a new domicile either by long residence or the clearest possible indication of a settled purpose is necessary. And the petitioner has not yet even removed his furniture from Scotland. He has himself stated that he has not decided not to return. Hence his domicile is Scotch, and this Court has no jurisdiction. The petition must be dismissed and costs will follow the event.' There was a pause. 'In using the phrase "instructions from the Lord Chancellor," a few moments ago, I expressed myself inexactly. The Lord Chancellor does not "instruct" judges of the High Court. But he has placed facts before me which carried their own result, facts which were stronger than "instructions," although not in the sense in which I used the word.'

His lordship sank back in his chair. He had delivered an interesting, ingenious and irrefutable judgment. He had impressed the Bar. He had behaved honourably to his Scotch brethren of the Bench. And he was not ill-pleased with himself.

'Smalls *v*. Smalls and Jackson,' a voice announced.

He directed his intellect to the next case.

For Lawrence the issue was not merely a disaster; it was a disgrace. He could not meet the eyes of Wray or of Bowes. He had concealed an essential fact from his advisers! And he was a lawyer! He ought to have foreseen all consequences, provided against all risks. Yet it had never even occurred to him that his domicile was not English. He had left everything to Pennington, and of course Pennington was not aware of the circumstances of his birth. He, a lawyer, acquainted with the dangers of the vast judicial machine, had allowed himself to be caught and crushed in the machine. In vain he cursed the barbaric rule which visits the irregularities of parents upon absolutely innocent children! In vain he cursed the antique jealousies existing between English and Scottish courts. In vain he cursed all that was mediæval, illogical, clumsy, and cruel in the fabric of legal systems. He was a lawyer, and he ought to have known. He lived on the law; he saw the law from within, and he ought to have known.

Neither Wray nor Bowes nor Mark could say anything to him. But the expression of Wray's face was not benevolent.

Lawrence had only to leave the court. He left it, in company with Mark, and stood hesitating in the corridor, full of his shame and his anger and his self-condemnation. Then Phyllis emerged on the arm of a chivalrous Cyples, her mother behind. She had won; she was triumphant; and the tragedy of her lover's death, bathing her form in poetic grief, seemed to sanctify her revenge.

'I'll begin again in the Scottish courts,' Lawrence cried passionately. 'If it costs me every cent I have I'll be free of that da——d woman.'

'Let's get out of this, my boy,' said Mark quietly.

CHAPTER X

ON THE LEAS

Towards the end of the month of August, long before the trial of Ridware *v.* Ridware, Charles Fearns knocked one evening at the door of No. 77, Sea View, Sandgate. It was the bravest, or the most desperate, act of his life. The progress of his own divorce baffled and maddened him. It went on, like some inevitable scheme of evolution, and he could not arrest it, do what he would. He had appealed to Cyples and failed; he had appealed to Lawrence and failed. He had written to his wife; he had even written to Annunciata, having the address typewritten so that she might open the envelope unsuspectingly. These letters had elicited no answer whatever. At the same time, on the legal side, he had fought his wife's action step by step, except the petition for alimony, leaving nothing undone that might aid his ultimate victory. As to alimony, he had at once agreed to the sum demanded by Cyples on behalf of Alma. He had contrived to remain friendly with Cyples. In short he had conducted himself unexceptionably. But he had not succeeded in stopping the case. The case, indeed, was set down for trial, and would be reached during the Michaelmas sittings. Soon it would be necessary to draw the brief for counsel, and decide in detail the lines of defence. The final calamity was to him almost inconceivable.

So on a certain afternoon he suddenly jumped into a train at Knype and went to Sandgate. He would see his wife. He would insist on seeing her. Either he would see her or he would do something terrible. He would certainly convince her that he was in earnest. And after all, she was still his wife, the same woman who had lived in subjection to him for over twenty years.

As he walked down the exposed sea-road from Sandgate Railway Station, with the sea restlessly lapping at his right, and vague yellow walls and escarpments to his left, in the hot and feverish evening, he knew and realized that he had never in his life felt as he felt then. It was exactly as though the tip of his head must blow off like the lid of a boiler. What relief that would have been! The feverish summer night nourished and exasperated his fever. He was damp with perspiration, and yet sometimes a shiver chilled him. And he kept muttering, 'My God! My God! This is awful! This is awful!' and sighing and pushing his straw hat back and then forward, and wildly rotating his cane. His condition was extremely pitiable. He pitied himself acutely. He sincerely thought that he was suffering far beyond his deserts, and that, if women were not beings too often incapable of genuine compassion, his wife could not but yield after a single glance at him. Decidedly his wife had surprised him. He imagined that he had known her to the marrow of her bones, but she, in common with all the other women, she, the sacred exception, had proved incalculable, femininely incalculable.

He approached a terrace of houses; the gas lamps increased. His pace slackened. He pretended that he was walking more slowly in order to decipher the numbers on the house doors; but it was sheer cowardice that had got hold of his legs. At length he discovered the number, made doubly sure that it was the right number, passed on a few paces, returned, and, sick with apprehension, rang a very loud and startling bell. The house was between the road and the sea. Cyples, who had been down there, had once told him, with a kind of wonder, that at high tide the sea washes the wall of the garden at the back of the house.

He heard quick footsteps within the house. 'By God!' he murmured in a passion of fear.

Martha opened the door; not the unkempt Martha that he had known, but a finished and rather natty Martha. In a few months Martha had grown up. The change in her was quite remarkable, and, distracted as he was, he observed the style of her black frock and white cap and apron. A feeble jet of gas burned behind her in the narrow hall.

She peered at him.

'Mr Fearns!' she said in her broad Five Towns voice. She showed no emotion at seeing him. She just continued to stand at the door, occupying the whole width of the narrow hall. Her primness and her obtuseness robbed him instantly of his heroic desperation, and forced him to behave in a manner which was even an exaggeration of the casual and the everyday.

'Mistress in?' he demanded, wondering whether he ought not to step boldly forward and assume possession of the house.

'No, sir,' said Martha.

'Where is she?' he asked, and he was aware of an instinctive relief on learning that Alma was not in. But why did not Martha make way for him to enter? What instructions had she received?

'Missis is gone to the Folkestone Leas, sir, to hear the band play, with Miss Annunciata and Miss Emily and Master Charles, Master Frank and Master Sep are in bed.'

'Oh!' said Fearns. 'Well, perhaps I'll go up there and meet them.'

'Yes, sir. They haven't been gone long.'

'I say, Martha.'

'Yes, sir?'

'Have you any brandy in the house?'

'I'll see, sir. Will you come in, sir?' She softened. She, Martha, the least of his servants, was actually according him permission to come into his wife's house! She introduced him to a small sitting-room and raised the gas. It was the ordinary furnished sitting-room of summer commerce; but his wife's books, and some toys, and a hat of Annunciata's were lying about. The experience was like that of a dream. He gazed at himself in the looking-glass. Save that his hair was damp and disarranged, he could not perceive in his appearance any trace of the unusual. He looked as strong and well as ever. And yet he was almost fainting, and he felt very sick and absolutely empty at the same time.

Martha came with a travelling flask and a glass, and he drank some brandy.

'Now give me a crust of bread, will you, and I shall be all right.'

'A crust of bread, sir?'

'Yes, it's all I can eat.'

And Martha brought him a crust of his wife's bread on a small plate, and he ate it, breaking it first into small pieces and then, violently stimulated by the brandy, and his digestive organs busy with the bits of hard crust, he left.

'If I miss them, I shall come back, Martha,' he said.

'Yes, sir,' she agreed impassively.

She mystified him. She even awed him slightly. He would have liked to see Sep and Frank in their bed, but he dared not suggest to Martha this project of taking a glimpse at his own children.

And he continued eastward, through the silent main street of Sandgate in the direction of Folkestone. There were little fancy-shops in Sandgate, where such foolish things as postcards were bought and sold; and there was a milliner's, with the window full of women's hats, and there were grocers' and butchers' and other establishments that spoke of domesticity and family appetites and orderliness and weekly bills. It happened to be the quiet hour which precedes closing, when the shop-keepers sit idle and languorous behind their counters, glad to see customers but not expecting them, and waiting only for the clock to strike. The High Street dozed decently in its blue electricity, and the passage of the Folkestone motor-bus scarcely disturbed it from its doze. And Fearns traversed all this quiet, regularized respectability with the idea that he was a dark and obscure and tortured thing utterly foreign to it and to all that it represented. Yet once, he too had been just such a pillar of society as upholds Sandgate and hundreds of places like it round the coast of England. He grew excessively sentimental.

Then he penetrated into the gloom of the lower Folkestone Road, and he had passed the funicular railway that climbs to the level of the Leas, and was amid larger houses that stood unassailable in gardens, throwing the radiance of their peaceful inner life through yellow blinds across the roadway. And now and then he caught the wide sheen of the sea, and the flash of the Gris Nez light. And then at a particular point – for he knew the route well – he struck a winding path going zigzag up the steep, bushy face of the high cliff on which newer

Folkestone is raised. The path was very dark and mysterious, and at every corner, hidden in low trees, was a bench, and seated on every bench was a couple, murmuring, or more often silent, in ecstacy under the August night – a couple that hated him for intruding and desired the whole rapt, beautiful world to themselves. And he savagely hated all the couples, with their stupid illusion, their obstinate continuance in self deception, their bland, idiotic regard. He would have liked to shout fiercely in their silly ears: Do you know what it is – this damnable sex? Do you know what it leads to?' and thus he went upwards, and the immense expanse of the Channel was unrolled before him, and it was so still and so lovely, and so suggestive of the tranquillity of pure souls, that he loathed it; he could see no beauty in it, as he stared at it in disgust, watching steamers and fishing boats crawling imperceptibly across it. 'Why have I come up here?' he growled viciously. 'I shall never find them in the crowd. I shall only have to go back again and hang about till the children are gone to bed, and then knock at the door, and begin the whole infernal thing afresh. And supposing I do meet them! We can't have a scene on the Leas. It would be as awkward as the devil, Alma or Annunciata might do something absolutely monstrous. There is no counting on them – and then where should *I* be?' And the sense of delay, of uncertainty, of suspense, angered him profoundly. He wished he had not left the Five Towns. And the temptation to plunge into debauch openly, and let her get her cursed decree *nisi* and her cursed decree absolute, wandered into his mind and wandered out again.

Suddenly he reached the summit, and out of darkness and mystery he emerged on to the large tableland of the Leas, stretching under the crude effulgence of electric globes east and west in apparently endless vistas. This emergence had the disconcerting swiftness and surprise of something dreamed; the enormous well-dressed crowds seemed to be walking silently to and fro in a dream over dreamy grass; and the huge crimson hotel and the great boarding-houses with their bellying windows and floor above floor of exposed interiors were like the architecture of some impossible theatre. From a raised bandstand an orchestra exhaled into the night wafts of music which gently stirred the vague sentimentality of ten

thousand breasts, appealing irresistibly to the secret
romanticism of the race. Jews and Gentiles were gathered
together in a formidable array of wealth and self-importance at
the famous resort. The women were elaborate in white or pale
toilettes of surpassing fragility, the men either in evening dress
or in the lesser correctness of flannels and of Panama hats.
They walked sedately to and fro, or they sat sedately on the
innumerable chairs, and they might have been creatures
dreaming in the dream of Charles Fearns, whom agony had
made a poet. No sound was heard but the melody that spread
over the Leas from the bandstand hidden among many rings
of chairs, a melody, banal, and yet sincere in its expression of
some fragment of the universal longing. Feet trod noiselessly
on the withered grass. In the heat of the night the supine
pleasure-seekers found scarcely energy to speak, allowing
themselves to be lulled by the faint music into reveries that
were sad and delicious. It is perhaps in such moments of
torpor that the soul is most intensely and truly alive, most free
within the bonds in which the exigencies of society have
swathed it.

And Charles Fearns surveyed this multitudinous throng
with a cold and heavy stare, loathing it yet comprehending it.
He too had experienced the power of the drawing-room ballad
rendered by a few fiddlers in the warm obscurity of an August
evening. He too had felt the magic of a glimpse of a woman's
face lit up for an instant by the red glow of a cigar, and the
strange significance of a murmured word or a half-achieved
gesture. He too had known the savour of those exquisite
moments when, by the sea, overlooking the sea, it is impossible to distinguish between joy and sorrow, and all feeling is
simplified into a unique emotion that defies analysis. But now,
in the extremity of his woe and of his punishment, he could
have wished that Venus had never risen from the wave. He
would have refused all that he had ever accepted in order to
possess the apathetic calm which refusal alone can give. And as
he looked bitterly at the scene, and the glittering rosy interiors
of the boarding-houses, and at the broad steps of the hotel
which men and elegant women were continually ascending
and descending, and at little lighted windows shining here and
there high up in the dark façade of the hotel, there was but one

thought in his heart. 'Fools! Fools!' he ejaculated angrily in his heart. He imagined that his was the wisest mind in that assemblage.

He strolled along eastwards by the side of the cliff. The sounds of steamers came up from the harbour; beneath him, on the cliff's face, warm airs meandered in the branches of trees; and by listening intently he could hear the regular fall of the sea on the shore hundreds of feet below. Then, with a wrench, he tore himself from the asphalt path and immersed and lost himself in the crowd. His wife and children were somewhere in the crowd. It seemed curious! He could not expect to find them. He did not wish to find them. He feared to find them. His energy and his initiative had deserted him. He approached the bandstand, could not tolerate its music, and made his way doggedly out of the crowd again, meaning to return at once to the quietude of Sandgate and there reflect upon what exactly he should do.

And then he saw Charlie and Emily, his two school-children, whom he had not seen since Easter. They were chasing one another with laughter, and he could detect a hoarse note in Charlie's voice. The lad was actually growing up. And Emily's long legs were longer; she was nearly as tall as Annunciata. Yes, Annunciata stood close by, leaning against the rail of the cliff and gazing out to sea. She was in white, like Emily, and astoundingly graceful, he thought, with her fair face and the enchanting curve of her cheek, which he could just see. And this was the girl that had spied on his iniquity and ruined him! This was the girl who would denounce him before the law! And there were persons who would persuade him that he could not stop it! Of course he could stop it. She was his daughter. What good-looking, healthy, well-brought-up children he had! They would hold their own on the Leas with other people's children. And he was their father. It was not to be forgotten that he was their father. He speculated, as often he had speculated before, as to how their mother had explained to the younger children the changed circumstances of the family life. Had she told them bluntly that their parents had separated, or had she merely temporized? At any rate Charlie and Emily did not seem in the least sad; they did not seem to miss him; their days went on as if he had been nothing to them. Yet he was their father. He was the author of the family, the responsible founder of it! And he stood apart, a sort of outcast, a mere visitor to Folkestone, one among the crowd of pleasure-seekers on the Leas, an undistinguished item. His children did not even glance in his direction. He was not more than fifty feet off them, but they had no suspicion of his arrival, and he might as well have been fifty miles off.

There was a large hooded chair on the grass quite near him, but presenting to him its left side and part of its back. Alma was concealed in that chair. He knew she was in that chair. He could see her white skirt, and one of her feet extended in front of the other. If he had called out she would have recognized his voice. She was watching over his children, and dreaming perhaps. What should he do? Should he fly? Or should he join his family and let happen what might happen?

Charlie and Emily ran away along the path, Charlie pursuing Emily. They appeared to be very fond of each other. This mutual fondness hurt him. It somehow wounded his vanity. With a swift resolve he walked boldly up to Annunciata and stood by her against the rail. She instinctively drew back from this affronting stranger, and then she recognized him. He looked at her, at his daughter, quietly, and it was as if they were meeting for the first time in their lives, after having known each other always by reputation. He noticed the fear in her face.

'Ann!' he said.

'Father!' she whispered tentatively. He thought her voice hard and cold.

'Go and take Charlie and Emily home,' he said, 'I want to talk quietly to your mother, and I can't if they're about. Go along,' he repeated in a commanding tone. 'Tell them I say they are to be off home.'

'Yes, father,' she acquiesced, still in that voice hard and cold, and without meeting his eyes. And she went, slowly, hesitatingly. He breathed a sigh, and turned towards the hooded chair. His wife, who had seen him in colloquy with Annunciata, was approaching him with quick nervous steps.

'Charles!' she murmured. She was excessively agitated, but he could not be sure whether by resentment or by mere surprise. She stopped about a yard from him, with lips twitching. And he looked at her and she at him, and each strove to read the other and neither succeeded. They had been profoundly intimate for over twenty years. At certain seasons, in the far past, they had been as intimate as a man and a woman can be. And now the historic fact of this intimacy seemed to rise up between them and utterly confound them. They had parted with a kiss. They met, and in the tumult of their feeling they could not decide on what plane they stood. Habit worked its powerful spell and forced them at last to speak in the tones which they had always used when misunderstandings occurred – a tone not tragic nor heroic.

'What were you saying to Annunciata?' Alma asked in troubled apprehension.

'Surely I can speak to my own daughter!' he said, not angrily but rather with a dull bitterness.

He was relieved that he had encountered her, and that the first words of the interview had passed; it was a beginning. He was decidedly less oppressed by the sense of his own wrongdoing than he had expected. Indeed he almost had the astonishing illusion that his was the grievance.

'I suppose you can,' she agreed gently. He could see that she was mastering herself. He too must master himself. He must do nothing clumsily. All depended on his skill in managing her. And he thought that he could manage her; he thought that if any human being could manage Alma he was that being.

'As a matter of fact,' he said, 'I was just asking Annunciata to take the children so that you and I could have a chat, Alma. I've come down specially to talk to you. I went to the house and saw Martha. She gave me some brandy. I've had no dinner. She told me you were up here, and I came up on the chance of meeting you. Walk along with me this way, will you?'

He indicated the direction of Folkestone.

Would she obey? A group of people moved close by them, and he waited for her response. Her face had a pained, a tormented expression, and she looked at the grass and then at the sea. And then the distant orchestra softly breathed a new melody.

'I suppose I had better,' she said, 'as you are here.'

And they walked along together by the cliff's edge, close together. She had yielded, and without any fuss. He had got her. She was an instrument on which he had to play. Often, during recent weeks, he had desired intensely such an opportunity, and now he had won it. Nevertheless her tone disturbed him; it even frightened him. It was too amicable, too philosophical. It was the tone of a woman who was convinced that she knew precisely where she was and whither she was going.

'There's something I must say to you,' he muttered awkwardly. Certainly the situation was infinitely more delicate than he anticipated. He simply could not use the phrases which his brain had formed in advance.

'What?'

'Look here, Alma, this action must stop. It really must. You are bound to regret it afterwards.'

'I don't think so.'

'But surely anything is better than the scandal?' he argued.

'No,' she said. 'I don't think anything *is* better than the scandal. That's just the point that I really have settled in my own mind.'

'You've never given me any opportunity of –' he hesitated. He wanted to conduct the conversation in a proper manner, moving logically from point to point, and leaving no point until it had been definitely argued out. But he could not. His brain was already in disorder.

'Opportunity of what?' she asked.

'Of letting you hear *my* side of this affair.'

'Well,' she said. 'What is your side of the affair?'

'Of course –' he commenced lamely. He perceived that by requesting him to state his side of the affair she had compelled him at once to expose his weakness. He could not state his side of the affair; it was not to be stated.

'You don't mean that the whole thing's an error and due to a misconception?' she said, with a touch of grimness. 'You aren't going to ask me to credit that?' And she continued to walk regularly by his side, gazing in front of her with a fixed stare. There was a pause in the talk.

'You're terrible,' he murmured. 'Terrible! I wouldn't have thought you could have been so – Well, let's assume I've made a fool of myself. Let's assume that. Think the worst of me you can – though it's not so bad as you imagine, Alma. It isn't really. But assume it is – assume it is. What then? By God, Alma, there's many and many a husband worse than me, if you only knew! I could tell you things . . . You know I'm frightfully fond of you. You know I think the world of you. Don't you?'

'Yes,' she admitted, 'I believe you do.'

He was pleased. He had scored a little advantage. And he continued with a slight access of confidence: 'And then there are the children. I'm just as attached to them as you are, every bit. I never get as much pleasure as I get in my own home.'

'Evidently!' she ejaculated. And he detected in her voice a note of callous bitterness – that was startlingly new in his experience of her. He had said something stupid, something that left him exposed to an obvious and extremely cruel retort. And she had not hesitated to fling the dart. He was wounded. Alma was not sportsmanlike, after all: she was like other women. She was destroying his ideal of her. Yes, he had said something incredibly stupid, but that Alma should have seized on it and used it against him, pained him even more than the wound she had dealt. He was dashed, shaken. He staggered, and rallied his forces.

'You *must* think of the children' he insisted, with a pathetic air of wisdom and authority.

'I've been thinking of nothing else,' she replied. 'It was because of the children that I left your house, and it is because of the children that I am bringing the action. Don't fancy that I have any other motive, please.'

'But it will cling to them all their lives,' said he.

'What will cling to them all their lives?'

'The scandal of the action – if you let it go on.'

'Not it!' said Alma. 'People like you are apt to give too much importance to scandal.' 'People like him!' What did she mean? How bitter she was, in spite of the gentleness in her voice! He had told her that he had had no dinner, and that Martha had given him brandy; but she did not seem to care. How well and calm she looked! 'The scandal won't attach to your children and it won't attach to me. And in any case it will soon be forgotten. One doesn't discuss a divorce case for ever, even in Bursley. Do you suppose the scandal will keep the boys from getting on in life, or the girls from marrying? I've thought a good deal about the scandal, and it seems to me that it will only be like an illness. It will cure itself. It will be absolutely forgotten long before the children are old enough to understand it.'

'Not Annunciata,' he put in.

'No. I wasn't thinking of Annunciata. Annunciata isn't a child. She was. But she isn't now.'

It was extraordinary how nearly everything his wife said hurt him acutely.

'You know me, Alma,' he said in a low voice. 'You know the sort of man I am. If you go on with the action, I shall fight it – tooth and nail. Have you realized what the trial will be to Annunciata? For that poor girl?' He almost wept. 'She'll never get over it. It will be too shameful.'

'I don't agree with you,' Alma replied. 'Naturally it will be very painful. But as she says to me, nothing else can possibly be anything like as painful as what she has already been through. She will feel that she is doing her duty to me.'

'Then you talk about it?' He was shocked.

'We have talked about it.'

'What does she say about me?'

'Nothing. You don't suppose I should discuss you with Annunciata, do you?'

This pleased him. Here was a ray of light, 'Alma,' he cried, 'you'll never let that girl give evidence at the trial; you'll never do it. It will be too monstrous.'

They were approaching the eastern end of the Leas; no one was near. Alma stopped suddenly and clutched the rail with both hands.

'And if I don't,' she said, 'what then? Are we all to come back to you, and live together again? You and I and Annunciata? Are we to see each other every day, and talk just as if nothing had happened?'

She threw her head back, defiant.

'No, no!' he said hurriedly. 'I don't mean that. I didn't mean that for a moment. Only drop this action. Live where you like for a year or two. I won't worry you. I'll leave you absolutely alone. We can easily keep up appearances. Perhaps Annunciata will marry, or go out into the world and do something. She's the kind of girl that often does. Then you could come back. Alma, I'm cured. I'm certain I'm cured. You can trust me in future. I'll do anything you like. You can't suggest anything I won't do to satisfy you. I shall never – treat you badly again. But to see Annunciata in the witness-box will simply kill me.'

'Yes,' said Alma coldly, but always gently. 'It's yourself you're thinking of. My dear man, I can't trust you. I know you too well. We shall never talk like this again, and so I may as well say what I have to say. I can't trust you. What you tell me now is perfectly genuine, no doubt. But you're incurable. A man who has done what you've done must be incurable. Suppose I were to say that I forgave you – I might have even worse to go through later on. You've gone too far. Oh, yes!' She shuddered. 'You've gone too far. I'm sorry. But there it is. You say that anything will be better than the scandal. I say that anything will be better than not being absolutely free of a man like you. No! You must try not to mind me talking in this way. You came to me, and I'm bound to tell you. Mind, I don't blame you. You can't help it. I know you can't help it. I'm sorry, that's all. I'm dreadfully sorry. I wish I could do something for you. But I can't. We all have to go through with the thing. And please don't forget that *I* suffer,' she added proudly. 'All the humiliation is mine. Oh! Charles, I don't believe you will ever guess what the humiliation was! And here you come and ask me to forgive you! Well, I do forgive you. But I must have my freedom. I will have it. It's my right. No woman ever suffered more than I've suffered. I'm the mother of your children, but I'm just a woman too!'

She hid her face for a moment in her hands, and sobbed.

Despair settled on him. 'The Court will never grant you a divorce,' he muttered feebly.

'It will be infamous if it doesn't!' she exclaimed, revolted. 'But if I can't get a divorce I shall take a judicial separation. And I shall have the children. Goodbye!'

She turned abruptly in the direction of Sandgate and hurried off. For a moment he was at a loss. Then he followed her, like a pertinacious beggar following a person of wealth.

'But Alma –'

'Goodbye!' she repeated.

'What about me?' he demanded poignantly.

She shook her head. 'Ah!' she breathed.

The orchestra had ceased playing and the Leas were nearly deserted. All the concentric rings of chairs were empty; the bandstand rose up in the middle of them like a mushroom. The electric globes were extinguished, but the boarding-houses and the hotel maintained their illuminated brilliance.

'What do you say to the children?' he questioned, sticking to her side.

'I tell them not to ask questions,' said Alma.

'I must ask you to leave now, Charles,' she announced, after a long period of silence, when they had reached the Sandgate end of the Leas.

Obeying a sudden savage impulse, he wheeled round and turned to the Leas again. When he looked for her she was out of sight. He gazed at the sea, and he considered himself the most ill-used creature on this earth. Quite apart from its result, the interview had not passed at all as he intended. He had meant to meet her arguments with arguments; he had meant to appeal to her heart as well as to her mind. But she had baffled him. There was no doubt that Alma had completely changed; she was a different woman. And he, Charles Fearns, had ended by running after his wife like a beggar hysterically bent on getting a halfpenny!

If anyone had told him that he admired and respected her more than ever, he would have denied it furiously ; but he did.

CHAPTER XI

A PUBLIC APPEARANCE

'Shall you see faver?' Sep cried shrilly, at the open front door of No. 77, Sea View, Sandgate, one cold, dark morning early in December.

Mrs Fearns and Annunciata were getting into a cab, which was to take them to Folkestone to catch the 8.30 express for London. Sep and Frank stood on the white step; behind these infants were Charles and Emily, conscious of superior age and gravity; and in the background was Martha. The two elder children were now day-scholars at their respective schools.

'Perhaps,' said Mrs Fearns, calmly; and she smiled on Sep and Frank with benignity, and told them to go in at once lest they should take cold, and enjoined Martha to the same end, and nodded to Charles and Emily. And Emily, who had been pouting because she had failed to obtain any information whatever from either Annunciata or her mother as to the object of this mysterious visit to London, at last deigned to smile in reply. Mrs Fearns pulled up the windows of the cab, and the vehicle drove off with a rattle unjustified by its speed.

The two veiled women addressed no word to each other. Each sat with her muff on her lap, and furs round the shoulders, and by the muff a small satchel; and leaning in the corner of the cab were two umbrellas. At Folkestone Central they were a quarter of an hour too soon for the train. 'Why, mother!' exclaimed Annunciata, 'we've got a quarter of an hour to wait!' 'Yes,' said Mrs Fearns, after she had paid the cabman, 'but I have the tickets to see to.' 'Give me the money, dearest,' said Annunciata, 'I'll see to the tickets.' And Annunciata, with a couple of sovereigns in her hand, tripped to the ticket-office and through her veil demanded in her thin girlish voice two first returns to Charing Cross, and received them, and meticulously counted the change. And the habitués of the morning express, who went to town every day and were always on the lookout for interesting and agreeable phenomena to diversify their tedious routine, glanced at Annunciata and then at her mother, and thought how pleasurable it would be to have charge of such nice creatures during the journey; their masculine susceptibilities were outraged to see a young and attractive woman buying her own tickets and teasing her pretty head over the change. A solicitous porter came along and inquired about luggage, and when told that there was no luggage he seemed disappointed, as though Fate had robbed him of a legitimate opportunity to show his devotion to the sex. The guard himself put the two women into the train. Three heavily-coated men in the same compartment examined them furtively over the tops of newspapers, and then gradually lost curiosity as they settled to the perusal of 'Special Law Reports', or other matters equally absorbing.

The wife and daughter of Charles Fearns, sitting in opposite corners of the compartment, maintained an absolute silence. They did not even read newspapers or magazines. From time to time they gazed idly out of the window at the naked, brown December landscape; and that was all. They had, as a fact, scarcely discussed the affair which had been uppermost in their minds since the flight from the Five Towns. Between two intimate and profoundly affectionate souls there exists often a shyness, an unconquerable modesty, which prevents freedom of converse on certain subjects. Had Annunciata and her mother been separated by distance, they would most probably have written freely about the divorce; but to speak freely was impossible. After Annunciata's candid recital to her mother on the day of the governess's departure, hardly a word had passed. Nevertheless, without words, the situation was clearly understood by both. A letter from Cyples occasionally shown in silence to Annunciata kept the girl abreast of the proceedings. Though she did not grasp the exact nature of all the legal steps, she perfectly comprehended that the issue of the trial would depend on herself, that she would be the principal witness against her father, and that consequently her rôle would be an exceedingly painful one.

She could scarcely be said to shrink from it. She shrank from it even less than her mother imagined. Her love and admiration for her mother were boundless, and this testimony which she was to give in court, this ordeal which she was to suffer, presented themselves to her young mind as it were in the light of religious acts and sacrifices. She, who was by nature decidedly sentimental, stangely enough did not at all regard her share of the matter in a sentimental way. Her heart was extraordinarily hard about it. She had taken her mother's part with passionate enthusiasm. Her mother had become an angel and her father had become a devil. She had deliberately encouraged in herself a righteous and relentless animosity against her father. Whenever she thought of him she thought of him with bitterness; she forced herself to think of him with bitterness. She had developed a holy fanaticism. She would have been capable of condemning him, for his infamy towards her mother, to everlasting punishment and shame. She deemed her mother entirely right and wise in bringing the action, and in calling upon her, Annunciata, to end her father's career as a married man. She saw no other course open to her mother. In her soul she said that her mother would have been guilty of cowardice and worse if she had refrained from bringing the action. She had no doubts, no uncertainties. With the fierce absoluteness of her years, and of her ignorance of the world and human nature, she judged her father much more severely than her mother judged him. And the justice of one's children is terrible.

On the night in August when her father had spoken to her on the Leas, her attitude had been, after recovering from the first shock of seeing him: 'He *dares* to speak to her!' And she had fostered this attitude in herself, she had insisted on it to herself, in order to nullify certain instincts which the sight of him had awakened in her – instincts which she had thought to be dead and buried. And she had hurried the children away, not (so she explained to herself) in obedience to his command, but because she could not tolerate that they should breathe the same air as that monster of wickedness, the torturer of her angelic mother. She had been very cross with Charlie and Emily for venturing to demur at her orders, and there had been a little revolt; but Annunciata had triumphed; she was the

elder sister, and, however they might seek to disguise it, the
rest of the family went in awe of her. She had seen Charlie and
Emily to bed, and waited alone for her mother's return. And
even on that poignant occasion, Alma and Annunciata had not
mentioned the adulterer. Annunciata had merely questioned
her mother with her liquid eyes, and Alma had replied with a
grave kiss. And Annunciata knew from the silence that her
father's visit had changed nothing of her mother's intentions;
and she was glad.

So it occurred that Annunciata journeyed that December
morning to London with a proud and composed mien, the
mien of one who is conscious of duty, of righteousness, of a
full knowlege of affairs, and who is capable of looking at life in
a purely practical manner.

Cyples met them at Charing Cross. At the first glance Mrs
Fearns almost failed to recognize him, for he was wearing a
silk hat and frock coat, ceremonious attire in which the Five
Towns never had the opportunity of seeing him. He appeared
to be just a little nervous and shy, and this diffident
demeanour commended the big, stout man at once to
Annunciata, who, though she might have caught sight of him
once or twice in the streets of Hanbridge, had not met him
before and knew nothing of his immense reputation in his
own circles. He assisted the ladies to alight, and put them into
a cab which he had previously secured, and drove with them
to the Law Courts. During the passage down the Strand he
made none but the briefest remarks, of a general nature; he
was unrecognizable as the easy and ebullient Cyples; he might
have been going to a wedding or a funeral. He led them into
the courts by the principal entrance from the Strand, and had
the strange caprice, as Mrs Fearns thought it, of showing them
over the great pile as if it had been a museum and he the guide.
He was unhurried, and conversational now, in a style gravely
cheerful. He told them the dimensions of the great hall, and
the total number of rooms in the entire building; he related to
them the tragic history of the architect. Then he preceded
them upstairs and made the round of the courts, and outside
the portals of one court he said in impressive accents:

'The Lord Chief Justice is sitting there.'

There were pomps that could move even Cyples.

The mother and daughter, bewildered by the corridors and the crowds, followed him meekly from point to point, wondering when he would broach the fearful business of their visit, and not daring to broach it themselves. At length, in a wider corridor, where groups of men were staring at printed lists exposed on stands, they met a young man whom Cyples stopped. The young man, who was carrying a bag, raised his hat, as much to Cyples as to the ladies.

'Give me my bag,' said Cyples, in the curt tone of one used to authority.

'Here it is, sir,' said the young man, hastily yielding the bag.

'Court sitting?' Cyples questioned in a low voice.

'Yes, sir. Just started.'

'Well, be about. And let me know instantly the defence is closed in the case before ours. That'll do.'

'Yes, sir.' The young man vanished down a side corridor.

'Now will you come this way, ladies?' said Cyples, resuming suddenly his deferential air. And he conducted them to an empty consulting-room with which he was evidently familiar, and, begging them to sit down, asked whether they were in need of anything. Being assured that they were not, he placed his hat carefully on the table, sat down himself, and opened his bag.

'Everything is in order,' he said looking at Mrs Fearns. 'I had quite a long conference with our leader this morning, and he is very hopeful that we shall get the – er – full decree; very hopeful. Anyhow he'll make a good fight for it, and at the worst a decree of judicial separation is a certainty. You see, as I have explained to you before, we're trying for the full decree, but the judge has power, if he refuses us that, to grant us a judicial separation, which we really aren't asking for. You understand, don't you?'

'Oh, yes!' said Mrs Fearns. 'Then you really think I shall succeed in getting a divorce? You think the judge will regard it as sufficient cruelty?'

Cyples was astounded at the freedom with which even the nicest women will employ unpleasant words to say what they mean. His own delicacy had prevented him from uttering the word 'divorce' in Annunciata's presence, and as for the word 'cruelty,' it sounded shocking amd monstrous from Mrs

Fearns' lips. Yet she had spoken with apparently the blandest
unconcern. And Annunciata was looking her mother straight
in the face, unashamed. Really, women were an ever fresh
source of surprise to even the most experienced and inured
males.

'I think so,' said he, unfolding a large white paper. 'If you
ask me my opinion. I should say that the chances are distinctly
favourable, distinctly so! But the point is a new one – at least
in certain aspects.' He half turned to Annunciata. 'Now if I
might suggest, it would be well for both of you to stay here
quietly until you are actually needed. There is no necessity for
you to be in court except while you are actually giving your
evidence – especially Miss Fearns,' he added.

'Quite so,' Mrs Fearns concurred. 'We should much prefer
that.'

'Yes, much,' said Annunciata, behaving herself most
deceivingly like a woman of the world.

'Here is a note of your evidence, Miss Fearns,' said Cyples
in a low solemn voice. 'Perhaps you will look carefully
through it to see that it is all right.' And he handed her the
large white paper, with the legend in large caligraphy at the
top. 'Proof of Annunciata Fearns.'

Annunciata, in the primness of her dark grey coat and skirt,
seated there so calmly in that bare and formidable chamber,
did not realize how nervous and distracted she was. She
imagined that this new, strange, mysterious, hard, masculine
universe in which she suddenly found herself had produced on
her nothing but the most superficial impression, and that her
calm was unimpaired. And even when she attempted to
decipher and make sense of the contents of the paper, and
failed, she would not admit to herself the sway of any unusual
emotion. She forced her eyes to run along the lines, in a
semblance of reading, and after due delay, she remarked to
Cyples:

'Yes. This is perfectly correct.' And let the paper fall on her
knee.

It puzzled her how Cyples had obtained and caused to be
reduced to writing the particulars of all that she knew
concerning her father's conduct and the conduct of Renée on
the catastrophic night and the next morning. Certainly she had

told her mother everything, and Cyples had seen her mother immediately afterwards, and, at a later date, during a professional visit of Cyples to Sandgate, a few questions had been put to her. But that was all. And lo! the precise details of her evidence filled a large sheet of paper. She noticed with a start that her mother was perusing a similar paper. She picked up her own paper again, and now succeeded in reading it. The facts were recorded perfectly correctly. But the sight of them set down in crude, direct language, in black and white, disconcerted her excessively. Qualms of terror visited her.

Cyples left the room.

'Are you all right, Ann?' her mother asked, anxiously scrutinizing her.

'Yes, mother, of course I am,' she replied in a cold voice.

And she resumed her courage, picturing to herself the aspect of the court and the demeanour of the persons present therein. She had never seen a tribunal; but she had seen pictures of tribunals, and portraits of judges and barristers whom she had encountered that morning in the corridors confirmed a fanciful, childlike conception which she had of the unhuman quality of justice. With her characteristic lack of imagination, she failed to appreciate the fact that human nature could no more be kept out of a divorce court than air could be kept out of it. In her mind she foreshadowed something arid, formal, awe-inspiring, almost supernatural, and perhaps terrifying; but not emotional with simple human feeling. If she could have analysed her vague ideas she would have perceived that she expected herself, and perhaps her mother, alone to be human in the court, and that she was relying on the austere majesty of legal procedure to lend to her weakness the strength which it needed, or to shame her into frigidity. In a word, she envisaged the ordeal that lay before her in a manner which was not merely inadequate but false.

The public gallery of the court was neither more nor less full than usual, but the ground-floor certainly showed signs of a special animation and interest when the case of Fearns v. Fearns was called, about three-quarters of an hour before luncheon. It had become known, through the agency of either solicitor's clerks or barrister's clerks, that the case of Fearns v.

Fearns would be delectable, from both a scandalous and a legal point of view. The Junior Bar was richly represented, and the floating clerkly population of the Courts, which devotes its ample spare time to the tasting of titbits of all kinds, crowded the gangways and the witnesses' benches. The Press Association's shorthand writer prepared himself to produce a report which had been specially ordered by the *Staffordshire Signal*, and which would appear piece by piece in successive editions of the daily organ of the Five Towns, under some such heading as 'Local Divorce Case. Astonishing Revelations.' Several Five Towns faces, quite unconnected with the action, were to be seen in court. Business, by a happy chance, had summoned these faces to London at the very time when Fearns *v*. Fearns appeared in the Cause List. The court was filled with a pleasant anticipation, an anticipation which was without misgivings, for there could be no fear that the judge would spoil everybody's pleasure by deciding to hear the evidence *in camera*. According to rumour – and rumour was correct – there could be nothing in the case that might not be listened to by all the world and read without abridgement in evening trains or at morning tables. There would be nothing to shock the most easily-shocked nation in Europe, no disgusting physical details, no perverse eccentricities, no history of disease; merely the spectacle of a young virgin compelled to relate, in the presence of public and Press, exactly how she had caught her father in adultery. It was an affair not by any means to be missed, an affair which it would have been wrong to keep from a race at large accustomed to such things. It was neither a bull-fight nor an indecency, and no one could take exception to it.

The initiated looked around for the heroine and the outraged wife, and, the sight being for the moment denied to them, they comforted themselves with the thought of the dramatic entry which these women must ultimately make. And in the meantime they could see Charles Fearns, who sat in the well of the court, with Apreece on one side of him and young Bowes on the other, and Lawrence Ridware next to Bowes. Fearns *v*. Fearns was a truly important case; its importance could be judged by the mere fact that the venerable and astute Apreece, the guiding brain of Apreece and

Company, Fearns' London agents, had thought well to be present in person. Fearns wanted support, and all the support that he could get, and he had asked Apreece to attend to the matter himself; he had not had to ask twice. It was apparently for the sake of support, too, that Fearns, in defiance of Lawrence's wish, had insisted on Lawrence accompanying him to London. Lawrence had suggested Pennington, but Fearns would not hear of Pennington. Fearns had never mentioned his divorce to Pennington. Moreover he required someone to whom he could talk as an equal, who had a brain beyond documents and ledgers. He had talked incessantly about the case for several days, and Lawrence, on his part, had several times spoken with a bitter freedom that had angered his employer. But Lawrence did not care. Since the failure of his own action for divorce, Lawrence had become morose and defiant: it was his way of restoring dignity: and he was pushing forward the preliminaries of a fresh action in the Scottish Courts with a feeling that might be fairly described as virulence. He bore malice against Fearns for having forced him to breathe again the atmosphere of the matrimonial court, which poisoned him by its humiliating memories; and he scarcely concealed this malice. Yet Fearns did not seem to care. All that Fearns seemed to demand was companionship.

Behind the Fearns group was one of the two King's Counsel engaged; the other was close by, with Cyples at hand. Expense had not been spared by either of the parties, and these aged forensic ornaments of the Probate, Divorce and Admiralty Division were of the costly kind, the kind that lends lustre to a trial and that, beneath a mask of exaggerated deference, does not fear to try to intimidate the judge himself. The chosen of Cyples, with his junior at his back, and Cyples and Cyples' agent in front of him, opened Mrs Fearns' case with cautious elaborateness. The experts instantly perceived the direction of the line upon which he was moving. If the President of the Division had a slight weakness, it was his tendency to read new meanings into old precedents, while professing, and sincerely feeling, a deep respect for those precedents. In order that Mrs Fearns might win her action, the legal significance of the word 'cruelty' would have to be somewhat broadened, and already, even at that early stage, the eminent pleader was subtly preparing the judge's mind. And the judge at intervals raised himself up in his chair according to his habit, and said to himself: 'This man imagines he is influencing me.' And nevertheless the judge was indeed being influenced.

And when the King's Counsel, in his mild, conversational tone, had laid down the foundations of his argument, there was some whispering in each of the opposing groups, and then the name of Alma Fearns resounded in the court and in the corridor, first loud and then faint, and Mrs Fearns was led in by a clerk deputed to that office by Cyples. She was absolutely self-possessed. She gave her unimportant evidence, and produced the letters which she had received from her husband, without an external trace of emotion. She caught her husband's glance, and did not flinch. She breathed the name of Annunciata, and her voice did not tremble. And after the barristers had done with her, she did not forget to bow to the judge on leaving the box. She impressed everybody. Cyples' eye shone with appreciation of her fine stern qualities as an ideal petitioner. Her ordeal was finished, she walked straight out of court, passing as quickly as she could and with averted gaze, along the peopled gangways. Between the inner and the outer swing-doors Annunciata was standing, the clerk by her side. The inner door was closed with a faint bang. And at the same moment there came the voice of the usher.

'Annunciata Fearns.'

'Go, dear,' said Mrs Fearns. The clerk held the door open, and Annunciata went into the court. Her mother followed her a few steps, and then halted near the door.

The girl blushed deeply as she moved forward, obeying the pompous gesture of the black usher, the only being whom at first she clearly distinguished in what was to her a confused mass of faces. He directed her up the steps to the witness-box; and, having once stumbled to her appointed position, she turned and fronted the assemblage with tight lips and frightened eyes. The court-room did not at all coincide with her vision of it. Every gaze was fixed on her. And what rude, bold, hard, human glances! She looked at the public gallery and saw what might have been the audience of a theatre gallery, examining her with intent and leering curiosity. The

thing about this audience which most annoyed her was that it
was ill-dressed, shabby, an audience of loafers. Her modesty
was outraged by the implacable, ignoble, prying stares that
beset her from the gallery. And, below, it was not much better.
The barristers had a terrible air; they seemed to be banded
together for her undoing. And behind the barristers was
another public, among which she recognized several acquaintances. There was, for instance, Mark Ridware. Had he come
simply to gape at her? Was it possible that people had come all
the way to the court to appease a disgraceful inquisitiveness
concerning her family's private affairs? She saw also a notorious
middle-aged spinster from Bursley, whose indefatigable
tongue was famous in the Five Towns. The idea that the idle
and wealthy spinster had journeyed to London in order to assist
at the shaming of the Fearns pierced Annunciata like an arrow,
changing on a sudden her whole estimate of human nature.

She thought the usher was a horrid man. She did not like his
untidy beard, and when he gave her the black Bible and threw
a form of words at her in a thick unpleasant voice, the aspect
of his hands offended her. She took the volume and kissed it
through her veil and the usher forced her to kiss it again. She
had to raise her veil in the presence of the entire audience, and
humbly obey the usher, whom she could plainly perceive to
be a most commonplace creature in a torn and dirty gown; the
usher was not nearly so distinguished as Martin, the gardener
at Bleakridge, and here he was issuing his instructions to her,
while the audience waited in shuffling silence. As she was
kissing the Bible she caught the eye of the judge, and even the
judge appeared to be regarding her with a masculine and
impious interest. There was not the grave and godlike
ceremonial of justice which she had expected. All that met her
gaze hurt her susceptibilities. She sought her mother's form
where she had left it near the door, and it was no longer there.
Mrs Fearns, unable to bear the sight of Annunciata solitary in
the witness-box, under the fire of that coarse curiosity, had
retreated to the corridor. Then Annunciata saw her father,
sitting below her in front of the old, clean-shaven barristers.
His eyes were fixed on the floor, his legs stretched out, his
hands in his pockets. The expression on his features was one of
intense pain and grief.

And suddenly she was aware of a desire, at once powerful and irrational, to rush down to him and fold him in her arms and let his arms enfold her. She remembered how sometimes at meals she used to clasp his great hairy fists, out of sheer affection, and then caress the back of his hand as it lay immovable on the table. And as she stood in the witness-box he seemed to her strangely and surprisingly the most lovable man in the world, and she forgot his misdeeds; his misdeeds lost importance. She choked with an emotion which she could not comprehend.

One of the aged barristers was waving a finger at her.

'Your name is Annunciata Fearns?'

'Yes,' she whispered.

'And you are the daughter of the petitioner and the respondent in this case?'

'Yes.'

Every pair of eyes in court was glaring at her.

She saw her father rise from his seat and walk out. He pushed violently and as it were angrily through the people obstructing the gangway. Her glance followed him. Then she gathered that the aged barrister was addressing her again, and she recognized, in a confused series of phrases meaningless to her brain, the sole word 'governess.' She gazed blankly and stupidly around her, with smarting eyes and a lump in her throat. The aged barrister addressed her a second time. Her lips did not move.

The judge coughed slightly, and turned a little sideways on his chair so as to look at her; and she looked at him, expectantly.

'You must answer,' said the judge, in a kind, firm avuncular voice. He did not resemble a judge to her in the least. He was scarcely six feet away from her, and merely a mysteriously and disconcertingly shrewd old man in a rather ridiculous headgear. Her eyes continued their appeal to him.

'You must answer,' he repeated.

Something broke within her.

'What?' she asked him in a simple, very quiet, colloquial tone. 'Here? Before all these people?'

'Yes,' said the judge.

'Oh, no!' she cried, 'I can't! I didn't know!' And in the unreflecting madness of her torment she sprang down the steps from the witness-box, like a wild deer that terror has made desperate and dangerous. At the lowest step she stumbled, and

Lawrence, jumping to his feet, caught her. Lawrence was the last person fitted by nature to carry a fainting girl out of a crowded hall, but he did it, knowing not how he did it. And there ensued that rare and thrilling phenomenon, beloved of all publics, a genuine 'scene in Court.' Within an hour or so it was on the contents-bill of every evening paper in the three Kingdoms, including, of course, that of the *Staffordshire Signal*.

Annunciata did not actually swoon. In the corridor she fell into her mother's arms. Her father had gone to the bar to find strength in a brandy and soda.

'What is it my darling?' asked Mrs Fearns in desolate accents. 'Mr Ridware!'

'Oh, mother,' Annunciata moaned. 'I've ruined you. Let me go back.' And she burst into sobs.

The corridor was blocked in a few seconds with a crowd, eager to see anything that was to be seen. Charles Fearns, oblivious, gulped down his brandy and soda in the bar with the gothic arches. And the imperturbable judge, the hour being within ten minutes of lunch, adjourned the sitting after a word or two with the two King's Counsel. Cyples and Lawrence, aided by sundry liege clerks and some officials, got the women away to a private room, where Annunciata seemed quickly to resume all her self-possession.

'If you will leave me alone with her for a few minutes,' Mrs Fearns murmured to Cyples. And Cyples and Lawrence withdrew.

Mrs Fearns smiled gently on her daughter.

'Mother!' Annunciata asked grievously. 'What are we to do? If I go back now, I shall be all right. It was – I don't know what it was. But I am better now.'

The mother shook her head.

'No, dear,' she said very quietly. 'I have been wrong; that's all. I've been quite wrong. I ought not to have put you to such a test. I didn't realize it would be quite so bad as it was.'

'But what shall we do?'

'We will go home,' said Mrs Fearns. 'There's nothing else to do. We'll just go home to the children.'

She opened the door. Only Lawrence was outside. Cyples had vanished to confer with his counsel and to assure them that the crisis was over and that the hearing could be proceeded with after lunch.

'Mr Ridware,' said Alma, 'can you get us a cab?'

Lawrence hesitated. 'Certainly,' he replied. 'Where do you want to go to?'

'Charing Cross,' said Alma. 'We are returning home at once.'

'But Mr Cyples doesn't –'

'Perhaps you will kindly tell Mr Cyples, will you? Tell him I dared not stop here another moment, and that I give up the case. I'll write to him tonight.'

Lawrence noticed that she was breathing hard.

'Very well,' he said. 'If I may, I'll see you to the station. You'll be needing something to eat.'

In the restaurant of the Law Courts, Mark Ridware was eating a mutton chop at a table by himself when Cyples came up to him with a worried and pre-occupied air. They knew each other slightly.

'Good day, Mr Ridware,' Cyples began. 'I suppose you haven't seen Mrs Fearns, have you?'

'No,' replied Mark. 'I've been looking all over the place for my brother, without finding him, and I've seen nothing of her.'

'Curious!' Cyples muttered reflectively.

'Miss Fearns isn't ill I hope?'

'No. She recovered immediately. A very brave girl.'

'Then they're probably gone out somewhere to have lunch, and they'll be coming back soon.'

'I expect so,' said Cyples.

'Better eat something yourself, Mr Cyples,' Mark suggested in a friendly manner.

And Cyples sat down, and ordered cold meat to he brought instantly, together with half a pint of bitter, and tucked the corner of a serviette between his chin and his ample collar.

'Very unfortunate, that little scene?' Mark hazarded, determined to talk.

'Yes,' said Cyples. 'Yet I think we took every precaution.'

'It's a pity that divorce cases can't be heard in private.'

'In private!' Cyples exclaimed, somewhat shocked. 'Justice must be public. Mr Ridware. All sorts of abuses might creep in, otherwise.'

'What abuses?' Mark blandly asked, and as Cyples made no response he continued in his best conversational, persuasive style: 'You see, a divorce case is different from ordinary cases. Why shouldn't a divorce case be heard in private if all parties consent?'

'Well,' said Cyples. 'It wouldn't do. As a matter of fact, they do keep the divorce court as private as they can.'

'They might succeed a little better, I think,' said Mark. 'That court this morning was like a blessed theatre. It's a regular spectacle, that's what it is – one of the stock sights of London. Why wasn't I stopped from going in? I just walked straight in, and no one said a word.'

'Hm!' Cyples muttered.

'It would have upset a man, to say nothing of a young girl,' said Mark further. 'It's a most singular thing that some sorts of divorce cases can be heard in private, and others can't. If the case is likely to upset the susceptibilities of the public, then the judge will clear the court like anything. But if the public is only likely to upset the susceptibilities of the parties principally concerned, the judge is powerless. How do you justify that? And then there's the newspapers. They ought not to be allowed to print reports of divorce cases. As things are, some of the most respectable papers in London, papers that are like people who wouldn't miss going to church on Sundays for untold gold, make a speciality of divorce cases; live on them indeed, except in the silly season, when they have to find other food.'

'This is a free country,' said Cyples. 'One can't muzzle –'

'It isn't a free country at all,' Mark interrupted him, with a certain heat which was characteristic of him when in the midst of an argument. 'Let a newspaper try to report a divorce case that had been heard in camera, and you'd soon see if it was a free country. Now I lived in Paris, once, for a year or two. You'll see pretty nearly everything in a French newspaper, but you'll never see a report of a divorce case.'

'Why not?'

'Because it's forbidden. And a jolly good thing too! In England, what with the sickening curiosity of idlers – Oh yes! I know I'm in a glass house! – and what with the newspapers waiting to give names and addresses and everything that's really tasty, a witness in a divorce case is likely to be frightened out of his life. And that doesn't help justice, does it? The truth is that justice is sacrificed to the lascivous tastes of the great enlightened British public. If that girl had been put in a room with the judge and the lawyers and nobody else, especially no reporters and no loafers, she wouldn't have had to go through what she did.'

'Pooh!' said Cyples, with his mouth full of meat. 'She only had a fit of nerves. She'll be right enough this afternoon.'

'That's not the point. Hallo! Here's Lawrence.'

Lawrence approached nervously.

'I've been looking for you, Mr Cyples,' said he. 'Mrs Fearns and Miss Fearns have gone back to Folkestone. Mrs Fearns asked me to tell you. She'll write you tonight. She says she'll withdraw from the case, give it up.'

Cyples lowered his half-raised glass.

'Gone back to –! ' he exclaimed aghast. 'Well, I'm damned! Well, I *am* damned! She asked *you* to tell me? . . . Damn me if I ever act for a woman again!'

Mark signalled a private grimace to his brother, and he thought: 'It's not your day out today, Cyples my boy!'

After lunch a formal verdict for the respondent was entered in Fearns *v.* Fearns. The venerable judge and the venerable counsel mused for a few moments upon the strangeness of women, and then they completely forgot the case. The public considered itself robbed. And Cyples went back to the Five Towns a beaten man, with a grudge against the universe. In the same train was Charles Fearns, in whose breast hope blossomed once more.

CHAPTER XII

THE SOLUTION

Nearly three years later, in the dusk of a Saturday evening in autumn, Lawrence Ridware sat alone in the parlour of a house in Knype Road, Hanbridge, near the new Hanbridge Park. His history in the meantime had been simple and characteristic. After the failure of his divorce action in the English courts, the idea had possessed him of leaving the Five Towns for ever and settling in Glasgow. But his native lethargy in front of an uncommenced enterprise, his instinctive unwillingness to begin, had kept him in Staffordshire. And rather than give notice to Charles Fearns and seek new employment in the city of his mother, where his furniture and principal books lay, and where he was known, he had doggedly lived through and lived down the notoriety which Phyllis's disclosure in the witness-box had brought about. It was simpler to do that than to move. Nevertheless, stung to an active and incurable hatred of his wife, he had instituted a new action against her in Scotland. Enlightened by her evidence as to the line of her defence, he had procured further evidence of his own to rebut it, and he had triumphantly won the action. Phyllis's rancour, coupled with the singular jealousies between the English and the Scottish courts, and the mediæval state of the law concerning illegitimate children, had cost him, after all, nothing but a few hundreds of pounds and his reputation as an entirely respectable man in the Five Towns. He had achieved his object, freedom. Soon afterwards, Phyllis's mother died, and Phyllis departed to London, an injured woman to the last. She was no more seen in the Five Towns. She disappeared as completely as Renée Souchon had disappeared.

Then Lawrence's ageing cousin Sarah fell ill. Her heart was wrong – angina pectoris – and she had an inclination to dropsy.

She could no longer live by herself. The sole persons upon whom she had any claim were Lawrence and Mark, and Lawrence accepted her. He did not hesitate for an instant. Sending at length for his furniture and books from Glasgow, he took the small house in Knype Road and established himself and her. Her condition varied. Sometimes she was well enough to render the house almost habitable for both Lawrence and the servant. Sometimes she was ill enough to occupy all their combined energies as nurses. Irritability was one symptom of her disease. Occasionally her nights were awful. Still, Lawrence was not altogether unhappy. He had probed life. He had attained calm. He was performing what he conceived to be his duty. He was intellectually and morally free. He had his books. He saw Mark now and then. He had deliberately discarded the most disturbing element in existence. Then Cousin Sarah grew steadily worse. There had recently come a moment when he had been forced to decide whether he should send his cousin to the hospital or engage a nurse from the Nurses' Home attached to the County Hospital at Pirehill. He engaged the nurse. She had arrived that Saturday afternoon. She was upstairs with her patient, and he was expecting her to come down to him and report.

He had to wait a considerable time, and putting a book which he had been reading on a pile of other books on the table, he stepped to the window and gazed out, drumming on the pane. Exactly opposite lived the doctor, who called in when he could, at odd hours, to see this conveniently-situated patient.

Then Lawrence heard the door of the sitting-room open and a step. And he turned to meet the nurse.

'Well?' he demanded, with a equable, friendly smile.

'She seems a little better this evening,' said the nurse brightly.

'How long do you think she'll last?' Lawrence murmured.

The nurse who was young and inexperienced, put on a grave, meditative expression. 'Perhaps about two months,' said she. The doctor had intimated as much.

'Won't you sit down for a few minutes?' Lawrence suggested. 'The servant is up with her, isn't she?'

The nurse nodded, and sat.

They were old acquaintances, she and Lawrence. Her name was Annunciata Fearns. The history of the Fearns family had been as simple as Lawrence's own. And Annunciata had made that history. She it was who had stood between the parents, and she stepped away so that they might meet face to face. Charles Fearns had realized his wish. A few weeks after the celebrated scene in court, articles of peace were signed between him and Alma. Alma surrendered. Alma forgave; she forgave unconditionally, but she forgave with proud dignity, and Fearns poured out humiliation on himself. It became known in the Five Towns that the Fearns' house at Bleakridge was to be sold. After the sale the next news was that Fearns had brought a house at Sneyd, the fashionable residential village which lies three miles south of the Five Towns. And then people whispered that Alma was in the new house, with all the children except Annunciata. And slowly the violent episode of the abortive divorce trial lost its salience in the general mind and passed into the social history of the district, and was discussed quite quietly at tea-tables as an affair not more astounding and scandalous than sundry other affairs. And old ties of friendship and acquaintance were resumed. And everybody tried to behave as if nothing had happened. And nearly everybody ultimately succeeded in behaving as though nothing had happened. Charles Fearns certainly succeeded. Rumour had his name again between her scandalous teeth ere a year had elapsed. But he was very discreet, and very attentive to his wife; and he never began to vary from the path of rectitude till he had reached London, where all things are hid.

Annunciata was obviously born to be a nurse. She had the intense seriousness, and the strictness, and the inward fire, that mark a woman for a vocation. The solution of her particular problem leapt to the eye. She accepted it gladly, earnestly. She never saw her father again. She would not. Nor did her mother urge her to do so. It was part of the family tact that she and her father should not meet. She frequently inquired about him from her mother; but Charles Fearns never mentioned her name.

When Lawrence Ridware had telephoned to Pirehill for a nurse, he had been informed that he could have one and that Nurse Fearns would be sent.

And now they sat together in his parlour in the blackening dusk of a Five Towns autumn. With her pale, tight-bound hair, and her clear blue costume and spotless cap, and large apron with the chatelaine jingling against its whiteness, she looked a comely and desirable creature, wistful, fragile, and yet very stern. Something stirred in Lawrence an impulse that had not stirred in him for years. His mind went back – to what should it go back but to the sudden interruption of the trial and to the feel of her thin body in his arms? He had held her in his arms. And he could recall the sensation precisely. Yes, something stirred in him. He remembered his divorced wife's vicious: 'Supposing I were to ask you about Annunciata Fearns?' How amazing was the penetration of women! He was nearly twenty years older than Annunciata.

And time was marking him. He did not belie his age as he sat there, nervously stroking his fine chin with his heavy, reddish hand. But he recognized candidly that for years past Annunciata had had a strange attraction for him. And for a moment a notion visited him of trying to win her, thus rounding off his life and hers despite the difference in their ages. But the notion vanished whence it came, even as he gazed at her placid features. Why trouble her career, why trouble what was left of his, letting loose again that force, terrific and ravaging, which through the agency of others had already embittered and poisoned their existence? Why awaken desire, which destroys calm – the most precious thing on earth, as it seemed to him? Why not be content with the fact that Annunciata lived, a beautiful activity on which all that was most pure in his soul might dwell?

He was sick of love. And she, he reflected, might have the good fortune never to know it. And so he allowed the notion of wooing her to vanish whence it came. And for him and for her it was best.

'You prefer Pirehill to a hospital in London?' he questioned.

'Yes, much,' she replied. 'You see, mother can come to see me, and it's so easy for me to go and see her.' Annunciata's eyes shone at the thought of her mother. 'Not to mention the children,' she said. Naturally she did not add that her visits to the house at Sneyd were carefully timed in order that she might avoid her father.

THE BISHOP AND OTHER STORIES

ANTON CHEKHOV

The last week in the life of Bishop Pyotr in 'The Bishop' introduces the themes of clerical abuse, social class, religiosity and poverty which are taken up and explored in these six brilliantly conceived and characterized tales.

The bishop is consumed with loneliness in his high position as he is rarely spoken to 'genuinely, simply, as to a human being', and he experiences a powerful sense of having missed that which is most important. Bishop Pyotr is witness to the drunkenness and discontent of the clergy, such as Father Demyan, nicknamed 'Demyan Snakeseer', and Father Sisory, as well as the poverty of his own family as Katya, his niece, begs for money.

Chekhov paints a world where the undignified and pitiful priests fail 'to satisfy the ideals which the Russian people have in the course of centuries formed of what a pastor should be'; the 'aged-looking faces' make the young look old; and the 'well-intentioned but unreflecting and over-comfortable' point to greed where there is grinding poverty.

THE BITER BIT & OTHER STORIES

WILKIE COLLINS

This collection contains five skilful tales of detection, mystery and suspense, from the author of *The Moonstone* and *The Woman in White*.

The title story is an investigation into the curious circumstances of an unusual robbery, revealing Wilkie Collins's lesser-known comic talents. 'The Lady of Glenwith Grange' is an intriguing mystery, while 'Gabriel's Marriage', set during the French Revolution, looks into the lives of a Breton fishing family after a storm at sea . . . In 'Mad Monkton' we have a fine thriller, and 'A Terribly Strange Bed', set in a Parisian gambling den, presents the dilemmas and delusions of a young Englishman who encounters a 'fiendish murder machine' after breaking a bank.

COMETH UP AS A FLOWER

RHODA BROUGHTON

Wild, endearing, unconventional Nell Le Strange is a misfit in mid-nineteenth-century society. But the individuality which makes her so different delights both the reader and the man with whom she discovers a powerful, enduring first love.

Must Nell bow to the constraints of poverty and marry to please others, or should she defy sense to follow her heart? Ironically it is not she but her sister Dolly who decides.

In a disturbing chain of events told with disarming honesty, Nell finds herself helpless in the face of Dolly's selfish ambition. Dolly is the epitome of ideal womanhood who turns out to be little better than a fiend: a fiend prepared to sacrifice the life of even her own sister.

THE DEAD SECRET

WILKIE COLLINS

Rosamond Treverton lay dying at Porthgenna Tower, the family mansion in Cornwall. But what was the terrible secret from her past which was about to go with her to the grave? Calling her lady's maid to her side she confesses but dies before she can extract a promise from Sarah to reveal all to her husband.

Hiding the written confession in a remote part of the mansion, Sarah carries the burden alone for fifteen years. Worn out by the strain, it is at this point that she is pitched headlong into a chain of events which could lead to discovery by the innocent she is trying to protect.

Will the secret be revealed? What lies in store for the young Rosamond, her blind husband and their infant son, heir to Porthgenna?

THE MATADOR OF THE FIVE TOWNS

ARNOLD BENNETT

When Mr Loring, a visitor from London, is forced upon the hospitality of Dr Stirling, he becomes caught up in a sequence of totally unexpected events, and ends up experiencing the frenzied atmosphere of a football match in which Jos Myatt, 'The Matador of the Five Towns', is playing. But when the finest full-back in the league arrives at the doctor's house, events become more sombre . . .

Will Arthur Cotterill make it to London in time for his appointment? He doesn't think so when he wakes up, believing he has twenty minutes to get to the station. Fortunately his brother, Simeon, had put the clock on and disaster is averted. But this is only the first of many occasions on which Arthur's heart is set racing. 'Catching the Train' is Arnold Bennett at his most entertaining.

Both tragic and humourous, the stories in *The Matador of the Five Towns* chronicle events in the everyday lives of the Potteries' citizens.

No
Thoroughfare
& Other Stories

Charles Dickens and
Wilkie Collins

When Walter Wilding the London wine-merchant discovers the true significance of his name from an unexpected source, he sets out to uncover and put to rights the confusion which occurred at the foundling hospital of his childhood. That 'No Thoroughfare' seems possible indicates only the beginning of a story of adventure and romance which sets the tone for an exciting collection that ranges from the comic festivities of 'The Bloomsbury Christening' to the tense 'Hunted Down', based on the character of a real-life forger and poisoner. Moreover, many of these stories, including the 'Lazy Tour of Two Idle Apprentices', which (along with 'No Thoroughfare') was written in collaboration with his friend Wilkie Collins, become almost confessional in their auto-biographical revelations of Dickens's private life.

THE PRETTY LADY

ARNOLD BENNETT

The coincidence frightened her, but it also delighted her . . . 'Was it not astounding that on one night of all nights he should have been at the Marigny? Was it not still more astounding that on one night of all nights he should have been in the Promenade in Leicester Square? . . . The affair was ordained from the beginning of time . . .'

So starts a relationship which explores two contrasting characters and their incompatible approaches to life. A young French courtesan and a respectable, middle-aged Englishman pursue their lives against a back-drop of London, war committees and class-consciousness at the outbreak of the First World War.

The scene is set for another classic Arnold Bennett novel.

SILAS MARNER

GEORGE ELIOT

Silas Marner is viewed as an outsider by the
village of Raveloe, a rural hamlet where life is
lived according to long traditions: he is one of those
'pallid, undersized men' who work with machines,
a linen weaver by trade. Driven from his previous
community after being wrongly convicted of theft,
Silas seeks to cut himself off from a world he
distrusts, and when he discovers that all his savings
have been stolen from him, he becomes a recluse.
Then one snowy night, a small child crawls into his
lonely cottage seeking refuge after her mother has
died from the cold. Somewhat to his consternation,
the child's pathetic assumption of help awakens in
him lost feelings and he determines to do the best
for her and to bring her up as his own child.

One of her best-loved tales, George Eliot here
depicts the Industrial Revolution and shows how
Silas is restored into the affections and good
attentions of his neighbours through his love for the
child, Eppie. A story of warmth and compassion,
Silas Marner is as justly popular today as it has been
at any time since its first publication 130 years ago.

THE THIRTY-NINE STEPS

JOHN BUCHAN

JOHN BUCHAN

'The definitive story of espionage, intrigue and pursuit . . . terse, taut, endlessly inventive, and as delightfully fresh as the day it was written.' *New York Times*

'No one can beat Mr Buchan when it comes to spinning a good yarn.' *Manchester Guardian*

Richard Hannay, a South African mining engineer, finds the adventure he craves when an American, Franklin Scudder, to whom he offers sanctuary, warns him of an evil conspiracy afoot. Shortly afterwards Scudder is murdered. Pursued by both the police, who suspect him of Scudder's murder, and the murderers, Hannay flees to Scotland where he is chased over the Galloway moors as he follows the clues that will eventually lead him to the final denouement at 'the thirty-nine steps'.

UNFINISHED NOVELS

CHARLOTTE BRONTË

Charlotte Brontë is best known for the hugely popular *Jane Eyre* and for the novel of her mature years, *Vilette*, written in 1847. Less well known are the unfinished novels, which exhibit those characteristics for which she became famous, and in which she can be seen writing with both wit and subtlety.

Ashworth, discovered in the early 1980s and published here in book form for the first time, is set in the West Riding of Yorkshire, and recounts the fortunes of an impressionable and dissolute young man and the fate of his children. In *The Moores*, first published in 1902, are described the difficult beginnings of a marriage. Also included here is *The Story of Willie Ellin*, and the first chapters of *Emma*, Charlotte's last novel, which was published just after her death, in 1860, in the *Cornhill Magazine* with an introduction by William Thackeray.